PENGUIN BOOKS

1390

THE IMPREGNABLE

ERIC L

By the same author

WHITE MAA'S SAGA
POET'S PUB*
JUAN IN AMERICA*
THE MEN OF NESS
RIPENESS IS ALL
MAGNUS MERRIMAN*
THE SAILOR'S HOLIDAY
JUDAS
PRIVATE ANGELO*
A SPELL FOR OLD BONES
LAXDALE HALL
THE HOUSE OF GAIR
THE FAITHFUL ALLY
A DRAGON LAUGHED
THE DEVILS IN THE NEWS
GOD LIKES THEM PLAIN
BEN JONSON AND KING JAMES
JUAN IN CHINA*

Also available in Penguin Books

The Impregnable Women

ERIC LINKLATER

PENGUIN BOOKS

Penguin Books Ltd, Harmondsworth, Middlesex
AUSTRALIA: Penguin Books Pty Ltd, 762 Whitehorse Road,
Mitcham, Victoria

—

First published by Jonathan Cape, 1938
Published by Penguin Books 1959

Made and printed in Great Britain
by Wyman & Sons Ltd,
London, Reading, and Fakenham

TO

EDWIN MUIR

an Orkneyman

Contents

The intolerable futility of mankind obsessed her like a nightmare, and she gnashed her teeth against it. 'I do well to be angry', was the burden of her cry.

Lytton Strachey

Where is the man who has the power and skill
To stem the torrent of a woman's will?
For if she will, she will, you may depend on't;
And if she won't, she won't; so there's an end on't.

Anonymous

οὕτω γε λεπτὸν ὥσθ' ὅλης τῆς Ἑλλάδος ἐν ταῖς γυναιξίν
ἐστιν ἡ σωτηρία

(By virtue of this triviality the saving of all civilization is in the power of us women.)

Aristophanes

CHAPTER ONE

The Crisis

I

A COUPLE of hours before the start of the bombardment, a young man called Julian Brown, who was a teacher of English in a Secondary School in Brixton, and lived in lodgings in Plotinus Road, was wakened by his landlady, who brought his breakfast on a tray and the Sunday papers. It was his habit and philosophy to live with all possible luxury, and though his salary was so small that his luxuries could be neither many nor impressive, they were sufficient to give him an air of superiority that most of his colleagues resented. They also gave him an appetite, which he could not satisfy, for other and more splendid luxuries.

Getting out of bed, he brushed his hair with ivory brushes, and took from his wardrobe a yellow silk dressing-gown that he had bought in the rue du Quatre Septembre. He was a devoted Francophile, and had on several occasions enjoyed short holidays in Paris, the Loire district, and Chamonix. In a pocket of his yellow dressing-gown, which he had not worn for several weeks, he discovered, indeed, a relic of his last visit to France: a copy of *Le Sourire,* so folded that a page of small advertisements was on the outside. Ignoring both newspapers and breakfast tray, which his landlady had put on a small table in the window, he began to read for the fortieth time these curious announcements, and by one in particular his eyes were attracted and his imagination captured. It read:

Spirituelle, raffinée, et sympathique, délicieuse blonde aux gds yeux noirs pleins de rêves troublants . . . Un adorateur heureux de connaître la magie des baisers, des caresses voluptueuses et exquises, peut lui écrire. Mlle Suzy, P.P., 43 Chaussée d'Antin.

Where but in France, he thought, was delight in sensual love so honestly admitted and so capably expressed? Where but in France did the lover prize beauty for her wit, and where else

did wit, among its other witticisms, devise the most exquisite
caresses? Ah, France! Let other countries teach how this or
that may most profitably and swiftliest be done; yours is the
better part, the teaching how to live. Let other nations serve
their neighbours; you, alone and always, will delight them . . .
There could, in fact, be no doubt — or so it seemed to Julian —
that the French were not only the most agreeable of people,
but also the most sensible, the most truly cultured, and the
most deserving of England's friendship and admiration.

It was therefore with great displeasure that he discovered
in the morning's news, when he had settled down to his breakfast and the papers, that England, by the agency of certain
financiers, had just acted in a way that might easily give
offence to her dearest neighbour. It was announced that a
loan of £50,000,000, for cultural and educational develop-
ment in Germany, had successfully been floated in the City of
London.

The *Observer,* in which Julian read this unwelcome news,
was careful to explain that the loan had, of course, no political
significance. It was not anticipated, said the report, that even
the most suspicious of foreign critics could suppose there was
any connexion between it and — for example — the current
crisis. There had been, as it happened, no less than three successive crises in as many weeks, and the papers, according to
their several tempers, were either desperately calm or hys-
terically agitated.

In the first week of July an Australian journalist called
Ferret had been killed in Moscow in mysterious circumstances.
The people of Russia, of their own free will, had recently
demonstrated their loyalty and solidarity in a remarkable
fashion; they had offered as a personal tribute to Stalin a
year's income, if they were urban workers, and the year's crop
if they were peasants. This gesture had been much admired,
until Ferret revealed that some forty thousand urban workers,
and rather more than that number of peasants, had been
liquidated in order to make it really spontaneous, and that
the nation's gift was now being rigorously collected by the
Commissariat for Internal Affairs. Ferret was given twenty-
four hours in which to leave Russia, and during that time he

was unfortunately assassinated. It had been proved beyond doubt, however, that his murderer was insane, and had no more connexion with the Government than any other member of the Secret Police. The Soviet Government, indeed, expressed profound regret for what was a most unfortunate accident; and their apology was somewhat grudgingly accepted. But the affair had created a bad impression, and some of the newspapers had gone so far as to demand that diplomatic relations with Russia be immediately broken off.

A week later, the Italians, having newly signed with other powers a non-intervention pact in respect of the small civil war that was raging in Rumania, had permitted Bucharest to be bombarded by twenty-two Savoia-Marchetti aeroplanes that carried, in addition to their bombs, the Italian colours. By certain rather doctrinaire observers, this was held to be an infringement of their promised neutrality.

And thirdly Herr Hitler, whose energy the years had nowise diminished, had again startled the world, and France in particular, with a tendentious speech. Since the alleged theophany at Berchtesgaden in 1971 his manner had become increasingly Messianic, and he had shown a curious fondness for Israelitish metaphor. He had more than once mysteriously referred to the fact that Moses, or Mosheh – one who leads or draws – was merely the Egyptian for Führer; and he persistently spoke of the land of Canaan. In his latest speech it became evident that Canaan was bounded on the west by the Bay of Biscay, on the east by the river Dnieper; and the whole of France was roused to indignation by this immoderate geography. In Paris several people were killed when a gigantic demonstration of protest – called by no less a body than the Institute – came into collision with rival processions, equal in size and as patriotically angry, summoned by Catholic and Communist organizations.

French fears, moreover, had hardly been allayed by a pronouncement of Sir Joseph Rumble, the British Foreign Secretary. The accumulated gravity of the situation had been recognized – and even, it was hoped, dispelled – by a statement broadcast by him as spokesman for the British Government. It was officially understood that he had promised that

Britain would stand by all her commitments. Actually he had said: 'We desire peace, and come what may we shall continue to desire it. But we would hardly be accounted wise if we were to purchase peace at a price which would invalidate the rewards of peace; and though I may safely say that this country will never lightly disregard the mutuality of its obligations – should we be confronted with the alternative of military action or seeming acquiescence in a war of apparently unprovoked aggression – yet I repeat, what I have so often said before, that our policy is and must be, in the largest and most generous interpretation of the term, a matter of accountancy. Nevertheless, our word is pledged, and should an act of aggression be proved against any nation subject to, or acquiescing in, such judgement, then the world may rest assured that this country will view such an act with its most grave displeasure.'

This statement was ill-received in France, and the *Matin* declared that a far sterner warning was needed to make insensate Germany pause. The *Écho de Paris* went further, and said that all France would deplore so bald an admission that England's policy now, as always, was nothing more than self-preservation. In vain had France fought so long her noble and unselfish battle for Peace and Liberty and the Democratic Principle; she need no longer look to England either for help or sympathy, but must depend on her own strength, and draw closer to her great ally, Russia. . . .

In these circumstances, thought Julian, it was monstrous that a few bankers and other financiers in London had been allowed to lend Germany so large a sum of money as £50,000,000. A representative of the group, Mr Cyril Mordecai, had explained that the loan was made in the ordinary course of international business. But would France believe that? The French, despite their many good qualities, were inclined to a rather tiresomely logical interpretation of events. They were apt to believe that deliberate actions were not wholly meaningless, and they nearly always took a serious view of financial operations. Would they accept Mr Mordecai's assertion that sums of £50,000,000 travelled insignificantly across the continent in the normal course of international business? It seemed very unlikely.

The succession of crises had been taken more seriously in France than anywhere else. It was reported that M. Blum – breaking the silence which traditionally surrounds a President – had solemnly stated that France, now wholly and deliberately isolated, was surrounded by enemies; and certainly this belief, though it might have been incorrectly attributed to M. Blum, was fairly general in Paris, where the atmosphere was by turns infected with prodigious gloom and bellicose excitement.

Much perturbed by the indiscretion of Mr Mordecai and his friends, Julian paid little attention to the rest of the day's news, and failed to see a small paragraph that described a shipping mishap at Toulon.

The *Araby*, a British ship of 5,600 tons, had collided with a French destroyer and then rammed the breakwater. Both vessels had sunk, and were lying in the fairway in such a position as to endanger incoming traffic. The *Araby* had been leaving port about nine o'clock on Saturday night, and the destroyer had been inward bound. There had been, it was feared, considerable loss of life, and the captain of the *Araby*, Mr Peter McCombie, of Leith, was under arrest. He was very angry when arrested, and had assaulted the police so violently that two of them had required medical treatment. The Press Association stated that Captain McCombie was alleged to have been drunk at the time.

II

The motionless sunny air was already tainted with a little smell of urban heat, and Plotinus Road, as always on a Sunday morning, was quiet and peaceful in a sort of yawning emptiness. There was neither traffic on the road nor hurrying people on the pavement; but under his window Julian could see half a dozen attentive children. They were patiently staring at the house opposite, which for the last three days had been the object of unusual and almost national interest. Rose Armour was there, watching by the bedside of her dying mother.

Not for many years had an English actress been so well loved in England or so highly esteemed in the more critical atmosphere of America. She had become famous at the age of eighteen, when she had been given a small part in a poor comedy at the Garrick Theatre. She had little to do. She had to laugh and be kissed. But so infectious was her laughter that half the house joined in, and a moment later, being most casually kissed, she had kissed in return, quick and passionate, with such ardour in the movement that half the house felt, as though it were an electric shock, the full force of young love. She had become the chief attraction in the play, and by pro-longing its unworthy life had conclusively demonstrated her talent by saving for its backers a considerable sum of money. But her career on the legitimate stage had been short, for it was soon discovered that she had a charming voice, and there-after her public had preferred to see and hear her in musical pieces.

She had also acted for the films, and in the cinema her success had been as immediate as in the theatre. Unlike the great majority of cinema actors, she had resisted the flatten-ing effect of her new medium, and her playing was so lively that many of her more simple admirers used to say, 'She comes right out of the picture and sits in your lap'. Her vitality was irrepressible, her physical charm more than sufficient, and she never forgot, or was tempted to conceal, her humble birth. Now, when she was world-famous and exceedingly rich, she had come rushing home at the first words of her mother's illness, and because her mother had always refused to leave the little house in Plotinus Road – to her mother, indeed, since she had stopped the taking of lodgers, it seemed a house of extravagant dimensions – Rose Armour had returned to its narrow rooms, and might have been happy enough had it not been for the nearness of death.

At her arrival, and for some little time after it, the street had been crowded with reporters, press photographers, and the general public. But Rose had pleaded for quietness, for her mother's sake, and now she was visited only twice a day by half a dozen of the most tactful newspaper-men in London, and the street had emptied of all her clamorous warm-hearted admirers except the obstinate children of the neighbourhood, whom no human power could keep away.

To Julian Brown her coming had been unusually disturbing. In the privacy of his own mind he admitted without shame that he wanted above all things to be a great lover. To go with splendid ease from this proud mistress to her who was more gay, from one who was *spirituelle et raffinée* to another whose *grands yeux noirs* shone with a melting warmth; there surely was the top of luxury and the very heat of the sun. But now the nearness of Rose Armour had driven all his other dreams away, and he curiously resented this enforced fidelity that put him on the same level as half the love-sick hobble-dehoys in Britain. Despite his passion, he regretted his lost freedom, his heroic and never-achieved promiscuity; and once, essaying to break the spell, he had with a reddened face refused to look at Rose when they happened to pass in the street. But in truth it mattered very little whether he looked at her or not. Her image was too clearly fixed upon his mind to need renewal.

Having finished his breakfast, Julian took from his wardrobe a uniform tunic and a Sam Browne belt, and began to polish brass and buttons and the already gleaming leather. He was a lieutenant in a Territorial battalion of Royal Fusiliers, and this Sunday was the occasion of their annual Church Parade. His colleagues, at the school where he taught, disapproved of Julian's military enthusiasm, for most of them were inclined to a pacifist doctrine and Left-wing politics. But Julian appreciated the sensation of power that he had when his commands were instantly obeyed by tall and disciplined men in uniform – by tautly attentive men who marched and turned or stood immobile at his word – and he knew that war, if it came, would produce other excitements than those of the battlefield. War was a moral laxative of the strongest kind, and one who was fighting his country's battles, if he avoided being killed in them, might well become a great lover in the intervals of sterner service. He would also have the profound satisfaction of fighting for France; most probably on the very soil of France. For England, of course, would be on the French side.

The uniform suited him. He had a good figure and carried himself well. His long thin jaw and high-bridged nose had a very soldierly appearance under his service cap, and his uniform, which had cost more than he could properly afford, was as smart as that of any Regular officer.

And how excellent it was, he thought, to wear a sword! It had been the proudest of all weapons, and though it might now be regarded as little more than an ornament, it was still the most gallant of ornaments. No one who carried a sword was not ennobled by it. He wished that Rose Armour could see him, no longer a schoolmaster, but an officer with a sword at his side.

III

The auxiliary ketch *Freya*, with her sky-darting white Bermuda sails and shapely hull, made a charming picture on the ruffled blue water of the Channel. There was a light south-westerly breeze, and she was reaching easily, with St Catherine's Point about three miles on her starboard quarter. Sailing the boat was her owner, Colonel Scrymgeour, lately in command of the 2nd Grenadier Guards and now Deputy Director of Military Operations and Intelligence; and with him in the cockpit were his wife, Lady Lysistrata, and Mr Eliot Greene, the Parliamentary Under-Secretary of State for Foreign Affairs.

In appearance they were distinguished – and oddly distinguished – by very striking and curiously dissimilar features. The Colonel had a flat Mongolian countenance, with heavy eyelids and a broad and heavy mandible; Mr Eliot Greene was Latin and loquacious, dark and aquiline, with raven hair and brilliant eyes; and Lady Lysistrata might have sat as a model to Praxiteles. Her Grecian features were inherited from her great-great-grandmother: after playing a notable part in the defence of Missolonghi, her great-great-grandfather, the eccentric third Marquis of Lovenden, had married an Acarnanian peasant girl.

For some time the pleasant sounds of sailing – the soft shearing hiss of cloven water and the returning melody of the little bow-wave – were uninterrupted by speech. The day was very fine, a tempered sunlight being enclosed by distant haze, and the circumstances favoured peaceful contemplation rather than gossip or debate.

But presently Lady Lysistrata, whose active mind was proof against any environment, turned to Mr Eliot Greene, and said, 'Oughtn't you to have stayed in London, Eliot? And wouldn't you have stayed if you had any sense of responsibility?'

'I have a very definite sense of responsibility,' he answered, 'but I have taught it not to diffuse itself.'

'You mean you can leave it in a pigeon-hole and forget about it. But who's in charge, if anything happens during the week-end? The Prime Minister and Rumble are both at Loven Bister, and I don't believe there's a Minister left in town.'

'I shouldn't worry, Lysistrata. The political prophet is less certain than the meteorologist, and even the best of depressions can tumble off its isobar. There's time enough to put up your umbrella when it starts to rain.'

'I think,' said Colonel Scrymgeour reflectively, 'that I'll try out the new Genoa.'

'There are occasions,' said Lysistrata with unfriendly vehemence, 'when I come to the conclusion that masculine authority is always either cynical or incompetent; and often it is both together.'

'That sounds well, but it isn't true. Tony, for instance, is most decidedly not a cynic, and his competence is notorious.'

'If you're in the Army, it isn't very difficult to get a reputation for competence. Even a cripple looks fairly fast where everyone else is bedridden,' said Lady Lysistrata.

Colonel Antony Scrymgeour's reputation was comparable to that of Lord Kitchener in the early years of the century. To the general public he was a hero, to the Army a teacher and reformer. While still a junior captain he had fought, under an assumed name, in the Spanish Civil War, of which he had later written a history that was admitted to be a major work of military criticism. A few years later, when the Guards went to India to hurry things up in the last Afghan war, Scrymgeour became the hero of the battle and long-drawn siege of Ghazni. Having been seriously wounded, as well as decorated and promoted, his health broke down, and he was given a year's sick leave. To encourage convalescence he entered Parliament at

a by-election, and fought a fierce and successful battle on behalf of Army reform. His purpose achieved, he resigned his
seat and returned to his military duties. At the same time
his popularity with the general public, and his influence in
certain other quarters, were augmented by his marriage to
Lady Lysistrata, whose father had just won the Derby with
the most heavily backed favourite there had been for a
generation.

His marriage, however, was not the most successful part of
Colonel Scrymgeour's career, for his wife had a character of
great independence, and her mind was so much her own that
it not only resisted the victor of Ghazni, but often attacked
him. She was, at times, most wantonly opinionative. She would
question the Colonel's innermost beliefs – he was conventional
by nature, and enough of a scholar to give orthodoxy an his-
torical defence – and try to undermine him, to worry him
out of them. He, not unnaturally, was bored by her questions
and angered by her criticism. He was also, on occasion, exasperated by the indignity of being in love with a woman who
so persistently annoyed him. He was very passionately in love
with her.

Now, ignoring his wife's last remark, he said to Mr Eliot
Greene, 'You made rather a hash of your speech at the Dinner,
didn't you?'

'It was unpopular, and perhaps indiscreet,' Mr Greene
admitted. 'Nevertheless, if ye know the truth, the truth shall
make you free; and it is time, I think, that we recognized the
instinctive Machiavellianism of the English character. My little
speech' – he addressed Lysistrata – 'was a laudation of that
injunction of our pious Founder, which has since become the
College motto, *Be Loyal.*'

'Loyal to what?' asked Lysistrata. 'That has always puzzled
me. Time and again we English have discarded our kings,
broken our contracts, and forsaken our principles; yet we are
all agreed that loyalty is not only one of our favourite ideals,
but one of our established habits. It's very mysterious.'

'That was precisely the point I raised,' said Mr Greene,
'and my old school-fellows were very indignant when I
suggested that the only real object of our loyalty was self-

interest. Nor, as I hoped it might, did I wholly soothe their feelings by saying that the English, being a comparatively illiterate people, are susceptible to the magic of words rather than to their meaning. Consider the word *character*, for instance. No one bothers to observe that *character*, like *loyalty*, needs definition. We are satisfied with it, all unsupported, because it has acquired a numinous quality. It is a good word. It is one of those magical words which mean so much to us English that when they are spoken with proper solemnity they induce in all who hear them a willing suspension of the critical faculty.'

'Another good word,' interrupted the Colonel, 'is balderdash.'

'An excellent word,' said Mr Greene. 'It used to mean a mixture of beer and buttermilk, and heaven knows that that was a nonsensical conjunction. It is a word that the Foreign Secretary and I must use more often. – Thank you for the suggestion, Tony. – I think Sir Joseph could have found a place for it in the speech that he broadcast on Friday.'

'To sum up what he had said?' Lysistrata coldly enquired.

Mr Greene looked at her reproachfully, 'You didn't approve of his aery message?'

'It was so ambiguous as to be quite meaningless, and his manner was heavily self-righteous.'

'That is the precise description of a really useful political announcement.'

'You're infuriating, Eliot. The situation is serious, and I want to talk seriously about it. I'm worried, and no one will help me, neither you nor Tony.'

'Isn't it enough to be assured that appropriate action is being taken by the responsible authorities? – There, incidentally, is a really numinous sentence. – And surely, on a day like this, it is abundantly evident that God's in his heaven and the situation is well in hand.'

'In which hand, right or left? Are we going to stand by France? Have we a policy, and if so, what is it?'

'To ride in the whirlwind and direct the storm,' said Mr Greene with a pleasant smile.

'Or raise a storm and then run away from it?'

Colonel Scrymgeour smothered a yawn and said, 'Take the tiller, Eliot. I'm going to help Bulmer set the new Genoa.'

He swung himself over the coaming of the cockpit, and going forward shouted to a paid hand who was busy below.

'We talk about our commitments and our friendship with France,' Lysistrata continued, 'and at the same time the War Office is having Staff Talks with Germany.'

'How did you hear of that? Did Tony tell you? They're entirely secret, and it was only in confidence, in return for another secret, that I learnt about them myself.'

'Tony never tells me anything till I've read it in the papers. It was Mary Rumble.'

'Oh, of course, Sir Joseph has always believed that bed-time is the time for confidences, and she knows everything that's going on. How lucky we are that he's faithful to his Mary, and no other pillow hears his secrets. What did she say about the Staff Talks?'

'She hadn't time to tell me very much, but apparently we want to do a deal for their new anti-aircraft guns.'

'I can't help thinking that that's a good idea. But of course France will hear about it and accuse us of perfidy. We had a look at their new guns, two or three months ago, and didn't think much of them. I'm devoted to the French, most truly devoted, but their insistence that the welfare of France should be the first charge on European statesmanship makes our relations with them rather difficult. As a matter of fact, my relations with you are getting more difficult.'

'There's no reason why they should be.'

'Except the fallacy of the half-loaf, my dear. It feeds, but it doesn't satisfy, and I'm more deeply in love with you every day.'

'But you mustn't think that. You must be reasonable. I love you, but I'm not indifferent to Tony's welfare, and I'm not going to do anything that would spoil, or even interfere with his career.'

'I'm quite prepared to abandon my own.'

'You can do as you please about that, but you won't make me think any more kindly of you by a show of irresponsibility.'

'Love has nothing to do with responsibility. It ignores it and overrides it.'

'On the contrary, it conforms to it – if love has grown up, that is.'

'You complained, a few minutes ago, that I could put away my sense of duty in a pigeon-hole. And now you're doing the same with love.'

Lysistrata turned away, and leaning her arm on the coaming, faced the warm breeze and the sunny ruffling of the sea. She spoke over her shoulder: 'Dear Eliot, don't let us quarrel on a day like this. It's so wholly beautiful. Don't let us argue any more, about love or politics or anything. Nothing matters that doesn't upset our peace, and nothing is worth while that does. We can live happy and quite complicated lives so long as there's an arch of peace above us.'

'Listen!' said Eliot suddenly.

Muffled by the distance and dimly drumming against the leisurely wind, three or four shocks of sound had come faintly to his ears.

'I don't hear anything.'

'Listen,' he repeated.

Small and dull, like the coughing of a distant lion heard by drowsy men in a tent, the sounds were repeated and a moment afterwards innumerably multiplied. Now it seemed as though the far-off jungle were full of lions, dryly coughing, roaring with anger that was muted by many leagues of air.

Colonel Scrymgeour, with Bulmer behind him – an agile but melancholy-seeming man with long arms – came hurrying aft, and another hand, emerging nimbly from the forward hatch, went to the jib-sheets.

'In mainsheet,' commanded the Colonel, and took the tiller. The hiss of softly cloven water and the lap of the little bow-wave became a brisker noise, and they felt the wind in their faces.

'Hard-alee,' exclaimed the Colonel, and put her about. 'Get below, Bulmer, and start the engine.'

'What do you think has happened, Tony?'

'I don't know, but we'd better go and see.'

Thudding softly on their ears, the noise of the bombardment

was like the petulant bursting and the sullen fall of ripe fruit.

'It isn't – it isn't war?' said Lysistrata. But no one answered her.

'Well, if it is,' she cried angrily, 'I'm going to have nothing to do with it, and you, Tony, are certainly not going to the front!'

IV

Julian Brown had gone as far as the corner of Plotinus Road and Clapham Road before he became aware of an uncommonly loud noise in the sky. Then, looking up, he saw part of a glistening fleet of aeroplanes, flying high, half-curtained in the sunny mist. For a second or two he stood awkwardly, his head bent back, his chin up, his neck taut; and suddenly he felt in his throat a choking sensation, that was not caused by straining muscles, but by a strange and swift perception that something of fearful horror was rushing earthwards.

The blast of the explosion knocked him off his feet, and for a moment or two of dreadful chaos he lay in a state of half-conscious bewilderment. In this semi-comatose but yet terrified condition he heard three more explosions – earth-shaking detonations that stupendously beat upon his ears – and then, a tiny sound after that enormous thunder, the fretful crying of wounded or frightened people. Painfully he sat up, his head ringing and his stomach rising, and saw that half the street was in ruins. On one side of him was a broken lamp-post, on the other a stuffed owl that had been blown irrelevantly out of a demolished parlour. Houses were raggedly disintegrated, walls had been thrust apart and were still falling, and pieces of genteel furniture lay tattered in a sudden brickyard. Through the reddish dust, that swayed and counter-swayed to his giddiness, he perceived figures running agitatedly to and fro. Some of them were only half-dressed, and a fat man in his shirt-sleeves, his braces hanging down, was shrilly blowing a whistle.

Julian got unsteadily to his feet. His sword was between his legs and he nearly fell again. But the encumbering weapon reminded him of his responsibility. He caught and steadied his still swaying consciousness. He stiffened his shoulders, he straightened his cap, and hurried towards the gathering crowd.

A man with blood on his face was crying insanely, and no one took any notice of him. A thin and tremulously angry woman, with a hair-brush in one hand and a sobbing child in the other, screamed hoarsely to a small boy, 'Come 'ere, Stan! Come 'ere this minute and get your gas-mask on!'

'Good for you!' shouted Julian with unnecessary vehemence. 'You're all right. You've got sense in your head!'

He felt within himself a surging of strength and angry competence. He had been waiting for this for years. He was still sick and dizzy, but no longer afraid of bombs, and he had no doubt of his own ability. He ran to meet a group of three people. Rose Armour, in a green linen dress, was one of them. The others were a woman in nurse's uniform, and a young man with a very pale face, very red hair, and heavy horn-rimmed spectacles.

'You're not hurt?' asked Julian.

Rose Armour shook her head. 'I'm all right. Thank God, mother didn't live to see this. She died half an hour ago. This is Dr Binning.'

Julian shouted to the young man with red hair – northward, across the river, the bombs were dropping in a pandemonium of abrupt and echoing thunder – 'We've got to collect the wounded and take everybody to the nearest Clearing Station. I want you to take charge of this side of the street, and the nurse to look after the other.'

The fat man in his shirt-sleeves, who had been blowing a whistle, came puffing towards them and clumsily saluted. 'I'm the Air Raid Warden for this district, sir. I don't smell any gas in the air, but I've sent 'em in to get their masks and emergency rations, just in case. Some of them are sort of excited – took 'em by surprise, on a nice morning like this – but we'll soon get things tidied up a bit.'

Julian hurriedly gave him further instructions. He had the gift of authority. He had always known it, and never been able to exercise it without restraint. But here was his opportunity, and he was taking it, fully, and despite its horror, without hesitation.

He felt, with a curious indignant pride, not merely capable of dealing with the situation, but of exploiting it.

The Warden again saluted, and Julian turned to Rose Armour. 'Do you feel able to help me?' he asked. 'I must go and see what other damage has been done, and I'd like you to come with me. You might be useful. If there's any panic, it'll quieten them to see you walking about – if they're calm enough to recognize you, that is.'

She nodded, and spoke in a dry breathless voice. 'I'll do anything I can. It's lucky I've got a good nerve, isn't it?'

They walked quickly towards Clapham Road, and turning into it found there, and in Petunia Street, conditions similar to the ruin they had left. They picked their way through familiar wreckage, through a desolation of broken walls and shattered furniture, the savage brittling of tidy homes. But already the more stout-hearted inhabitants were controlling their fear-stricken neighbours, and rescue work had begun. The sheets of a large double-bed, with brass rails and an abundance of covers, that had been hurled from a collapsing house into a tiny privet-hedged front garden, were being torn into bandages, and Julian quickly organized a systematic search among the ruins for dead and wounded. Everyone was ordered out of the remaining buildings, and an ex-sergeant of police, who carried, rolled up like a truncheon, a copy of the *News of the World*, took charge of the able-bodied survivors.

The value of the air-raid drills, which for several years everyone in London had been obliged to attend, was sufficiently demonstrated. The first panic quickly subsided, and grief had less chance of utterance when those who had most cause for sorrow were given familiar work to do. Julian was an efficient organizer, and Rose Armour, though unable to help the wounded – for the sight of blood sickened her – was bravely useful in calming the frightened children. Her face was white, and her voice strained and shrill. But children stopped crying when they saw her, and she gathered them about her as easily as if she had been the Pied Piper.

Policemen and a fire brigade arrived. Some small thermite bombs had been dropped, and a dozen houses were ablaze. Julian found a score of volunteers to assist the firemen, and the police helped him in the dangerous last stages of the search for wounded or imprisoned survivors. The flames grew hotter, and they worked more desperately. They rescued a child from a burning house, a moment before it collapsed, and Julian decided they had done all they could.

The loss of life was remarkably small. The younger people of the neighbourhood, taking advantage of a fine week-end, were nearly all far afield, afoot or on bicycles, walking the Downs or sitting under sunny hedges. They had saved their lives for another day. Only their elders and their youngest brothers and sisters were left at home, and it was a slow-moving company that Julian presently mustered and led towards the 23rd South London Clearing Station. But they were not without spirit. Anger had enlivened some of them, and many felt, as a wild and drunken delight, the joy of having escaped such near and dreadful death. They were alive! They felt their limbs moving, sweaty but whole, and smelt the bright day, and there on the pavement beside them, walking with a fine young officer, was Rose Armour, their darling.

They were all her admirers, her distant lovers, her worshipful public. A fat waddling woman, shameless in a meagre bodice and petticoat, cried in a great voice, 'Good old Rose! We'll look after you!'

Rose Armour turned and waved her hand. They answered her in cracked and doubtful voices. Some were hysterical, and others on the edge of hysteria. But here and there was a note of true defiance, of honest bravado, and an oldish man, wearing a steel helmet that was his souvenir of the last war, shouted from the far side of the column, 'Stick to us, Rose, and you won't go wrong! Are we down-'earted? *No!*'

The children, crowding to the head of the procession, were now wildly excited. They began to sing, and the song they chose – the first that was heard in the new war – was as vulgar and inappropriate as *Tipperary* in 1914. But Rose Armour had sung it in *Happy Hampstead*, her latest and liveliest film, and the English, their spirit yet blissfully unregimented, and as totally illogical as ever, found it more to their liking than any battle-hymn could be. It was destined to be sung by all the regiments that went marching on English roads and foreign

highways, and finally its triviality, by repeated association
with heroism, appeared to wear, like an ill-fitting mask, a
certain aspect of greatness. The words of the chorus were:

> Up in the morning and fry the bacon,
>   Make him a nice cup of tea:
> Who would think yesterday I was forsaken,
>   Now I'm as happy as happy can be?
> If you feel rotten because you're a woman,
>   Seek for a suitable spouse –
> Say what you like, but we're all of us human,
>   And better for having a man in the house!

The neighbouring streets were full of shouting, crying, and
stampeding people. They were more panic-stricken than the
streets which had been bombarded, and neither police nor
their Raid Wardens could control them. But when they saw
the procession of survivors, and heard the children singing,
they fell back before them. They drew to either side, on to
the pavements, back to the dusty railings and the blind shop-
fronts, and the retreat put on a disguise of triumph. Seeing
they had an audience, the children sang louder than ever,
and their elders, in quavering or raucous voices, took up the
song to show their neighbours they were undefeated. While
the warring aeroplanes, now homeward bound, were still over
English soil, their victims were chanting with indefeasible
sentiment and brazen incongruity,

> Say what you like, but we're all of us human,
>   And better for having a man in the house!

To Julian the song was exhilarating. It was an army in
retreat, a poor and ragged army, that he commanded; but
his motley troops were singing, and therefore they were not
beaten troops. The streets they had left were a battlefield,
and northward the summer sky was dark with heavily rising
smoke. The raiding aeroplanes had gone again, leaving a
ruined city behind them, but not a defeated people. This
simple troop of his, untidy women and men not drilled, had
faced the sudden terror from the sky – unarmed and having
no defence – and stood their ground; the common people of
England, the little street-bred heirs of Agincourt and Mal-

plaquet, had shown their mettle, and he – he turned his head and stared fiercely at a saluting constable – he had shown them the old trick of leadership.

In this brave mood he was disconcerted to find Rose Armour crying. She held tightly to his arm, and like a child, the tears running down her face, sobbed without concealment. 'It's mother,' she said. 'I must go back and walk beside her.'

'Of course,' he said quickly – ashamed of pride, contrite in a moment, and feeling his love for Rose as though it were a wave that would take him off his feet – 'Of course. I'll come with you, shall I? Because of the crowd.'

He called to the fat Raid Warden, who with a rolling stride was marching behind him, and said, 'I'm going back to see that the wounded are all right. I want you to take the head of the column. And don't hurry them too much.'

'Not likely to do that, sir,' said the Warden affably. 'You 'aven't ever seen my veins, or you wouldn't think I'd go hurrying anyone.'

Julian nodded, and with Rose Armour beside him, stood while the dishevelled column went slowly by.

She dried her eyes, and catching her breath between every few words, she said, 'I'm sorry I began to cry, but we've gone through rather a lot this morning, haven't we? And then they started to sing that song of mine. They're such darlings, aren't they? If only mother could have heard them! But she's better off where she is. She was always so frightened of another war, and I used to think she was just getting in a flap about nothing, like old people do. And now it's started, and we don't even know who we've got to fight against. Oh, but you're an officer. You're sure to know.'

'Germany, of course,' said Julian, and felt as he spoke a violent interweaving of emotions. There was hatred of the country that had treacherously broken England's peace, and a feeling of excitement so pleasant that he could hardly help being grateful for it. Rose Armour was beside him. She held to him, and looked to him for protection. The whole world had changed in the last half-hour. The schoolmaster had become a soldier, and Rose Armour was only a woman.

On improvised stretchers the wounded were carried past.

Julian, still and erect, looked at them gravely, but hardly saw they were in pain. More keenly than a wound, he felt the tight hand on his arm, and a thrill of triumph in his blood. He had wanted a war, and now it had come.

V

When Julian told Rose Armour that the enemy was Germany, he was as far wrong as the man who calls *Heads* when *Tails* has fallen. That is to say, as wrong as he could be. The raiding aeroplanes were French. It was France that had so summarily declared war on her former ally.

To Julian and other Francophiles – who included all the most agreeable and intelligent people in Britain – the revelation of the identity of their enemy was an even greater shock than the fact of being at war. It was of small significance that they felt they had been betrayed; many of them, secure in Britannic righteousness, would have thought that, no matter who their opponents were; but their feeling of disorientation was overwhelming. They were like exiles in a harsh unfruitful land when they found that Paris was the hostile capital, the language of Stendhal and Proust the enemy's tongue, and claret became inimical to their patriotism. It could not be, they said, and being by tragic evidence assured it was, a small minority accepted the situation with the hopeless fortitude of passengers on a sinking liner, and the vast majority, after an interval for reaction, discovered an anger against France that was fiercer by far than the wrath of original Francophobes.

It was not for several months that anyone in Britain had the opportunity to study in detail the case for France, and to learn the immediate cause of her unheralded aggression; and by that time the war was being so widely and intensively waged that very few could find sufficient detachment to be interested in its origin. But France had not acted without reason, though whether her reasons were sufficient will always be a matter for dispute.

In the first place, her historic fear of Germany had compelled her to take a serious view of Herr Hitler's speech and the new map of Canaan; while Britain's threatened breach with

Russia, almost coincident with this, and closely followed by the elaborate ambiguity of Sir Joseph Rumble's statement, had caused further perturbation. Then, on the Saturday preceding the outbreak of war, the Quai d'Orsay had received information of no less than three occurrences, any one of which, in the circumstances, was sufficient to strain Franco-British relations to a state of acute discomfort.

At midday news was received of the Mordecai £50,000,000 loan to Germany. It was found impossible to get official confirmation of the report – official sources in London had been sealed for the week-end, and Berlin's reply was that Germany could not and would not permit any interference with her private affairs – but by late afternoon it was confirmed beyond all reasonable doubt.

Then, at six o'clock, M. Thevenin, the Minister for War, was asked by a Colonel Bizet, of the Bureau of Military Intelligence, to consider a statement newly received from a man whose name was either Gody, Pückel, or Ramírez – subsequent investigation never identified him, nor proved his nationality – and discovered, to his great consternation, that a series of Staff Talks had recently taken place between the English War Office and its opposite number in Germany. He at once communicated with the Premier, and the Conseil des Ministres was summoned for nine o'clock. M. Thevenin himself questioned the man Gody, who told him that Britain had offered, in the event of war and under certain conditions, to admit Germany's territorial jurisdiction over the Baltic east of a line through the Aland Islands; and had got in part exchange the secret design of the new German anti-aircraft gun. He would not give any further details of the pact, and refused to explain how he had acquired his information. He was then put under arrest and removed for more intensive questioning.

The Conseil des Ministres had barely had time to express its anger and dismay, when a Secretary laid before the Minister for Marine a report of the collision at Toulon between the British steamer *Araby* and the destroyer *L'Aiglon*. Both ships had sunk, it said, and were lying in the fairway. The entrance to the port was blocked.

It was easy to see more than an accident in this unfortunate occurrence. In the circumstances, indeed, it was difficult not to regard it as a deliberate act of war. In recent years the major Powers, when pursuing a forward policy, had invariably refrained from the ostentation of any formal declaration of war; and several Ministers, recalling similar incidents in the past, were absolutely convinced of Britain's hostile intention. They were the more sure they were right because the British Fleet, not yet dispersed after its summer cruise, was ostensibly engaged in tactical exercises off the coast of Morocco. The Premier, after some difficulty in making himself heard, pleaded for patience and said he anticipated, at any moment, an *éclaircissement* of British policy. This untoward concatenation of events, he said, might yet be capable of friendly interpretation, and the most sinister implications be happily dissolved. It was unfortunate that the British Ambassador was in London – he had gone there to attend the Old Hattonian Dinner – but an attempt was being made to get into touch with Lord Pippin, the Prime Minister, or Sir Joseph Rumble, the British Foreign Secretary. It had been ascertained that they were spending the week-end at Loven Bister, the seat of the Marquis of Lovenden.

This honest and well-intentioned move, however, was nullified by an unfortunate accident. The secretary, who had been trying to telephone to Loven Bister, was given a line to a notorious road-house with the fanciful name of Love-in-a-Mist, where his inquiry for the Prime Minister was regarded as a joke. He got a rude and facetious reply, which he reported to the Conseil des Ministres with natural indignation. His anger was shared by the Ministers, and at midnight orders were issued for general and immediate mobilization.

An hour later the Conseil reassembled to hear the result of the questioning of Gody. His examination had apparently been conducted with some brutality – the British War Office subsequently denied his allegations, and stated that testimony exacted under duress was of no value whatsoever – but his story was coherent and told with so much detail that it commanded instant belief. According to him, the fullest plans had been made for collaboration between Britain and Germany in the event of any move, that might be construed as unfriendly to either, by any one of the countries commonly supposed to represent the Left ideological front; and this understanding was to be made public by an Anglo-German denunciation of all alliances based on political ideology.

The Premier continued to plead for time and caution and an open mind, but the other Ministers were in no mood to welcome a policy of moderation or to listen coolly to anything; they preferred the lusty violence of M. César Baradat, the Minister for Labour, a huge, trumpet-toned, mustachioed Pyrenean, a passionate Communist, a poet, duellist, and enemy of everything that smelt of indecision and double-dealing and Germany. It was he who demanded war. He asked them what had been, for the last twenty-five years, the foreign policy of Great Britain? A cold, calculating, bargain-hunting purchase of time, he said. Time to recuperate, rebuild, and rearm – as now Britain had rearmed – and now at last she was showing her true colours. All the prudent expediency of British policy he denounced as the covers of a Machiavellian programme. Britain's careful avoidance of trouble, its cautious belief that honesty was not always the best foreign policy, its sensible perception that where honour conflicted with self-interest, honour was the lesser sacrifice: all this sagacity he arraigned, in a manner that would have bewildered and infuriated English listeners, as cunning progress to the clearly envisaged goal of unchallengeable power. And now, so the English thought, they had come to that state of power. But France, undaunted, would accept the challenge!

He addressed the Ministers for thirty minutes, and long before he had done, France was committed to war. But M. Baradat had not finished. He demanded not only war, but the instant commission of a decisive act of war. In the name of humanity he demanded this seeming outrage. Let France strike such a blow as would paralyse the heart and brain of England, and the war would be over while the echoes of its first assault were still rumbling in the sky. The head and power of Britain would be destroyed, but its people would scarcely be injured. They would, on the contrary, be far better off, for such a war would be like a surgical operation, removing from the body politic that which was poisoning it: namely, the oligarchy that had for so long misgoverned, thwarted, and enchained the people of Great Britain. And so on.

Stressing again the ultimate humanity of his proposal, M. Baradat said he had no intention of asking for the use of any form of poison gas. France was the soldier of civilization, and had a natural abhorrence of that fiendish Germanic invention. But in spite of this clemency he had considerable difficulty in persuading the Ministers to authorize an aerial bombardment of London without the formal declaration of war; though in the decade that had gone since Italy's conquest of Abyssinia, no such declaration had preceded any of the several wars which history had recorded, save a brief campaign between Honduras and Nicaragua. At last, however, he succeeded, and the fateful order was given.

Though M. Baradat's faith in the finishing power of an air-raid was unwarranted, his belief in its relative humanity was apparently justified. In all that made it a capital city, London was destroyed; but the loss of life was no more than the sum of a few weeks' road casualties. Between seven and eight hundred killed, and two or three thousand wounded; that was the human total, for the City was empty and the docks almost deserted in their Sabbath quiet when the bombs fell on them.

But Whitehall was practically demolished – what remained of Downing Street was mere debris – and two large bombs that fell in the Star Chamber Court and the Peers' Inner Court laid the Houses of Parliament in ruins, which the subsequent fire reduced to rubble and a few desolate stalagmites of stubborn masonry. In the City there was hardly a building left intact, though St Paul's escaped without other damage than the wrecking of the Dean's Vestry. The Bank and the Guildhall and the General Post Office were completely destroyed, and from Tower Bridge to Gallions the docks were bombarded with pitiless accuracy. It was in Poplar and Silvertown that most of the human casualties occurred.

When the raid was over, London was left without a head or a spine. It survived as a huge and shapeless deposit of irrelevant domestic architecture. Its nucleus had been extirpated, and the periphery remained with nothing to justify its existence or direct its activities. That which had given life to the whole and united its teeming millions in a semblance of corporate existence, had been deleted.

But the annihilation of London – of its source of motion and action – was not the end of the war. It was only the beginning.

CHAPTER TWO

Arma Virosque Cano

I

By the end of August the war had become general. All Europe, except the three Scandinavian countries, was more or less involved in it, and on all fronts there had been perforce a return to the conventional use of trenches and the orthodox principle of attrition. The war had settled down.

During the period of aerial activity, the most appalling damage had been done to almost every large city from Glasgow to Stamboul. But this phase of the war was of brief duration. Its horror was too much, and the people rose against it. In those countries especially where war had been glorified, and whose citizens for many years had by government instruction seen themselves only in the destined role of conqueror, there was dismay and a wild resentment when their towns were bombarded, and their children who had been called the heirs of the future lay dead in the ruined schools that had taught them to think always of victory. Their newspapers told of the burning of enemy towns, and stories of triumphant carnage were broadcast nightly. The air vibrated with tales of victory, and the streets were humming with news of the destruction of Paris and London and Moscow. But the voices that told of foreign death and the enemy's collapse, were in the same words shouting their own domestic losses, and there was blood in the streets to prove it. Call Paris Berlin, and the story was as true as ever. Aeroplanes flew over both, and dropped their bombs, and between the ruins they left there was no longer any difference. The aeroplanes came, the bombs fell, houses broke asunder, and women and old men lay dead. Then who should say, This was French, this was German? The little difference, so dear and perilous, had been destroyed, and that spilt envelope of blood had no nation. But the aeroplanes were the enemy of all. The aeroplanes came – no matter whose, there was no more difference between aeroplanes than be-

tween bodies that had been French and German, and now
were nothing – and when the aeroplanes went again there
were more ruins, and children dead or screaming their intolerable pain. The aeroplanes were death itself.

The people turned against their own men and destroyed
their own machines. They burnt hangars, and broke bombers
and pursuit-planes with pokers and axes. They set upon the
pilots and trampled them underfoot. Scores of them were
murdered.

The madness infected all Europe. It began in the countries
where sanity and freedom of thought had been driven under-
ground, and sanity, breaking its shackles, came out like a
maniac. But the other countries, the remnant democracies,
caught the frenzy too. It set quiet men and decent household
women to lynching and burning. A fury possessed them, more
dreadful than the ancient lust of witch-finding, but fed like it
on crazy fear and finding like it relief in cruelty and violence.
At many stations and encampments of the air services – in
France and Britain, Russia and the Balkans – there were
pitched battles, and soldiers joined with civilians against the
airmen. For a few days there was chaos throughout Europe,
and when order was re-established a flying-machine was as
rare a thing to see as it had been thirty years before.

But the war went on. The governments of Europe had committed themselves, and were not to be deterred by a few days
of internecine killing. The huge machinery of war had been
set in motion, and was more difficult to stop than it had been
to start. Had the revolt against the airmen had leaders, they
might have turned it into a campaign against war of any kind.
But the revolt had been leaderless. It was a general rising of
the people, undirected and spontaneous, and for that reason
all governments had been helpless against it. They could not
quell it; but when it had spent itself, they could ignore it.
Having destroyed the aeroplanes, the people were again
amenable to discipline. The mainspring of their rising had
been fear, and when they had dispelled their fear they were
ready once more to be dutiful citizens. They were, indeed,
eager to show how sensible and submissive they really
were, being already deeply ashamed of all they had done in

the lust of witch-hunting. They flattered their rulers with cheerful obedience and protestations of loyalty; so the governments returned implacably to their muttons, and the war went on.

The United States remained neutral, but not idle. The American Government, in somewhat ironical coincidence, had made a humane and self-sacrificing attempt to limit aerial warfare at the same time as so many fear-stricken people were destroying the instruments of it. Three days after the bombing of London, the President of the United States had signed a decree forbidding the export to any destination whatsoever of American petroleum; and forty-eight hours later his representatives had persuaded Mexico and Venezuela to impose a similar ban. Out of a world production of about 215,000,000 tons, this accounted for 150,000,000; and the European oil-fields were meanwhile being ruined by saboteurs. Though the people's rising had been undirected, it had not been wholly unintelligent, and the idea had occurred to many of attacking aerial warfare at its source. The oil-fields of Poland and Russia and Rumania had all been so badly damaged that there was little hope of their resuming production for many months; and wreckers had caused similar havoc to the wells of Iraq and the Dutch East Indies. And so by sanctions in the New World and sabotage in the old, the combatants' supply of petrol was restricted to what they had in store and to the products of a little hazardous bootlegging.

By this unexpected dearth the warring armies were soon robbed of their mechanized transport. Motor-trucks and tanks and armoured-cars all died of thirst like cattle in an Australian drought; and the speed of the armies was reduced to the old pace of men and horses. They took to trenches again. On the Western Front the line ran from Nieuport to the Swiss border, and in many places trenches were dug in the ground that had been scarred by the war of 1914. The British Expeditionary Force occupied positions not far removed from those that had once been defended by Old Contemptibles and Kitchener's Army; but with the material difference that they were now facing the other way round. They were to find, however, that Ypres was just as difficult to take or hold from one side as the

other. The stubbornness of the French resistance there, together
with the rain that fell throughout October, persuaded everyone of the folly of supposing that hostilities could be quickly
terminated. So trenches were deepened, more comfortable
dug-outs were excavated, and both sides prepared for a long
and satisfactory war of attrition.

II

Nearly three months later, Lady Lysistrata Scrymgeour and
Mr Eliot Greene were dining together at the New Carlton
Hotel in Blackpool. Most of the male diners, in the crowded
restaurant, wore either uniform or the evident mask of war-
time prosperity. The noise, presumably of gaiety, was loud
and sometimes strident. In nearly all the larger cities of Europe
there were, on the same evening, similar scenes and a comparable note of stridency wherever the soldiers and profiteers
sought entertainment; for in every country and every kind of
human activity the war had destroyed all reason and moderation. As grief had become excessive, so gaiety had grown
extravagant. As uncountable women were weeping in bitterness that knew no solace – mothers for their only sons, and
girls for their dear playmates – so others, hot with the world's
excitement, were laughing and making love in a sightless
frenzy. And because soldiers in the line were living in constant fear and the squalor of a badger's den, so those on leave,
and they who were under orders for the front, must fare as
richly as they could, drink deep, and snatch with boisterous
hands at every passing luxury. Good sense and temperance
had been lost with peace, and now there survived nothing but
extremes, of faith and ugliness, of fortitude and passion, of
greed and lies and tenderness and cruelty, of utter misery
and fevered glee. Nothing was the same as it had been, and
most things were altered for the worse.

Neither Eliot Greene nor Lady Lysistrata showed any sign
of gaiety, however. He, who was leaving for Germany on the
following morning, wore a dinner jacket, as if it were a life-
belt thrown from the sinking ship of ordinary existence, and
an expression of gloom that was nearly as dark as his coat;
and she, who was almost too tired to eat, maintained with

evident determination a precarious composure. From the outbreak of war she had ceased to be his lover, but he was still
unwilling to accept his dismissal.

'My dignity!' he said bitterly. 'What's the use of appealing
to something that no longer is? Dignity was my first discard
when I joined the Army. I swore instant obedience to anyone
who happened to have three stars on his shoulder. I took an
oath not to reason why. And having abjured reason for England's sake, it's absurd to suppose I can recapture it for yours.
I know that pleading isn't the way to win anyone's love; but
I don't want to win your love, I want to be admitted to it.
I'm reduced in circumstances, you see. I'm like a beggar,
grateful for scraps. I'd take your morsel of love, and be thankful, if you offered it with no more emotion than in giving an
old coat away. A coat that meant nothing to you, but was
comfort to the beggar who got it.'

'It's no use, Eliot. I've told you again and again that I
can't do it. And even if you've thrown away your dignity,
won't you, for my sake, have the decency to keep quiet about
it?'

'I may as well, I suppose.'

'I'm so very fond of you. From childhood I've been fond
of you. And we –'

'We can still be friends.'

'We could. And you're very foolish if you sneer at friendship.'

'There's nothing wrong with it, except that it isn't enough.
No, I'm not going to be importunate again. I'm really quite
happy. I'm off to war tomorrow. That's enough to make
anyone happy. But what I can't see is why, if Tony was
unaffected by our love before –'

'Eliot!'

'Yes, I know. I wasn't trying to persuade you. When did
you hear from Tony?'

'This morning. They've had heavy losses, but they're still
advancing.'

'Aren't our Generals fine?'

'Tony is,' said Lysistrata calmly.

Antony Scrymgeour was now a Major-General, and the

Fifth Division, which he commanded, was the spear-head of
an attack recently launched against the strong French position
on Passchendaele Ridge. The Division had already made a
name for itself – the popular newspapers referred to it as the
Fighting Fifth – and General Scrymgeour's fame had grown
correspondingly. So had his wife's love.

She had ceased to be critical of him on the day that he was
given a brigade in the first Expeditionary Force. She had,
indeed, ceased to be critical of nearly everything except the
iniquity of France and the neutrality of the United States.
She admitted that the war was a tragedy, but she passionately
believed that the only way to stop it was to win it. And because
Tony was in danger – because he was a soldier, and soldiers
were now of such paramount importance – her love for him,
that previously was so impatient and capricious, had become
whole and certain. It had acquired an almost idolatrous
fervour.

The cause of her presence in Blackpool, with Eliot Greene,
was the exigencies of the war. Within forty-eight hours of the
bombardment of London the Government had transferred
itself there. The move had been quickly and efficiently made,
because it was according to plan. The numerous departments,
services, and ancillary organizations of government found
ample accommodation in the spacious amusement halls and
countless boarding-houses of the Lancashire resort. Though
certain hypercritical observers thought its associations might
impair the dignity of administration, Blackpool was strategically
an excellent choice; and none of the dozen or so surviving
French raiders, who still occasionally and extravagantly flew
over England, had so far succeeded in reaching it.

Eliot Greene was in Blackpool for two reasons: because
Lysistrata was there, and because his regiment was not far
away. He, a natural Francophile, had been thrown into such
insensate fury by the French bombardment of London, that
he had immediately resigned his under-Secretaryship and
obtained a commission in the Rifle Brigade. The violence of
this behaviour, the desperate attempt to give his emotions the
freedom of a pendulum – which finds fulfilment in either ex-
treme – had for a little while brought him solace. But then

the monotony of his military duties had begun to affect his spirit, and the constant instruction in bayonet-fighting – which grew in importance as the war became more obviously an affair of infantry – reduced his mind to the dimensions of an irritated shellfish. It hid within an integument of deliberate indifference, and he refused, as though he were cutting his oldest friends, to recognize anything in life he had previously valued.

Unfortunately his battalion was sent for its last month of training to Fleetwood, and Eliot Greene found himself within easy visiting distance of Lady Lysistrata, who had become an Area Commandant of the V.A.D., with headquarters in Blackpool. He had sought to renew his broken love affair, and succeeded only in aggravating his wretchedness.

Lysistrata, though by long habit fond of him, found his rather dreary persistence increasingly trying, and with difficulty maintained an exasperated sympathy for his altered temper. Now, in the crowded restaurant, she said, 'You had better drink a lot of champagne, and see if that will help you. I don't know what to think about you, Eliot. I've never seen anyone so much changed for the worse in so short a time.'

'Not even in the wards of your hospital?'

'What is the point of saying a thing like that?' she demanded angrily. 'There's a war going on, and we're in the middle of it, and we can't stop it. Nobody wanted a war less than I did – I was practically a pacifist before it started – but now that it's come, there's only one thing to do, and that's an honest job of work that will help to finish it.'

'Send us victorious, happy, and glorious,' said Eliot.

'I suppose you would like France to win?'

'Nobody can really win a war as big as this. One side will be the first to admit defeat; then the others will realize what they have lost, and try to conceal their despair in savage reprisals.'

'It hasn't taken you long to admit defeat.'

'There were special circumstances that helped me to see things clearly.'

'That means that I am to blame for your early collapse.'

'No, not really. It's the war that turned me into a sort of spaniel, whining for love, because now love is more desirable and more important than ever before. There's peace and forgetfulness in it. A lover in the arms of his mistress is like a dead man at the bottom of the sea, and that's what I long for. To let my spirit drown in the last stillness of love.'

Lysistrata was silent, and Eliot said irritably, 'Say something, for God's sake.'

'It won't help you, whatever I say . . . Look at that girl over there. Have you ever seen anyone more beautiful?'

'And look at the brute she's with. Have you ever seen anything more revolting?'

The girl she had indicated was in the first bloom of her beauty. Twenty-two years old, perhaps, she was golden-haired, white of skin, full bosomed, her face was exquisite, her bare arms a treasure to behold, and her grey eyes under a calm brow were serene. The man she was with was between fifty and sixty, bald, red-eared, brutally fat, ferret-eyed, and vulgar as a pig in its sty.

'That's what we're fighting for,' said Eliot, 'so that swine like that can furnish their beds with beauty.'

'It's horrible, I know, but it isn't only in war time that rich men buy lovely girls.'

'No, but it happens more often in war, when there's easy money to be made for those who don't mind the taste of corpses in their food, and when there are more girls for sale, because the men who ought to have them are in the trenches. Look at the profiteers! Couldn't you tell them a mile away? Don't you smell hyenas in the room?'

Gross or grim of feature, assertive in their demeanour, loud of voice, the profiteers sat at wine-laden tables, and with them were resplendent women. Scattered among them, the officers in service dress had the lean ascetic look – though some were little more than schoolboys – of an arduous priesthood.

'A thousand years ago,' said Eliot violently, 'war could possibly be justified because it meant the survival of the fittest. But now it means the survival of the hyenas, and the fattening of those who've got an appetite for carrion.'

Lysistrata put down her fork. 'Why,' she asked coldly, 'did you ask me to dine with you if your only intention was to take away my appetite?'

'I'm sorry,' said Eliot, and sat for a minute in melancholy silence.

The leader of the orchestra, which had been playing, unregarded, Schumann's Pianoforte Quintet, rose and spoke into a microphone. The metallic voice announced: 'Ladies and gentlemen. We have now a very pleasant surprise for you. Miss Rose Armour, who, as you know, is appearing this week at His Majesty's Theatre, has found time to come over here for a few minutes, and will sing two of her latest songs. Miss Armour is taking a special interest in the National Fund for sending comforts to our boys in the trenches, and at the conclusion of the entertainment there will be a collection. Miss Armour has come over here at considerable inconvenience to herself, and I hope your response will be generous. Ladies and gentlemen: Miss Rose Armour!'

Rose was wearing a white evening frock that closely fitted her slender figure. She stepped into the blueish glare of a spotlight, and was greeted with a great roar of applause. She smiled, and bit her lower lip, and clutched her hands in front of her as though she wanted to embrace everyone there. It was her well-known gesture, and the applause rose to a storm of delight.

'Ladies and gentlemen,' she said in her sweet husky voice. 'Or do you mind if I call you dears and darlings? Because that's how I feel, and I just can't keep anything to myself. Well, Mr Silberstein has told you that I want you all to help me send another cheque to the National Fund for Our Boys, and I know you're going to be as generous as you always are. I can depend on you, can't I? Well, I've only got time to sing two songs and the first one – I expect some of you have heard it already, but you'll just have to listen to it again – it's called *I'm in love with a soldier now*. And there he is, if you want to see him.'

She blew a kiss to a young fair-haired subaltern, who blushed bright red, and when the laughter quietened she began to sing.

And it's true, she thought as she sang. It's true, true, true, and she felt the stiff edge of Julian's letter moving against her round breast. It had come to her dressing-room that night, and there were phrases in it that seemed to her the most wonderful she had ever read. She felt them like arms about her, and his lips on her mouth. *I love you*, he had written, *I love you as you were meant to be loved, with all the strength of my body and the passion of my mind. I love you*, he had said, *because you are more beautiful than anything else on earth, and more kind.* They sang in her heart to the tune of the silly words she was singing, but turned to the sweetness of a lark in the summer sky. Julian was her lover, and Julian was in the front of battle. He had written his letter in the acrid danger of a trench. He was fighting for England, and for her, and he loved her more than anything else on earth. She felt her body softening, desire with a morning softness woke in her limbs, as though he were there to embrace her. Her lover was a soldier in the front of war. He was a captain now. Captain Julian Brown of the Royal Fusiliers.

She sang another song, but her audience would not be satisfied. They refused to let her go. Waiters went round the tables, and their silver trays were filled with rustling largesse by the profiteers, and the officers' half-crowns. A man with the blunt head of a tortoise and a laugh like the snarling of a baboon – a man with diamond studs in his shirt and champagne in a bucket beside him – shouted raucously, 'How about *A Man in the House*?'

'Well, that's the very last,' said Rose, 'and you've got to give me some more money if I sing it.' – Money for Julian's men, she thought. Socks and cigarettes and Balaclava helmets for the Fusiliers who follow him into battle. There were tears in her eyes, and her vulgar little song was compulsive as a wave-borne air of the sirens.

> Up in the morning and fry the bacon,
>   Make him a nice cup of tea!
> Who would think yesterday I was forsaken,
>   Now I'm as happy as happy can be?

A major in the Argyll and Sutherland Highlanders, somewhat

excited by wine, rolled a couple of pound-notes into a ball and, threw it to her. 'It's worth it, Rose!' he cried. 'You're worth a war all by yourself, my dear!'

She laughed, and bit her lower lip, came swiftly towards him, put her arms round his neck, and kissed him. 'You're a darling,' she said. – He was a soldier, she meant. He was Julian's comrade, fighting beside him.

A bald-headed Canadian captain, waving a fist-full of dollars, shouted, 'They're yours for another, Rose!' and the fair-haired subaltern, to whom she had pointed, got up so hurriedly that he knocked over his chair, and ran towards her with a pound in his hand.

She kissed them both, and a dozen others, till her hands were full of money, and still there was a queue of eager suitors.

The fat ferret-eyed profiteer who was dining with the handsome fair girl had pushed his way to the front of the queue. He flourished a five-pound note and shouted for attention. But Rose shook her head. 'Soldiers only,' she cried, and stood tip-toe to kiss a tall Australian.

'My money's as good as theirs, isn't it?'

'Maybe it is, but you've got to get into khaki if you want to be kissed. Come on, Gunners, your turn next.'

The profiteer continued to argue, but a Gunner subaltern pushed him out of the way and a Naval officer trod heavily on his foot. He began to shout – still flaunting his five-pound note – and suddenly those about him grew angry. He was pushed and jostled, and finally daunted. He reappeared, and glared resentfully at the still-seated diners. The fair-haired girl raised a long white arm and beckoned to him, but before returning to her he wanted to argue his case and justify himself. Angry and unhappy, he spoke to a middle-aged, quiet-looking officer whose eye he caught: 'My money's as good as theirs, isn't it?'

The middle-aged officer, a tallish heavily built Scotsman with a red square face and short red hair, was somewhat embarrassed. He answered cautiously, 'I don't suppose there's very much difference.'

'I've earned it, and I've got a right to spend it,' said the profiteer, and began to explain the nature of his business.

'Hogpool's Barbed Wire, that's who I am. The war would be over in a week if it wasn't for me and my wire.'

The officer wished he would go away, but did not care to draw attention to himself by telling him so. His wife was with him, and her young brother, who, till recently a medical student at Edinburgh University, was now a Surgeon-probationer in the Navy. They were not accustomed to dining in expensive hotels, but this was a special occasion. His battalion was leaving for Germany on the morrow. He would probably be in the trenches within a week. Well, he had escaped death in the last war, and he might survive this one, though active service would be harder on him than in 1918. Even the saying good-bye would be immeasurably harder now. He had been married for ten years – happily married – and to live apart from his wife was like being in prison. It deadened him. He seemed to have no faculty of enjoyment unless she was beside him. But he was no weakling. For several years after the last war he had played Rugby football, and after giving that up he had become a golfer of very respectable achievement. No one had ever thought of impugning his manhood. But his wife had the stronger mind and the stronger spirit, and though he had never been aware of domination, she had ruled his life from the day he married her to the day when, as an officer in the Territorial Army Reserve, he had been mobilized for the war against France. She was twelve years younger than he, and handsome in a hardy Scots fashion. Now, he could see, she was getting very impatient with the fat blethering stranger who had interrupted their dinner-party; and he nerved himself to say some polite but decisive word of dismissal.

Before he could think of a suitable phrase, however, the fat man declared, with the force of what was meant to be a conclusive argument, 'Money's money the whole world over, and that you can't deny.' He held out a red thick-fingered hand. 'Hogpool's my name,' he said. 'Tom Hogpool,' he repeated.

'And mine is Graham,' said the officer weakly.

'Him and his five-pound notes!' said Mrs Graham disdainfully, when the fat man had gone.

'I could do with a few of them,' said her brother.

'Wait till you've earned them, and then you'll know their value. Aren't you going to finish your pudding, Charlie? You won't be getting anything as good as that for a long time to come.'

Her voice faltered, and the shadows of fear and separation darkened her eyes. She caught his hand and whispered roughly, 'Oh, Charlie, Charlie, I don't think I can bear it!'

Tom Hogpool, slowly returning to his table, stopped beside Eliot and Lady Lysistrata, and showed them the crumpled note.

'I suppose you saw what happened?' he said. 'If you ask me, this war's going to be the ruin of some people. It's gone to their heads, that's what it's done. Did you see what Rose Armour did? Behaving like a duchess when I offered her a five-pound note? She's nothing but a little tart, either.'

Lysistrata paid no attention to him, but Eliot in a harsh intolerant voice told him to go away and get back to his own table.

The fair-haired girl beckoned to him again. Unwillingly he returned. 'It's showing people up in their true colours, this bloody war is,' he grumbled. 'You never saw such a pack of dirty snobs in the whole of your life. Rose Armour and all. Would you say my money's as good as anyone else's, or wouldn't you?'

'Of course it is,' she answered in a comforting voice, and taking the five-pound note put it in her bag. She half-filled a claret glass with Chartreuse, and pushed it towards him. 'Have some more of this stuff, and forget about it. What does it matter to you what soldiers think?'

Eliot looked at his watch. 'It's time I was getting back to camp,' he said wearily, and called a waiter.

There were no taxis, for lack of petrol had immobilized them all, but a few ancient cabs and victorias with moth-eaten blue cushions had reappeared on the streets. Lysistrata offered to see Eliot off at the station, and they sat together in the stale darkness of an old four-wheeler. She took his hand and said, 'Eliot, will you believe me if I tell you that I have only two wishes in my heart; and one is for Tony's safety, the other for yours. If I hadn't been so worried – but no, I don't think that would have made any difference. The whole world has changed, and I've changed with it. I keep thinking of Tony — and now I shall think of you too.'

He lifted her hand and kissed it. He tried to speak more cheerfully. 'And remember, when you think of me, that I added myself to the war for the most nonsensical reason under the sun. I became a soldier to fight against France because all my life I have been in love with France. If I am killed, France must be acquitted. It will be a *crime passionel*.'

III

Lysistrata lay awake for much of the night, because she could not forget the sight of Eliot, his head and shoulders framed in the dark window of a dingy little local train. He had regained his self-control, but at the expense, in the end, of some human quality. His face was lifeless, as though, to spoil it of satisfaction, he had already anticipated death. But the deadness of his expression was hard, not yielding. The outer part of him was a kind of shell, or a suit of armour, in which the real Eliot, shrunk in size, hid from view. If I took him by the shoulders and shook him, she thought, I would hear him rattle like a dried-up hazel-nut. Never had she seen anyone suffer so great a change . . .

Not even in the wards of your hospital, he had asked, where youth comes home without its limbs, all broken and drained of its bright blood? But that was not Eliot talking. That was the bitterness which had shrivelled his soul and distorted his good sense. There was a war, and wounds and death were part of it. There was a war, and the only way to end it was to win it, and it did no good to think of wounds. She had no fear for Tony. In the last battle, she knew, he had gone forward every day to an artillery observation post to see for himself how his battalions were faring. He had been in danger like any subaltern. But he would never be hurt. She knew that. It was not his destiny to be maimed or killed in battle. It could not be. She must not think of wounds and death, or be afraid for Tony.

But Eliot was different. She was afraid for him because she could see his peril so clearly. Was that because his life no

longer meant much to her? But it did, it meant a whole world
of memory. He had been her gay lover and most witty friend,
and all their time together had been like the morning and the
evening of a fine day, the morning sun and the bright darkness of a starry night. He had loved her, and his wit had made
of their two minds an instrument on which to play the sweet
absurdities, the dappled beauty of the world. He had said this
and that. He had made her laugh, and made her see the little
cause and enormous consequence of something passing by.

But what had it been, and what had he said? She could not
remember. The tune had gone, and was now only an echo
in her mind, because her mind was too thickly crowded with
thoughts of Tony to have room for much else. Tony was in
the front of war. The most brilliant of our generals, the people
said. He is marked for promotion. He is in the line of great
soldiers – Marlborough, Clive, and the young Wellesley – and
perhaps not the least of them. His conduct of the operations
extending from 14 to 26 October showed a perfect grasp of
the situation and outstanding ability to exploit to the fullest
its succeeding phases. Scrymgeour's division, the Fighting
Fifth, is again the spear-head of our attack. Scrymgeour's
Division. Tony's men were the heroes of the war, and Tony
was her husband.

She felt her love like a receding wave that leaves a smooth
rock all naked to the sky. Like a wind that bows down the
corn and shows it quivering to the sun . . .

'*Young Seton went on leave, met a girl whose looks he liked, and
married her within the week. He has probably been foolish. But I
can't blame him, because I would have done the same had I been in
his place, and you the girl. My only complaint against the war is that
it keeps me away from you. Seton himself, with the unction of his
wedding still on him, is no more devoted or desirous than I am. But
the war . . .*' He had written that after a long day's work, after
endless planning, poring over maps, gathering information,
talking with his Brigadiers, with German Staff Officers, making
grave decisions. The war had given him fame and the happiness of liberating his talent for war. But he complained because
it kept him away from her. His love was still bridegroom-
strong, and hers was no longer changeful and capricious, but

hot and faithful. The war had made it so, and now the estranging war denied what it had taught her to desire. But not for long. It would only be for a little while. It would not, dared not do more, do worse. It could not do that.

She slept for a few hours, and woke to the cold prospect of another day. But habit had given her discipline. She got up at once, without more than a moment's return to the troubled and luxurious thoughts with which she had fallen asleep. She had promised – not Eliot, but herself – to go to the station and see the passing of the troop-train that would take his battalion on the first stage of its journey to the front.

There was a long mirror in the room, and she looked at her tall reflection. Her beauty had always given her a deep and satisfying delight. But is beauty, she wondered, anything more than a refinement of utility? A yacht and the Ionic column are serviceable things. Passionately, with sudden conviction, she thought: I must have children. I have been foolish, and blind and selfish, but when Tony comes home I shall tell him that I am wiser now. I cannot live childless and die a barren stock. . . .

Though rain was falling, and the grey of early morning was still laggard in the slow-rising light, there was a huge and murmurous crowd at the station to see the troop-trains pass. A whole brigade was moving. The most of the crowd were women, and many in a state of strong excitement. Here and there was a mother's uncontainable misery, tear-stained, and clinging without shame to an embarrassed husband or unavailing daughter. Grimly intent on reaching and keeping a place in the front of the crowd were women who, by the preternatural severity of their expression, showed clearly the bitterness of their feelings and the strain of controlling them. But far more numerous were girls and shrill young women whose emotion was quite simply that of animals in heat. The passing trains were full of men. They were men more positively male than dull mechanics, pale docile clerks, and tradesmen busy with their prices and their profits. They had been segregated and trained to kill. They had been hardened and fed for a primal function. And as the trains went slowly through the station – a myriad faces at the glancing windows, the noise of brave shouting, the smell of khaki and leather – the hundreds of waiting girls, pressing against the barricades and shrieking as the fly stung deeper, cheered their lovers to their death.

Lysistrata was in uniform, and a policeman, after making way for her through the crowd, had let her on to the platform in front of the barricades. It was cold and draughty. A Railway Transport Officer stood talking to an elderly Quartermaster who was indignant about the non-arrival of four thousand blankets. A couple of red-capped Military Policemen walked stiffly up and down, and two St John Ambulance men, elderly volunteers, shivered in the doorway of the Refreshment Room. There was another woman on the platform. She was good-looking in a hardy Scots way, and she wore an oddly defiant expression on her high-coloured face. She was manifestly ill-at-ease when Lysistrata spoke to her, and a moment or two later, with a nervous laugh, she said, 'I'm afraid I've no business to be here, but I simply had to get a last look at my husband. I told a lie to the policeman at the gate, and just walked on.'

'What did you tell him?'

'I said Charlie – my husband, I mean – was the Colonel of the 9th Royal Scots, though he's a Captain really: Captain Graham. But I looked the policeman right in the eye when I said it, and I spoke in the sort of way you English do. That did it. I just walked past, and he gave me a salute as I went.'

Lysistrata laughed. 'You earned it, I'm sure, and I hope you manage to see your husband. But none of the trains will stop, you know. You will only be able to wave to him.'

'I know that. We said good-bye last night, but I couldn't miss the chance of seeing him again, though it's only for a second.'

With a brazen whistle and a harsh escape of steam another train came in and passed slowly through the station. Heads thrust from the windows wore tufted Balmoral bonnets, and in the corridors could be seen the paler khaki of kilt-aprons. 'It's them!' exclaimed Mrs Graham, and watched with painful apprehension the passing of close-crowded, cheering soldiers fearful lest she miss the quieter carriages where their officers sat. Then loudly she cried 'Charlie!' and lost her voice in a sob. With quick ungainly movements she began to run along the platform. But in a moment she stopped, for Charlie's brother officers were in the carriage with him, and he would not like them to see her behaving in this indecorous fashion, and looking dishevelled in consequence. So she stood as still as she could, with a dignified demeanour, and waved in a friendly, almost casual fashion to her solemn and swiftly vanishing husband. But in her heart she was thinking, 'I may never see him again,' and her breast rose and fell with the violence of her fear.

Presently, with urgency in the iron sound of its wheels, another train came in. There was more cheering, more shrieking at the barricades. Soldiers wearing the black buttons of the Rifle Brigade leaned from the passing windows and shouted to the hoarse excited girls. There was a burst of laughter, the fragment of a joke, a few words of a song. Then the wheels grew louder and more urgent. The blind walls of a luggage-van went by, and nothing more could be seen of the soldiers but a few small and backward-looking heads that still protruded from the windows. Swiftly they were drawn out of sight, and the last of them vanished.

'Did you see your friend?' asked Mrs Graham dully. It was politeness, not curiosity, that prompted the inquiry.

'No,' said Lysistrata. 'I hadn't told him I would be here, so he wasn't looking out for me.'

'Oh, I'm sorry.'

They walked slowly from the platform and through the now rapidly dispersing crowd of spectators. 'From the way that some of them behave,' said Mrs Graham bitterly, 'you'd think that a war was a fine thing for women. But they'll find their mistake out when there's no one left in the country but old done men, and weaklings, and those that were clever enough to dodge the fighting. It'll be a wintry world to live in then, for that kind's no use to women, and never will be.'

IV

There was hard frost in December, and the whole of northern France listened in a chill white silence to the sounds of war.

The ploughed and furrowed mud of the battlefields was powdered with snow, and every shell-hole, every hoof-mark, was sharp-edged with ice. In the morning a brownish fog obscured the desolate landscape, and at midday and in the early afternoon a thin blue sky looked down at the soldiers in their bitter trenches, and a distant sun as pale as guinea-gold made redly to glisten the twisted acres of barbed and rusty wire. When shells burst in the frozen trenches they threw out lumps of earth as hard as shrapnel, and at night the sentries on the fire-step, peering into the cold and haunted darkness, felt their elbows freezing to the parapet. The battle had been renewed, and the British were again advancing with a stiff and sullen vehemence.

On the eastern front their German and Polish allies had been heavily defeated. The Russians had taken Vilna and Lida in the north, and Lemberg was threatened on three sides by the coordinated advance of Soviet troops and the armies of the Little Entente. Czechoslovakia, though hindered in the first few weeks of war by internal dissension, was now showing unsuspected strength, and after furious fighting along the Böhmer Wald had on the whole front pushed forward its front line into Bavarian territory. The German High Command, having already sent troops to stiffen their half-hearted Polish allies, had now to withdraw many divisions from the western front to meet the menace to Bavaria. Their whole position in Lorraine – where, in August, they had advanced with astonishing rapidity after the French fortifications had been destroyed from the air – was now seriously weakened by these withdrawals; and the British Command had been urgently requested to do all it could to keep France busy in the north.

The Fifth Division, hurriedly reconstituted after its losses in the last battle, was again in the line. It was, however, no longer directly commanded by Antony Scrymgeour, who had again been promoted when Lieutenant-General Sir Hugh Kew-Godleigh, an elderly gentleman commanding the IInd Corps, had succumbed to war strain and been invalided home with shingles. But the Division was lucky in its new general. He was an Indian Cavalryman called Brannigan, whose promotion Scrymgeour had been diligent to secure. He was brave to the point of recklessness, the sort of man who inspired devotion wherever he went, and a brilliant soldier.

Two battalions of the Division had been so badly punished in the October advance that their remnants had been withdrawn and sent home as training cadres for New Army units of their regiments. In their place the Division received two Territorial battalions, the 9th Royal Scots and the 24th City of London Royal Fusiliers. It was in the latter battalion, which had already seen active service, that Julian Brown was a Company Commander.

The heaviest fighting was again in the neighbourhood of Ypres, and though by the second day of the battle appreciable gains were reported all along the line – in one or two places the troops had gone forward about half a mile – the British losses had been severe. The Fusiliers had reached their objective, a low mound south of the village of Voormezeele, at the cost of their Colonel, nine officers, and nearly three hundred other ranks killed or wounded. But the French still occupied part of the village, which was wholly in ruins, and on their left flank the Fusiliers were dangerously unprotected. To the right the line ran in front of Hill 60 to Sanctuary Wood, but to the left, where the attack had been less successful, it leaned backward towards Wytschaete. The attainment of this rather perilous but otherwise satisfactory position had been largely due to the gallant and soldierly behaviour of Captain Julian Brown. . . .

He had started badly. It was so cold that he felt his body like an empty shell. He was cold inside. His clothes hung loosely on him, not snugly related to his skin, but separated from it by little draughts of winter air. It was the cold, he thought, that made him frightened by chilling his blood, and fearful of betraying his feelings he looked along the crowded trench to see if anyone was watching him. But nobody paid much attention to him. The men had a starved and wolfish look. Their faces, twitching a little, were almost the grey hue of the frozen sandbags. The drab earth was frost-flecked, the soldiers' khaki had no colour. It seemed as though their life were already being drained away to leave dry husks in the sunless air; and in that dying vacancy, piercing the splintered thunder of the barrage, Julian heard the remorseless ticking of his watch and saw with horror the second-hand flit nervously over the zenith of the last minute. He was galvanized by a stronger fear, and with a shuddering movement put his whistle to his lips. The men, with a sort of groaning cheer, clambered swiftly out of the trench, and Julian, turning aside, vomited bread and tea on to the fire-step. Then, as if released of fear, he had followed them, still retching, but possessed of an agonized valour that was half his terrified recoiling from cowardice, half a destructive and barely specified hatred.

The barrage was thinnish in front of them, not quite the curtain of thunder and smoke and steel it should have been, but more like a furious and irregular screen of scouts. It had silenced the French artillery, but not wholly daunted their machine-guns. Stuttering in mortal rage, the *mitrailleuses* traversed the forlorn and frozen ground, and the Fusiliers wavered. There was uncut wire before them, a few yards in their rear the battered remains of a half-dug trench. They fell back to its doubtful shelter. Their spirit of aggression failed, and the bloody fragments of their dead lay in front of them and behind. They were more than half beaten. They hugged themselves to the rough winter-stiffened earth, and the thickness of their breath rose like a mist.

Julian went forward alone, crawling till he reached the wire. The frozen earth cut his wrists, but he did not feel it. There was a wildness in him, not so much of aggression as of a wild thing trapped. He was trying to escape from the memory of fear. He found an opening through the wire, and turning, waved to a savage little cockney sergeant called Raikes. Running and stumbling, they were barely conscious of the spitting, the plucking at the taut air, the ripping sound of bullets. They were close-furled to a single thought. Their minds and senses were drawn in to the hard core of one fierce intention; and the miracle that will sometimes go with desperate men – making, it would seem, their bodies unsubstantial by the intensification of their spirit – took them alive to the French machine-gun post that was immediately responsible for holding up the attack. Julian carried a dead private's rifle and bayonet. From close range he shot a gunner through the face, and leaping down – man, rifle, and bayonet all one piece – drove the thin steel through the body of another. They fell together, and Julian, blinded by his helmet that tumbled over his eyes, could not release his rifle from the corpse it spitted. He fired a shot to clear it, and got up quickly and warily. But Raikes had killed another of the gun-crew, and the last was running down the sap – a T-shaped projection – to the trench behind it. They followed, and bombed the trench with French grenades. Then with the captured guns they silenced another machine-gun post, and Julian, leaving Raikes to supply covering-fire, ran back to the waiting Fusiliers.

He was aflame now with a terrible unwitting anger – roaring like a house afire when the wind fans it – and the men, curiously abashed, had no hesitation in following him. Stiffly they rose from the broken ditch where they had been lying. They were clumsy figures, the same yellowish-brown colour as the shell-turned earth. They were helmeted with round steel basins; encumbered back and front with gas-masks, ammunition-pouches, and bulging haversacks; their legs were thickened by coarse puttees. With jerky movements they ran forward over the hard ground. The grey steel of their bayonets wavered in front of them. They cleared the trench that Julian had bombed, and went forward again. They were in fighting mood now. They were in the grip of a brutal restlessness that made it easier to go forward than to stay where they were. A quiet-seeming man, a bus-conductor in civil life, showed a sudden savage initiative, and crawling from shell-hole to shell-hole succeeded with half a dozen bombs in dispersing an enemy support-company that was preparing to make a local counter attack. A boy with blood running down his face leapt to his feet and shouted wildly to troops advancing on their right. Action and the daring of danger had quelled all fear, and within a strangely short time their fierce temper was changing to a precarious good humour.

An hour after the advance had begun they were on the mound that lay to the south and a little to the west of Voormezeele. They had captured eight hundred yards of ground, on a narrow front, and lost three hundred men. It might be thought an expensive victory. To their left, however, a Lancashire battalion had had nearly five hundred casualties and gained less than half as much ground.

The shortness of the winter day was a relief to the Fusiliers. They had no chance to suffer from the colder air of night, for as soon as darkness fell they set busily to work at strengthening their position. It was no easy task, for the earth was too hard for digging except where shells had broken it, and to build their new parapet they had little but the tattered, scattered sandbags of the old one.

Julian had a sleepless night. There was much to be done, but he was in a mood now of elated confidence that could not be wearied. He made a hurried journey to Battalion Headquarters, which had been established in a dug-out about three hundred yards to the rear, and discussed the situation with the surviving major, a calm and dullish man called Teggatt. He listened with mild approval to Julian's report, and as mildly agreed that it would be a good thing to reconnoitre the nearer ruins of Voormezeele, and if possible establish a forward position there.

'Do you want to go yourself?' he asked.

'Yes,' said Julian. 'I thought of taking a sergeant and one other man to have a look round first. I've got a good fellow called Raikes who'll be glad to come. There's no use taking more than that, because in the darkness and among the houses I couldn't keep in touch with them. But if everything goes well I'll get a couple of guns moved up.'

'Well, I leave it to your own judgement, Brown. But don't get into trouble. Oh, by the way, I've got some rum for you, which I'll send up in time for stand-to.'

'Thank you, sir. And about our left flank . . .'

'We've done all we can. We're still rather in the air, I'm afraid, but there's no need to worry. It's a nasty position to be in, but not really serious.'

'Have you any orders, sir?'

'No, nothing really. You'll hold on, of course. I dare say the Frog will try to kick you out in the morning, but you'll be all right, won't you?'

'I hope so.'

'That's good. I knew I could rely on you. And you'll let me know how you're getting on, of course. Have a drink before you go?'

The patrol had an easy task. On the near side of the village street the ruins, black as charcoal under the starry sky, were deserted, and Julian got his machine-guns up without any trouble. They would have a small but useful field of fire. Then he went to the left of his front and lay for an hour with a listening-post that he had sent out. Everything in the immediate neighbourhood was quiet. The French line was discontinuous, and here was a small patch of country, littered with the debris of war, but of human beings seeming empty as a desert. Farther south, however, between Wytschaete and Kemmel, he could hear the rumble and see the multiple flash of gunfire. They were fighting there all night.

Major Teggatt came up in the morning, a few minutes before stand-to, when the men, grey-faced and shivering, lined the trench. His nose was pink with cold and he was puffing slightly. His breath emerged in little clouds.

He took Julian aside and said, 'A nasty thing happened yesterday. Brown. Poor Brannigan's dead, and most of his Staff too. A shell got the lot of them, somewhere behind Wytschaete.'

'What bloody bad luck.'

'Yes, isn't it? A good fellow, Brannigan.'

'He was shaping to be about as good as Scrymgeour himself.'

'I know. It's a damned shame in one way, and pretty serious in another. Higgins has taken over the Division temporarily, but Higgins isn't Brannigan, not by a long chalk.'

'What's been happening on the left?'

'We're doing rather well. The Welch and the Cambridgeshires came up at Wytschaete and went forward at a run. Well, they were held up a bit here and there, but they got through generally. The Welch have got a post about three hundred yards away in a bit of wood over there. You could see it if it wasn't for the mist. We're still held up in front of Kemmel, of course, and this hole in the line, between us and the Welch, is giving Brigade cold feet. But I told 'em I didn't think there was any need to worry. What have you done about the dead, by the way?'

'Put them behind the parapet; the French, and ours as well. We couldn't bury them, and they're useful there. The ground's so hard we had the devil of a job to make a parapet at all.'

'Yes, I suppose you had. Poor fellows, though, Makes you think a bit, this war, doesn't it, Brown? Still, it doesn't do any good to think too much. Oh, I nearly forgot to tell you. I'm going to put you in for a Military Cross. You did very well yesterday. I don't know whether you'll get it, of course, but I think you ought to.'

With a long crescendo scream and a dull bump, a shell came over and burst some two hundred yards behind them. It was followed by half a dozen others bursting like iron bubbles and shaking the earth as they landed; and a minute or two later an English battery replied. But presently the shelling stopped, with as little reason, apparently, as it had begun. It was not the bombardment they had feared – the bombardment that would herald a French counter-attack – but merely a convention of the war. Morning had come, and the white dawn must be saluted.

The Fusiliers took their rum and felt life returning to their frozen limbs. 'Roll on, Christmas!' they said, for though they no longer believed that the war would be over by then, they felt sure that in so kindly a season they would be taken out of the line and given a little holiday. They might get back as far as Roulers or Courtrai. Some place where they could look at a girl and drink a pint in peace. That was what they wanted. A pint or two, a little peace, and a clean shirt instead of the lousy rags they were wearing.

'Roll on, Christmas!' they said.

'Think of getting down to it in the old scratcher for a 'ole bloody night!'

'I 'ope to Christ I ever get thawed again,' said a tall weedy youth with a shrapnel-dint in his helmet.

'I 'ope to Christ we get out of 'ere before the bloody thaw comes,' answered an older man.

'Frightened of drowning, are you?'

'There'd be a bloody lot drowned if the ice melted, and all those shell-'oles filled with water, and we was getting out in a bit of a 'urry.'

'And a drowning man sees all 'is past life go by. No wonder you got the wind up. Be a nasty sight for a dirty old man like you, wouldn't it?'

'Shut up, you noisy bastards,' said a corporal as Julian came into the bay.

'Did you get your rum all right?' he asked.

'Yes, sir.'

'Everybody fit?'

'Private Topliss says 'e's got aneroids, sir.'

'Got what?'

'Piles, sir.'

'Well, we can't do anything about that, can we?'

'No, sir.'

'We'll be going out tonight, Topliss. You can carry on till then, can't you?'

'Yes, sir. It's sitting on this cold ground that's done it, sir.'

'Well, don't sit so much. There's plenty of work to do. All right, Corporal Harris, you can stand down here.'

Julian visited his listening-post on the left and the forward position in the ruins of Voormezeele. He took tapes with him, to make sure of finding his way back through the mist. Sergeant Raikes reported all quiet.

'But the boys don't like it, sir, sitting 'ere in the fog,' he said. 'They say it gives 'em the creeps, everything being so quiet and lonely-like.'

Julian spoke to a tall brown-haired boy of nineteen or so. 'How do you feel about it, Jenkins?'

'I'm all right, sir.'

'And you, Humble?'

'Nothing to complain about, sir.'

'Then it's only Sergeant Raikes who's got the wind-up, is it?'

There was a little subdued laughter. The notorious courage of the Sergeant made the joke a good one and pleasantly obvious.

'I'll come over again in an hour's time, if the fog still holds,' said Julian, 'but probably it will have lifted by then. I expect our relief about eleven o'clock, Sergeant.'

'Very good, sir.'

''E's in a good mood this morning,' said Private Humble when Julian had gone.

''Ave you ever seen 'im any other way?' asked Sergeant Raikes.

'Too bloody true I 'ave. What about last week, when 'e 'ad me on the mat for a dirty rifle, and nothing wrong with it except a speck of rust, the size of a pin's 'ead, under the leaf of the back-sight? He's a bit too bloody regimental at times, is our Captain Brown.'

''E's the best officer in the battalion,' said the Sergeant. . . .

The day passed in a strange eery silence. The battle had apparently come to a stop. It seemed as though both sides, aghast before their dead who could not be buried, had withdrawn a little to look with horror at the evil they had done. The frozen soil would not receive their dead. They lay stiffly in their altered uniforms, mouth frostily agape or half their bowels a pallid blue on the winter earth. They were all young, these shattered and untimely dead. They had been swift of foot, and laughed easily. They had been strong. Yet by reason of their youth they were dead, and because of their strength their bodies had been torn asunder. This clearly was madness, bred by evil out of a wilful folly, and the earth, to punish men for their sin, would not admit the bodies of those they had slain. She had closed her doors with winter, and barred them with an iron frost. Also, to bring shame to the living, she had medicined the young dead against decay. She had sealed them with ice, and stiffly frozen their mutilations and the agony of their death. Now should winter last a year, and the front continue hard enough, and the war still slay its two hundred thousand every month, then Europe would be seen, not as Golgotha, a place of decent skulls to play at loggats with, but a madmen's charnel to the dullest eye of all, littered with the everlasting corpses of all the youths in the world, that had killed each other because their minds were poisoned, and women, not knowing what they did, had screamed them forth to show their manhood in a mortuary . . .

Eliot Greene took off his helmet and wiped his forehead. Despite the intense cold, he was sweating slightly. He was afraid, not of death, but lest he should be going mad.

His battalion had taken part in the attack on Kemmel Hill. They had gained a fair amount of ground, but not their final objective, and after the failure of their last assault they had fallen back, leaving a good many wounded behind them. In the early morning, Eliot, with a couple of stretcher-bearers, had gone forward again through the fog to where cries for help could be heard, and found in a crater with two dead *poilus* three badly wounded Riflemen. He and the stretcher-bearers had tied up their wounds, and then, before he could get them out, the mist grew visibly thinner. Hurriedly they lifted one of the wounded men, but as soon as the stretcher-bearers rose into sight a machine-gun opened fire, and both, with their burden, fell back into the crater. One had been killed outright, the other had died an hour later. By midday two of the wounded Riflemen were dead of exposure, and the third was delirious. Nor could Eliot leave them, for the machine-gunner was still watchful. Twice, when Eliot made a rash movement, he had fired savage bursts. Till night should fall there was no escape from the frozen crater and the little company of dead men. He was safe enough so long as he kept still, or moved with caution, but when he thought of the massacre of youth and the earth's refusal to receive the dead, he grew frightened of going mad unless the night came soon to set him free.

V

Huddled to the side of the road behind St Éloi, the relieving battalion of Royal Scots stood in the darkness while a diminished column, with strange alacrity for weary men, hurried past them.

A voice with a Scotch accent, young and curious, inquired, 'What's it like up there?'

'Bloody 'ell, Jock.'

Here and there along the line of men who were about to take their turn of duty in the trenches were others who asked the same question. They all got the same reply: 'Bloody ' ell, Jock.'

The column re-formed and carefully it moved forward into danger. Over the shell-pitted fields duck-boards had been laid to make a road for wet weather, but on the hard ground they were only a hindrance. The men walked beside them. They were in file, and between each platoon there was an interval of about sixty yards. The night was dark and the weather milder than it had been for nearly a fortnight.

Two companies went into trenches a few hundred yards in front of the ruins of St Éloi. The remainder went on. There was a longish halt while the leading platoons found their way into a shallow communication trench, and some of the older men, who realized the danger of standing about, grew fretful and nervous. But the majority, who were going into the front line for the first time, were too innocent to feel anything but an excited curiosity. They looked at a dead man, laid on his back with arms outspread, seen dimly in the dark, with a strange and thrilling interest, but with no apprehension that a like fate would be theirs.

They stumbled into the communication trench, and in that long slow progress many lost all sense of direction. Then at last they found themselves in a deeper and more warlike ditch, where men stood silently waiting for their coming.

The officers commanding the relieving companies were shown the extent of their front, and formally took over the responsibility for its defence. But for nearly an hour the trench was doubly manned, because the Fusiliers, to avoid congestion in the rear, had to wait till an appointed hour before they went out. This last hour seemed the longest they had ever known.

In a small dug-out, miserably lighted by a couple of candles, Julian sat talking to a captain of the Royal Scots, a tallish heavily built man with a red square face and short red hair. He was old for his rank, but he had been quick to appreciate the position, and his manner showed the mild confidence of experience. He took the mug of tea that Julian offered him, and drank gingerly from its hot rim. 'I never thought to see Voormezeele again,' he said.

'When were you here before?'

'Twenty-six years ago.'

'You mean in the last war?'

'Yes,' said Graham, 'the last war. And that's what we thought it was going to be. We were innocent then. I spent my eighteenth birthday a couple of hundred yards from here, and got wounded two days later. That was in April 1918. I was a private in the Black Watch.'

His deep-toned slow Scots voice showed no trace of emotion, but he was in fact excited by the coincidence of returning to war in the very place where, as a boy, he had been seriously wounded, and his excitement was making him talkative. Twenty-six years ago he had fought among the ruins of Voormezeele, and now it was again in ruins, and after a quarter of a century he was once more a soldier. The intervening years had been earnest and busy, filled with arduous endeavour and laudable experiment. Inventors and mechanics had innumerably multiplied the comforts of life; poets and scientists had enlarged the store of humanity's self-knowledge; mankind had grown a little, here and there, in beauty and wisdom and in charity. And now the world was at war again, and again the western Powers were fighting for the ruins of Voormezeele. Progress had stopped and their objective had shrunk to that. This shattered village was now the goal and scope of all their effort.

Julian, with not much interest, said, 'You were facing the other way, then, of course.'

'We were facing all ways, for the war had got rather out of hand about that time, and the Germans were everywhere. It's an odd feeling to be fighting on their side now, for I've always had a sort of liking for the French.'

Julian answered with unnecessary vehemence: 'It's their fault we're fighting them. They started the war. I was in London when they bombed it, and I saw the old women and children they killed.'

'Yes, that was a bad business. But I can't believe they did it wantonly, and if we knew the whole story we'd likely find that our Government was a bit to blame in some way or another.'

T – C

'Perhaps it was, but nothing can excuse the bombing of London.'

'I suppose you're right.'

Julian had again spoken in the loud and dogmatic voice of one who must convince not only his audience but himself. The discovery, on the morrow of that Sunday in July, that France was the enemy, had been a dreadful blow to him, and the bruise was still tender. Like other Francophiles – but he had been immoderate in his romantic regard – he had turned against France with the blind anger of a lover betrayed. Like Leontes in *The Winter's Tale* he thought: 'Say that she were gone, given to the fire, a moiety of my rest might come to me again . . .' But this feeling had to be preserved, and he would not willingly hear a word in defence of his former love.

'They asked for trouble,' he said stubbornly, 'and by God they're going to get it. Look here, have a drink instead of that filthy chlorinated tea.'

Graham refused the whisky. For a minute or two neither of them spoke. Then Graham, untidily filling his pipe, said, 'There's another difference between this war and the old one. In the old one we thought we were fighting for the rights of small nations. We were going to put a stop to war, and make the world safe for democracy. Well, we didn't, of course. We didn't do any of those things. But we had good intentions. The ordinary people, like you and me, had righteous hopes. But there's none of that feeling nowadays. We're simply fighting for survival and the ruins of Voormezeele. There's no suggestion of anything else, and though you may say that that's a sufficient purpose, it seems a pity to have lost the larger motive.'

'We're at war because we were wantonly attacked, and we're fighting to win.'

'But what's going to happen after we have won? Are we going to waste our victory and all the men who've been killed, as we wasted them before? I'm not given to crying over spilt milk, but I come near to it when I think of the opportunities that Britain had and lost in 1919. We could have led the world to better things. We had the strength and the prestige – we and the United States – and we could have taught peace and justice. But we shirked our responsibilities. We took the narrow view, and America was narrower still, and we thought only of our own profits, not seeing that we took our profits from everyone else, and their welfare was just as important as ours. Security was what we wanted in the first place, being international traders; but we didn't like the notion of collective security, which was the only kind possible, because we thought that other people might get some of the benefits. We were selfish and stupid, and I'm afraid that we and America are much to blame for the misery and confusion in the world today.'

Julian took another drink. He had begun to find Graham a little tedious, and now he felt a sudden spurt of anger. He did not wish to be reminded of misery. For thirty-six hours he had been trying to thrust out of memory his humiliating fear at the moment of attack; and the word misery was a mnemonic of his shame. He wanted to shout it down, but with an effort he controlled his voice, and leaning over the ramshackle table – tapping the rough wood with irritable fingers – he said, 'I don't agree that the war has brought only misery, or even that misery is what it has chiefly brought. To many people, and I'm one of them, it has meant life as well as death. I used to be a schoolmaster, teaching English Litera- ture to cretinous small boys. Do you think that was life, or had any flavour of it? To know life you've got to know love and poverty and war, and I've learnt two of them in the last six months. "The fighting man shall from the sun take warmth and life from the glowing earth" – but perhaps you don't believe in poetry?'

'I've always had the impression that most of it was meant more for pleasure than instruction,' said Graham cautiously. 'And I don't think much of a soldier's life unless he's fighting *for* something. I'm not a pacifist, or I wouldn't be here, but I think a soldier ought to have a peaceful end in view. And what end do we envisage now? That's what puzzles me. Is the war going to teach humanity anything of sense and under- standing? That would be a proper sort of victory. Teaching is what we need, because the great weakness of the world is the ignorance and sheer feeble-mindedness of humanity at large. We still need a great deal of elementary instruction.'

Julian looked at his watch. Then he got up and put on his helmet. 'You sound like a schoolmaster yourself.'

'No, I'm in Insurance, or was,' said Graham with a sigh.

'Well, it's time I was going.'

They passed through the double doorway of the dug-out – a greasy blanket at the foot of the steps, canvas at the top – and came into the cool darkness of the trench. 'It's milder tonight,' said Julian. 'I hope you get out before the thaw comes.'

After the Fusiliers had gone, Graham visited his sentries and for a long time stood looking into the hostile night while memory returned, more vividly than for many years, of that other war in which he had fought, and of his last days in the ruins of Voormezeele. He remembered the faces and the rough voices of men whose existence he had long forgotten, and the morning mist, and the huge grotesquely helmeted shapes of Prussian infantry coming suddenly out of the mask of white-ness. He remembered the halt and the fall of a man he had shot in the belly, and the friendliness of a sergeant when he had behaved with unrealized gallantry, and the post-corporal coming with a bag of letters, nearly all for men who were dead. His battalion, after desperate fighting on the Somme, had been reduced to something less than the strength of a com-pany, and they had formed a composite battalion with – the Cambridgeshires and Cheshires, wasn't it? He could not quite remember – but he heard, as an echo in his mind, the pipers playing *The Flowers of the Forest* in the square at Poperinghe, and with a shock he remembered how young they had been, those boys in the black kilts and the red-hackled bonnets, who had fought a wasted war for freedom and justice and decency. As young as these other soldiers, in the trench beside him, who were fighting for no one knew what, except the ruins of Voormezeele. . . .

A couple of miles away, marching wearily with the remain-ing half of his battalion, Eliot Greene was also seeing visions; but of the enemy. In his fevered brain rose the figures of the two Frenchmen whose drained and mutilated bodies had laid beside him in the shell-hole, and now he thought someone told him that the one had been a painter, the other a poet. Their trade had been the creation of beauty in the colours of the sunflower and the sky, and in words that pealed like smitten bronze. Their pale dead faces were lilies in the dusk of his mind, a whiteness whose eyes were darkly brilliant, a pallor that framed eloquent young mouths. They were the beauty of mankind, and they had died to make a desolation with smiths and ploughmen, with little men from suburban streets, and tall drum-majors with enormous plumes. They who were artists, and the sons of a land that lauded intelligence and beauty, had created a hideous desert and died in the battle for its possession.

He stumbled in a rut in the road, and his body yearned for rest; but keener than that desire was the wish of his mind for sanity.

The soldiers, verminous and cold, marched heavily with sunken heads and empty brain. They came to a group of low-roofed huts, a shabby hamlet of corrugated iron, and found their billets, and fell asleep. But Eliot could not rest, for his mind was still haunted by the vision of a monstrous destruction, and he thirsted for sanity like a fever-patient crying for water. In the darkness before morning he heard the guns again. For a minute or two his heart raced, and then, utterly exhausted, he slept. . . .

But the bombardment continued. The battle for the ruins had begun again, and Graham, head down, went to and fro among his men and saw that they were calm and ready. The earth shook and the paling sky was filled with fury. Tight-lipped and grimly patient, the young soldiers waited. They were the Royal Scots – they were the Right of the Line, they were Pontius Pilate's Bodyguard, their colours bore the honours of Blenheim and Alma, Waterloo, Mons, and the Hindenburg Line – and they would fight like veterans and die like heroes though it were only for the broken stones of a Flemish village.

The shells were all falling behind the trench. The sky grew lighter. A sergeant, stocky, square-shouldered and square of jaw, looked through a little embrasure in the parapet, and saw a grey-blue line of men rise menacing from the earth.

Their individual movement was jerky and irregular, but the line came steadily nearer. Athwart their forward-stooping bodies they carried, up-pointed, their long rifles, and above their heads their bayonets were like a long fence of steel. Then, as the fierce faces grew more distinct, the long steel points came down.

Half-turning from the embrasure, the sergeant shouted to Graham: 'Here they come, sir!'

VI

The Right Honourable Percy Small, P.C., Minister for Munitions, came down the steps of the Palace of Fun in Blackpool, and stood for a few seconds arm-in-arm with Tom Hogpool while half a dozen press photographers trained their cameras on the Man of the Moment and his faithful friend.

The fidelity of the faithful friend was, as a matter of fact, a source of considerable annoyance to Mr Small. It often robbed him of the luxury of reminiscence. He delighted to describe, in his own way, his humble origin and the rigours of his early life; but his narration of that heroic struggle was never quite confident when Hogpool was there to hear it, for Tom had been born in the same street, and gone to the same Elementary School, and he remembered many details of their formative years – their having been runners to a street bookie, for example, and their skilful manipulation of the funds of a working-men's Christmas and Holiday Club – which the Minister had tactfully forgotten. It was Hogpool's belief, moreover, that friendship had its obligations, and that he was therefore entitled to a higher price for his barbed wire than that established in open market. For these and other reasons Mr Small entertained a lively hatred for him; but as his practice had always been to mix an air of hail-fellow-well-met with a profession of Christian charity to the meanest of mankind, he concealed his feelings and took what compensation he could from his reputation for never forgetting an old friend.

The photographers liked him because he was patient, friendly, and obliging. His photographs always showed him in a manly attitude, either broadly smiling or impressively serious. He was smiling now, and so was Hogpool, though the latter's expression was too frankly porcine to make a favourable impression on anyone but a pig-fancier. They had good reason to be pleased, for Mr Small had just succeeded, by alternate rhetoric, tears, and cunning proposal, in settling a serious strike of munition-workers.

The munition-workers, perceiving the ever-increasing wealth of their employers, had got the idea that they were entitled to some share in their profits, and demanded a fifty per cent increase in wages. The community at large, however, had been quick to see the impropriety of this demand, for munition-workers were already paid twice as much as employees in the pacific industries, while soldiers in the line, who were drawn from the same social strata as both, seemed perfectly content with a mere fraction of the latter's earnings. The greed and selfishness of the malcontents were obvious to everyone except themselves, but they, with wilful obtuseness, declined to see any difference between their position and that of their employers, whose profit, as any reasonable person could readily perceive, was the unavoidable increment of patriotic endeavour; and when their demands were refused they went on strike. .

The strike almost immediately had the most unfortunate effects. At the front the supply of shells was interrupted and many additional lives were lost through the artillery's failure to protect the infantry with a proper sort of barrage; while at home the profits of heavy industry alarmingly declined. The strike, it was clear, had to be settled with the minimum of delay. But the strikers were stubborn and their employers with adamantine logic declared that it was impossible to raise wages without diminishing profits and thereby throwing suspicion on their patriotism – unless, of course, the Government was prepared to pay fifty per cent more for the products of their labour. But this the Government was unwilling to do, and the situation was then aggravated by a virulent campaign in the popular press against the octogenarian Prime Minister, Lord Pippin. He, however, when the crisis appeared to be threatening the life of his Cabinet, if not of the country as a whole, emerged from his characteristic quiescence to settle it with customary ease. He gave Mr Small *carte blanche* to deal with the dilemma as he thought best.

The war, like the boiling of a pot, had thrown to the top of affairs a number of men more suited than the older politicians to the peculiar difficulties of the time. These newcomers, by the vigour of their constitution and the business-like quality of their minds, had impressed the public and secured some excellent jobs. Two or three had attained Cabinet rank, of whom Mr Small was one; and even his political opponents found it difficult not to admire the manner in which, without loss of time, he now proceeded to negotiate a settlement of the dispute.

He summoned a meeting, in the Palace of Fun at Blackpool, of employers and the strikers' leaders, and laid before them an initial proposal for a general increase in wages of twenty-five per cent. He also intimated that in all the affected industries there would have to be a comb-out of men of military age up to a figure representing forty per cent of the whole number employed. These on being drafted into the army would be replaced by women, and boys under the age of eighteen, whose wages would be fixed at five-eighths of the existing standard wage. There might be, he admitted, some disorganization as a result of this large displacement of labour, but in return for a guaranteed output he proposed for the compensation of employers the derating of all premises used in the production of munitions. These offers, which at first were doubtfully received, he supported by a display of oratory that greatly impressed the employers; by tears that gradually melted the resistance of the strikers; and by a private request, to the wealthiest of the employers and the leader of the strikers, that they would accept a Barony of the United Kingdom and a Knighthood of the British Empire respectively. It was then discovered that the proposals were characterized by the triune spirit of Christianity, fair play, and British statesmanship; and the strike was called off. The men who escaped conscription returned to work, and their employers to counting their profits; and Mr Small, after receiving the congratulations of everyone, went smiling out of the Palace of Fun to be photographed by the united press of Great Britain. The only flaw in his happiness was the adhesive presence of Tom Hogpool.

But it was Hogpool who suggested a bottle of champagne

to celebrate the occasion, and Mr Small, who was always glad to eat or drink at anyone else's expense, accepted the invitation and together they walked among audibly admiring passers-by to the New Carlton Hotel.

'There'll be another friend of mine there,' said Hogpool complacently. 'A young lady, as a matter of fact, and she'll be glad to meet you, Perce. She's of good family herself, and she likes to meet people that's well up in the world like you. Though she might think different if she knew as much about you as I do. Eh, lad?'

'What you know is neither here nor there, Tom, and you ought to realize that as well as I do. I'm a Cabinet Minister now, and all that matters to me is the welfare of the whole country, and the speedy victory of our boys over there in Germany and Belgium.'

'Well, do you think I don't understand that as well as you, Perce? Hogpool's Barbed Wire was down to 52s. 6d. the day before yesterday, and it's up to 61s. this morning, and I know it's you that's done it. You and the backbone of the English people, that is, which can always be trusted to see common sense in the end. God strike me silly, I'm a patriot as well as you, Perce, and all I was saying was that you'd make a hit with my friend Miss Ivy FitzAubrey. You haven't lost your sense of humour, have you?'

'I've got a very conscientious sense of humour, Tom, which you should know by this time.'

'That's your proper self speaking now, Perce. And you'll be feeling better still after a glass or two of bubbly, just you see.'

They entered the pink granite doorway of the New Carlton Hotel, and in the cream-and-scarlet lounge Hogpool introduced the Minister to the orchidaceous young woman who was waiting for them. She was the beautiful blonde creature who had been with him in the restaurant when Lysistrata and Eliot dined there before the latter went to Germany; and Mr Small acknowledged her charm by immediately displaying for her benefit all his well-known affability, a pleasant condescension, and some evidence of his familiar acquaintance with the chief dignitaries of the land.

Ivy was visibly gratified, and determined to make the most

of her opportunity. 'It must be an awful strain, being Prime Minister at a time like this,' she remarked with sympathy in her voice.

'Oh, Pippin takes things pretty easily, just like he always has done. He leaves the work to us younger men.'

'Pippin?' she asked. 'Who's that?'

'Lord Pippin, the Prime Minister,' he explained. 'But I call him Pippin, of course, being in the Cabinet myself.'

Ivy looked puzzled. 'I thought you were Prime Minister,' she said.

Mr Small, after a moment's indecision, laughed loudly and said boisterously, 'Did you hear that, Tom? Your friend Miss FitzAubrey's having a joke at my expense. Prime Minister indeed! Fancy a little girl like you trying to pull *my* leg!'

He patted her thigh to show that he took the joke in good part, and Ivy, quickly recovering herself, said with a playful petulance, 'Well, everybody seems to think you're the most important man in the country, so naturally I thought you must be Prime Minister.'

'He will be, if the war lasts long enough,' said Hogpool, and told the waiter to bring tumblers instead of champagne glasses. 'You can't drink champagne and brandy in those shallow things,' he explained, 'and somehow I don't seem to like a neat champagne as much as I used to. I generally take a drop of brandy in it nowadays, to buck it up a bit.'

'You're getting quite a connoisseur, Tom,' said Mr Small.

'Live and learn: that's my motto, and always has been.'

'Fancy you and Mr Hogpool knowing each other when you were boys,' said Ivy, 'and still being friends. I do think that's funny. Well, not exactly funny, of course, but it seems funny, if you see what I mean.'

'The world,' said Mr Small sententiously, 'is not only a little place, but a very strange place. To a young lady like you it must seem a great adventure simply to be alive in such a world as ours.'

'Yes, I suppose it must,' said Ivy brightly; and then, lest brightness had not been the proper response, she sighed so deeply that the globes of her superlative bosom pushed into sight above her frock a narrow segment of their loveliness –

a double crescent of their twin white moons – and Mr Small, profoundly moved, repeated hoarsely, 'A very great adventure indeed.'

Tom Hogpool summoned a page-boy and told him to fetch a newspaper. Perce and Ivy, he thought complacently, were getting on together like a house on fire. She'd be grateful to him for introducing her to a Cabinet Minister – she had her ambitions, had Ivy – and if Perce fell for her, well, so much the better. There was nothing like a good-looking young woman for exerting a useful bit of leverage now and then, and Ivy knew her stuff all right. He drank a little champagne and brandy. What a girl she was! A lovely figure, skin like a two-year-old, and clever as well. Good manners, too. He gave a shilling to the page-boy who brought him his newspaper, and flapped it open at the financial page. Hogpool's Barbed Wire was quoted at 62s. 3d. Well, that was better than a slap on the belly with a wet fish. He'd be able to branch out a bit more in another month or two. Not munitions, though. There was too much competition there, and if they weren't careful they'd find prices being cut. But something more general. Something connected with the war, of course, but that would still go on when the war was over. You had to think of the future. Real estate, or something in that line. He looked through the paper to see if there was anything there that might give him an idea. But there was little more than war news. Casualty lists, and a story by Our Special Correspondent about how a corporal of the Sherwood Foresters had brought in fifty-six French prisoners, who were all of a twitter because they expected to be shot – just like the French did to their prisoners – but our boys gave them cigarettes, and then they shouted '*Anglais très bons!*' Well, maybe it was true. You never could tell. Then there was a picture of General Scrymgeour looking at a map, and a mother who had given three sons to England reading a War Office telegram to say that another was wounded, and Some of Our Boys in Khaki lining up for dinner, and a Bishop who had said that the English were always God's chosen instrument for doing anything big. And more casualty lists on a back page. There was nothing to interest a business man.

He threw down the paper and asked, 'What would you put your money in, Perce, supposing you'd a few thousand to spare?'

Mr Small, who had been listening with rapt attention to Ivy's story of her childhood – she had been brought up in a country vicarage, or else a rectory, she could never quite remember which – looked up with a frown and asked what Tom had said.

Hogpool repeated his question, and Mr Small, after an interval for thought, said slowly, 'Well, it's secret information, Tom, and I wouldn't tell it to anyone but you and Miss FitzAubrey here. But as a matter of fact there's shortly going to be chance for a really nice little bit of speculation, and I hope you'll remember who gave you the tip. We're going to shift our quarters. The Government, that is. You see, Blackpool's all very well in its way, but the surroundings aren't what you would call dignified. Take the Ministry of Munitions, for example. We're in the Palace of Fun. Well, it's invidious, to say the least of it, and I told the Prime Minister so more than a month ago. Then there's the Exchequer in the Crystal Palais de Danse, the War Office under the Flip-flap, and the Admiralty in the Swimming Pool. It's not good enough, Tom. If a government's going to be dignified, it's got to have dignified surroundings, and I was one of the first to say so. Blackpool for holidays, but not for Cabinet Ministers in a time of crisis. That's what I said. Then fortunately that French aeroplane, a week ago, got through and dropped a couple of bombs not far from the Flip-flap. That brought the War Office round to my side, and now it's all settled. We'll be moving as soon as the necessary arrangements can be completed.'

'Where to, Perce?'

'Edinburgh,' said Mr Small.

'That's in Scotland,' said Ivy cleverly.

'You'll be taking over all the big hotels,' said Hogpool.

'And we'll want a good lot of other accommodation too. The rent of furnished houses will go up, Tom.'

'That's an idea, Perce.'

'Well, don't forget who gave it to you. Have you ever been in Edinburgh, Miss FitzAubrey?'

'No, I don't think so. I used to go motoring a lot with a friend of mine – he was my cousin, really, and his mother was there too – but I don't think we ever got as far as that.'

'I'll be making some changes in the Ministry when we go north, and I could give you a nice important little job if you'd think of taking it.'

'Oh, I'd like to ever so much, Mr Small. I've always wanted to do war work of some kind or another, but Mr Hogpool always says that he doesn't think I'm strong enough.'

'This job that I'm thinking of wouldn't need much strength, Miss FitzAubrey. Just charm. The sort of charm that you exercise without ever thinking about it. Oh, yes, you do. You see already I know you better than you know yourself. Well, let me tell you about the job. Now as you know, most of the Ministries have got very big, and some of them have appointed what they call hostesses, to look after visitors, and so on. But *hostess* is too American a word for my liking, and what I want is a young lady to act as *receptionist*. Now, how would that suit you? Receptionist to the Ministry of Munitions.'

'You mean just receiving people – gentlemen and so on – and being nice to them?'

'That's the idea.'

'Oh, I could do that!'

'Well, I'll engage you. Tom, I've given Miss FitzAubrey a job with the Government.'

But Hogpool was lost in a dream of riches. In imagination he had mobilized all the profits of barbed wire and with them bought or rented innumerable houses in Edinburgh, which presently he would let at extravagant prices to secretariats and civil servants and the horde of industrialists who would follow the Government as hotly as Mr Jorrocks after the bag-fox. Here was easy money, and the figures of it moved before his eyes like houris to a hashish-eater.

'He's thinking,' said Ivy reverently; and then exclaimed, 'Oh, look! There's Commander Lawless, the V.C.'

A tall lean figure in a shabby Naval uniform, stooping somewhat, went by with a pretty, slim, fair little woman. A lock of yellow hair hung untidily over his forehead, and he had a wild blue eye.

'They say he's quite mad,' whispered Ivy. 'I wonder who's that he's with?'

'Mrs Curle,' said Mr Small. 'Her husband's the Secretary of State for War.'

'Her hat's all wet. It must be raining,' said Ivy.

VII

Rain was falling on the flooded battlefields. It came on whirling gusts of wind and beat upon shelving trenches and a myriad dark lagoons and the hooded soldiers. When the frost went the earth had collapsed as though its ribs were melting. Soil and sandbags, losing their rocky form and crisp security, had resolved into shapeless puddings and a soft floor of mud. In tiny holes and crannies the water gathered, and overflowed their crumbling edges, and ran in turbid little rills to fill a larger pool or join a deeper rivulet. The grey lids of ice dissolved, that had covered shell-hole and hoof-mark, and opened filthy tarns and innumerable small brown puddles. The soggy earth was pocketed with water-holes that filled from subterranean springs and over-filled with rain. Duck-boards that had been frozen to the hard earth now lost their hold and slewed in the yielding mud, or moved uneasily in rising water, while the straight sides of deep-dug trenches, flattened from the clouds, bulged weakly out and their diminished strength let parapets collapse and scarps fall sullenly.

The dead were yielding to corruption now. They no longer lay gaunt and rigid, but huddled softly in the mud. When the frost melted in their flesh the starkness of their last agony had relaxed and the icy preservation of their youth dissolved. They no longer showed how young they had been, nor any likeness to any of the ages of man, but buried their faces or let the rain fill their mouths like any puddle of the fields. Sometimes when a shell struck a flooded crater a dead arm would rise, like that of a drowning man, or a body heave slowly into sight. But that was all that suggested they had once known strength and movement. They were no more to be recognized as the sons of men, but as parcels of the troubled earth.

In the lowering sky the whistle of the flighting shells was

a little muted. They had a wilder but more melancholy note, and the noise of their bursting was muffled by mud and water. They came only at intervals, like a rare skein of geese on a stormy day, and they seemed to be fired for no better reason than petulance, as if now and again the soaking gunners, rebellious at inertia and the quagmire of their pits, let fly at the elements which had brought them such wretchedness. But in the trenches there was no warlike activity at all. A steady watch was kept, but except for that the men did nothing but try to maintain their crumbling walls and keep life enough in their bodies to go out when they should be relieved. Dugouts were flooded, and in many trenches the men sat on the fire-step with water up to their knees, or splashed slowly to and fro as if they were walking in the bed of a stream. They were hooded in dark waterproof sheets, and their rifles were tied round the breech with old rags to keep the mud out. No one could move without being smeared with mud. It dried in the joints of their fingers and the wrinkles of their clothes, and old mud was coated with new. They ate and drank it, though in the front line there was little enough eating. The ration-parties were unable to get up, and all that the men had was a mouthful of beef from a muddy tin, a loaf – fished out of a muddy sack – among six, and distasted tea.

A little while after the fall of darkness, on the night of the Royal Scots' relief, the rain stopped and the wind died away. The wind died suddenly, leaving a silence behind it. But then into the silence came the sound of a hundred little watercourses, the tinkle and babble of rills and brooklets, the chuckle of deeper streams. The splashing steps of Graham walking along the trench were as loud as the struggles of a seal among salmon nets. The men listened anxiously, nervous as poachers of being discovered. They were like poachers in a maze of running water, and the chuckling of the brooks bewildered them. A star or two came out, and were faintly reflected in dark pools.

The relief arrived, and twenty minutes later the Royal Scots began to file out of the trench. Many of them had taken off their kilts and tied them like capes over their shoulders. Their shirt-tails and bare thighs showed palely in the darkness. They were in a hurry to be off, and more careless of noise now that all were moving, they splashed and stumbled as quickly as they could down the communication trench.

Graham brought up the rear of his company. With difficulty he kept in check a rising elation, for in a Scotch way he was superstitious about the confessing of optimism till the event was concluded. But they had been lucky so far. They had done well and fortune had favoured them. His young soldiers, standing firm as veterans, had beaten off three French attacks with great loss to the enemy and few casualties of their own. They had acquitted themselves like seasoned troops, and when the floods came they had suffered that misery with quiet endurance. They had done well, and deserved their good fortune. He prayed that it might continue, and wished that their patience would last a little longer. 'Steady in front,' he implored. 'Take your time there, and don't bunch like that.'

They came into the open, into the country of the dead volcanoes whose flooded craters showed darkly on every side, and clustered in confusion to a halt. There was shell-fire to the right, but far off, and a few shells had fallen about half a mile away. They saw before them a dim rank of silhouettes, all close together. They grew angry, and a little frightened. What had gone wrong? 'The bloody fools!' said someone. 'Why the hell don't they get a move on?'

The guides of the other battalion, that was also going out of the line, had lost their way, and the far-off shell-fire had alarmed them. A muttering rose from the congested ranks, and some wrathful shouting.

'Get a move on!'

'Get a bloody move on!'

'For Christ's sake get a move on!'

Squelching through the mud, officers came quickly to restore order, and the other battalion, assured they were going in the right direction, continued clumsily on their way. But they had hardly started when, with a shriek and a bursting thud, a shell landed fifty yards to their right. Another followed, and half a dozen more. The waiting soldiers forgot their discipline and began to run. They spread out fan-wise from the narrow duckboard-path and scrambled through the mud. In the trenches, when they were facing the enemy, their patience had been tireless and their bravery beyond suspicion. But now they had come out of the line, and because their objective was a place of safety they had grown more aware of danger. A dozen men had been killed by the falling shells, and twenty or so wounded. And all because the bloody fools in front had lost their way. They were stuck there, huddled together to be killed, though they had done their job in the line and were entitled to a little rest and security. And still the fools were bunched like cattle, and the road was blocked. The road was blocked, and they had to get out. They had to get out quickly, before more shells came to blow them to pulp in the mud. They began to run.

With a shout of despair a man fell face-forward into a flooded shell-hole, and even as he was falling he felt the boots and the knees and the weight of another man on top of him. The water went over their heads. It filled mouth and eyes with its foulness, and they floundered, drowning, in the mud at the bottom of the hole while more boots and the weight of other men trampled them down. In the darkness the quagmire opened its gulfs, and men who had been brave enough till a moment before made bridges of their fallen comrades. The faint starlight flickered on thick black water that was heaving with the death-struggle of dying animals. The babbling mockery of dirty little rills was drowned by the splashing feet of the panic-stricken herd. They had turned their backs to the enemy, and fear was behind them. . . .

The distant shells, the first they heard, had fallen near the huts where Eliot Greene's battalion was billeted. Forty yards in front of them was a so-called safety-trench in which, according to standing orders, everyone had to take shelter in the event of the camp area being fired on. At night, however, the troops, unimpressed by a danger to which they had become habituated, were sometimes averse from leaving the comparative comfort of the huts for a cold and muddy ditch. They had to be driven out by an officer or a sergeant.

The ground between the huts was a water-logged marsh, spanned and intersected by duck-boards. Eliot, who had been writing to Lysistrata when the iron walls of the camp were shaken by the first explosion, stumbled along one of these slippery tracks with the half-finished letter in his hand. He had found a few sullen and disdainful men still in their beds, and ordered them out. He turned a corner and dimly saw a figure struggling in the mud and trying to haul something out of a slimy pool. He thrust the letter into his pocket and went quickly to help.

His boots slithered and sank in the soft earth. He stooped, and putting his hand into the filthy pool felt a cold and naked limb. He repressed his nausea. 'Who is it?' he demanded.

The young soldier beside him, hauling away and sobbing with the effort he was making, said tearfully, 'It isn't a who, sir. It's rations.'

'What do you mean?'

'I was carrying it from the Quartermaster's store, sir, and when that whizz-bang came over I got a bit of a fright, and let it fall. It's beef, sir, the 'ind leg of a cow, and if I leave it 'ere I'll be crimed for losing it.'

Eliot, in a violent revulsion of feeling, began to laugh, but the boy was still serious. He had a clean crime-sheet, and his only military ambition was to keep it clean. The loss of a quarter of beef would be a serious offence, and he was most reluctant to abandon it. Eliot spoke sharply to him, but the boy answered triumphantly, 'I've got it now, sir!' and dragged the lump of filthy meat on to the duckboard.

Eliot with a slight shudder stooped to look at it, and at that moment heard the whinnying of another shell, the whining irregular crescendo of its approach.

'Get down!' he shouted, and they drew themselves flat beside the quarter of dead cow.

In the fraction of a second the whine rose to a vivid shriek that burst into thunder as it met the ground, and into the ribboned air hurled a black mephitic fountain. Eliot was thrown from the earth as if by a giant wave, and through the shock came a scarlet flash of pain. He felt the mud again, cold and wet to his hand, and with the lurching of an earthquake in his head, consciousness left him.

VIII

Lysistrata woke with a start. She had come home, tired out, and fallen asleep in a chair. . . .

For the last month she had been living in Edinburgh. The Government had successfully transferred itself, with all its apparatus and appendages, to the Scottish capital, and none could deny that in appearance at least the city was more congenial than Blackpool to imperial and warlike administration; though many found the climate uncomfortably severe. Edinburgh from her high place overlooks the windy estuary of the Forth, and is sometimes buried under a cold sea fog. She stares northward to the nearer Highlands, and frequently is pelted by a Highland snowstorm. The Castle, crowning the great crag that rises in the midst of the city, is like a challenge to all the winds of the sky; and often the challenge is answered. But it was a portion of Edinburgh's climate – a kindly fog – that had saved her unscathed from the air-raids; and the high-set Castle had a look of authority that was very welcome after the Flip-flaps and Giant Wheel of Blackpool. It was agreed that on the whole the migration had been a wise one. . . .

Lysistrata's dinner was ready. The maid who announced it was a middle-aged woman, sharp-featured and of yellowish complexion, whose apparently sour temper concealed a character that was capable of the most violent and contradictory sentiment. Horrocks had been in Lysistrata's service since her marriage, and before that in her mother's house. She was devoted to her mistress, and for several years had been passionately in love with a hand on General Scrymgeour's yacht, a long-armed melancholy-looking man called Bulmer. It was her misfortune to believe that she was necessary to the happiness of both, and in order to satisfy the wholy different demands that each made on her time, she had been compelled to practise a duplicity that was abhorrent to her intensely respectable aspirations. Under cover of the fiction that Bulmer was her nephew – which Lysistrata very dubiously accepted – they had for long been illicit lovers, and the more frequent their misdemeanours the more fervidly loyal grew Horrocks to her mistress. When shortly after the outbreak of war

Lysistrata dispersed her household, Horrocks refused to leave her, and now, in a small flat in Edinburgh, she was maid, housemaid, butler and occasionally cook.

Lysistrata did not linger over her dinner. Her V.A.D. command had accompanied the great migration to Edinburgh, and its rehabilitation was still giving her a lot of extra work. Every night she carried home a sheaf of documents and conscientiously attended to problems of organization, economy and discipline, and to the ever-present possibilities of reform. She took her duty seriously, and harshly criticized herself if she allowed her own feelings to interfere with her work. But she was finding it more and more difficult to keep her feelings in the background.

Horrocks brought coffee, and said in a flat uninterested way, 'Bulmer's been sent to that place Rosyth. He says it isn't very far from here.'

'That will be nice for you.'

'Yes, madam. He's in a destroyer now, and his captain is Commander Lawless, who won the V.C. He says it's a big change from a battleship, where they didn't use to do anything but gardening and drill.'

In addition to some ill-natured criticism there was much sympathy for the predicament of the Navy. The stoppage of oil supplies had not seriously affected it, for the Admiralty had accumulated an enormous fuel reserve, and many of the ships were capable of burning coal-oil, which was being produced in increasing quantities. But the submarine menace, the danger of floating mines, and the extravagant price of capital ships, had made it impossible, or at least impolitic, for a battleship to leave port without the protection and preliminary manœuvring of cruisers, light cruisers, destroyers, smaller destroyers, coastal motor-boats, and mine-sweepers. The larger cruisers themselves required, in the rare event of their going to sea, the very extensive cooperation of ancillary craft, and in certain quarters it was thought that even the latest sort of destroyer, which was a large and expensive vessel, should not be allowed to leave harbour without at least a preliminary reconnaissance by sweepers and the new sort of boats called Pilot Fish, to see that conditions were reasonably safe. But as all the smaller vessels were needed for the protection of convoys the capital ships were unable to secure protection, and were consequently immobilized. They had become, in fact, a string of floating forts, principally on the south coast, and their crews spent much of their time in foot-drill and the cultivation of allotments. The French fleet, in similar circumstances, had been forced into comparable inactivity.

Among the general populace, which was wholly ignorant of the difficulties of naval warfare, there had at one time been manifest a feeling that the Navy was not living up to its reputation; but this had happily been dispelled by the gallantry of various junior officers commanding small craft, and in particular by a dramatic affair off Cherbourg. A certain Lieutenant Lawless, in command of a flotilla of the fast motor-boats called Pilot Fish, had torpedoed a small French cruiser which had had the temerity to leave harbour, and closing in on the partially disabled ship he had, with the genius of his kind, given the perfect order: 'Out cutlasses and board!' Cutlasses, of course, had long ceased to be an official weapon, but Lawless, who had the courage of his convictions and a small private income, had bought a hundred at a sale of surplus stores and issued them to his crews. His foresight was amply justified. His men, ennobled by his faith in them and fired by the apostolic touch of steel, had boarded the astonished Frenchman, and sweeping to victory with irresistible valour, had completed the operation by bringing their prize triumphantly into Portsmouth. This heart-of-oak exploit had restored the wavering faith of Britain in its fleet. The spirit of Nelson, if not his strategy, was still alive, and again the French had yielded to the Nelson touch. That was the news that the people needed, and the moral effect of the action was probably worth a new Army Corps. . . .

'A lot of them were sick the first time they went to sea,' continued Horrocks, 'but Bulmer was all right, of course, being used to yachting.'

Lysistrata thought of her last cruise in the *Freya*, on that morning in July, and saw for a moment, in the decisive clarity with which memory sometimes unhoods the past, the huge arch of the peaceful sky; and heard herself saying to Eliot,

'Nothing is worth while that upsets our peace.' Was that true? she wondered. It could not be wholly true, or the war was merely a waste of life and effort and the fruits of time; and to admit that was to be torn at the roots from the very soil of credence. She could not believe that. . . . Yet for Eliot, if one thought of him as an individual and not as a subaltern in the army, it had been waste and nothing else. He had lost nearly everything. His life lay in ruins, that had been the expression of a long and prosperous culture, pleasant to himself and not unprofitable to the community. He had inherited a tradition of public service which he had exercised in fact to the best of his large ability, and minimized in conversation with agreeable cynicism; his birth and education had given him ideals which he would neither have forgotten in the excitement of self-aggrandizement, nor overestimated in the emotional habit of the intellectual *arriviste*; he had been humane because he knew the way of humanity, and witty because he was aware of its deviations; he had the faculty of pleasure and a mind to criticize it. But like a tidal wave the war had swept him from his habitation, and now he was a maimed and legless derelict.

They had expected him to die, but with amazing tenacity he had held on to life, and now with bitter irony he was said to be out of danger. He might keep what was left of life. He had lost his legs, and therefore could not go again into battle. He had paid the price of safety.

To Lysistrata the news of his being wounded had come as a confirmation of her continual fear for him. For him the peril of war had always seemed curiously aggravated, and death or some close congener inevitable. He had been more obviously vulnerable than most, more certainly a destined victim, and day after day she had read the casualty lists with a growing dread, that had almost become a morbid eagerness, of finding Eliot's name among the killed or wounded. It had been a relief to find it among the latter, and despite her sorrow and in the midst of a grief more poignant than she had ever expected, she was conscious of relaxation and freedom from strain. Fear had gone, and for a night or two she slept as soundly as though the world were at peace. But then, with the mysterious imperceptible motivity of a snake, fear returned; and now she was afraid for Tony.

She had never feared for him before. He had seemed to her as immune from danger as Eliot was vulnerable to it. But her fear for Eliot had been cut off and now, as though it were a spring that flowed without ceasing and must find a channel somewhere, it ran towards Tony. His imagined security disappeared, and again she lived in the shadow of imminent disaster.

He had come home on short leave at Christmas, and for a few days they had enjoyed intense but hatefully imperfect happiness. Even when on leave Scrymgeour's time was not his own, and he had had to attend conferences at the War Office, to visit training camps, and dine with political hostesses. The war was still his master, and what little time he had alone with Lysistrata was like illicit hours with a mistress. His ardency, indeed, had been the passion of a lover, and she had said nothing of her desire, so lately born and so importunate, to have children; but had met him in the fashion of the time, which was a desperate engagement – attack and surrender all in one – with the fleeting minute. It was no season for begetting, no world for bearing. Peace must come, with its calm horizon, and promise of long months ahead, before hope and love could set to breeding. Peace must come. ... And now for the first time she was conscious that her wish for peace was stronger than any desire for victory. Peace was the first necessity, and such a peace as would be consonant with England's greatness in the past.

It seemed to her that the English heritage was above all characterized by abundance. It was a tale of plenty, and the nation with such a history should be generous. Its sailors had circled the globe and brought into common parlance the gold and musk of the Orient, the coral names of the huge Pacific. Its soldiers had given to every childhood the colour and clash and chivalry of Agincourt and Malplaquet and Waterloo. Its poets had rivalled God with their creation, and made of English speech a treasury richer than Golconda. Its common people, in whose veins ran the blood of easy Saxon, the proud and sharp-edged Norman, the unpredictable dark Celt, had bred mysteriously liberty and the love of liberty; justice, and a high regard for it; and their innocent delight in gardens. Its destiny had given it material wealth to which half the world contributed. – Its heritage was abundance, and therefore its obligation was the bequeathing of plenty. The heirs of Drake and Raleigh should explore the mind for new worlds of richness and delight; the sons of Blenheim and Trafalgar should make a peace more glorious than any battle; the people for whom Shakespeare and Donne had written, whose penny poets were Milton and Blake and Shelley, should leave a wealth of life for their wealth of verse; and the heritors of the transient riches that came of trade and industry should buy with the brevity of their fortune the enduring name of good deeds. Let England spend its abundance in generosity. Let its future be as splendid as its past, but very different. Let England realize its strength, and its history to come should sound more gloriously than all the trumpet-pages that were turned. . . .

It was a noble vision. Its splendour was so bright that Lysistrata could not work for thinking of it.

IX

'I nearly forgot my words the other night,' said Rose, 'because I kept thinking of you, and it was so exciting just to *think* of being with you again, that nothing else seemed to count.'

'Nothing has ever counted more than love.'

'And we've got so short a time! Less than a week. And if I was just a few years older, you wouldn't be able to love me like this, would you?'

'Of course I would.'

'You wouldn't. You think you would, Julian, but you wouldn't really.'

Turning wantonly from her contentment, Rose looked with open eyes – but only for a minute – at the old sorrow of fleeting time and life that slips so fast away. It was a perverse indulgence, the result perhaps of an overdose of happiness; for Julian was on leave, and for a little time they could be together. He had come straight to Edinburgh, where for the

past two months Rose had been playing in a musical piece
called *Red, White, and You*. Edinburgh, since becoming the
seat of Government, had apparently doubled in size, and
despite the war multiplied its gaiety tenfold. Rose found it a
pleasant town to live in, though a little cold; but since Julian's
arrival the climate had been heavenly. Yet stubbornly now,
for a little while, she would uncover her heart and shiver at
the sadness of youth, and love that is short-lived.

'I've seen it happen,' she mournfully continued. 'I mean
I've seen a man and a girl who were desperately in love, and
they got married, and then two or three years later she was
older looking, she had a different kind of look, and he was
tired of her, because it was only her being young that he'd
fallen in love with. That's true, Julian. It's being young
that matters, and now, because of the war, even that's
wasted; because your man's away, and he may never come
back.'

'My darling. . . .'

'Yes, I know. I'm being silly, aren't I?'

'You're being adorable.'

'I don't often get like this. It was just the strain of waiting
for you, and I've got an awful lot to do in this new show, and
I suppose I'm a bit tired.'

'Then we'll have a long rest, shall we?'

'It must be terribly late. We ought to be getting up.'

'There's no hurry.'

'Julian! You don't care a bit what other people think, do
you?'

'Well, I've learnt some useful lessons in the last few months,
and one of them is to take my own line, as far as possible, and
use my own judgement. It pays every time.'

'Tell me about the war.'

'You said last night you didn't want to hear a word about it.'

'Well, I do now.'

'Really?'

'Really and truly. How long is it going to last?'

'Another couple of years at least. We're doing well,
better than could be expected perhaps, but we can't get
guns.'

'But everyone says we're making thousands of guns nowadays.'

'Yes, and we need still more. The problem's simple enough: we've got to smash our way through the French, and to do that we need artillery and plenty of it. The men are simply grand, but you mustn't expect them to work miracles. In modern warfare the infantry can't go forward without artillery preparation, and even the politicians ought to have learnt that by this time. But they haven't. It's they who are letting us down, the politicians and the people at home.'

With a comfort-seeking movement Rose wriggled nearer to him. She had very little interest in the actual conduct or problems of the war. To her it was only an emotional experience, something that filled her alternately with gloom or a glorious excitement. It had given her a lover, and kept him away from her. In the very hour of its beginning, when her heart was softened and distressed by the death of her mother and the world was literally falling about her, Julian had been there, strong and capable, to take charge of everything. She had seen him use his authority and exact obedience. The war had not daunted him. His confidence had been like a place of shelter, and then, when he declared his love and pleaded with her to become his lover, his confidence had vanished, and he was shy and clumsy and dependent on her. She had loved him all the more because of that, for it gave her the mastery and made him her very own. Even now, when he was no longer diffident, she felt a proud sense of possession, almost of creation. It delighted her to see and hear his assurance, for much of it was what she had given him. The war, of course, had hardened his manner and exercised him in authority. She could see a difference in his appearance. But it was she as well as the war who had made him what he was, and she grew a little jealous as he continued to speak of guns and brigadiers and the virtues of his men. He had six days' leave, six little days, and surely for so short a time he could forget about his soldiering. She pulled him towards her and kissed him on the lips.

'I thought so,' he said. 'You don't know what you want.'

'Yes, I do.'

'A couple of minutes ago you wanted me to tell you about the war.'

'I know I did.'

'I keep thinking of it anyway. It isn't easy to forget it overnight.'

'You're not trying.'

'Rose, my dear. Rose, I'm utterly in love with you. Utterly and starkly and for ever and ever.'

'My sweet, my darling . . . '

Love was the sovereign lenitive of the stricken world, its refuge and unfailing bliss. Never had love more closely, universally been sought than now, when the dirt and squalor of the war made by contrast its luxury more dear, and dread of Sergeant Death, who was everyman's own neighbour, drove him to the Cyprian for sweet forgetfulness. Love meant release of all that turbid and tumultuous feeling which the shouting of the patriots and fear and thought of vengeance had aroused; and was the remedy for coldness and despair. Ares had come back to overstride the ruined fields, but Aphrodite Pandemos ruled the air.

A few miles south of Edinburgh a battalion of English infantry was marching along a straight road between winter-stript black hedges. Their rifles were slung, they marched at ease, but soldierly. Their heads were high, their bearing gallant. Rank after rank, they trod the road in the precision and iron discipline of a Roman Legion, but their stride was the swagger of free men. In all the history of military service there was never a general from Hannibal to Charles the Great, from the Italian captains to Napoleon's marshals, who would not have been proud and thankful to command them, and boasted they were wholly dedicate to war. But the road turned a corner and passed a little house whose garden broke the long line of the hedge, and running to the gate, waving their hands to the soldiers, came a woman and her daughters. Then the brave music of the band, the martial drums and high-pealing fifes, were shouted down by a sudden outcry, and all the soldiers as they swaggered by called loudly to the blushing woman and the laughing girls. They began to sing, no warlike tune but a common air of the people; a music-hall song:

If you feel rotten because you're a woman,
      Seek for a suitable spouse –
Say what you like, but admit you are human,
      And better for having a man in the house!

Rose Armour's vulgar song was acquiring an unexpected bitterness, however, as more and more women became lonely through no fault of their own, and girls when their lovers left them for the war saw loneliness haunting their middle years. The song was less popular than it had been, and many women who heard it saw in their imagination those haggard Birds, with women's faces pale and hungry, who waited for the next to die. In the orchards and forests of Europe and the meadows of England they sat on the trees, the Harpies waiting for their meat, and fouling all they could not take.

There were, too, ghouls of another sort, many of whom were much esteemed by the uncritical world, and leaders of fashionable society. They consumed the dead with relish, and unexceptionable manners. Late in the afternoon – of this day when Rose Armour had been sad for half a minute, and the marching soldiers had sung her song – about thirty of them were gathered in a house in Heriot Row; of whom three or four were listening to a Mrs Losel and her story of a distinguished General.

'He was so amusing about their last Conference,' she said, speaking to Mrs Curle, Colonel Hotspur, and Mr Sanfoy, who with sherry glasses in their hands were crowded close to her by the surrounding throng. 'He said that none of the politicians had the vaguest notion of the number of effectives in the Home Command, and all of them had utterly erroneous ideas not only about the reinforcements needed, but those we are actually sending to the front.'

'I believe the wastage from all sources is about a hundred and twenty thousand a month,' said Mr Sanfoy.

'Yes, I think it is. And then Puffles said, "If you want to know the truth about the war, we're not fighting the French at all, but the Home Office and the Treasury."'

'Poor Puffles is *mal vu* with everyone except the soldiers now.'

'They say the Prime Minister still believes in him.'

'My dear, the Prime Minister believes in anyone who leaves

him alone. He slept for fourteen hours after the last meeting of the Conference, and when he woke up he refused to see anyone till six o'clock, because he was reading *Pride and Prejudice*.'

'How I envy him! The war gives me no time for reading, literally none.'

'Didn't I see you lunching with Lionel and Myra yesterday?'

'Yes, we had a marvellous talk. Lionel is terribly bitter against the War Office. He says nobody has made any plans for the future, and even if they got the divisions they're asking for, there isn't maintenance for them, and no one would know what to do with them.'

'It's an absolute certainty, I believe, that poor Puffles will be *dégommé*.'

'I suppose you've heard the marvellous story about von Schmerding?'

'About his attempt to convert poor Sir Joseph to Wotanism?'

'No, better than that. Our unfortunate allies, as you know, have had heavy losses in the Böhmer Wald ... Lysistrata! I haven't seen you for ages.'

'I have been rather busy lately,' said Lysistrata.

'You mustn't kill yourself, my dear. That won't do anyone any good.'

Lysistrata had gone to Lady Oriole's sherry party because of a suspicion that loneliness was making her morbid. For some weeks she had been living very quietly, seeing few people except those with whom she associated in her war-work, and because more solitude than she was used to had been making her think more profoundly than was her habit, she had begun to fear that her mind was getting unhealthy. She had gone to the party in the hope of finding it tonic and restorative, but it had only made her angry and more unhappy.

They were enjoying the war, these fortunate people. They had such fine material for gossip now, such hot expensive pies to dip their fingers in. The difficulties of all the world were translated for their pleasure ... The Prime Minister, they said, knew nothing of the military arrangements between our several allies – the soldiers had muddled everything – the politicians were ignorant of strategy – the Generals had never heard of economics. They had had the most fascinating discussion with someone who knew all about Italy and Rumania – and the most marvellous Bridge – and the last time they saw him Sir Joseph had looked like a peacock in a thunderstorm, and screamed like one too. Their lives were rich with all the news they heard, and the agony of nations was their table-talk. Europe on its death-bed fought for another day or two of life, and they were all agog to be told its latest symptoms. Already, they said, the quality of recruits was deteriorating, and Puffles had called the new officers a parcel of tailors. The life of a subaltern was only six weeks, however, so perhaps it didn't matter. – They would be short of men in another year. They needed twelve more divisions on the western front. The C.-in-C. had said he was no longer worrying about reserves, because he hadn't got any. The politicians knew nothing about strategy, and the soldiers had muddled everything. – The heavens were falling, and such a harvest of gossip had never been reaped before.

Lysistrata was fond of her hostess, however, who was a busy, nervous, hospitable woman, with a habit of keeping too many irons in fires of her own igniting, and a husband, sometime in the Brigade but now commanding a Territorial battalion, who had gone to Germany, though ten years too old for the line, and was enjoying himself prodigiously there. Camilla Oriole hated the war, and was constantly endeavouring to hurry it to a satisfactory conclusion, either by fomenting intrigue against the Prime Minister and Sir Joseph Rumble – or against Sir Archibald Puffin-Lumkyn, who was in command of Home Defence – or by touring the United States with propaganda of her own devising – or by extravagantly subscribing to every charity she heard of. There was an abundance of virtue in Lady Oriole, and its unassociated surplus might have healed Lysistrata's infirmity had Lady Oriole had time to talk to her; but she was too busy conversing with Colonel Siegfried Fleischhauer, a new military attaché, a person with such highly polished manners, magnificent appearance, and automatic supply of lubricant information that he resembled rather an expensive motor car than a human being.

'We interrupted you,' said Mrs Losel to Colonel Hotspur, 'when you were *sur le point de te gausser de von Schmerding.*'

'It is a sad story,' said the Colonel complacently, 'and von Schmerding was very upset about it. Our allies, with all the thoroughness of the Teuton, had prepared a splendid attack along the Regen. It was to be a lesson in the art of war, a model battle that would be quoted in the textbooks. Every detail had been planned, even to a review of the successful troops.'

'And what prevented it?'

'The impetuous Czechs. They launched their attack just twenty-four hours before the Germans were ready, with what results you know. But the joke was von Schmerding's reaction. He was still tearful when I saw him, and he said – you know his manner – "It would have been such a beautiful battle! We had made every arrangement, we had many of our best troops there, and then everything was spoilt. It is heartbreaking to fight with an enemy who cannot be trusted!"'

'They used to be so clever,' said Mrs Curle with a sigh. 'But I suppose they've had too much mass emotion and muscle-building and Wagner, poor things.'

'My dear!' exclaimed a tall marcid woman, very smartly dressed, with brilliant dark eyes and a thin scarlet mouth, who came shrill-voiced through the crowd, her bony brace-leted hand held high. – 'My dear! have you been to Madame Corvo? She's the most marvellous fortune-teller I've ever known. I had her round to my house the other day, when all the Admirals were there after their conference about the Medi-terranean – just as useful to confer about the moon, so I told them – and every one consulted her, and you should have seen their faces when they came out of the room! A smirk, you know, terribly happy but very decently controlled. Each one like the last, I give you my word. She'd told the whole lot of them they were going to be Commander-in-Chief, it was plain as a pikestaff, whatever that is. She's really wonder-ful, and she says the war's going to last another five years at least. You should go to see her . . . Lysistrata, darling, where have you been all this time? I thought you had died or taken vows of some sort, I haven't seen you for so long.'

Mechanically, conscious how dull she was being, Lysistrata again said she had been very busy, and a minute or so later protested she must go.

'Poor Lysistrata,' said Mr Sanfoy. 'She's looking rather pulled-down, don't you think?'

'And no wonder,' said the tall marcid woman vivaciously. 'You've heard, of course, of the storm that's brewing round the ears of her *preux chevalier*? You haven't? Good heavens, you ought to cultivate a few Socialists, they're the people to give you news. You get more information from a Socialist M.P. in an hour than you do from *The Times* in a week. It was my Mr Marchpane who told me about Tony Scrymgeour. He's losing too many men. Very successful and all that, but far too expensive. My Mr Marchpane wrote an article about him, calling him a butcher or something of the sort, but the Censor wouldn't pass it, so he's going to ask a question in the House next week. I do think there's this to be said for the war, that so many men have lost their reputation that a fallen woman feels quite respectable again. It's an ill wind that blows nobody good, isn't it?'

CHAPTER THREE

Councils of Mutiny

I

OUT of a silver-plumed swiftly moving sky and from the new-green lands beyond the Forth, the wind blew brisk and cold in the challenging way of a northern spring. The window had a far chill view. It rattled in its frame, and Eliot, half-turning in his bed, felt the humiliation that came from every movement as he shifted the diminished weight of his body. The bandaged stumps of his legs, not yet resigned to impotence, sought for resistance and could not find it. His mind was still conscious of knees and feet, but when he tried to reach the mattress with them, they were not there, and his mind grew ashamed and miserable.

The bold sky's brightness taunted him. Not with soft fingers, with flowers at foot and plainsong in the hedge, does spring come to Scotland; but with a blow and a challenge. With the challenge, he thought, of cock-crow in the dark of a cold morning, or pipers loudly through the dawn-grey tents blowing reveillé. It shocks, not woos, the earth awake, and one day dazzling the feathered streams with the sun in splendour, the next will beat the shivering trees with a white storm of hail. But the leaves grow brighter green for their whipping, the rare sun colours the brooks that go leaping over granite boulders, and summer when it comes is lovelier under translucent tall skies than the lazy charm of the south. – April, icy-shod, hammers at the door, the reeds in the lake bend down and whip the pointed waves, the pale sun tossing through the clouds rolls like an Indiaman in stormy seas; and it's time to be out and catch the tide of the year. Faith, the old hunter stretches his legs; Hope, his old bitch, strains at her leash; and against all modern likelihood, despite the bankrupt spirit and the shabby heart, belief renews in beauty and the bright shining beneath her cloak that may be reality. April, icy-fisted, the braggart pipers rousing the tents, the thought of summerlit mountains and long Atlantic beaches . . .

The renewal of life and the other year were flaunting their finery in the north. Eliot with a thrust of his arms shifted his stumps and turned away from the window. There was a knock at the door and Lysistrata came in.

'Thank God!' he said. 'I've been feeling the *renouveau* in my legs, and as my legs no longer exist, it was damned uncomfortable. What's the news? Talk scandal, rumour, gossip – tell me what's agog in Edinburgh – anything to take my mind off that confounded sky and the time of the year. *Por la saison, qui se change et remue, chacune, fors moi, s'esjoïst et revele.*'

Lysistrata stooped and kissed him. Her cheeks were cold. 'Surely the weather isn't so inviting as that,' she said. 'The wind's like a knife.'

'Not inviting, but compulsive,' said Eliot. 'That's the note of Scotland. I think my legs must have been true Saxon, and now the blood of my Border grandmother has a preponderance in my curtailed body. I've been in the damnedest, silliest mood of romantic excitement, Lysistrata. I've been talking poetry to myself. Lush, high-falutin poetry that none of the words I know will fit, but look like a schoolboy's jacket on a grown man. It's my Scotch grandmother who's done it, and being in Edinburgh. If I'd gone to Birmingham, I wouldn't have felt anything at all.'

'You mustn't get excited, Eliot.'

'Do you think it matters?'

But he lay back on the pillow, and his face was suddenly drained of the strength that had filled it while he was talking. The bone showed white and fragile through his skin, his hollow cheeks were bloodless, and his thick dark hair had the dead look of a hank of black cotton.

Lysistrata sat without speaking, his hand in hers. She had visited the hospital a dozen times since his coming there, and she still found it difficult to hide her distress when she saw him, and the flatness of his bed revealed the enormity of his mutilation. The uncontoured coverlet, tightdrawn over nothing, was horrible to look at.

'You don't feel it, do you?' said Eliot suddenly. 'The spring, I mean. The challenge of that sky?'

'Not as a challenge. As another wound, and a joke in the worst of taste, yes.'

'The grass coming to life, and men going to their death. Yes, it's a joke against *homo sapiens*, who can think of so many clever things and make such ingenious toys, but has never been clever enough to grow up and give himself the chance to enjoy them. What do you live for, Lysistrata?'

'For peace, and Tony coming back to me. That's all, at the moment.'

'You don't care, now, who wins the war?'

'Of course I do. But not so much as I care about Tony. They're attacking him again, Eliot.'

'The Labour people?'

'And some of the newspapers. I know his losses have been heavy, but how can he help that? He has to do his duty like any subaltern, and no one can win a battle without casualties.'

'That's true, unfortunately. But it's also true that some of Tony's successes have been rather expensive. They say he has never lost a trench, but he's lost more men than any other general in the war.'

'So you hate him, too?'

'No, that's too crude a simplification. Tony is a good soldier, and a good soldier is like a good mole; wherever he goes, his progress is shown by little mounds of earth. But I hate the war, that sets good people to grave-making, because I believe with all that's left of me in the goodness of life; or its potential goodness. I don't like to think of young men – men with legs, my dear – being deprived of it without gain or purpose. I asked you a minute ago what you were living for; and you said Tony's return. Well, why do you want him to return?'

'So that I can be happy again.'

'Precisely. And isn't happiness what everybody wants? Isn't happy living the very point and justification of living? Even the Scotch Presbyterians – my grandmother was one, and nobody ever accused her or them of frivolous thinking – agree that enjoyment is one-half of man's aim in life. *Man's chief end is to glorify God and enjoy him for ever*. That's what they say. Well, if God is anything at all, he's the creator, and to enjoy him is to enjoy his creation, which is life and the world. To enjoy that for ever. But instead we go to war and get our legs shot off, or die face down in the mud, or cough our lungs out, rotten with gas. It's not a joke, my dear, it's sheer bloody farce. What does a man want? Happiness. And what does a nation need? Peace. So we go to war and blow each other's guts out. A farce, by God! Do you realize that I lost my legs when I was trying to rescue a quarter of beef? That's farce, isn't it? Roaring, blood-boltered farce. The grass knows more than we do. It grows!'

'But, Eliot . . .'

'What can we do? That's what you're going to say, isn't it? Well, I say: stop it!'

He had thrust himself upright again, and his face, sharpened by late nearness to death and animated again by excitement, was lighted by the bright northern sky. Lysistrata was half taken by his enthusiasm, and half afraid of it. Leaning forward she put a restraining hand on his shoulder, and tried gently to make him lie down.

But he pushed away her hand, and exclaimed, 'It's life that's making me talk like this. Life coming back to my demi-carcase. And life can't do me any harm . . . Stop it, Lysistrata! Stop this damned farce before the whole world is a shambles, and even the grass is poisoned.'

'But who am I, Eliot? How can I do anything? Half the world's at war, and nobody thinks of anything else. What can I do to stop it? You might sooner expect a mouse to stop a charging lion.'

'There's a fable of a mouse that set free a captive lion. You could do it, Lysistrata. You're clever and beautiful and your husband loves you. Tony is a person of importance, and you, because of yourself and because of him, would have a lot of influence if you cared to use it. But the question is, do you really want the war to be stopped?'

Lysistrata got up and went to the far-sighted window that still rattled in the sash when the wind beat on it. Between the bright feathers of the clouds were patches of dancing blue, and the pale green lands beyond the Forth were gilded with the stormy sun. The world was renewing itself. The fields were quickening and the twisted hedges putting on their leaves to shelter a quire of birds. The earth was burgeoning, and the wind was a blast of trumpets crying that man's chief end was to glorify God for his creation and enjoy it for evermore. But war that shattered the limbs of tall young soldiers and left them in the mud to die was blasphemy and the bitter end of folly.

'Do you honestly want to stop it?' said Eliot.

'Yes,' she answered.

'Then listen,' he said, and lying back on his pillow began to talk in a reasonable, calm, and surprising fashion.

Lysistrata grew angry. She could not believe that he was serious, and her mood was ill-suited to a joke. Then by her repeated questions and his simple uncompromising answers, she was unwillingly persuaded that he must be in earnest; and became yet more sceptical, for what he proposed was fantastic and preternatural. It was a plan that by its very simplicity appeared outrageous, and was indeed more drastic than any precept of the most violent and radical of political revolutions.

'But it's impossible,' she said at last.

'It's the only way,' said Eliot.

'But it's farcical. No one would take it seriously.'

'The war is a farce. The most huge and imbecile farce that ever was, because it enlists the strength of all the world to destroy what all the world most dearly values. And hundreds of millions of people are taking it seriously.'

'But that's different.'

'It is indeed. Because war can achieve nothing, and what I propose may bring sanity and happiness.'

'It's impossible,' she said again. 'It wouldn't work. No one would ever believe it could work.'

'Try it and see. Or submit to the mass-suicide that will continue unless you put an end to it.'

Insistent in a mind still bewildered by an outrageous suggestion – a suggestion that she could not yet take quite seriously – was the thought that if she did what Eliot urged her to do, she would be betraying Tony. So at one moment swung the balance, and the next tipped over to the other side when she thought of the hatred gathering about him because he won his battles with so great a loss of men. If the war were stopped he would be saved from hatred and perhaps disgrace. And then with the buoyancy of her strong vitality the thought sprang up that it would be glorious to rebel against the folly of the world and the hateful forces that threatened Tony: to lead rebellion, to bring to their knees, so simply and with certitude, the bull-headed, arrogant, dull men who were destroying the world and themselves. Rebellion was a fine breath-taking thought, but its very splendour made her cooler self mistrustful of it.

She was excited, and her mind was confused with emotion and reason struggling somewhere for a foothold, when she said good-bye to Eliot and left him. Not thinking where she was going, she turned to the right, down a long corridor that led her away from the officers' wing into a noisier and more crowded part of the hospital, where the wards were full of wounded soldiers who philosophically endured the close company of death, gangrene, and the high spirits of convalescence. She passed a wax-faced boy who was being wheeled on a trolley into the operating-theatre; a high-coloured, tall, and bustling nurse; a couple of cheerful blue-coated men on crutches; a sergeant of the Royal Army Medical Corps with a file of papers in his hand and a pen behind his ear; a whistling youth with an empty sleeve – and came into the entrance-hall, where the air more coldly circulated with an odd smell of soap and poverty and carbolic acid.

To the right of the hall was a waiting-room. The door was open, and Lysistrata could see half a dozen women sitting on benches. They sat motionless, prisoners to dread or fearful hope. They were silent, and their faces would have seemed lifeless had they not been so tired. Their clothes were poor, but all held tightly a few flowers or a little paper parcel.

Stopping for a moment by the open door, Lysistrata felt compassion like a blow, and with it a burning anger. She wanted to go in and put her arms about them. But what real comfort could she give? There was only one way to help them, one thing that would put an end to the fear in which all women lived.

She heard steps behind her, slow shuffling steps, and a sound of dismal weeping. A small, thin, oldish woman, her eyes red, her cheeks furrowed with grief, her body drooping, was supported by the arm of another woman hardly taller than herself but thick-set on short fat legs, whose own round face was incongruously chap-fallen. Both were dressed in shabby black clothes, that looked older and dirtier than they were by contrast with the white starching of the hospital Sister beside them.

She looked into the waiting-room and said, 'We can't take her there. We'll go to Matron's room – it's just round the corner – and she can stay there till she's feeling a bit better.'

The stout woman lugubriously agreed, but the other with a wailing cry slid from her grasp, and crouching on the stone floor as though to escape an unseen enemy, rocked to and fro in the extremity of her sorrow. Lysistrata with a protesting cry against the horror of such grief, stooped quickly and pulled her to her feet. She seemed no heavier than an old coat.

The Sister, sympathetic but worried by the knowledge of other duties that waited for her, led them to a small sparsely furnished room, and Lysistrata, half-carrying the little woman, made her lie down on a leather couch.

'Her son or her husband?' she asked.

'Her son,' said the Sister. 'The second in three months, she says. She's a widow, and they were all she had.'

The stout woman, kneeling clumsily beside her stricken neighbour, turned her sorrowful moonface and said, 'I lost my own boy six weeks ago.'

Her stupid eyes filled with tears, and her lower lip everted, down-drawn and quivering like a child's. 'It's a pity all those Generals and Prime Ministers can't do their own fighting, instead of leaving it to us and ours,' she sobbed.

There was nothing to redeem such grief as theirs, no grandeur or beauty or assurance that loss would bring some ultimate reward. Their sorrow was absolute. They had had so little wealth of life, and all had been taken. They were ugly in their loss, and infinitely pitiable. Lysistrata knelt and kissed the thin woman's tear-salt cheek. Her own tears fell on it.

She had made up her mind. This desolation of the innocent and brutal robbery could not go on. No matter how, the war must be stopped, and dignity was a little thing to sacrifice for such an end. She would be ridiculed and hated and conscious of naked impropriety. But what did that matter? War was an outrage, and outrageously she would put an end to it. If poor and wretched women could breed soldiers, then women could bring soldiers to their knees.

II

Three weeks later Lysistrata stood at one end of Lady Oriole's drawing-room in Heriot Row, and confronted a close-packed audience of more than a hundred women. It was a remarkable gathering. The least susceptible of male observers could not have failed to remark, and be moved by, the beauty of all but a few of the assemblage; and a moderately discerning witness would have perceived that the company had been drawn from widely disparate classes of society. There were women whose manner and appearance – their insolent *bienséance* and quotidian elegance – showed long familiarity with the world of fashion, with the attention of press photographers, and the flattering discipline of royal courts. There were others, no less *soignées* and at least as lovely, who by their demeanour in contiguity with such neighbours betrayed a more modest experience of provincial society and the suburban skating-rink. A few – Rose Armour was one of them – exhibited at once a livelier composure, a happier knowledge of pre-eminence and welcome in any circle, than even the youngest of the fashionable ladies; and there was a score of ingenuous or semi-ingenuous beauties whose remarkable charm of figure, features, and complexion must have been the delight and despair of a multitude of postmen, sailors, sergeants, policemen, and other humble but virile citizens. The small minority undistinguished by physical virtue were patently influential by reason of their social position or force of character.

Lysistrata stood like a storied queen as she addressed them. Standing alone, her height was exaggerated, and in repose her face had a masterful nobility. Under the spell of enthusiasm or other emotion – friendship made all its lines easier, her eyes lambent – her aspect would change to a thrusting fierceness or a lovely intimacy, for her lips were mobile and apt in smiling. She used no gesture except, at rare intervals, an odd fluttering movement of her long hands, raising them only waist high, and with so small a movement giving the impression of great strength with difficulty controlled.

'Till a few weeks ago,' she said, 'I believed with all my heart and mind that our duty was to win the war. But I have changed my mind. I do not apologize for that. A mind that cannot be changed, when facts reveal that its position is untenable, is only a dead mind. I say now that our duty is to stop the war, and I speak as a woman to other women, for we can bring it to an end.

'I do not want to talk of politics. Politics are a male invention. When men have interests that must be defended, they contrive a screen of words which they call a policy, and if they can persuade a few simpler people that their screen is of general value, then they are ranked as politicians. But we are women, and our concern is not the defence of any clique or faction or vested interest. It is the defence and happiness of all humanity. A man may have many interests in life, and never know which is the greatest. But a woman, though she has as many interests as any man, always knows that her chief concern is with the preservation and reproduction of life itself, and with happiness, which is the only justification for life. We can be politicians, but only in our spare time. We can be theorists, but only in our leisure moments. We are fundamentally and always, by reason of our nature and constitution, humanitarians and realists.'

There was a little rather puzzled applause. Lady Oriole, sitting beside Lysistrata, clapped vigorously; and a dozen or so in the audience followed suit – Rose Armour because she was warm-hearted and loved to be applauded herself, and the motherly Mrs Graham because she heartily approved what Lysistrata was saying. But the majority were lukewarm. The lovely young women of the upper classes felt that any display of reason and sincerity was probably subversive; the beautiful frequenters of the skating-rink and the provincial drawing-room were willing enough to agree with Lady

Lysistrata, but naturally cautious about committing themselves to any definite opinion; and the exquisite servant-girls, barmaids, and cinema attendants hadn't the faintest notion what she was talking about.

'Nobody can deny,' Lysistrata continued, 'that war is an evil thing. But many people, perhaps most people, believe that it is a necessary evil, and we have to put up with it. Well, to my mind that is simply defeatism. Many things combine to create a war, and perhaps the most powerful of them all is stupidity. And when a war has been started, it is allowed to continue only because everybody gets more and more stupid the longer it lasts. We lose the habit of thinking for ourselves; we take a distorted view of things; we become inured to evil and callous about human misery; we accept words like *loyalty* and *patriotism* as something holy and compulsive, and never stop to ask ourselves the proper object of loyalty, or the true path of patriotism; we forget what we really want, and believe what our leaders tell us we ought to want. – But is it necessary to behave so foolishly? Is our stupidity really incurable? I don't believe it is. I believe it can be cured, and now is the time to cure it. To effect a real and lasting and radical cure. And you are the people who can do it.

'I want you, for the next few minutes, to be thoroughly selfish. To think only of what the war means to you, and what it will mean to you for the rest of your lives. But if you're going to be truly selfish, you must be absolutely honest. You must acknowledge your real feelings, and confess your strongest, your innermost desires. Well, what do we all want from life? Will anyone here deny that her dearest and most constant wish is for happiness? But we are women – most of us are young women – and what we most often mean by happiness is love. We want a home and babies and the tenderness of a husband. It is right and proper that this should be so. Our whole nature was so designed that a man's love and the love of children should be our crying need and our deepest thought. But what is the war doing to our husbands and the fathers of our children? It's killing them. They're being mutilated, and ruined in health, and killed.

'In the last war there were more than a million British

casualties. But that was not all. As well as the million dead, there were hundreds of thousands of young men whose health and strength were destroyed, whose nerves were shattered, whose sanity was undermined. And so, when the war was over, there were countless women condemned to a loveless barren existence, and countless others whose lives were ruined because the war had wrecked the mind or body of the men they married. The agony of the dead soldiers was unspeakable, but it lasted only a little time. But the misery of the women, condemned by their death to hunger and loneliness, lasted all their lives. That was the legacy of the old war. And now, a generation later, we are in the midst of another war at least as destructive, a war that may last as long as the old one, a war that will leave another legacy of bitterness and starvation. The men are suffering today, but we shall suffer tomorrow. We are young, and our lives are before us. But how shall we endure them if we are to be robbed of all that makes life dear to us? The men who are being killed are our lovers, and the fathers of our children. It is our happiness that is being thrown away on every battlefield. Our leaders say there can be no peace without victory. But every victory means that thousands of women are being condemned to barren misery, to wasted years, to jealousy of their neighbours, to life unwarmed by love and the children their bodies demand, to a lonely and unwanted old age. Is any victory worth such a price as that? Are you yourselves prepared to pay that price? Or will you join together to bring the wickedness of war for ever to an end?'

There was a good deal of applause as Lysistrata sat down, but most of it was still doubtful. Some of the more ingenuous young women of humble station were openly weeping, but many of the betitled and much be-photographed beauties in front were hostile or sceptical; while the loveliness of the middle-classes had been somewhat upset by Lysistrata's frank reference to the nature of the female constitution and their private aspirations. They had been impressed and frightened, but they were as yet hardly willing to admit, by open applause, that their feelings were indeed so natural.

Lady Oriole, leaning towards Lysistrata, whispered her

congratulations and suggested that this was the time for her to say a few words. But before Lysistrata could reply, a tall and remarkably beautiful girl in the middle of the room rose and began to speak in an accent of uncertain refinement and a mood of obvious defiance. Her appearance was striking, and Lysistrata, searching her memory, suddenly remembered where she had seen her before. It was in the New Carlton Hotel in Blackpool, on the night before Eliot went to Germany. She had been with a stout brutal-looking man who had behaved badly and made a great nuisance of himself.

Miss Ivy FitzAubrey had no lack of confidence. 'I don't want to say anything against what Lady Lysistrata has been saying,' she declared, 'because everybody is entitled to their own opinions. But I would like to ask her what does she mean by saying that the war is wicked? A gentleman-friend of mine, who happens to be in a very important position, was telling me only the other day that it was a very stimulating thing to happen, which brought out all the best in everybody, and didn't leave any time for selfishness or unnoble thoughts. Well, that's what it seems to me, because I've been doing war work myself for quite a long time now. And what's more, it isn't true to say that everyone has a boy-friend who's in the army, and so is likely to get killed. Because the gentleman-friend of who I was talking is much too important to ever get sent to the front, so that changes a girl's point of view, doesn't it? I mean, there isn't any fear of things happening the same as Lady Lysistrata said they would happen, and a good lot of us have decided not to have any babies anyway, because there are other things in life besides, and it takes so much out of a girl who isn't as strong as other girls are. I mean, you've got to allow for what everyone thinks herself, haven't you?'

Miss FitzAubrey sat down feeling very pleased at having so clearly stated her opinions. But immediately the stout and motherly Mrs Graham, whose husband was in the Royal Scots, got up and indignantly exclaimed, 'Lady Lysistrata said we all had to be selfish. But there's two kinds of selfishness, and one's sensible and the other's not. And what the last speaker said was just nonsense, and nasty nonsense at that.'

The meeting grew more animated. Little arguments shot

up like the spurting of steam, and there was a general turning about, a scraping of chairs, and babble of conversation; during which a girl like a Botticelli painting, all white and gold – but now the white was stained with a spreading rose – got up and exclaimed in a sweet piping voice, 'I don't think we should be selfish at all, I think we all ought to be unselfish!'

Lady Oriole grunted and hoarsely inquired, 'What does that mean? Is she for us, or against?'

Lysistrata shook her head. 'I don't know. For us, I think. You'd better speak now.'

In her own way Lady Oriole had a presence as commanding as Lysistrata's. Her face was long and pale, her eyes and eyebrows pitch-black, her hair a bright badger-pattern of black and white. She carried a sheaf of papers that she rolled into a stick and smacked against her leg as though it was a hunting-crop.

In a loud husky voice she exclaimed, 'There'll be an opportunity for questions and discussion later on. But before the meeting's thrown open, I'm going to give you my views. This is my house – anyway I've rented it – and I'm going to tell you my reasons for having this meeting here. Lady Lysistrata is an old friend of mine, and I've always had the greatest respect for her charm and ability, and wondered why she didn't put 'em to more use. Well, now she is. She's putting 'em to the noblest use of all. I've been against this war from the beginning – I'll tell you why in a minute – and when she came and told me she was going to stop it, I said, "Lysistrata, you're using your ten talents at last!" But when she told me *how* she was going to stop it – when she explained her plan for stopping it – I said, "Lysistrata, you're a heaven-sent genius!" And so she is. Because her plan is sure, safe, and simple, and there isn't a man in Great Britain, or the whole world for that matter, who can stand up against it.

'Now about this war. As soon as it started I said to Tatters – that's my husband, who's in France, poor man, though he's fifty-seven and old enough to know better – as soon as it began, I said to him, "Tatters, we're making a big mistake. It's suicidal to go to war with France. All my life I've bought my clothes in Paris" – and I dare say most of you have, too.

Very pretty frocks you're all wearing, so far as I can see from here – "and at my time of life," I said, "I'm not willing to make a change." Well, he didn't see my point as clearly as you will. But think what's going to happen if we and Germany go on till we win this wretched war. We'll have to be loyal to our gallant ally! That's what the politicians will tell us, and little enough will they care what it means. But we know! It means that we'll have to buy our clothes in Berlin! Think of that! Models designed for hausfraus and javelin-throwers! The sort of frocks that Hitler likes! Well, I don't like 'em, and you won't either. So that's the first thing I've got against the war, and because of that I played my part in arranging this meeting. I invited about thirty of you myself, choosing the prettiest I could find, as they're the sort who are going to be most useful. And now, as soon as we're all agreed that the war has got to be stopped, and that we're going to stop it, Lady Lysistrata will tell you her plan, and explain how we're to go about it.'

With a triumphant glance and a final smacking of her thigh, Lady Oriole sat down; but after a brief muttered conversation with Lysistrata, she hurriedly got up again and exclaimed, 'I forgot the most important part of my speech! Tatters – my husband – always says I've got a brain like a sieve, but it's better than his, and he knows it. He can't get on for long without me, and I don't want to try and do without him, though I'm forty-six, which is a lot older than most of you. If I was twenty-two again I'd feel that way about any good-looking young man without blemish and able to sit on a horse and dance without walking on my feet. And that's how *you* ought to feel! A decently built young man, with a tongue in his head and a good leg, is something that every woman on earth ought to take care of. But instead of that you let 'em go out and get shot for no purpose at all except to make us buy our frocks in Berlin!

'Well, I'm a sensible woman, whatever you may be. I know what I want, and I'm prepared to go to any length to get it. Lots of you think that love is something that only matters when you're young. But that's nonsense. It matters long after you don't want to stay up all night jigging to a Dago band. It's a thing that lasts all your life, in one way or another, but it's a thing you ought to start before you get too long in the tooth. Men know that, even if you don't, and that's why we've been going round mustering young 'uns and lovelies for the last three weeks. And now we're ready to start business . . . Will that do now? What? Of course, I'd forgotten again. Just a minute, ladies.

'I dare say a lot of you are worried by the thought that you'll be disloyal if you work against the Government to bring this nonsensical murdering to an end. Well, that's just because you've been made to think that loyalty means doing what you're told. But God knows that if women had believed everything, and done everything that men told 'em to do, we'd still be in the harem or at the back of a cave! I like 'em, and always have done, but as soon as they get high-falutin, I just stop listening. The truth is this: that what we've got to be loyal to, is ourselves. If women are starved and miserable, and haven't got men to look after them – and another couple of hundred have been killed since we started talking – then the whole world goes off the handle. The world needs good, sensible, contented women, and plenty of them; and women, to be contented, need men – and plenty of them! There's the situation in a nutshell. But this damned war, and every war, is killing off all the best of the men, so the only sensible thing to do is to stop it. Otherwise the world will go to pieces like a racehorse if you try to feed it on sawdust.'

Lady Oriole's speech was a great success with the betitled young women. To begin with they had laughed – but in the friendliest way – and when she sat down they all most seriously and vigorously applauded. But the servant-girls and the cinema attendants were vaguely antagonized by her manner, and the loveliness of the middle classes was still a little constrained in its approval.

Lysistrata rose again. 'I think we should spend the next ten minutes or quarter of an hour in informal discussion,' she said. 'Won't you all consider that you know everybody here, and talk the matter over among yourselves? If our movement is to succeed you must get to know each other, because you are meant to be its leaders. You have all been carefully chosen, and if you have the will to lead, we feel sure that you have the necessary ability. You are the potential leaders of a great movement, the officers in a new army. Please remember that.'

These remarks were received with general approval. A gratified and multitudinous noise, like the honey-fed buzzing of a warm hive, rose almost visibly above the hundred lovely and excited heads, and though the audience was slow to break its ranks, it immediately began to exchange friendly smiles and amiable remarks.

Lady Oriole beckoned to eight or ten of the betitled beauties and said hoarsely, 'Go and talk to those nice girls behind you. Work 'em up, and they'll do anything we ask 'em to. They're shy. Tell 'em not to be. Be nice to them, and the whole lot are with us. You believe what Lysistrata and I have been saying, don't you? Of course you do. You know what we are – women, I mean – and so do I. It's those nice girls who've been so damn well brought up that won't listen. So go and talk to them and make 'em loosen up a bit.'

Lysistrata, meanwhile, was talking to Mrs Graham, who presently gathered the servant-girls and cinema-attendants, and in five minutes had made them all her sworn adherents. But Lysistrata had a more difficult task with Miss Ivy Fitz-Aubrey.

'You see,' she said in her most careful accent, 'I felt it was only fair to myself, and to my gentleman-friend as well, to put my case before you. Because it's rather exceptional, don't you think? You see, he's got a very important position. Well, you won't let it go any further, of course, but actually he's a Cabinet Minister, and it wouldn't be fair to him to let him down about the war, because he's got such a lot to do with it, of course. I mean, he feels responsible about it. And then there's myself to think of. You see, I'm working at the Ministry of Munitions – I'm the receptionist there – and it was only yesterday that one of the secretaries – simply a dowdy old woman, the sort of person you'd never notice – was given the O.B.E. So I said to my gentleman-friend, "Well, why can't I have one too?" But he said I'd have to wait for another three or four months, and then he'd see what could be done about it. So naturally I don't want the war to stop before then, because it would be such a nice thing to have, wouldn't it?

I mean it would show what you'd done, and the ribbon looks ever so nice, though it's a bit difficult to match, of course.'

'The O.B.E. ?' said Lady Oriole, who had been waiting her chance to speak to Lysistrata. 'If that's what you want, I'll give you one tomorrow.'

'Oh, really? How terribly sweet of you.'

'You can have mine, it's no good to me.'

'But that wouldn't be quite the same, would it? I mean . . .'

'Just the same. They're all made in the one factory.'

'But . . .'

'It would be a greater honour,' said Lady Lysistrata, 'to get a medal from Lady Oriole than from the Government. Lady Oriole is a far better judge of merit than a lot of civil servants and politicians.'

'Well, of course, I hadn't looked at it in that way before.'

'So you'll join us if you get an O.B.E. ?'

'Well, I think I owe it to myself, don't you, to get some sort of recognition before the war's over?'

'That's another,' said Lady Oriole triumphantly, and waving her sheaf of papers nearly struck someone in the face. 'Sorry!' she exclaimed, 'Miss Armour, isn't it? My husband would give anything to be here. He dotes on you, my dear, and so do I. You're with us, aren't you?'

'Oh, of course I am,' said Rose earnestly. 'That's what I came to tell you – you and Lady Lysistrata. I think the war's a dreadful thing, though of course I've been singing all the time and pretending to be happy about it. But the theatre does a lot of good, don't you think, because it takes people's minds away from it – except when we try to cheer them up and make them think we're going to win. But I'd much rather help to stop it.'

'That's splendid,' said Lysistrata. 'I was hoping for your support more than anyone else's.'

'She'll propose a vote of confidence,' said Lady Oriole, 'Won't you, my dear? I think it's time for one now. Always cheers things up a bit, a vote of confidence.'

It was no easy matter to get the audience back to its seats, for the informal discussion, broken into twenty parts, had become twenty warm and absorbing conversations. The audience had been mixed like the ingredients of a plum-pudding, and though when they sat down again they resumed something of their previous individualism, they gave the impression of being not averse to benevolent coalescence. 'We've got 'em,' muttered Lady Oriole.

Rose Armour got up to propose the vote of confidence. 'I don't want to make a long speech,' she said, 'because I'm not very good at making speeches, and I don't think it's necessary anyway. All I want to say is that if Lady Lysistrata knows of a way to stop this dreadful war, then I'm with her, through and through, and I hope all of you are too. I've got a sweetheart who's in the trenches now, and if he was killed, I think I'd die. And I don't want to die. I want to live, and get married, and be happy. Well, that's a very small and selfish view to take of things, but nearly every woman has the same view about somebody, and if we all get together and say honestly what we think and hope, then our view is going to be the biggest in the world. And the most sensible, as well. So I ask you all to express your confidence in Lady Lysistrata, and say that you'll help her to stop this horrid war before it's too late.'

This artless avowal was more potent than either Lysistrata's eloquence or Lady Oriole's compulsive heartiness. The whole audience clapped and applauded, warmly and without reserve, and Lysistrata rose to face, as it seemed, the already converted.

'The only way,' she said, 'in which we can be sure of stopping the war, is this . . .'

III

Graham woke, sweating slightly, from a brief afternoon sleep. It was a Sunday. His battalion had just come out of the line, and both officers and men were in a bad humour. They had been compelled to march three miles that morning to attend an open-air church service, at which a lugubrious and untidily-uniformed minister, in a series of melancholy prayers and a long Presbyterian sermon, had told them they had naught to fear – since God had in his keeping all who were fighting his battles – save the uncleanness of their own hearts and the carnal temptations of the foreign land in which they were living. They were, as it happened, billeted in a war-stricken village where there was neither an estaminet nor a living woman under forty; and the sermon was regarded as a piece of heartless mockery, for during twenty-eight days in the trenches every man in the battalion had been most earnestly looking forward to temptation, and the opportunity of yielding to it.

The service over, they had marched back behind the scornful music of the pipers to their barren village, where the Colonel had ordered a kit inspection. After a month in the line there was a great shortage of forks and knives, of button-sticks and tooth-brushes; and a total absence of spare socks. The Colonel lost his temper, and showed it; the men lost theirs, and had to conceal it. The battalion ate its Sunday dinner – a thin bully-beef stew and a watery mess of rice and raisins – in a bitter temper and with many a mutinous comment.

Graham, both tired and depressed, had sought comfort in sleep, and even there found disappointment. He had dreamt that he was in a trench, waiting for the signal to attack. The men about him were strangers, but he had seen them all clearly, as if under bright lights. He had seen their faces and their hands, the shape and posture of their bodies. They had been such an odd mixture as any company would show: here a loose lip, heavy eyebrows, and a sallow skin, there a bullet-headed little man with thickened cheekbones and tiny eyes, a sparring-partner to some second-rate boxer perhaps; now a solemn fellow, older than the rest, worried because he could get no oil for his rifle, but accepting without much concern the whole circumstance of war; a schoolboy, open-mouthed and eager, reckless and miserable by fits and turns; a sergeant, a big loosely-built freckled man with a mothering nature and careful heart; a corporal who was a bit of a blackguard, brave enough but something of a drunkard, something of a bully, yet a soldier born; a dumb youth with white eyebrows and a manner of perpetual bewilderment; an old bricklayer cross-grained, who had fought in the last war, and was fighting in this for no reason save that he could not stay out of it . . .

Graham had seen them all, the texture of their skin, the mud and dirty buttons on their tunics, the rough hands holding their rifles. They were strangers to him in everything except their familiar humanity. But the feeling grew in him, during those last seconds of excitement before the whistle blew, that these men were his blood and flesh of his flesh, and he could not lead them into death. His visionary mind, that saw so clearly their unknown and common faces, shrank horribly from the thought of the changing of those rough features to agony and cold clay. He could not do it. Rebellion stiffened in him. He fought against sleep and shouted through the blanket of his dream, 'Stay where you are! You must not die! You shall not, shall not die!'

He woke, his head damp with sweat, and saw through dusky glass the buttercup light of early evening. He heard beneath the window a murmuring antiphony of soldiers' voices and the sound of metal-shod boots crossing a cobbled yard. He saw his belt and map-case slung on a chair, his helmet and gas-mask on the table. A far voice, its hoarseness fading in the distance, bawled with a gentle suddenness, 'Guard! Turn out!' – The guard-house was too far away for him to hear the answering clatter of hurrying feet and briskly handled rifles, but his accustomed ear tricked him into thinking it was audible; and thankfully he realized that for a little while he and his men were out of danger. For guard-mounting was a harmless occupation. It was only when they were truly in safety that soldiers could afford to make a ceremony of security. . . .

Over all Europe the sun and the warm winds of early summer had dried the interminable trenches, and filled the polyglot countless soldiers with impossible sweet thoughts and a hopeless longing. The fields were green again. Woods shattered and laid waste by shell-fire had put on new leaves, and birds in the midst of war had sung their song and mated in the torn branches. The rusty wire that marked the edge of No Man's Land, and the dead who had died in places too dangerous for burial, were overgrown with grass and flowers and yellow weeds. Everywhere, as though to conceal the horror made by men, the earth had put on bright-waving garments.

Among the soldiers there was no longer any hatred for their enemies. In civilian society, it is true, the politicians, the newspapers, the relentless *embusqués*, and women starved of love fomented where they could a wild factitious rage; but the brave and honest men in the trenches had no such feeling, nor was there any chance of its developing unless it were directed against their far-off leaders and those who told them it was their duty to put rancour in their killing. The soldiers in the trenches obeyed their regimental officers and used their rifles or their bayonets, sternly and conclusively, as they were told; but save in the heat of close conflict they had long discarded the idea that the poor devils in the opposite trench were their personal and deliberate enemies. England and Germany were at war with France and Russia; Italy – having at the last moment changed her front as she had in the old war – was fighting Germany and Yugoslavia; Turkey was at war, and Poland and Rumania and all the rest of them. But the common soldiers of the warring nations had only one enemy, common to them all; and that was the war itself. They continued to fight each other because they were simple men, trained to obedience; because discipline compelled them, and they had not the wit to escape it, nor even to question its purpose or necessity. They did not fight for pride of their own country or hatred of another, whose conscript forces, like themselves, did only what they were told, and grinned happily when as prisoners they were given cigarettes. Had their officers left them, on every front the soldiers in opposing trenches would have gathered peacefully together, swapping their wine, tobacco, pidgin phrases, and spare shirts, and tearing down the barbed wire to fraternize and learn each other's songs. But their officers were bound by discipline more straitly than the privates. They had been taught to believe that discipline in itself was a virtue. And behind the regimental officers were the Generals with their gold and scarlet tabs, and behind the Generals were Governments implacable, resolute, and pitiless; being blind and without understanding.

All these warring governments were in their nature evil. They had imprisoned their people and diminished their humanity by giving to a whole nation the likeness and single purpose of a machine. They had made, of communities that delighted in creation, machines that were capable only of destruction. They had forbidden the telling of the truth, and diligently commanded the teaching of lies. They lauded murder, and made mercy a thing of shame. Having suborned their clergy to announce that God was their stay and companion, they had blackened God's face by making him their confederate in spreading falsehood, doing murder, and wasting his creation. They had robbed both strangers and their own people of decency and happiness and life; and they made a virtue of their resolution to continue a policy of spiritual destruction and corporal death.

Nor could the common people do anything against their governments, or resist their evil doing; because their governments were part of themselves. However it had been nominated and elected, in Russia and Britain, in France and Germany and Yugoslavia, the government was a piece of the whole nation and represented it; and the evil done by the governments was evil extracted, as though by a centrifuge, from all mankind.

IV

'But how could we *tell* them? How could we *talk* to men about anything like that?'

Red as a peony, and furious with her own embarrassment, a little neat pretty woman hurled her angry questions at Lysistrata; and in the babble of other questions, expostulation, and indignant comment, they disappeared like pebbles tossed into the loud and ceaseless billows of the Atlantic sea.

Lysistrata's plan had raised a storm. Nearly everybody was opposed to it, and most of them were very violently opposed.

'It wouldn't be right!' exclaimed a tall dark girl with the sinuous grace and the wild eye of a black swan. 'My husband's coming home on leave next month, and how – how could I treat him like that?'

'No, it wouldn't be right!'

'And I couldn't do it! Even if I wanted to, I couldn't do it!' The new speaker was tearful, and amid little sniffs dabbed her eyes, and now her nose, with a small wet kerchief. Her hair was pale gold, her eyes like hyacinths, and her chin was inconspicuous. 'I've always been so warm-hearted,' she sobbed.

Infected by her example, another young woman began to weep, and fumbling in her bag – which carried the badge of the Royal Artillery – she let fall a gold powder-box decorated with the crest of the Gloucestershire Regiment, and found at last her handkerchief under a cigarette-case with the inscription, *HMS Valiant*. 'I'm sure nobody could have a warmer heart than mine,' she averred.

'You can't deny them anything when they come home on leave,' protested an ox-eyed barmaid with dewy lips and a bosom of oriental luxury.

'And even if you did . . .'

'It wouldn't do any good, would it? She doesn't know my Tom, or what he's like if he's only been away for a week.'

'And think of your own feelings. We're human too, aren't we?'

The tumult increased, and then, having risen to a ragged height, subsided with strange celerity to a muttering quietude that was almost silence. Many of the ladies who had given loudest vent to their feelings were now a little ashamed of themselves, and by coughing in a small artificial way, and looking round them with haughty curiosity as if to see who had been making all the noise, they tried to wipe away their consciousness of having been startled into a very vulgar display of emotion; while others with greater candour considered their appearance in small mirrors and deliberately repaired their smirched complexions.

A young woman in the front row, one of the small minority that had heard Lysistrata's proposal without obvious dismay, took advantage of the quietness to offer an unpopular criticism. She was as calmly and exactly beautiful as a drawing by Ingres, and her voice had the clear cool sound of a convent bell.

'The real difficulty,' she said, 'is that none of us can be trusted. You may persuade us to adopt your plan, though it doesn't seem likely at the moment, but put us in a position to keep our promises, and we'd either honestly forget or find a dozen excuses for breaking them. No woman was ever bound by a promise, and no woman in the same room with her lover is going to give two thoughts to common sense or the common weal. Forgive my putting it so crudely, but all your prettifying won't conceal the fact that we're selfish, shallow, and quite untrustworthy.'

This brutal denigration of the female character aroused even greater, because more homogeneous, opposition than Lysistrata's proposal; and the Botticellian young woman, who had previously made so brave an appeal for altruism, got up and cried with a sweet disarming passion, 'That's a shameful thing to say! Any woman worthy of the name is true and thoughtful of others. When I first heard Lady Lysistrata's plan, I didn't like it, because I – well, it seemed rather immodest, though really, of course, it's just the opposite – but now I see how necessary it is, and when my fiancé comes home . . .'

'You'll go down like a ninepin,' said the young woman who might have been drawn by Ingres.

Lysistrata rose hurriedly and began to speak. 'We have been told that no woman can keep a promise,' she exclaimed, with rhetorical indignation. 'Do you accept that statement, or do you reject it?'

'Reject it!'

'It isn't true!'

'It's men who are liars . . .'

With various phraseology and general agreement the allegation was rejected.

'We have also been told that women are utterly selfish, and take no thought for the future, no thought for their neighbours. That women, like animals, are ruled only by their appetites. Is that true or false?'

'False, false!'

'Then I *can* rely on you, and we *will* stop the war!'

Diverse incertitude and numerous doubt, like the smoke of a wetted pentecost, descended again upon her audience; but very earnestly Lysistrata continued.

'You will be surprised,' she said, 'by the ease with which we shall win our victory. Only be resolute, and the future is ours, our happiness secure! For a little while give up the joy of love, and you will make love safe for ever. I know that for

many of you it will not be easy, because your husbands and
your sweethearts will plead with you, and you will find it
hard to deny them. But for their own sakes you must! Not
only your happiness, but their lives, depend on your stead-
fastness and determination. You must be strong – but you
mustn't show your strength till the proper time. Make yourselves as lovely and attractive as you can. Wear your prettiest
clothes. Use every aid to beauty, and all the graces. Be
glamorous, alluring, irresistible. And then, then draw back,
and make your denial! Then be strong and refuse your love
till the war's over and peace has come again. Tell your husbands and your sweethearts they must choose between love
and war. Have strength and courage for a little while, and
whether you are married or single, be cold as icicles to proffered love, and flaunt your chastity like a banner!'

Miss Ivy FitzAubrey rose to put a question: 'Wouldn't it
be more fair if it was only girls who are already married who
were asked to disappoint their husbands? Because I mean, it's
going to cause a lot of hardship to girls who want to go on
pleasing their gentlemen-friends, and if they don't please them
will perhaps wake up to find themselves in the soup. I myself
am very anxious to help Lady Lysistrata, because I feel she's
made it ever so clear that people don't fully realize the importance of we women. But I think that when it comes to
deliberately making an enemy of your gentleman-friend, then
a married girl is in a much stronger position than the rest of us.'

Lysistrata gravely answered that such discrimination would,
she feared, invalidate their whole campaign.

Then a tall gipsy-looking girl, with dusky eyelids and a
sulky mouth, after much whispering with her friends at the
back of the room, inquired in a sing-song Scots voice, 'What
do we do if he'll no' tak' no for an answer?'

'I beg your pardon?'

'*What do we do if he'll no' tak' no for an answer?*'

'You mean your husband?' Lysistrata inquired.

'Ay. Or your lad.'

'If your manner is really determined and obviously resolute,
I don't think that any husband is likely to be so insistent as
to cause you physical anxiety.'

A protestant murmuration at the back of the room showed there were some who did not share Lysistrata's facile optimism. A snort of laughter, a scornful remark half-heard, and a derisive giggle angered her, and warmly she exclaimed: 'Though by sheer physical strength you may be compelled to acquiesce – but I think it highly improbable – you can still maintain a most discouraging attitude, and pointedly show your displeasure. In which circumstances the incident is not likely to recur.'

Over many a lovely face there appeared to settle a kind of film, of thin ice or transparent wax, that gave to those who wore it a lifeless look, and so advertised their utter detachment from the sort of existence with which the gipsy-looking girl and her friends were so unhappily familiar. It was Lady Oriole who first saw the spreading of this protective indifference, and realized its danger. If these charming frail creatures turned cold and frigid, then the meeting was a failure, and their crusade was finished before it had begun. Hurriedly she got up, and with a manner compounded of easy friendship, worldly wisdom, and the truculent confidence of a racing tipster, she began to exhort, bully, and cajole her difficult audience.

She got them presently into a high-hearted mood, and made them think that abstinence from love would be a gay adventure. She made the modest smile, and put the brazen on their mettle. She laughed half a dozen pretty hypocrites to shame, and stiffened the backbone of ten shy but honest creatures. Then Mrs Graham delivered herself, not without difficulty, of a speech that was full of sterling good sense and candid passion; and made a great impression. But in the end it was Rose Armour who brought the still uncovenanted to the very edge of agreement, to all-but-unanimity and the shedding of penultimate reluctance. Rose Armour spoke simply as before, and because she was an artist, her simplicity was more compulsive than rhetoric. She could be as sentimental as a Christmas card, speak platitudes worn smooth as a pebble; but she made her sentiments echo like cunning arguments, her platitudes gleam anew. She took the stubborn remnant of her audience to the threshold of consent, but there they stuck and no one had the power to push them over or the wit to lure them.

Then the cynical girl who might have been drawn by Ingres – and who had said that no woman could be trusted – got up, and with two or three vigorous puffs lighted a cigarette from the red stump of another, and said abruptly: 'I may have been wrong. Or rather, I may have got the wrong notion of how you mean to go about this chastity business. Are we expected to be chaste in comparative solitude, and privately, or with plenty of publicity and in whole battalions? If it's chastity *en masse* that you're thinking of, then I dare say we might make something of it. But you'll have to give us more details before I'm going to commit myself.'

'I can reassure you on that point,' said Lysistrata. 'Our campaign will include both action *en masse*, and individual guerrilla warfare. But for the latter we shall ask for volunteers. We intend to start the campaign with an act of open aggression in which I want about three thousand women to participate.'

'Yes, that should be enough,' said the cynical girl. 'To keep an eye on each other, I mean.'

'Then if we are now all in agreement, I can explain in detail what we propose to do. . . .'

CHAPTER FOUR

The Shock

I

THE College of St Cecilia, in Hatton in the county of Kent, was the creation of an English king whose life had otherwise been remarkably free from sentimentality. It was founded by Richard III in honour of his mother, and the original establishment consisted of a provost, fourteen priests, four clerks, six choristers, a schoolmaster, ten poor scholars, and a like number of bedesmen. Becoming wholly secular after the Reformation, the College had rapidly grown in size, and its endowment was doubled by the Elizabethan Chancellor, Sir Christopher Hatton, presumably by command of his royal mistress, for his nature when unprompted was parsimonious. His compulsory beneficence was unexpectedly rewarded, for there began a popular tendency to identify the College – situated as it was in a townlet of his name – with its newest patron rather than the holy person to whom it had been dedicated; and by the late seventeenth century, and always thereafter, it was universally briefly known as Hatton College. As such it increased from year to year in glory and good report.

From the Restoration its supremacy in the scholastic life and public esteem of England was unchallenged, and for nearly a century it had been pretty generally accepted as the most famous school in the world. The Prime Minister of Great Britain – unless he happened to have been born in poverty or Scotland – was always educated at Hatton, and so were most of his Cabinet. The eldest sons of European monarchs were sent there, with the favourite offspring of Oriental despots; and though many of its pupils had of course no such authoritarian background, the majority soon acquired the air and manner of it. The College set its mark on them, a sigil of authority, so that a great number on leaving immediately took to ruling over negroes, Asiatics, or – what was easiest – their fellow-countrymen.

That the public ceremonies of the College, and in particular the Annual Dinner of the Old Hattonian Society, should become occasions of national, or even international interest, was inevitable. Membership of the Society, restricted as it was to the most eminent of Old Hattonians, was one of the most coveted of all distinctions, and the elder statesman who was invited to speak at the Annual Dinner regularly found it an opportunity to make some announcement of policy or opinion that would capture the attention of a much wider audience than the one he was addressing, and promote in them a favourable impression of his prescience or wise humanity.

In this year of far-spread war the Dinner was smaller than usual, and robbed of a little splendour by the absence of European monarchs and Oriental potentates; but its importance was enhanced by the circumstances of the time, and there was a general feeling that those present were truly the inspiration and the leaders of Britain in arms: the acknowledged and legitimate *patres conscripti* of their people.

Because the seat of Government was in Edinburgh, the Dinner also was held there, under the dignified roof of the New Club, whose members had been proud to lend it for such a purpose. It was the first of July. The war had now been going on for nearly a year, and the end of it, after twelve months of fighting, seemed more improbable and remote than ever. But the Old Hattonian *patres* showed no sign of perturbation or distress. They were on the contrary, the image of calm assurance, the pattern of untroubled dignity, the unshaken though slightly withered flower of English civilization.

More than half of them were quite old. Their heads were smoothly, pinkly bald, or thatched with a tenuous bright silver and their colour was either pale – a legal pallor of new parchment, a yellowish Indian hue – or red with good living and the air of many autumns spent in pursuit of the fox or awaiting the pheasant. The minority of young men there were all making a name for themselves in the Foreign Office, or rising politicians who looked more like members of the Guards Club than of the House of Commons, and among those of middle life were several distinguished soldiers. Many of the soldiers were of handsome appearance – their small heads, cavalry moustaches, and well-drilled shoulders contributed to the effect, but regular features also appeared to be characteristic of the military temperament – and many of the oldest men had an appearance of great benignity that was somewhat invalidated by the stony look of their eyes.

But all the many differences, of complexion and the curve of a nostril, were slight in comparison with the strange obvious alikeness – the almost massive similarity – that bound together these notable two hundred Old Hattonians. The lawyers, it might be, had a more ascetic look than the bishops; the bishops, perhaps, had less noble noses than the soldiers; the soldiers, within the limits of correctitude, were better dressed than the representatives of the Foreign Office: and the young Conservative politicians were clearly twice as clever as the Elder Statesmen: these, it is true, were differences, and worthy to be noted. But this, on the other hand, was their alikeness: that all were marked with the knowledge of their authority and responsibility, the sigil of their school. They were the rulers of the land, the almost-hereditary senate, and had some hidden observer – sensitive, intelligent, and not of their class – been present to see them, he must have felt not only natural awe, but something of fear because on this night Great Britain was so vulnerable; for here, in one room together, were all its leaders, its principal and irreparable eggs – so to speak – in a single basket.

The observer, had he turned eavesdropper as well, would soon have discovered that no one in this gathering of the great was talking of the war; but over their whitebait and their *vol-au-vent*, their savoury aspic and their saddle of mutton, they calmly discussed the minor and agreeable topics that had occupied their tables before the war, and again would hold their attention when the war was over. They chose, in their wisdom, not huge ephemerals, but matters of small and eternal interest.

Lord Lomond, for example, who was a little deaf and in the fashion of deaf people spoke more loudly than was necessary, turned abruptly to his right-hand neighbour, who happened to be Sir Joseph Rumble, and politely shouted: 'Have you got heather-beetle still?'

The unwitting truculence of his query drew a look of mild surprise from the Bishop of Brighton and Hove, who was discussing with Lord Osselburt, one of the Lords of Appeal, the vexed question of the migration of butterflies, in particular of Red Admirals and Painted Ladies; and for a moment distracted the attention of Mr Pelham-Blair and Mr Denis Mowbray, two rising young Conservatives, who were listening with polite attention to old Lord Laffery on the revival of interest in the harness-horse, which was one of the few real benefits brought by the war and the prohibited use of motor-cars. 'A horse in leather *must* go high all round,' he was saying in the solemn tone of one dealing with fundamentals.

Nearer the Chairman was a little learned argument on wine, and a few places distant from the Prime Minister – the octogenarian Lord Pippin – grew some light and leisurely talk of politics: not politics of the day, but of fifty years before, when Mr Gladstone and Lord Salisbury had led their parties to the ballot-box and the assault. The talk was all of things, material subjects, and actual events; not of ideas and generalities, and less than usual of people, since people in large numbers were being killed, and talk of them might become talk of the war, and otherwise be embarrassing. They debated, safely and with commendable knowledge, of agriculture – the effect of a wet spring on root-crops – and of the breeding and diseases of fox-hounds and gun-dogs; they spoke of racing, so sadly diminished by the war – it had been a strange June without Ascot – and of bloodstock, and gardener's topics: aquilegias, eschscholtzia, and the neglected fruits of England. The Prime Minister, with great enjoyment, was discussing the merits of Jane Austen and the sound character of Mr John Knightley; while General Scrymgeour, a little moodily, listened to Mr Justice Bilbow's description of a Roman pavement that had recently been uncovered by workmen who were somewhere excavating a suburban swimming-pool.

Scrymgeour, though nominally on leave, had actually come home to give evidence before a Commission that was inquiring into recent losses on the western front. That casualites continued to be heavy was undeniable, but every soldier above the rank of colonel hotly disputed the allegation that they were excessive; and it was generally felt that old Pippin had been badly at fault in listening to the clamour of the Socialists and the popular press – an unholy alliance – and agreeing to the inquiry they demanded. It was intolerable that a General on active service should be questioned about his profits and losses, as though he were a bankrupt tradesman; and looking along the table Scrymgeour could almost persuade himself that the Prime Minister's cheerfulness was a sign of senility. But that was poor comfort, and Scrymgeour, much troubled in spirit, found it increasingly difficult to pay proper attention to Bilbow and his Roman tiles. As though unhappiness had made his senses more acute, he heard scraps of conversation from near and far, and more and more oblivious of Bilbow, took a melancholy pleasure in their strange irrelevant pattern.

' . . . at any rate it's quite certain that Painted Ladies get more numerous in the south as winter approaches . . . Sainfoin: yes, she's nicely made . . . cut-and-laid . . . but she ought to be a dog not a bitch . . . *saepes etiam* – how does it go? – *et pecus omne tenendum* . . . yes I know . . . the Romans show . . . when a farmer lets his fences go . . . Clos . . . in front he's got to show the knee and behind he's got to go . . . but the virtues of Clos Vougeot are the virtues not of burgundy but of claret . . . the Romans . . . off his hocks . . . had said their Local Government Act of 1894 would make life more interesting . . . my boy's last half . . . it's laminitis . . and the only novelist to have realized that the majority of men must inevitably marry silly women and thought it a very tolerable state of affairs . . . and Roman stairs . . . your boy's last half . . . then tell your keeper to worm them every six months . . . the Romans . . . and June she said . . . Lord Salisbury replied . . . no Richebourg . . . like Hamlet without the Prince of Denmark . . . if the Liberals really wanted to amuse the villagers he would rather recommend a circus . . . the medlar the quince . . . for unentered bitches . . . the medlar the bullace and barberry . . . George Wyndham said . . . he goes a good pace and quarters well . . . at Peterborough Peterborough? Peterborough . . . and the feeling of life and bustle when Mr Elton's marriage follows so closely . . . but Wyndham was the best that Ireland ever had . . . and there were Red Admirals round the lamp at midnight . . . and the Romans said . . . PRAY SILENCE FOR YOUR CHAIRMAN!'

But into the sudden silence, the waiting seconds during which everyone composed his mind and features to a proper solemnity, there broke, like a murderer through the arras, the rudest inconcinnity. To the deaf ears of Lord Lomond the toastmaster's voice had seemed no louder than the surrounding conversation, and while all the company but he were fingering their port-glasses in reverent anticipation, he turned to his left-hand neighbour, and addressed him in the jovial imperative voice of one shouting to a distant yokel to open a gate, 'Rumble says he's badly bothered with heather-beetle,' he bellowed.

But the interruption was ignored – Lord Lomond himself was nowise disconcerted – and the loyal toast was drunk, cigar-smoke coloured the air, and Mr Pelham-Blair, the Parliamentary Under-Secretary of State for India, rose to commend the Pious Memory of their Founder.

'Your Royal Highness, my Lord Archbishop, my Lords and gentlemen,' he began . . .

It was a tradition that one of the junior Ministers should propose this toast, and custom allowed him to lighten it with a little humour, an occasional discreet and cheerful witticism. A year ago, thought Scrymgeour, they had asked Eliot Greene to do it, and he had offended a lot of people by poking fun at their motto, *Be Loyal*. He had gone too far, definitely too far, that night. Well, there wasn't much left of him now, poor devil. He hadn't been a shirker, though he had talked a lot of subversive nonsense. And in his position he could have stayed at home with a clear conscience. As Pelham-Blair was doing. There was a clever fellow, with more balance than poor Eliot. He wasn't the sort to offend anyone for the sake of cracking a joke. He'd probably do well for himself. He had done well already, if it came to that. He looked a shade too sleek and well-fed, perhaps, but he played a lot of real tennis, and that must keep him reasonably fit.

Scrymgeour's mind, in half-idle speculation, stared like a wavering beam – a searchlight fumbling in clouds – at Pelham-Blair speaking with such smooth assurance; at old Laffery and young Mowbray, at Bilbow and Saint – a soldier like himself – and the Bishop of Brighton and Hove. Some had lived out

the greater part of their lives, others still nursed ambition. And
how many counted, or would count their lives successful?
How many here had felt the deep wound of public hatred? Or
worse, had seen dismay on the faces of their own officers? –
Yet in any major operation he had never failed, and in his own
mind he knew that he had done well. In his mind he knew it,
if not in his heart. They lived in his heart, those swift-marching
regiments he had sent to their death – and he could bear the
burden. He was a soldier, dedicate in all his being. Without
complaint his body had suffered discomfort and wounds and
now his heart in the same service would bear its burden. His
mind approved what he had done. His mind rejected the
whimpering and the angry clatter of the politicians and the
weathercock newspapers that censured him. They didn't know
what they were talking about. None of them had the smallest
elementary knowledge of strategy and the constitution of
modern war. But though his mind could despise them and
refute their silly arguments, it could not quite armour him
against their hatred.

He heard none of the earlier speeches; but when silence was
requested for Lord Pippin, he made an effort to hush the tiresome voices of his own brain, and listen to the old man. He
might be the victim of senile decay, as for years past his
enemies had declared, but he could still make a better speech
than any one else in the country. Or so it seemed while he was
delivering it. In print, on the following morning, it might have
a thinnish look, but while the words were still in the air they
had the strong sweet sound of honey-bees in a walled garden;
and a bit of sound, ordinary, English common sense, as he
spoke it in his powerful voice, was better than the proudest
rhetoric.

But before the Prime Minister had risen to his feet, while he
was still making his leisurely preparations – he unhooked a
thin gold watch and laid it on the table, he drank slowly a third
of a glass of port – an untoward incident occurred; or rather a
small but disturbing series of incidents.

Through a half-opened door could be seen a young officer
in excited contention with a person who looked like a policeman in plain clothes. Then the door was closed again; but in a

few seconds was re-opened, and an elderly Club servant, walking with unavailing delicacy in creaking boots, came carrying a silver tray on which were two letters that he delivered, with a low-spoken explanation, to the Prime Minister.

With an expression of elderly annoyance Lord Pippin opened first one and then the other. The second was a single sheet of typewritten foolscap in a long buff envelope. The Prime Minister read it with incredulity, anger, and impatience. He showed it to the Chairman, and looking along the table caught the eye of Mr Pelham-Blair, to whom he beckoned. The Prime Minister, the Chairman, and Mr Pelham-Blair then re-read the letter, discussed it with obvious distaste, and settled the matter by sending Mr Pelham-Blair to conduct a personal investigation. As the door opened for him, the excited young officer was again for half a second visible.

The Prime Minister slowly and deliberately drank the remainder of his port, and rose to speak. His theme was the English character. He said much in praise of it, especially as it showed itself in times of peril or difficulty, and in his own manner he revealed many of the ripe qualities that he found so laudable in his fellow-countrymen. It was an admirable speech; better than ever, thought some who had heard it several times in the past twenty years.

Lord Pippin was just coming to his peroration when Mr Pelham-Blair rather noisily re-entered the room. The temper of the Parliamentary Under-Secretary of State for India was clearly ruffled, as indeed was his smooth black hair. He came hotly in, impatient of ceremony or restraint, and immediately claimed the Prime Minister's attention; who, having marshalled several dependent clauses to their place in a long sentence and brought it majestically to its appointed close, turned to him and asked, 'Well, what news?'

'It's perfectly true,' said Mr Pelham-Blair. 'They've seized the Castle.'

'How very provoking, especially for poor Comyn Curle,' said the Prime Minister. 'Is anything the matter with your eye?'

'It was punched. It will soon be black, if it isn't black already.' Mr Pelham-Blair was very angry indeed about his injured eye.

'Then you had better go and bathe it, while I finish my speech.'

His peroration was shorter than usual, but he showed no sign of being worried by what he had heard. His voice was calm and strong; he induced the comforting feeling – as he so often did – that common sense might be the most profound of all philosophies; and he quoted with deep feeling:

> 'Friends, call me what you will; no jot care I;
> I that shall stand for England till I die!'

Rightly inferring that here was the end of the speech, and being pleasantly moved by it, the Old Hattonians began vigorously to applaud; but the Prime Minister remained standing, the applause died away, and he continued: 'You are right in thinking that I have concluded my speech, but too hasty in your assumption that I have no more to say. I have some news that you are entitled to hear. I do not overrate its importance, but as it is likely to cause some excitement, and thus give rise to many undesirable rumours, you will probably be glad to have an authoritative account of what has happened. A little while ago, as some of you may have noticed, I received a certain communication. Or, to be accurate, two communications; but the one did no more than introduce the other, which I shall read to you.'

Taking the typewritten sheet of foolscap from its long buff envelope, Lord Pippin slowly unfolded it.

'It is somewhat oddly addressed. "To the Prime Minister and all whom it may concern",' he said. 'And it reads as follows:

We, the women of Great Britain, have resolved that as the war is bringing nothing but misery to the world, it shall be stopped. We cannot afford to wait for victory, because victory can only be bought with the lives of our husbands, our lovers, and our sons. Victory therefore would come too late for them to hear about it, or for us to enjoy it. It is peace that we want, and in order to get it with a minimum of delay, we have decided to call a General Love-strike. We hereby declare in consequence our firm intention to abstain as far as possible from any contact with men, and we utterly renounce, repudiate, and abandon all marital relations; extra-marital association of a like or comparable nature; and casual intimacy whether for affection or hire, until such time as peace has been re-established. We have, moreover, in order to facilitate our task and to show the solidarity of women all over the country, taken possession in various towns of several strongholds or key-positions, and established garrisons in them. In Edinburgh we have occupied the Castle, which we shall continue to hold until you have stopped the war.

Signed: Lysistrata Scrymgeour
Camilla Oriole
Delia Curle.

The effect of this announcement was profound rather than spectacular. The Old Hattonians, though deeply shocked, retained on the whole a decent composure. Some natural incredulity that showed at first was dispelled when the Prime Minister explained that the proclamation had been brought him by an officer of the Royal Horse Guards, who with his men, the squadron on duty at the Castle, had been turned out of the Guardhouse by an overwhelming force of women, and that Mr Pelham-Blair, who had kindly offered to seek further information, now confirmed the officer's report and on his own person showed signs of the violent temper of the insurgents.

A darker red suffused the features of many present, and the politicians with difficulty restrained their instinct to jump up and ask a supplementary question. The mutter of two hundred voices had an angry note in it, and drumming in many ears were the ugly words Mutiny, Bolshevism, and Sex. With growing restlessness the diners began to divide and gather again in smaller groups, like peewits preparing for their flight to Africa. It was only the presence of Royalty that prevented an immediate migration.

General Scrymgeour and Mr Comyn Curle, the Secretary for War, had left their seats to examine the document which their wives had signed. Both were speechless with shame, bewilderment, and wrath. Mr Curle made without stopping a small chattering noise, rather like a wheatear, and Scrymgeour betrayed the state of his mind by the extraordinary tension of his skin, which was stretched so tightly that the bridge of his nose, his cheekbones and knuckles, had the dead look of ivory.

'I need not ask whether either of you had any inkling of what was about to happen?' inquired the Prime Minister. 'No, I thought not. A husband is so often the last to hear what his wife is doing. And now I must tell the Duke that he would be well advised to go home – it would be helpful if he got the Archbishop to go too – and then we shall drive to the Castle and see for ourselves what is going on.'

II

On the other side of Princes Street, on the cab-rank by the Royal Academy, stood some twenty or more aged victorias, broughams, landaus, and hansoms which had been resurrected since the dearth of petrol banished motor-cars from the streets.

Suddenly on the steps of the New Club appeared the hall-porter who whistled shrilly, again and again. One after another the bottle-nosed fumbling old cabbies climbed stiffly to their boxes, touched-up their shabby rack-ribbed old horses, wheeled into line ahead, and drove gingerly, jerkily, with a jingle and a slow clip-clop, across the street.

Out came the Old Hattonians, and the aged and most famous of them got heavily into the mousy old growlers, while the younger, keeping abreast of them on either pavement with dignity walked alongside. Slowly, like a belated funeral in the ebb of the long northern twilight, the procession of dark vehicles climbed the Mound. With an air of tall indifference and a cold anger in their hearts, the *patres conscripti* were marching against the rebel women. – They advanced with tranquil deliberation, without passion. There was an heroic quality in their dark unbannered cavalcade with its tophatted, tail-coated infantry. The slow clip-clop of the old horses' hooves struck from the stones an epic tune, and the Prime Minister reciting to General Scrymgeour and Mr Comyn Curle – who shared his cab – a favourite passage from *Pride and Prejudice*, was as much a figure of unshaken fortitude as Spartans titivating in their valiance on the sea-wet rock.

To their right, crowning the huge island that rose so abruptly in the midst of the city, was the Castle. It loomed enormous, and because the base of the crag was already lost in upward-creeping darkness, it appeared to be preternaturally high in a torn dove's-feather sky. Its great walls were nearly the same shadow-colour as the clouds, but the farthest battlement and little outflung turret had caught a yellowish gleam from the afterglow that still lighted the north-west. There was a light westerly breeze, and presently the Old Hattonians heard the confused vibrating hubbub of an angry crowd.

The cavalcade turned into the Lawnmarket, where its progress was hindered by an excited multitude, and forty yards short of the Castle Esplanade a solid mass of people brought it to a halt altogether. The news of rebellion had travelled fast, and from all parts of the town were coming curious, indignant, startled, or sympathetic citizens.

'What an excitable people are the Scotch,' said the Prime Minister, looking about him with mild interest. 'I am always amazed at their exuberance. There's Pelham-Blair trying to reason with them – I feel sure he will get another black eye.'

Half a dozen mounted police arrived. A mixed force of regular and special constables had already been making themselves impartially useful, having rescued a group of soldiers from a company of angry women, and a troop of impudent girls from an irate gathering of men; and now they secured a passage for the more eminent of the Old Hattonians and brought them safely to an empty space, from which with difficulty they had cleared the crowd, in front of the drawbridge and Main Gate of the Castle. The cabmen with their aged vehicles were herded into a corner, and the newcomers looked about them with guarded interest.

The great iron-bolted Main Gate under the archway was closed, and on the drawbridge in front of the statues of Bruce and Wallace stood a pair of raw-boned, six-foot-high young women who carried each, for a weapon, a steel-shafted heavy niblick. Some ragged cheering broke from the crowd – pressed heavily against the restraining arc of policemen – when Lord Pippin and the Cabinet ministers were recognized. There was also counter-cheering, with catcalls, groans, and other noises.

'Where is the Secretary of State for War?' asked the Prime

Minister cheerfully. 'Ah, there you are, Curle! Now this is your pigeon; how do you propose to carve it?'

With the transference of Government to Edinburgh, the Castle had become the War Office, and Mr Curle had hitherto been very proud that his Ministry was so magnificently situated; but now he would gladly have handed it over to the Minister of Transport, or the President of the Board of Education, or anyone at all. He was a smallish, rather ill-tempered man with heavy eyelids and a long thin nose, which gave him the expression of someone who would be very clever if he were only fully awake. He was, to be fair, a most able administrator, but rather inarticulate unless he had been given plenty of time to order his thoughts and consider his phrasing of them.

Now, with manifest and tetchy unwillingness, he approached the Amazonian young women on the drawbridge, and said shortly, 'I want my wife.'

'What, *already*?' said the one on the left, whose name was Miss McNulty.

'You've got no self-control at all,' said the other, who was a Miss McNab.

'I am the Secretary of State for War,' cried Mr. Curle, 'and I insist on seeing my wife!'

'Do you think there's any truth in that?' asked Miss McNulty.

'Of course there isn't,' said Miss McNab. 'A man like that would tell any sort of lie to get what he wanted. You can see how passionate he is by the way he's stamping on the ground.'

'I expect you're right,' said Miss McNulty. 'And if we did let him see his wife, there's all those other old boys who'd make up a story of some kind and come bothering us to let them in.'

'My identity,' said Mr Curle in a choking voice, 'can be established by any of these gentlemen here.'

'So you're all in the game together, are you?' said Miss McNulty.

'I can just hear that fat one saying he's the Prime Minister, and please can he speak to his sister,' observed Miss McNab.

'You are partly right,' said Lord Pippin, 'for I *am* the Prime Minister . . .'

'I told you so!' exclaimed Miss McNab triumphantly.

'. . . and I must ask you to inform Lady Lysistrata Scrymgeour, Lady Oriole, and Mrs Curle of my presence here; and to say that I very much hope to confer with any one or all of them.'

'You're too ambitious, grandpa.'

'He's just showing off,' said Miss McNulty.

'Enough of this nonsense!' shouted Mr Curle. 'I repeat that I am the Secretary of State . . .'

'Well, keep your distance,' said Miss McNab. 'I'm pretty good with a niblick, and if you come any nearer, I'll chip your appendix out.'

'I say,' said Miss McNulty tentatively.

'Now don't weaken,' said Miss McNab.

'I shan't. But I think the fat one does look like the Prime Minister. I saw a photograph of him once. Perhaps we ought to tell Lady Lysistrata.'

'Well, if you really think so . . .'

'You go, and I'll stay here.'

'No, you go, but hurry up. I can keep 'em out so long as there isn't a rush.'

Miss McNulty was more cautious, however. Kicking open a wicket in the great door, she shouted to the guard within, and three or four strapping girls, armed with golf-clubs and hockey-sticks, came to take her place while she hurried with her message to Lady Lysistrata.

During her absence there was a new and concerted movement in the crowd, and presently a body of soldiers, about three hundred strong, pushed their way to the front and assumed a semi-military formation. They were a mixture of many regiments, and conspicuous among the majority khaki were half-a-dozen glittering troopers of the Blues, whose white-scarred boots and dinted breastplates showed what rough treatment they had got in the recent battle for the Guardhouse. The commander of this irregular company was Julian Brown, now a temporary Lieutenant-Colonel whose tunic was en-nobled by the ribbons of the Distinguished Service Order, the

Military Cross, and a German medal. He was pale from a recent wound – he had newly left hospital – and in a state of considerable agitation. With obvious relief, however, he recognized General Scrymgeour, and approaching him in a very military fashion, he saluted with fierce precision.

Many of the Old Hattonians were now unhappily lost in the crowd, but those whom the police had shepherded to the front were either congregated about the Prime Minister; or conversing in small groups; or walking briskly to and fro after the fashion of people on board ship. Their manner varied from the apparent easiness of race-goers meeting in the paddock, to the icy calm of first-class passengers on a sinking liner; and some portrayed now one and now another of these styles. But Scrymgeour had no disguise. He walked alone, for he was in a state of tragic bewilderment that he could not conceal and would not willingly let others see.

He stopped reluctantly when Julian saluted. 'Well?' he asked dully.

'I've collected about three hundred men, sir. I think that ought to be plenty.'

'Plenty for what?'

'To arrest these women, sir.'

'Oh. How many women are there?'

'I don't know, sir.'

'But you want to put them under arrest?'

'It's the obvious thing to do, sir, isn't it?'

'Perhaps it is.'

Julian could hardly contain the rage of impatience that he felt. To hear Scrymgeour talking like this – the most resolute and percipient of soldiers – was infuriating. The situation was clear as the tropic sun and more intolerable. Rose was in the Castle, Rose had deserted him, and he must get her back. He had spent two days of his leave with her, and then, without warning or preparation, with no more explanation than a letter could give, she had packed her clothes and left him to join these lunatic women. ... His voice grew hoarse with emotion. 'We can't let them defy us!' he exclaimed.

'No, not indefinitely. But I'm not in command here. Half the Cabinet is over there, and politicians have their own way of looking at things. You feel strongly about what has happened, do you?'

'Yes, sir.'

'Do you know anyone among the mutineers?'

'Yes.'

'Well, come along and I'll tell the Prime Minister what you suggest. He may think it's a good idea.'

At that moment, however, the Castle gates were thrown open, and the crowd surging forward in renewed excitement, they were cut off from the Old Hattonian politicians by a great wedge of sweating turbulent humanity. The women were coming out. Over the drawbridge, under the lamps that spread a tent of yellow light, a column marched, wheeled left, halted, and faced its front. Another column formed the right flank. Then Lysistrata, Mrs Curle, and Lady Oriole appeared, and behind them came a solid mass of stalwart and high-tempered young women.

The near sight of his wife threw Mr Curle into a very violent unhappy temper. She looked charming. She was dressed in a tailored white flannel costume that accorded well with her type of beauty – she was a light blonde with rather protuberant blue eyes and a very short upper lip – and made her more conspicuously feminine than Lysistrata, who wore a workman-like suit of green corduroy; or Lady Oriole, who, rather oddly, wore hunting costume. But Mr Curle's passion did not give him words to express it. He could say no more than, 'Delia! What the devil! What the devil are you doing there!' And Mrs Curle found little difficulty in resisting his appeal.

Then the Prime Minister began to speak. He was much more eloquent. He said that he was always ready to consider the views, however widely they might differ from his own, of any reasonable and responsible body of citizens. He had never been tempted to believe that wisdom was born with him alone, or would die with him. In a free democracy everyone was entitled to an opinion, and enjoyed the right to express it. But there was a right way and a wrong way of expressing it. No one, in a free democracy, could be allowed to make an ultimatum of his opinion. No one could be allowed to hold a pistol to the head of the community at large. Given good will and an open mind, he did not doubt the possibility of their coming to an agreement. They would find a formula. But there could be no discussion, of course, until the ladies had evacuated the Castle and called-off their – ah! their ... The Prime Minister sought in vain for a euphemism.

'Our love-strike,' said Lysistrata firmly.

An expression of marmoreal impersonality appeared to indurate the features of the Old Hattonians, and guarded successfully their wounded verecundity.

'Your love-strike,' repeated the Prime Minister with manifest distaste.

'No surrender!' cried Mrs Curle, and stared with the prettiest and most provocative defiance at her unhappy husband.

'Stop the war,' said Lysistrata, 'and we shall call off the strike.'

'The war was not of our choosing,' observed the Prime Minister.

'Then let there be no doubt that peace is our choice.'

'We must face facts,' said the Prime Minister mechanically.

The three ladies laughed most scornfully. 'Why don't you?' they cried.

'War is the stupidest thing on earth, and there's a fact,' cried Mrs Curle indignantly.

'It's an evil thing, and does evil to all concerned in it; and there's another,' said Lysistrata.

'And it's killing off the best of our breeding-stock, and there's a third,' exclaimed Lady Oriole at the top of her voice. She had to shout, because the noise of the crowd was now increased by a terrible clamour of bells.

A fire-engine was coming up Castle Hill. Policemen blew their whistles and bustled about; the multitude divided and shrank away, pressing so tightly against their neighbours that no one had any breath to cheer; and into the road they had left came with a rising hullabaloo a huge scarlet engine.

It was now nearly dark, but not too dark to see that it was only lightly manned. Its crew consisted of two Naval officers and one elderly, bespectacled, and ponderously built gentleman in evening-dress. The Naval officers were the celebrated Commander Lawless, V.C., and the Captain McCombie – now

Lieutenant McCombie, R.N.R. – who had contributed to the outbreak of war by ramming a French destroyer in the harbour of Toulon. They had newly come ashore at Rosyth, and McCombie had fallen into a passion because his wife was not there to meet him. Then, hearing garbled rumours of the love-strike, both he and Lawless had been filled with consternation, and commandeering a fire-engine – because fire-engines were among the few motor vehicles still in use – they had driven to Edinburgh without loss of time.

Calling at the New Club for a drink, they encountered Sir Joseph Rumble, and learnt from him that the Castle was now occupied by insurgent women. He, poor man, had stayed behind, after the departure of the Hattonians, to telephone to his wife. But after patiently ringing-up his own house and several friends, he had been unable to trace her, and had come to the conclusion that she must be among the rebels; a redundant figure in the mutiny, perhaps, considering her sixty-five years, her domestic temperament, and maternal figure. But she had often, he remembered, spoken with admiration of romantic heroines, and hazarded the opinion that she herself might have done something in that line had the opportunity occurred. – Sir Joseph was excessively worried, and gladly accepted Lawless's offer to drive him to the Castle. They remounted the fire-engine, and roaring up the Mound, drove through the yielding crowd to the very edge of the ever-diminishing arena where Lord Pippin and Lysistrata stood in momentous debate.

For half a minute, while Ministers and mutineers and the silent multitude all stared at them, Sir Joseph and the two Naval officers stood on their lofty vehicle, and through the thickened twilight peered at the crowded scene below. Sir Joseph screwed up his eyes and saw little, but Lawless and McCombie had keener sight, and suddenly Lawless shouted like a trumpet from the battlements: 'Delia, my heart!'

He leapt from the fire-engine, a tall swift figure, and breaking through the several ranks of astonished Old Hattonians, pushed Mr Comyn Curle out of the way, and catching the palpitating Mrs Curle under the arms, lifted her up – she was small and slim – and held her high in an attitude of extravagant adoration. Then, bringing her down to his own level, he kissed her warmly, set her on her feet, and stooping now – he was well over six feet, and she but five feet two – enfolded her in his long arms and kissed her again.

Mr Comyn Curle, who had never suspected that Lawless was his wife's lover, nor indeed that she had a lover at all, uttered a cry of indescribable anguish, and ran furiously to her rescue. But Miss McNulty was too quick for him. Miss McNulty was ever watchful against any assault on Lysistrata, and she did not mean to let Mr Curle come too near. So with a neat little movement of her niblick, as if she were trying the balance of a new club, she tapped his ankle and brought him to the ground.

Almost at the same moment Lysistrata beckoned to the equally alert and faithful Miss McNab. When Lawless snatched his love aloft, a cry of rage had risen from the eight hundred armed women who guarded the entrance to the Castle; but when he kissed her, their voices grew like the howling of wolves in winter; and when he kissed her again, there came from them all a lickerish and dreadful sigh. The situation was dangerous, and danger threatened from both sides. Lysistrata beckoned and signed to Miss McNab, who with her heavy club struck the impetuous officer a blow of just sufficient strength behind his right ear. His Delia tried, but could not support him, and he fell senseless to the ground.

'Take him inside,' Lysistrata commanded; and four big rosy-cheeked girls in short blue tunics laid him across their hockey-sticks and carried him over the drawbridge.

Meanwhile Lieutenant McCombie, a thick-chested red-faced man of great strength and hardihood, had remained on the high driver's seat of the fire-engine to view the spectacle and see if he could find his wife among so many women. But when he perceived how cruelly they were treating Lawless, he forgot everything but friendship and anger; and shouting in a Western Ocean voice, 'Rescue! a rescue!' he jumped quickly down and drove his way through all who opposed him to what became, as soon as he got there, the front of battle.

Eloquently and with force he appealed to the Old Hattonians: 'Come on, boys! Engage the enemy more closely – that's the order. Tumble the bitches!'

Without waiting to see the effect of this hortation, he charged alone at Miss McNulty, evaded her deadly niblick, and grappled her round the waist. Two only of the Old Hattonians followed him. The rest of them, to their undying shame, continued to wear a look of cold distaste for all that was happening – or quickly assumed such a look if they had been taken unawares – and pretended not to have heard him. Most of them gathered more closely about the Prime Minister, and many urged him to come away, for the situation was clearly getting out of hand and might soon be embarrassing to all of them.

The pair of Hattonians who followed McCombie were Sir Joseph Rumble and Mr Pelham-Blair. The former had recognized Delia Curle when Lawless raised her aloft into the light of the drawbridge lamps; and immediately his doting mind decided that if the wife of the Secretary of State for War was in the rebel lines, then Lady Rumble must be there also. And puffing at the mere thought of exertion, but dauntless as well as breathless, he had joined the attack. After the briefest hesitation, Pelham-Blair had followed in a vain attempt to look after him. Pelham-Blair was most truly devoted to the welfare of all Cabinet Ministers and peers above the rank of Viscount. Already he had got a black eye for his zeal that night. But he was to suffer worse things for Sir Joseph than his bruises for the Prime Minister.

Neither Rumble nor Pelham-Blair, nor even McCombie, made any impression on the sturdy and numerous enemy. It was Julian Brown who saved the reputation of his sex and made a fight for it at least. He, when he heard McCombie shouting for a rescue, turned to his company of volunteers, and by voice and gesture and example lifted their hearts to battle-height and led them straightaway into action. He had waited long enough for orders, and no orders came. Scrymgeour had lost his nerve, the politicians had never had any. Then he, Julian Brown, sometime a teacher of literature in Brixton, now a lieutenant-colonel and a Companion of the Distinguished Service Order, would take command and beat the rebels home. He was full of righteous anger and a great desire to smack

Rose Armour's pretty bottom. He led his three hundred into battle with a rare spirit and stern determination.

They were in three divisions, and for a little way they advanced in line of companies. But when they had room they deployed and halted to dress their ranks, facing the enemy in line. The women were disposed in a deep crescent. Their centre lay in front of the drawbridge, where they were massed eight or ten deep. To their right and left their flanks were thrown forward in front of the low wall that guarded the empty moat. It was Julian's plan to push their forward-reaching wings back upon their main division, causing confusion where they were already badly crowded, and so drive them all before him. He himself commanded his centre company. His right was under a Canadian captain, scarred and lean, a soldier of fortune who had served in many wars, in Spain and Mexico and the mountains of Szechuan; while the left wing obeyed a gallant but headstrong young Scot, the Master of Ballantyne.

The mutinous women already outnumbered him by three to one, and they had reserves of unknown strength. But their discipline was poor, their strength unequally disposed. Lysistrata and Mrs Curle had been persuaded to seek safety in the Castle, and the defending army was under the command of Lady Oriole. She was a striking figure – booted, top-hatted, and veiled – as she reviewed her troops, and, where they were needed, uttered soldierly words of encouragement. She carried as her only weapon a hunting-crop with which, at intervals, she smacked her riding-skirt in a boisterous and defiant fashion.

Apart from the disparity of numbers and the difference of sex, the most noticeable inequality between the two forces was that whereas the men had no weapons but their natural strength, the women were all armed. For the most part they carried golf-clubs, hockey-sticks, or various domestic utensils; but a few had implements more dangerous, both to themselves and others, which they had found among the trophies in the Banqueting Hall of the Castle; such things as broadswords, halberds, and long Lochaber axes. Their temper, too, was more obviously hostile. They kept up a chorus of shrill defiance, now breaking into song that was soon abandoned because so few could agree as to what song should be sung; now shrieking the most scathing of insults; and now like howler monkeys in the jungles of India, yelling for the mere pleasure of listening to the savage reverberation of their own voices.

In contrast to this unruly behaviour, Julian was pleased to observe the calm demeanour of his men. Their mood was a grim humour. As they removed their tunics and rolled up their sleeves, they commented without rancour on the appearance and conduct of their enemy, and were seemingly without fear of the issue. Despite the odds against them, Julian felt sure that their quiet confidence was justified, and his assurance was equally shared by his two lieutenants.

When all were ready he gave orders to a saturnine tall piper, who had been one of the first to volunteer, to play *The Cock o' the North*. A cheer broke from his men, deep-throated and spontaneous, that drowned the shrill clamour of the women.

'Stand fast, the centre!' he commanded, and signalled to his lieutenants. Their voices rose together, the nasal tone of the Canadian captain, the warlike yell of the Master of Ballantyne: 'By your right, quick march! Double march! *Cha-arge!*'

Their feet thundered on the stony ground. They cheered once more, at the very moment of coming to grips with the enemy, and then for a long time nothing was heard but the multifarious clamour of close and savage conflict. The hoarse breathing of antagonists well-matched in strength; the small dull thud of a mashie meeting bone or muscle; the larger noise of a descending hockey-club; the cheerful exclamation of a hard hand smacking plump cheeks; the protesting scream of a girl whose Lochaber axe had drawn blood; the despairing cry of a soldier whom some gigantic Amazon had hurled into the moat; and the music, growing fainter, that the saturnine tall piper played – here was the noise of battle that rose in the darkness under the ramparts that had known so many battles, yet none as strange as this.

Julian watched keenly, and with growing anxiety, the fortune of his two companies. On the right, for a little while, the men seemed to have the advantage. The smacking of faces

T – F

and the cries of female pain were uppermost in the din. But then the soldiers, pressing home their advantage, began to go too far, and many were surrounded by women, and their strength was nullified by the close pressure of ponderous foemen. Here and there in the battle rose the head of some tall trooper or great Guardsman, towering above their adversaries, and there rose and fell again the huge fist and mighty arm – pale in the dusk – of a stalwart shoeing-smith who fought alone among his enemies; but they sank from sight, and were seen no more. Slowly the weight of numbers told. The attack had failed, and the survivors, still fighting stubbornly, began their sullen retreat.

On the left, where the women were more loosely ordered, the impetuous Master of Ballantyne had at the first shock led his company into the very thick of them. But the women, though yielding in all directions, had nowhere fled. If at one minute they gave ground, at the next they encircled it. Where they drew back, they lured forward, and when they fell they did not fall alone. Surrounded on all sides, the hundred soldiers of the left wing struggled vainly like explorers: lost among the clinging vines and too luxuriant foliage of a tropical forest. A steam of mingled perfumes rose above the fray, and so great was the heat of conflict that men felt their strength fail them, and their spirit swoon. They were pulled down by innumerable writhing arms, and disappeared beneath a billowing mass of uncounted bosoms. Here the battle was all but lost. Only some dramatic reversal of their fortune could save the men from utter defeat.

Julian took a gambler's chance, and resolved to throw his remaining division against the enormous strength of Lady Oriole's centre. It was his only hope. '*Allons! faites donner la garde!*' he muttered, and with a desperate valiance ordered his remnant to the attack.

He heard the staccato cheering of his soldiers and the answering cries of the defenders. He was gathered into the torrent of the charge, and flung against the solid mass of women. He saw faces flushed and wild, teeth gleaming, and fierce lovely eyes. A poker prodded him in the ribs, he gasped, and was flattened against a gigantic bosom. The breath went

out of him, and his sight darkened. He caught feebly at some
loose garment as he fell, but the fabric tore, and he was down
among frantic feet, and silk-clad ankles. He seized a shapely
leg, and saw the knees above him bend, and down came a
great hockey-player. But in her fall she stunned him, and as
she lay she stifled him, and he knew no more.

In the meantime the ever-diligent police had slowly driven
the great mass of onlookers away from the Castle, and dog-
gedly prevented them from joining the battle. The battle was
apparently a political affair, and therefore the police kept out
of it themselves, and exerted all their strength to keep excited
spectators out of it. Having escorted the Prime Minister and
his party to a place of safety, they drew their batons and drove
the obstreperous multitude to the lower end of the Esplanade,
and kept them there. With admirable self-control the police
kept their heads, and cracked no more than forty or so belong-
ing to the populace. But all the outward channels from the
Esplanade were hopelessly blocked. The narrow ways of
Castle Hill and Ramsay Lane and the steps into Johnstone
Terrace were swarming with people, and even the police could
not drive the crowd home.

Over the dark uneasy mass of humankind – still struggling,
tight-packed as herring in a drifter's hold – rose a gibbous
moon. It climbed slowly above the tall black houses behind
them, and grew brighter as it rose. The sky cleared, and the
great lop-sided lantern lighted equally the heavens and the
earth, and shone upon the Castle walls.

The battle was over. In a corner of the Esplanade there
stood, or lay wearily on the ground, the survivors of Julian's
little army. They were bruised and listless. Many were bleeding from deep scratches, and two or three had received a
trifling wound from halberds or the broad blade of a Lochaber
axe. More than half had been taken prisoner. Julian, who had
recovered consciousness when the battle ebbed away from
him, was stiff and sore, and his heart was bitter. But weary
though he was, he was counting casualties and taking, so far
as he could, the names of the missing.

One of his men spoke sullenly: 'What are they randies gaun
tae do next?'

He pointed to the Castle, and looking up they saw a dozen misshapen bundles being lowered over the parapet of the Half-Moon Battery, the high round wall a hundred feet above the main gate. The bundles swayed gently to and fro. The bright moon lighted them. From the closely penned crowd at the lower end of the Esplanade there rose a confused harsh noise of exclamation and inquiry. Curiosity gave them strength, and like a bursting dam they broke through the cordon of police, and charged towards the Castle. When they came nearer they saw clearly what the bundles were.

They began to laugh. – Feather-brained, weathercock-witted as always, they forgot that women were now their enemies, and seized upon a joke, no matter who had made it. – Their laughter came at first from little groups and individuals. The crowd grew rapidly larger and denser as more and more people rushed on to the Esplanade from the streets and lanes that led to it. The newcomers had first to see, distinguish, understand, and swallow their astonishment. Then they also began to laugh. The laughter spread. It swept like a wind across the crowd. It grew louder and louder, till it roared like a forest fire. It broke in waves upon the Castle walls, and reverberated with the thunder of an Atlantic tide. Men laughed until their bodies weakened, and when strength returned they wiped their flowing eyes and laughed again.

The bundles that hung from the Half-Moon Battery were some twenty of the captives that Lysistrata's mutineers had taken. In the very centre was Sir Joseph Rumble, and on either side of him Commander Lawless and Mr Pelham-Blair. Lieutenant McCombie was also there, and the impetuous Master of Ballantyne. They had been stuffed – not wholly, but as much of them as would go – into those large wire receptacles that are used, in parks and public places, for the collection of waste paper and other debris; and in these strong baskets they swung gently in the moonlight, the evidence of victory.

The women had won their initial trial, and the moon that had so many times betrayed them, now in their honour silvered the fruits of their first battle.

CHAPTER FIVE

The Love Siege

I

SHOWING a pretty taste in architecture, the Government had taken possession of the greater part of Charlotte Square, the north side of which housed in reasonable comfort the First Lord of the Treasury, the Chancellor of the Exchequer, and the Government Whips. Lord Pippin, who greatly admired the work of the Adam brothers, was delighted with his new residence, and often at some Cabinet meeting forgot the topic of discussion in more agreeable contemplation of mantelpiece, fanlight, or ceiling. The houses, too, reminded him of Bath, and rarely had he read the novels of Jane Austen in surroundings so congenial to himself and them. In a room which he called his *arcana curia* he had, indeed, recently taken to morning reading – an hour or so between eleven and twelve with *Emma* or *Mansfield Park* – a form of intemperance from which he derived intense though guilty pleasure.

It was three days after the battle for the Castle, and he had recently begun *Emma* for the twentieth time, when contrary to all orders he was interrupted – his *arcana curia* invaded – by Sir Joseph Rumble, Mr Comyn Curle, and General Puffin-Lumkyn. The last was a tall stout man with large pink cheeks, a small red mouth, a Socratic nose, and rather colourless eyes, one of which looked at the world in pale astonishment through a single eye-glass.

They came in without being announced, with no more ceremony than a loud knock at the door, and Lord Pippin had barely time to stuff *Emma* between the cushion and the arm of his chair before they confronted him with the determined aspect of honest men who were about to make themselves thoroughly unpleasant.

'This state of affairs, Pippin, can't continue,' said Sir Joseph, and selecting a chair, sat ponderously down.

'It must be stopped,' said Mr Curle.

'Before things have gone too far,' added the General.

'From all over the country,' declared Sir Joseph, 'reports are coming in of new disorder. This mutinous idea of a regimented continence is gaining ground.'

'It's spreading like wildfire,' said Mr Curle.

'It's playing the devil,' said the General. 'I never heard of such a thing. And it isn't only in public that these women are going in for chastity. They're practising it in their own homes, a lot of them.'

'The situation is quite intolerable.'

'And it must be stopped,' repeated Mr Curle.

Ruffled by their unmannerly intrusion, the Prime Minister permitted himself to show a little anger.

'Then why,' he asked, 'have you done nothing to mend it? – It would be supererogation, my dear Curle, to *stop* a situation. – But you are clearly too excited to appreciate such a nicety of language; and to be frank with you, I think your excitement is natural, since you must realize how much to blame you are for our present difficulties. The Castle was your War Office, and you failed to take proper care of it. Were you a soldier, like General Puffin-Lumkyn, you would certainly be court-martialled for losing Government property. And you, General, must feel as guilty as Mr Curle, for, as Commander-in-Chief of Home Defence, you are responsible for the conduct of the sentries and the squadron on guard who allowed the insurgents to dispossess them of their charge. Throughout the country, moreover, there have been mutinies similar to the one we have witnessed in Edinburgh; and wherever military action has been taken against the mutineers, it has resulted in the defeat of your troops. That is a grave reflexion on their discipline and training, and I quite understand how uneasy you must feel. Almost as uneasy, perhaps, as Sir Joseph? You, Rumble, are most culpable of all. In permitting yourself to be captured by the women you were guilty of criminal negligence, and your being displayed, on two occasions, I think, in a receptacle for waste paper, has seriously embarrassed the Government and sensibly weakened its authority. But perhaps it is unfair of me to – shall I say, rub it in, like this? For I suppose you have now come to tell me of some plan that will speedily – I think we agreed to say *mend*? – that will soon mend a situation which we all find extremely disagreeable if not positively intolerable.'

The Prime Minister had now recovered his normal equanimity. With open disregard for the opinion of his Ministers, he pulled *Emma* out of its hiding-place, laid it on a table, and settling himself more comfortably in his chair, looked from one to another of his colleagues with a blandly inviting smile. 'And now for your plan,' he said.

His visitors were engulfed in silence. Like cavalry in a quicksand, the indignation which the Prime Minister had set galloping down their arteries was now caught in the embarrassment of having nothing to suggest. Their fury struggled and sank in the shifting bottom of their impotence. Their breathing grew louder, they coughed, but were otherwise inarticulate.

Mr Curle was in a pitiable state of mind. Robbed of his War Office and deprived of his wife, he had had for three days little to do but mourn his double loss and regret his vanished felicity. He had laboriously prepared for the Prime Minister's information a statement of the difficulties of carrying on a war without a War Office – when he was even more concerned with the impossibility of being a married man without a wife – and now, abashed by Lord Pippin's jobation, he could remember none of it. Nor had he conceived any more likely idea for dealing with the love-strikers than to persuade them out of rebellion with some happy display of eloquence and logic – some irresistible mixture of rhetoric and reason – and unfortunately his tongue-tied condition did not give him a fair chance to bear witness to the power of words.

Sir Joseph, too, was in no enviable state. He had suffered, not in spirit alone, during his exposure in the wire basket. Never in his life had he been so humiliated, nor endured such discomfort in his legs. Twice those infernal women had hung him over the parapet; once in the moonlight, and again on the following morning. Then he and the other prisoners had been released, and the fickle crowd had met them with jeers and mockery. It was torture to be reminded of what he had gone through in the recent past; and as in all his political life he had never committed himself to any definite opinion nor failed in finding for his Party some way of securing release with honour from the more daring pledges of its rasher members, he had naturally no positive suggestion to make for the future. It was, perhaps, some comfort to him that Lady Rumble had not joined the insurgents; but not so much as it might have been, for she had announced her intention of starting a rival loyalist movement, and her first recruits, whom she had invited to dinner, were all phenomenally ugly, and most of them had so far passed the age of consent that it had long since become inoperative.

Not less unhappy was General Puffin-Lumkyn, though ignorant as yet that he was at last to be rewarded with a peerage and put on the retired list. The Prime Minister's criticism had not seriously upset him, for he tolerantly regarded all dispraise of the military as a symptom of civilian jealousy. But his private life had been tragically disrupted by the strike. He was a bachelor, a man of means, of taste and appetite as well, and his household staff had been famous. He had kept neither butler nor valet, but his tablemaid had been a regal brunette, and he was always dressed with loving attention. And now they had all gone, his gay domestic bevy, and his cook as well, who was worth the lot of them, and had gifts more lasting. The General was suffering severely; but discipline and a keen regard for decorum enabled him at last to break the embarrassing silence.

'We could shell them,' he said gruffly.

'Good God, no!' cried Mr Curle.

'You mean we could have the Castle bombarded?' asked the Prime Minister.

'Yes. It's not a pleasant idea, of course, but war's not pleasant either. And we've got to get on with it, haven't we?'

'Now that is a point worth considering,' exclaimed the Prime Minister, delighted by the chance of forgetting more serious discussion in pursuit of the General's *non sequitur*. But he was balked by Sir Joseph, who had been horrified by the suggestion, and now insisted on describing his revulsion, which, he said, would be shared by every decent man in

Britain. He was supported by a series of heartfelt ejaculations from Mr Curle.

'And yet,' said the Prime Minister, 'there is logically no reason why we should refrain from shelling those tiresome women. Many of their male relatives have been under fire for nearly a year, and the privilege of equal citizenship, for which their mothers fought so strenuously, should surely be accompanied by equal liabilities.'

'No, no,' said Sir Joseph. 'You can't be serious. The idea is intolerable. The populace would be up in arms. There is not a man in Britain who could be persuaded to fire on them, misguided though the poor creatures are. The unrest amongst our troops, to which you have already referred, is due to their reluctance to be used against women. The Englishman, and even the Scotchman and the Welshman, is essentially a chivalrous being.'

'I wonder,' said the Prime Minister. 'I sometimes think that the real reason why so many men refrain from hitting their sisters and their wives is simply fear of the consequences. You praise our fellow-countrymen for their chivalry; but I wonder whether we should not rather esteem them for their prudence?'

It was Mr Curle who brought them back to earth. 'You must have forgotten,' he told the Prime Minister, 'that my wife is in the Castle.'

'So she is. Then of course we cannot bombard it.'

There was a note of regret in Lord Pippin's voice, for he did not like Mrs Curle, and though his opinion of her husband was none too high, he had often wondered why Curle had been so foolish as to marry her. She was accounted pretty, he supposed, but she was not sympathetic. She had no brains, and he had been told that she had no money. But she had found a husband, and then a lover. Poor Curle. '"I feel that as to fortune, he might have done much better, and that as to a rational companion or useful helpmate, he could not have done worse",' he murmured; and wished that his colleagues would hurry up and go, and leave him in the pleasanter company of Jane Austen.

'Then what do you suggest?' asked the General.

'The ordinary industrial strike,' said the Prime Minister, 'often collapses when the strikers' funds are exhausted. This – ah! this love-strike – may expire when the strikers are bankrupt of resolution. A conventual seclusion is not agreeable to the majority of women. They prefer a mixed company. Marriage, as you know, was ordained as a remedy against sin, and women have discovered that a less binding association may be equally efficacious against boredom. I venture to suggest that we give them time. Time to be bored. Let us be patient, gentlemen. There are women in the Castle, I do not doubt, who are as capable of long-sustained resolution as any of us. But others, I am equally sure, are not so capable; and those who have not the gift of continency – how greatly the Prayer Book has enriched our common speech! – may defeat the rest and solve our problem for us.'

'But the war!' exclaimed Mr Curle, finding his voice at last. 'How can we carry on the war when we can't get into the War Office? How do you think we're going to maintain Organization? Or direct Operations and Intelligence when we don't know who's doing which and why? We don't know anything. For weeks past we'd been making elaborate calculations of enemy losses, but nobody can remember what they came to. What are the enemy's movements? We don't know. What are the movements of our own divisions? We don't know – and we can't find out, because even if we do get information it will be in code, and we've lost the code-books. What's going to happen to Personal Services and Military Training when everybody's records have disappeared and we don't know who or what we've got to train? How is the Director of Movements and Quartering going to move and quarter when he hasn't the least idea where anybody is, and where they ought to go, and how many there are? We may not have lost the war yet, but we've lost everything that proves there is a war. The C.I.G.S. is wandering about looking like a Belgian refugee, and the streets are full of G.S.O.1.'s without a home. At this very moment the Adjutant-General's playing snooker with the A.Q.M.G., because they've nothing else to do, and the Master-General of the Ordnance has started to write his reminiscences. You can't stir without running into private secretaries, under-secretaries, assistant secretaries, and deputy-assistant-under-military secretaries. Yesterday, my God, the D.G.A.M.S. and an A.D.O.S. were arrested for loitering! We can't go on like this, and the war can't go on either. We must face facts. Either we regain possession of the War Office, or we've got to stop the war!'

The Prime Minister wore an expression of appropriate gravity. His manner was both soothing and firm. 'The situation is difficult,' he said. 'None of us can deny that. But we all know, my dear Curle, that we can rely on you to do your best. We know, moreover, that the greater the task, the greater is your aptitude for it. Again and again I have seen you accept the challenge of seeming impossibility, and marvelled at your eventual triumph. You will, I feel sure, discover some device of – shall we say mollifying? – of mollifying the horns of the dilemma that you stated, and meanwhile, as I said before, we must exercise our patience. Time, gentlemen, is on our side, but a woman's chief enemy. The mutineers are young, and youth always demands: *Da nobis hodie*. – And that reminds me that I also have much to do. *Da nobis hodie*. Yes, indeed. And so I wish you good morning, gentlemen. Good morning.'

Three minutes later the Prime Minister was happily engaged with Miss Woodhouse and Mr Knightley, and his Ministers, slowly and somewhat disconsolate, were walking towards George Street. Before they had left Charlotte Square, however, they encountered Mr Percy Small, the Minister for Munitions, whose demeanour was even more melancholy than theirs, and whose manner was oddly furtive. Company was what he needed – human company, he sadly specified – but he feared it also, for what was human was likely to be critical. It was the strike, of course, that was to blame for his condition: Ivy's desertion had quite unmanned him. She was a lovely girl – he told himself so a hundred times a day – and she had always attracted such a lot of attention when he took her out to dinner. It made him feel that he was somebody important, important in himself, apart from being a Cabinet Minister. And now she had gone, and he was desolate.

He didn't really want to speak to Curle and Sir Joseph, and certainly not to Puffin-Lumkyn, but he was glad of the chance to postpone, if only for a minute or two, the visit to which he had nerved himself. He stopped, and without cordiality they exchanged a few casual remarks.

Then Curle said cruelly, 'I suppose you're going to see the Prime Minister?'

'Well,' said Mr Small uncomfortably, 'as a matter of fact I would like to talk over a few things with him. There's a difficult situation in the munition industry, now that a lot of girls have refused to work alongside of men, or take orders from them; and two heads are better than one, as they say. But what sort of a mood is he in this morning?'

'Relentless and irresponsible urbanity,' said Sir Joseph bitterly.

'The sort of mood that he talks Latin in?' asked Mr Small with growing unhappiness.

'Next door to it,' said the General.

'I'd only be wasting my time then, I expect.'

'Not if you succeed in worrying him another hour towards his grave,' said Curle.

But Mr Small, his courage failing him, went past the Prime Minister's residence with the air of a man who was walking only for the sake of his health, and turned with deep relief down St Vincent Street. He was afraid of the Prime Minister, but with obscure emotion deeply revered him. Old Pippin was one of the few people, he felt, whose mere presence could be a comforting thing – so long as you didn't want him to do anything, that is – and he wished that he had the confidence to go in and talk to him as man to man. Not that he'd dream of telling him about Ivy of course, but talking things over in a general way would help a lot. In a world gone arsey-versy all of a sudden, the P.M. was like something that knew how to keep its balance, no matter what happened. That was all he did do, perhaps; keep his balance. Still, it would be comforting to know how he managed it, if he'd only tell you. But he wouldn't, of course. He'd look at you like an old rosy-cheeked Buddha, and say something sarcastic. In Latin, if he was in one of his bad moods.

Mr Small made the circuit of Moray Place, tried to persuade himself that all men were born equal, came out at a tangent, crossed Queen Street with momentary resolution, and with a spirit already failing started up North Charlotte Street. He stopped at the corner, breathing heavily, and made a last effort to be brave. But with no success. A vision of the Prime Minister daunted him, and admitting his cowardice he turned eastward to walk to the North British Hotel, in which his Ministry was now situated.

Mr Curle and the General had in the meantime taken a cab to the Castle Esplanade to see Lysistrata's noon parade. This had become the most numerously attended event of the day in Edinburgh, though it was a bitter pleasure that it gave to the multitude who watched it. The two Ministers had a good long time to wait, for the rebel women did not always come punctually to their exercises.

II

In the Castle Lysistrata was making her daily tour of inspection, accompanied by Lady Oriole, her second-in-command; Mrs Graham, her Quartermaster-General; the Officer of the Day; a couple of buxom women who had been appointed Regimental Sergeant-Major and Regimental Quartermaster-Sergeant; and Horrocks, her faithful maid. It was rather unwillingly that Horrocks had joined the rebels, and for the first couple of days in the Castle she had been in a sour and petulant temper. But today she seemed so very happy that Lysistrata, when she had time to notice her, was puzzled by the change. Her attire was somewhat curious, but apparently designed to suggest that she was now an officer's batman rather than a lady's maid: she wore, in addition to a neat black costume, a Balmoral bonnet with a feather in it, and a sergeant's red sash.

It was part of Lysistrata's policy, however, that every member of her forces, except those in disgrace and certain duty detachments, should be encouraged to dress according to her own pleasure and style of beauty. The garrison, in consequence, presented a very gay and charming appearance, and its *morale* was daily strengthened by innocent competition and mutual admiration.

Lysistrata had made a circuit of the battlements, where the sentries stood like a border of tall bright flowers; she had seen the old military cook-houses, where by fastidious hands an excellent simple luncheon was being prepared; and she had inspected the ancient ablution-benches, whose dark severity was now concealed by a host of mirrors and a great array of powder boxes, skin creams and astringent fluids, sweet-smelling atomizers, crystal bottles, and many curious unguents, washes, and other nostrums. She had watched a score of defaulters doing foot-drill in khaki uniform; the uniform was a part of their punishment, as well as the sign of it. – All was going well, she thought, and she congratulated Mrs Graham in particular on her good work. As Quartermaster-General Mrs Graham had been responsible for the transport of thousands of wardrobe-trunks, hat-boxes, and suit-cases, for the mutineers had been told they would need all their best clothes; but she had not been able to provision the Castle against a siege of any duration. As yet the Government had not cut off supplies, partly because the Cabinet shrank from the inhumanity of such an action, and largely because it would be humiliating to admit that a mutiny of women was so serious as to call for really drastic measures; and so daily supplies of perishable foods were still brought to the Castle, and the butcher boys, the milkmen, and the greengrocers would stare through the great gateway with such a gnawing hunger as neither milk nor mutton nor new potatoes could wake or satisfy.

Having completed her inspection, Lysistrata with her Staff left the Citadel, and walked downhill toward the barracks. About a third of the garrison – perhaps a thousand women – were gathered on the broad causeway, of whom a couple of hundred were in military formation, while the rest walked to and fro or chatted in little groups. It was a spectacle bewildering to the eye, for all the colours of the rainbow and the laboratory were there, with the countless triumphs of the dressmaker, and such arms, legs, lovely bosoms, bright eyes, and glowing cheeks to show them off, that neither chemist nor couturier could suppose the Creator's art one jot the less ingenious than theirs. For more than a minute Lysistrata stood looking at them, and never a general, reviewing his Guards or Cuirassiers or Legion, had more pride in his troops than she.

Then, calling to Lady Oriole, she asked if they were ready to move off.

Lady Oriole, who still wore her hunting costume, was oddly conspicuous in the bright throng. She saluted Lysistrata, and in a loud mannish voice called the parade to attention. This was the signal for most of the young women to take out their pocket-mirrors and assure themselves that their lips and cheeks were nicely coloured, their noses not; and presently they set off down the cobbled road, round the steep corner, and under the old Portcullis Gate. The guard turned out, the Main Gate was thrown open, and laughing gaily, loudly talking, the lovely mutineers marched over the drawbridge and on to the Esplanade.

From the crowd of waiting men, several thousands in number, who filled the lower half of it, there rose a hoarse and indescribable sound. So many ejaculations of desire – such gruff and hopeless longing – a sort of wistful moaning – the sharp intake of breath – all these combined to make a noise more dreadful than the groan of breaking icebergs; but a noise that strangely did not frighten the marching women, who indeed now trod with a lighter step and laughed more delightfully than ever.

They were well guarded, of course. A hundred exceptionally stalwart young women, dressed severely in breeches and white shirts, stood in a long row across the Esplanade. They were armed with pikes and Jeddart axes, and they stood gravely still, bareheaded in the sunshine. Their serious demeanour and the simplicity of their attire gave them such a look of stern innocence as would have daunted most men; and their muscular arms, their formidable weapons, could probably have defeated any reckless minority. But for additional security there was a body of police on duty, a thin blue safety-line that tightly held in its place the reckless and unshapely mob of spectators. The police had retained their virtue and neutrality. They had, as always, a poor opinion of humanity, which to their understanding was divided into three sorts: the intemperate, the ill-conditioned, and the injudicious. But it was their duty to look after all sorts, prevent rioting, keep ideologues from each other other's throats, and spectators from rushing in to see the fun; and they did it. For seventy shillings a week and their boots, the police enforced several of the Ten Commandments which no authority, spiritual or temporal, had ever made effective before – as well as innumerable items of more recent legislation – and set an example to the whole world. The police were wonderful.

It was noticeable, however, that they turned their backs to the love-strikers. It was, perhaps, necessary for them to watch every movement of the impassioned spectators; they may, on the other hand, have thought it prudent to ignore a spectacle that others found so painfully exciting.

It was scarcely a parade in the military sense of the word, for most of Lysistrata's young ladies merely walked hither and thither in gay little groups, or slowly by two and two, talking so closely that everyone wondered what they could be discussing. The sun shone brightly in a clear blue sky, and a warm breeze blew softly with teasing eddies. The Esplanade was like the deck of a great galleon, almost becalmed in fine weather, and the Castle was its towering poop, the city far below was the murmurous level sea.

The tumult in the crowd grew still, and presently they stood in utter silence, hypnotized by the unsimple and allusive beauty of humankind. The strolling ladies, in their costumes like a parterre of tulips, withdrew to either side – to the parapet that overlooked the Grassmarket, to the pavement under the statues of Lord Haig and Queen Victoria's Uncle York – and a company of dancers came into the sunny space between them. The dancers were dressed in pale tissues that floated as they moved, like the wings of dragonflies or the morning shadows of a wood that hamadryads lived in; and their dance was like the mingling of the leaves and their shadows in a breeze, with the whiteness of the hamadryads glancing through.

Then followed a troop of rosy girls in short tunics who leapt and ran and rhythmically stretched their sturdy arms as though in training for the decathlon. Singers next, who sang a sweet and melancholy air; and after them, blowing very strongly for women and fingering cleanly, a square of pipers marched into the middle, and immediately everyone else, in the highest of spirits and with loud exclamations of delight, ran for a partner, and lifting their skirts and tossing aside their hats, danced in a hundred sets an Eightsome Reel, and followed with The Dashing White Sergeant, that filled the whole ground with a storm of colour and movement. Nothing could have shown more clearly their confidence and gaiety and beautiful long legs. Nothing could better have demonstrated their certainty of victory and supple figures. Laughing still, and still dancing, they swept in a broad tideway of chiffon and singing, of perfume and colour and white arms waving, into the impregnable Castle; and as they disappeared a desperate wild shout rose from the infuriated spectators, who hurled themselves, too late, against the thin blue line of ever-virtuous constables.

It was Lysistrata's habit to hold some such parade as this at noon, or soon after, whenever the weather was favourable. It was good for her rebels, who liked to show themselves off; and it kept the men, she thought, aware of what they were missing by their refusal to stop the silly war.

III

It would be an exaggeration to say that Britain was by now in a state of chaos. Some trains were still running, enough coal was hewed and distributed, milk was delivered, bread baked, and the postman came punctually. Indeed all but one of the essential services were decently maintained, and the Stock Exchange was still open; though prices had fallen as sharply as the spirit of its members, and there was a natural reluctance to provoke invidious attention by doing anything bullish. But despite an appearance of order and normality, the country was in a truly desperate condition. It was like a great ship that had struck a submerged wreck, and though the engines were still running, though the sailors dutifully went about their work, it was common knowledge that the water was gaining in every hold; and here and there a lesser riot broke out, the stokers were mutinous, the passengers but half-a-mood from panic.

The love-strike had spread with amazing rapidity. Lysistrata, in her few weeks of hurried preparation, had established centres of revolt in a dozen of the larger towns, and every one of them had been successful in creating an area of local rebellion. Prominent buildings had been seized and garrisoned. In Manchester the insurgents held the Midland Hotel; in Glasgow, the University; in Cardiff, the Municipal Centre; and elsewhere the women were in possession of other equally conspicuous or strategic positions. But even more important than these acts of large aggression was the wide diffusion of revolt. Countless women had declared a strike in their own homes. Others had made some little league and covenant among their neighbours, and in every street there was a house filled packfull of defiant women who with deliberate provocation advertised themselves to be marvellously inviolable.

Such tactics were, of course, responsible for many breaches of the peace, especially among the labouring classes. The labouring classes in Great Britain were distinguished from the rest of the world by their innate conservatism, and from the middle classes by their superior virility. They had therefore a double reason for being peculiarly incensed by the love-strike, and for a few days it was easy to distinguish a girl with whom some navvy or plasterer, miner or private soldier was deeply in love; for she would have a black eye or suchlike mark to prove it. In a very short time, however, working women discovered the flying column, and put a stop to corporal abuse. Their etiquette till now had prescribed non-interference with domestic quarrels; no matter how loud and distressing the cries from the next-door house or the adjacent room, a good neighbour would decently ignore them. But now policy demanded a new standard of manners, and presently a woman had only to scream once, fairly loudly, and all her neighbours came hot-foot to help her. Black eyes grew fewer and fewer, but more and more men were scratched and bitten and otherwise maltreated.

In a good many places pitched battles occurred. A Northumbrian mining village was the scene of a desperate encounter, in which the local rebels were rescued from defeat, in the nick of time, by a relief column from Newcastle. In the Black Country there was very severe fighting, and a Birmingham brigade, including a most redoubtable battalion from Edgbaston, won the highest praise for its mobility, the *élan* of

its attack, and its doggedness in defence. Its leaders showed
not only the most laudable resolution, but a strategic apprecia-
tion of the whole situation in the Midlands, and by fine co-
ordination with local commandants recorded notable victories
in such dangerous neighbourhoods as Walsall, Dudley, and
Smethwick. In London – the uncertain London that survived,
a great shapeless circumference about a core of ruin – the
women had everything their own way; and in Scotland, where
the inspiration of Lysistrata's leadership was most keenly felt,
they achieved a dominant position in spite of stubborn opposition. In Dundee, for example, there was a gruelling battle
when a hundred men of the Black Watch came home on leave
the day after the strike had started. They were met at the
station by their wives, mothers, and sweethearts, a committee
of the rebels, and a strong force of unattached mill-workers.
The Royal Highlanders, at first gratified by what appeared
to be a popular welcome, were sorely disappointed when they
learnt the truth of it, and the station became the scene of a
very wild and bloody affray. The mill-girls succeeded in taking
captive some twenty or thirty soldiers whom they shut in a
waiting-room. The prisoners immediately set it on fire, the
flames spread rapidly, and the fire brigade turned out. The
mill-girls then seized the fire-engines, and turning the hoses
against the infuriated soldiers, drove them off the field in much
discomfort and complete dejection. There was isolated bicker-
ing after this, but no major or concerted effort to break the
strike.

Among the middle and upper classes, however, in all parts
of the country, there was remarkably little violence. Stock-
brokers and teachers, doctors and baronets and temporary
officers, were on all sides defied and rejected by women with
whom they were mildly-to-madly in love; and they took the
rebuff with tears or a frown of annoyance, in a huff or a pique
or utter dismay; they were thrown into a state of derelict
gloom or a towering passion; they went off with a hurt or a
haughty expression; but not one in a hundred replied with a
swinging blow, with an elbow-smash, cross-buttock, or
effective body-slam. When the strike was over and Britain
again at peace, this mannerly forbearance was very warmly

commended, and critics of many nations and both sexes paid handsome tribute to the self-control, the natural chivalry, and well-taught reverence for womanhood of the British male – at least in the upper and middle classes. Their admiration, however, took no notice of another reason for his curious behaviour: which very often was sheer lack of imagination. Not for centuries had anyone in the politer circumstances of life done his wooing by the simple process of knocking a young woman on the head; and there remained no racial memory of this method. When, therefore, the well-brought-up British male was confronted by a love-striker, he was generally nonplussed. He found the ordinary means of courtship useless – the fussing about, the forestalling her wishes and giving her presents, the flattery of constant and close attention, the remembering her birthday and her relations, the listening to her little jokes and little opinions, the obedience to her likes and aversions – all these, the servile arts of love, were unavailing; and he knew no other, nor had one in a hundred of such gravelled citizens the gift of invention. Not one in a hundred, that is, had the wit to suppose a stubborn girl might have her ears boxed.

There were exceptions, of course. It was said that Lord Lomond had thrashed his wife, his three grown-up daughters, and most of his domestic staff with a rattan cane, when his deafness allowed him to hear that they were theoretically on the side of the love-strikers; and Julian Brown had immediately seen that such a rebellion could only be put down by force. Passion, too, had given to a fortunate minority instinctive knowledge of how to deal with the situation; but the great majority of decent men simply accepted defeat. It was possible, however – it was even probable – that their inertia would soon be thrown off. That they could endure so wretched a condition for long was hardly conceivable; but any considerable delay – occasioned by niceness of feeling, lack of initiative, and a masculine fear of ridicule – would be very dangerous to the women. Lysistrata could not hope to keep her rebels celibate for ever, and she as well as Lord Pippin knew that the longer the strike lasted, the less likely it was to succeed.

She had foreseen the danger, however, and lately made provision to meet it. The well-brought-up British male might suffer in gloomy silence and pitiable inaction the spoiling of his bed, but he was not likely to put up for very long with any derangement of his dinner-table. Lysistrata, therefore, had arranged that the strike should be extended to include domestic as well as connubial service; and a statement was also issued that women could give material help to the cause by upsetting the comfort of any men they knew in any fashion that might occur to them. This announcement produced some very ingenious and malicious devices, and the Edinburgh Ladies' Bridge Club immediately cancelled its forthcoming tournament with the Officers of General Puffin-Lumkyn's Staff.

On any fine morning – and a persistent anti-cyclone favoured Lysistrata's noon parades – the consequence of the embargo on domestic service could be seen in many strange effects in Princes Street, George Street, and Edinburgh's other shopping districts. Here was an irate solicitor buying a pound of sausages; there a haggard father endeavouring to placate an illdressed, unwashed, squalling child of four with a red balloon. An officer's batman went by, indignantly pushing a perambulator. A major of the Royal Field Artillery, spending cheerlessly his six-days' leave in a deserted house, could be seen buying a couple of lamb chops; and General Puffin-Lumkyn, superbly mounted on a tall bay horse and accompanied by a mounted groom, was bargaining with a fish-monger who, on the pavement beneath him, displayed for his inspection a large codfish. Not only had men to do their own marketing, but they had to carry home their purchases, because the shops were so short-handed they could not be delivered; and to many men the carrying of parcels was more irksome than any other effect of the strike. There was, indeed, a good deal of bad temper displayed as shoppers, heavy-laden, jostled each other in doorways and on the busy pavements; for some went about their errands with twitching cheek and burning eyes, walking with bitter haste as though to escape their present misery; and others with Byronic gloom would loiter, lost in thought, and dwell upon their unhappiness at every corner.

On the fourth morning of the strike there was an incident in Princes Street that openly betrayed the fretted nerves of the men, and gave the authorities some anxiety, not on account of any great damage that was done, but simply because it revealed the dangerously uncertain temper of the country.

A Professor of Edinburgh University – his name was Arrowburn, and his Chair the recently established one of Dialectic Materialism – came out of Mr Flockhart the chemist's with a large parcel under his arm; and collided with Mr Torquil Adair, a Chartered Accountant, who had also been shopping. Their impact was severe, and each let fall his parcel. It became evident that the Professor had just bought, among other things, four toilet-rolls; and Mr Adair's purchase had been a bushel or so of brussels sprouts.

'Where do you think you are going?' asked the irritated Professor.

'Oh, confound you!' cried Mr Adair.

They faced each other in anger, but both were timid men. The spirit of Mr Torquil Adair had long since failed beneath the burden of his romantic name; and the heart of Professor Arrowburn had been laid waste by Dialectic Materialism and his family of five young daughters. The incident might have been concluded in peace had not a Major Endive – whose love was in the Castle and his mind a furnace – taken a passing kick at one of the toilet-rolls, which opened into whirling streamers of white paper and wrapped itself round the stout figure of a certain Dr Prunty who was approaching from the opposite direction. Dr Prunty had spent many years in the East, and his disposition was inclined to be choleric. He too had been shopping, he disliked the burden of parcels, and felt strongly the indignity of being garlanded in paper. He hit the Major in the face with the large fowl he was carrying, and at the same moment Professor Arrowburn, endeavouring to escape from what was about to be a *fracas*, trod on a brussels sprout and fell heavily to the pavement. A small crowd gathered, and a subaltern in savage levity – he had recently been shell-shocked – tore open two of the remaining rolls of paper and flung their gross chaplets over the cinctured combatants; while a passing haberdasher who should have known better – but his wife was beautiful and she had left him – stooped to gather handfulls of brussels sprouts, and began to pelt everyone in sight because suddenly he hated them all.

The turbulence increased, and General Puffin-Lumkyn impatiently steered his horse into the middle of the road in order to pass it. He was following a plump and pretty young nurse. Nurses had remained on duty, and they were almost the only women, other than armed bands, who went freely about the streets. The General could not bear to lose sight of the charming creature, and when the agitated crowd discharged from its inner parts an uxorious teacher of mathematics in one of Edinburgh's well-known schools, who stumbled against the shoulder of his horse, he spoke rudely to him. 'Go to the devil yourself,' said the teacher of mathematics, and by a movement of the crowd was again flung against the horse, which grew frightened and reared. The codfish which the General was carrying – his groom was too heavily laden to take it – slipped from his hold and the paper surrounding it, and descended on the teacher of mathematics; who with a petulant remark threw it viciously at the General and caused him to tumble from his charger. The groom with a shout rode to his master's help, letting fall a number of parcels, and a plumber of Socialistic tendencies raised a shout of Tsarism. The plumber then picked up two pots of caviare, and with one of them stunned the groom, with the other broke a shop window.

The crowd by this time numbered at least two hundred, and many of them who had no reason at all for doing so, entered the combat with whatever missiles they had recently been buying; so that a shower of oranges might provoke the irrelevant throwing of a child's tricycle, and a pound of sausages counter the appropriate jaculation of a frying-pan. The psychological basis of the affray was obvious but interesting; and when by the discharge of their hated parcels the shoppers had eased a little of their repression, they grew suddenly quiet and ashamed of themselves, and wiping yolk-of-egg and vegetable fragments from their clothing, hurried away as fast as they could. The police arrested General Puffin-Lumkyn's groom, the plumber who had thrown the caviare, and Professor Arrowburn. The Professor would have escaped had he not thought it expedient to return to Mr Flockhart the chemist's in order to repeat his purchase.

During all this tumult, however, a long row of men, gloomily unaware of it, stood leaning against the railings on the south side of Princes Street. They stood there eternally, looking forlornly at the Castle enskied in bright blue air. Their faculties, it would seem, were completely paralysed by a catastrophe which their imagination, never having guessed at such a thing, could not wholly grasp.

IV

Hotels, though their staffs were much disorganized, did phenomenally good business during the strike, and every bar was always full of bereaved customers who bought each other drinks for the privilege of unburdening their hearts. They spoke of their wives as though they were newly dead. Never had there been such virtuous and splendid women, all in all to the husbands they had now deserted. Photographs were shown, and little anecdotes related that told, in simple words, of perfect happiness. A cynic would have hoarsely laughed; but there were no cynics left. They also were buying each other drinks, and talking of the Golden Age that once had been. Now and then some brash young man would say loudly that what was needed was vigorous action. The women, he would say, must be brought to their senses, and the sooner the better. But that sort of wild unfeeling talk was never popular in a pub. The other customers would look reproachfully at the brash young man, and shake their heads, and ask quietly for another drink. They showed more respect for tears, and if a man really broke down he was always given a drink on the house. Then, after another round, someone would look at the clock and say he must go now. He had to put the children to bed.

In the lounge of the Albyn Hotel, the largest and most fashionable in Edinburgh, talk went on much the same lines as in the humbler taverns. There was, perhaps, more solitary drinking – more who, like Childe Harold, nursed alone the sad knowledge that none did love them – but there was much unbosoming as well; and at any given moment the consensus of opinion would have been that the rebel women were unsurpassable for virtue, beauty, kindliness, and domestic efficiency.

About the same time as Professor Arrowburn was starting the riot in Princes Street, Julian Brown and Commander Lawless, meeting by chance at the main entrance of the Albyn, went in together. They knew each other slightly, for both were temporary members of the New Club – which had offered its hospitality to officers of the rank of major and upward – and they had shared in the first assault on the Castle.

Lawless looked even wilder than usual. His uniform was dirty, the crimson ribbon of his Victoria Cross was torn, a hank of bright yellow hair hung over his forehead; and on top of this habitual untidiness, he was strangely, unnaturally haggard, for he had just had all his teeth taken out. But he was in very good spirits, and the lugubrious widowers in the lounge looked at him reproachfully when they heard his cheerful lop-sounding voice.

'Here's to the strike,' he said over his gin. 'I hope it lasts a month.'

'If that's meant to be a joke,' said Julian, 'it's a poor one.'

'There's no joke about it. It isn't for beauty that my young woman loves me, but I don't want to try her affection too hard by letting her see me like this.' – He grimaced, and showed two naked gums. – 'For the present, being cheated of feature by dissembling nature and Surgeon-Bloody-Commander Runagate, a celibate life is what I want, and the veto on the Venerean ecstasy suits me down to the ground.'

'What was wrong with them?' asked Julian without much interest.

'Nothing, so far as I could see. But about a year ago I fell out of a theatre and hurt my leg, and every now and then I feel a sort of shooting pain in it. So I saw the doctor – Surgeon-Bloody-Commander Runagate – and he said I had rheumatism. Well, the next thing was an order to go to the dentist, who dredged up every tooth I had. But what I'm really sore about is that when I fell out of the theatre, it was Runagate who fell on top of me.'

Julian was a dull companion to this liveliness, for his mind, like a poor tightrope-walker, was balancing clumsily between self-pity and the impregnable Castle. It was a torment to think of Rose, but he coaxed and fondled every passing thought of her as though the image had been reality. And though he detested self-pity in others, he thought it excusable in himself, since he had lost so much. Her gaiety, the warmth of her loveliness, the proud and dear delight he had in her – and now this exile in a cold and ridiculous land where all who walked were figures of fun and the sky spelt only frustration! His loss – or rather the indignity of it – might have seemed more tolerable had he still been only a schoolmaster; but it was a bitter thing that a temporary Lieutenant-Colonel, with the Distinguished Service Order and the Military Cross, should be so treated. Nor did Julian conceal from himself this aggravation of his plight. He was a lover, passionate in his devotion; but he was also an officer, distinguished in his service; and these two could not be dissociated in the sum of his unhappiness. – Remembering his D.S.O., he felt more kindly towards Lawless. Lawless had the V.C., and in such times as these, when bravery was contemned, it was clearly desirable that those who had been decorated for bravery should stand together. He ordered another gin and orange bitters, and a second glass of sherry.

Presently they walked down Princes Street to the New Club, and had lunch together. Julian ordered cold beef and pickled walnuts, but Lawless, because of his toothless condition, asked for soup and a large whisky and soda. They had scarcely begun their meal when Lawless exclaimed, 'For God's sake change places! There's a man over there whose visage cloys the hungry edge of appetite. And if he sees mine, it will cloy his.'

It was Mr Comyn Curle whom he wished to avoid looking at, or being seen by. The Secretary for War was sharing a table with Sir Joseph Rumble at the other side of the room. He had a sour unhappy look, and from the evidence of his lunch – which consisted of a little steamed fish and half a bottle of Evian water – his digestion was upset.

'Are you married?' asked Lawlesss.

'No,' said Julian.

'There's something petty about a husband. Something petty and mean and selfish. – Soup!' he barked at the waiter who came to remove his plate. 'More soup, and another whisky and soda. – They're monopolists, and I hate the smug look of them. By God, when I ship my new dentures I'll go through their marriage service like a bull through a paper gate.'

Julian frowned, and began to wish that he had found other company for lunch. He looked forward to an exceedingly jealous lordship over Rose, if he should ever regain possession of her; and already his sympathy was all on the side of the married man who must defend his own against pirates. Lawless's mood, moreover, alternately an ebullient good humour and high-spirited irascibility, seemed to make his voice unnecessarily loud. He was attracting unnecessary attention. The waiter had obviously resented being shouted at, and clearly thought that soup and whisky was a strange meal for any gentleman to choose. As indeed it was. And now Lawless, letting his spoon fall with a clatter and leaning back in his chair, suddenly began to laugh uproariously.

'I'm sorry,' he exclaimed, 'but I can't help it. I've just remembered the look on Bulmer's face when he confessed to having broached the nunnery.'

'Who's Bulmer?'

'One of my honest sailormen. He's got the desperate melancholy look and the long swinging arms of an anthropoid ape. And a passionate nature. You ought to see him. And to think he went off all on his own, scaled the virgin rock, and penetrated the gynaeceum!'

'When?' demanded Julian. 'And how?'

'He's been in for the last two nights. He's got a young woman there. – Bring me another plate of soup, waiter. What? Well, if the last was ox-tail, make the next tomato. And another whisky and soda.'

'For God's sake forget about your soup for a minute, and tell me more about Bulmer. Don't you realize the importance of this? If he's found a way into the Castle, it will change the whole situation.'

'No, it won't. He goes up the side of the Rock, and then his young woman throws a rope over a wall somewhere. – She's Lady Lysistrata's maid, he told me. – But Bulmer's like a cat. You won't find anyone else who could tackle that Rock in the darkness.'

Julian was silent for a few minutes, while he considered with rising excitement and from different aspects the significance of what he had heard. Then he said, 'I've done some climbing myself. I used to go to Chamonix.'

'So you want to horn-in on the Romeo act? Well, I don't know. It's Bulmer's pigeon, and I can't promise anything, but he might take you along for a couple of quid or so. But don't blame me if you break your neck.'

'I wish you'd realize the importance of this, Lawless – you're not going to ask for more soup, are you?'

'I certainly am. – I'm going back to the ox-tail this time, waiter, and just a small whisky and soda. – That's Scrymgeour over there, isn't it? What's going to happen now that he's C.-in-C.? Somebody said he was going to break the strike by suing Lady Lysistrata for restitution of conjugal rights.'

General Scrymgeour was paying his bill at the desk. In the past twelvemonth his hair had gone grey, but his figure was as strong and soldierly as ever, and his flat Mongolian face showed no trace of anxiety or other emotion. His nomination as Commander-in-Chief of Home Defence, announced that morning, had been a surprise to everybody – though the supersession of General Puffin-Lumkyn had been long expected – and it was generally assumed that he had been appointed for the particular purpose of bringing the love-strike to an end. The fact that his wife was the leader of the insurgents did not lessen the interest with which his appointment was received; and even those who knew that his life had always been ruled by the most rigid and selfless conception of duty, could not help wondering what he would do if personal affection and public interest were now suddenly to pull different ways.

'I must tell him about Bulmer's discovery,' said Julian.

'Well, don't get one of my sailormen into trouble, will you?'

'You had better come and talk to Scrymgeour yourself.'

'No damned fear. I haven't finished my soup yet.'

'Then where can Bulmer be found when he's wanted?'

'Strictly speaking, he ought to be aboard my destroyer, but actually for the last few days he's been putting in most of his time – daylight time, that is – at 33 Rolyburn Place, Leith. That's the address of Lieutenant Peter McCombie, R.N.R., my Navigating Officer and one of our toughest hearts of oak, whose wife has petulantly blown. She's a striker. So Bulmer, being a handyman, is helping to look after the house and children.'

Julian inquired where Scrymgeour had gone, and found him in a small writing-room. He apologized for his intrusion, and said he had news of the utmost importance. The General listened attentively.

'Have you seen this man Bulmer?' he asked.

'No, sir.'

'It's the name of a fellow who was a hand on a small yacht I used to sail.'

'Lawless said that the woman whom Bulmer visits is Lady Lysistrata's maid.'

'Then it's the same man. He's got more initiative than I thought.'

A moment later he said, 'You were in my Division, weren't you?'

'Yes, sir.'

'And you organized the first attack on the Castle?'

'But unsuccessfully, sir.'

'We must do better the next time. Have you any experience yourself of rock-climbing?'

'I've done a little in the French Alps, sir.'

'Could you do a reconnaissance with this man Bulmer?'

'I should be very glad to try.'

Scrymgeour, in a leather arm-chair, sat with the solid un-relaxed immobility of a Chinese god. He did not lean comfortably back, nor tautly forward, but seemed in a rigid poise to simulate the petrified comfort of an idol. He was, to some extent, aware of the impassive appearance that he presented, for within the last few months, and especially within the last few days, he had cultivated it as a barrier against the outer world, and a stockade to guard his own feelings. To find Lysistrata in command of the women's rebellion had been for

him a tragic discovery. He cared little about the nature of the
rising. It might be undignified, ridiculous to some, in others'
eyes indecent. Such criticism did not affect him. It was the fact
of rebellion, the naked treasonable fact, that counted. In his
soldier's religion, treason was the largest sin, and to see his
own wife leading a revolt of such magnitude had not merely
wounded his love, nor astonished only his pride and confidence, but because of his integrity hurt him in his whole
being.

For a moment, but only a moment, he had been tempted to
refuse his new appointment. He knew the difficulty of the task
he was invited to undertake. He knew also that the Cabinet
was hopelessly divided, and no one would defend him if he
failed. Two of the Ministers had advised him to be quite ruthless; but their advice, they added, was strictly confidential.
Some thought he could be stern without being ruthless, and
others were of the opinion that military efficiency was, in the
circumstances, not incompatible with the utmost gentleness.
Several were flatly opposed to his appointment, others were
luke-warm, and the Prime Minister had pleaded for the re-
tention of Puffin-Lumkyn, a dilatory policy, and their old
alliance with time; but his opinion had been disregarded.
Everybody most earnestly desired that the rebellion should
speedily be put down, and nobody was willing to run the risk
of being charged with barbarism, or even unkindness, in putting it down. But the need was urgent to do something, and
finally they left Scrymgeour to deal as he thought best with the
more insoluble elements of the problem.

He had hesitated; and then, because Lysistrata was the
leader of the rebels and he had that disgrace to wipe out, he
had accepted the nomination they offered. He could, he
thought, quite easily defeat the rebels in their various strongholds; but he was not very sure of being able to do it in a
wholly inoffensive manner; and he mentioned this difficulty to
Julian. The discovery that there was an unsuspected, and
presumably unguarded entrance to the Castle, was therefore
of considerable importance. If he could take the garrison by
surprise, he need use a minimum of violence, and with its
leaders in captivity, the whole rebellion might collapse.

Making a sudden movement he got out of his chair, and thanked Julian most warmly for the valuable information he had brought. 'It may be very helpful indeed,' he said, 'and I'm particularly glad that it's one of my own officers – an officer of the Fifth Division – who has come to my assistance in this way. Now where can I get hold of Bulmer?'

A minute or two later Julian left him with the well-contented feeling of a man who has done his country useful service, and attracted the favourable attention of his Commander-in-Chief. He felt that Rose might not unreasonably be comforted for the failure of the strike by her pride in him, when she learnt that he had played no inconsiderable part in bringing about its collapse.

From the stairway overlooking the hall he saw Lawless in cheerful conversation with another Naval officer; and waited till they should go.

Their voices were loud, their manner was animated; but what was the meaning or relevance of their conversation it was impossible to tell.

'And then we tied 'em all up in bags,' said Lawless with a happy laugh.

'Sacks, old boy,' said the other officer. 'Not bags, sacks.'

'Well, we called them bags. Potato-bags.'

'There's no such thing, old boy. They were sacks. Potatosacks.'

'But it wasn't potatoes, it was men we put in 'em. Thirteen full-grown men. In potato-bags.'

'You couldn't put a full-grown man in a bag, old boy. It must have been a sack.'

'Well, what the hell does it matter, anyway?'

'It doesn't matter a bit, old boy. Let's go and play snooker.'

'Snooker! That's the very thing.'

And sacks, thought Julian, might be the very thing for which he had been canvassing his mind.

V

Lysistrata's orderly-room was the right-hand lower one in the Governor's House. It was there that she dealt with the perpetual task of administration and the recurrent problems of discipline. The garrison had, on the whole, behaved with remarkable virtue. There had inevitably been a few cases of insubordination – but very few, because the discipline was as mild as possible – and daily she had had to punish a score or two of impenitent young women who had stolen each others' stockings; or impugned the morals and complexion of some sensitive neighbour; or been surprised in a hurried cuddle at the gate with the milkman or the grocer's boy. There had been misdemeanours of this minor sort, and difficulties had several times arisen when some well-behaved girl began to weep on parade, and infected a whole company with the same disorder. Nor had it been easy to refuse to let a girl attend her father's funeral; till evidence was brought that her father lived in Neckarboo, some four hundred miles from Melbourne. Others had sought leave of absence from the Castle on various grounds; several declared they had left the light burning in their houses, or a tap running; others were filled with a sudden anxiety for the welfare of their mothers; and one ingenious young woman had by the use of bed-clothes given herself a curious figure and sworn she was about to have a baby. But on the whole Lysistrata could congratulate herself on the good behaviour of her garrison. No serious crime – except for the desertion of a couple of sentries – had been brought to light until this morning. And now the criminal was none other than Horrocks, her own maid.

At a quarter to four that morning, about half an hour before sunrise, Horrocks had been seen with a sailor. She was bidding him an affectionate good-bye, and presumably he had been in the Castle for some considerable time. They were standing under the wall behind and below the large building that had at one time been the Armoury. After helping him over she had pulled up a rope, tied it round her waist, and hidden it under a raincoat. She had then returned to her quarters. The sentry who saw her had reported the incident to the Sergeant of the Guard, who had immediately notified the Officer of the Day, who promptly put Horrocks under arrest – she had to be wakened from a sound sleep – and discovered the rope in her bed.

When formally accused she would neither deny her guilt nor

admit it. She stood speechless before Lysistrata, stubborn though ashamed. In the unfortunate position in which she found herself, her appearance did not materially help her. Her thin sharp-featured face was uncommonly sallow, and between the two exceptionally well-built young women who guarded her, her figure looked even flatter and less attractive than usual. She could not plead that beauty made her willy-nilly an irresistible lure. Neither to starry eyes nor Cupid's mouth nor snowy breast could she point and say, '*It is the cause, my soul.*' Though Leander had so much changed as to become a mountaineer, it was nothing to the difference between Hero and Horrocks. Yet beyond any reasonable doubt she had a lover so hot and resolute that he was ready to climb the formidable Castle Rock to come and see her; and Mrs Curle, who sat beside Lysistrata, stared at her in blank amazement.

'Who was the man?' asked Lysistrata.

Horrocks did not reply.

'Was it Bulmer?'

Horrocks made a defiant movement, as if about to speak; but thought again and said nothing.

'You are charged with a very serious offence, Horrocks, and you are not making it less serious by a show of obstinacy. I don't want to deal harshly with you, but you are not giving me a chance to deal leniently. If you have any good excuse for your behaviour, I shall be only too glad to hear it, because I am very unwilling to believe that you, whom I have known and trusted for so long, would deliberately endanger the garrison and the success of our whole campaign. On you, more than anyone else here, I thought I could rely to the utter-most. . . .'

'Oh, don't, don't!' cried Horrocks suddenly. 'Don't talk like that, I can't bear it! Send these women away, and I'll tell you everything.'

The orderly-room clerks, the sergeant, and the guards looked indignant. But after a moment's thought Lysistrata turned to Mrs Curle: 'Would you mind if I were to question the prisoner in private?'

'Darling, of course not,' cried Mrs Curle.

'It's irregular, I know, but the case is important, and I think we shouldn't let our investigations be hindered by formality.'

'Indeed we shouldn't, and it's sweet of you to apologize. – But you'll tell me afterwards, won't you? – Come on, sergeant. Tell the girls to quick-march.'

For a little while after they had gone there was silence; and then Horrocks, with a sniff and a brave attempt to justify herself, explained: 'I wasn't going to tell *them* about Bulmer. It isn't any business of theirs.'

'So it was Bulmer?'

'Yes, madam. And that's why I didn't want to say anything before *them*, because they wouldn't have believed the special circumstances of the case.'

'What circumstances?'

'Well, his being my nephew, madam.'

'Oh yes. Yes, I'd forgotten. But that is still the relationship between you, is it?'

'Yes, madam.'

'But Horrocks, you must understand this: we're a garrison surrounded by enemies, and even nephews aren't allowed to visit us. Especially nephews who are forty years old and seamen in the Navy.'

Horrocks grew tearful again. 'But I'm all he has, madam. He's an orphan, and he relies on me for everything. He needs me, madam! He said so only last night.'

'When is he coming back?'

'Tonight, if it's dark enough.'

'He's found a path up the Rock, has he?'

'Yes, madam. It used to worry me at first, thinking he'd be sure to fall and break his neck. But he says it isn't really dangerous, so long as you're active and don't lose your head. And Bulmer's got a very good head for heights, considering how full-blooded he is.'

With deliberate severity, and intentional repeated reference to the faith she had formerly had in her, Lysistrata chided her wanton maid till she reduced her to tearful penitence. Then she said, 'Now you must show me exactly where Bulmer gets over the wall, and tell me when you expect him tonight. Is there any signal that he uses, to let you know he's there?'

'He whistles, and I whistle back if the coast's clear.'

'Then you'll have to whistle in the usual way tonight, and reassure him.'

'Are you going to let him come in again?'

'Yes. But he won't get out this time.'

'You mustn't hurt him!'

'No, we shan't do him any harm.'

'You promise, madam?'

'I give you my word, Horrocks. In the meantime you will have to go back to the cells – I'll decide on your punishment later – and some time this afternoon you must help me to plan Bulmer's reception.'

Her guards returned, and Horrocks was removed. Mrs Curle, full of excitement and curiosity, wanted to be told immediately every word that had been uttered, and Lysistrata could hardly persuade her to wait until they had done with orderly-room. – There was one more case, said the red-haired matronly sergeant.

The last case was an application from Ivy FitzAubrey for release from the service in the love-strike and permission to leave the Castle on the grounds of ill-health.

'That girl has been nothing but a nuisance right from the beginning,' said Mrs Curle indignantly.

Ivy had given them a lot of trouble. She had complained about the food and the accommodation, and offended many of her fellow-strikers by an assumption of superiority which they thought unwarranted. Within twenty-four hours she had shown a talent for making mischief and enemies, and from the second day she had regularly attended sick-parade. Her health, she explained pathetically, had never been good, and the excitement of the strike was too much for her. Her heart was weak, she had fainted several times, and always at inopportune moments.

'I was talking to the Doctor about her this morning,' said Lysistrata. 'She said her heart-sounds are definitely not normal, but almost certainly she's not so ill as she pretends. What do you think about her, sergeant?'

'She's malingering,' said the red-haired matronly sergeant. 'But she's doing a lot of harm to the other girls, and you ought to get rid of her.'

'That's what I think,' said Mrs Curle.

'Well, bring her in.'

Ivy was looking pale and ill, for she wore no make-up and she had been eating a little toilet-soap to upset her heart. Her hair, brushed lankly down, made her face look thinner than usual, and her grass-green frock accentuated her pallor. Her only ornament was Lady Oriole's o.b.e.

'Oh, I do feel so ill!' she exclaimed. 'Do you mind if I sit down? I just hate to trouble you, Lady Lysistrata, but really and truly I'm not fit for a life like this. It's simply wearing me out, and I can't sleep at night, with my heart beating, and. . . .'

'Yes, I've seen your medical report,' said Lysistrata. 'I'm sorry you think you're not fit for garrison duty. According to the Doctor there is probably nothing seriously wrong with you, but you may need a rest. So I'm prepared to let you go if you will give me your promise to maintain the principles of the strike outside.'

'You mean, not to have anything to do with men? Oh, as if I would! Why, in the state I'm in, it would kill me, and anyway that's not the sort of thing that appeals to me in general. There's more in life than that, I always say.'

'Are you able to go out by yourself, and is there anyone who can look after you when you get home?'

'Oh yes, I can still walk, thank goodness, and a breath of fresh air'll do me good, I think. – Well there's plenty of air here, of course, but it seems different, being cooped-up, doesn't it? And my landlady will look after me. You ought to see the way she mothers me. Breakfast in bed, and everything. – But there, you're busy, aren't you? Well, I do think it's sweet of you to see my point of view, because after all I owe it to myself to look after my health, don't you think? It's all that a girl has, in a way. And really Lady Lysistrata, I'm ever so sorry that I can't help you any more, and it's been such a pleasure to know you. But perhaps we'll meet again some time, and if we don't there'll be no ill-feeling, will there? Well, ta-ta. Ta-ta, Mrs Curle. I'll send for my things, sergeant.'

'My dear,' said Mrs Curle, 'she's simply a bitch!'

'Yes,' said Lysistrata, 'but I'm sorry to let any of the

garrison go. It may give the other side an idea that we're weakening.'

'She can do less harm out of the Castle than in it,' said the sergeant comfortingly.

VI

Ivy went lightly down the causeway, singing as she went, and having triumphantly shown her exeat to the sentries, halted on the pavement beyond the drawbridge to make up her face. But she was in a hurry to get home, and paused only for a hasty application of rouge and powder and lipstick. How good it was to be free of that ghastly nunnery! She hated women. And had she not been wise when, as a girl at school, she had learnt how to faint when she liked! And it was brave of her to have eaten so much soap, for the taste was horrible – she opened her bag and threw away a thin violet cake – and for all she knew it might be dangerous. But it had worked. It had deceived the Doctor, and now she was free. She wondered how she had ever been so silly as to join that dreadful unnatural strike. Why, it would be quite a treat to see Mr Small again.

She had a flat in Howe Street. She went straight there, and taking off her shoes and her green frock, put on a dressing gown and mules, and got a bottle of brandy and some ginger ale from a cupboard under the stairs. She mixed a horse's neck and drank it with great enjoyment. The Castle was dry – another sign of the unnatural nature of the strike – and she hadn't had a drink for days. God, what a fool she'd been! She got up and wandered about the flat, opening a drawer here, and a cupboard there, and found a strange enjoyment in the sight of her familiar things. She opened a window, and leaning out saw two men walking in the direction of Heriot Row. She could hardly restrain a temptation to whistle to them.

Then she had another drink, and wondered if she would ring-up Mr Small or wait till the evening. She decided to wait, and lighting a cigarette lay down on her broad comfortable bed. It was lovely to have a bed like that. She had never had a decent night's sleep in the Castle. She stretched herself luxuriously, and thought she might as well undress properly and have a really good rest. At first she was too excited by thoughts of freedom to sleep, but she finished her second drink, and presently grew drowsy. She turned on her side, drew the quilt to her ears, and curled up like a cat.

It was a little after six when she woke, and her first thought was of Mr Small. She reached for her telephone and dialled the number of his flat.

And unknown voice answered her, the voice of a discharged soldier whom Mr Small had engaged when his female staff went on strike. No, it said, he's just gone out. It didn't know where, nor when he would return. It was a rough unsympathetic voice, and offered no help.

Ivy telephoned to the Ministry of Munitions. After a long time a caretaker told her that Mr Small had left about five o'clock, and said she would probably find him at his flat or perhaps in the Conservative Club. She rang-up the Club first. He had not been there. Nor, when she tried again half-an-hour later, had he returned to his flat.

She was feeling hungry by now, and disappointment always made her furious. She went to the larder, but found nothing fit to eat except a bottle of olives, which she opened. After eating a couple she poured out another drink. She felt the room colder than it had been, and switching on the electric fire began to feel sorry for herself. 'Oh, hell!' she exclaimed, and drank half the brandy at a gulp. Then she went back to the telephone, and stood uncertain which number to call first.

VII

Had Ivy telephoned a little earlier, Mr Small would have welcomed her with rapture and an immediate invitation to dinner. He was in a state of profound melancholy, and loneliness compelled him to explore its blackest caverns and most abysmal gloom. The horrors and chimaeras that he discovered in this fearful darkness were none the less real because he knew that they and all their noisome tenement would promptly vanish if he had some true congenial friend to stand beside him. But he could think of no sufficient comrade except Ivy, or Tom Hogpool. And Tom Hogpool had never quite forgiven him for stealing Ivy; while Ivy, so he believed, was still in the impregnable Castle.

The love-strike had robbed him of all his confidence and a host of easy friendships. It had filled him with a superstitious fear, as though he had seen nature renounce its laws and proclaim a cosmic anarchy. Had the sun taken to rising in the west and moonlight become hot as day, he could hardly have been more pitiably astonished. And in this mood he was no company for the easy friends he had attracted by an appearance of genial success, and kept in the magnetic field of his jocular vitality; they had, moreover, their own troubles, that made many of them live miserably in a loneliness from which they could not escape; and when the magnitude of so much that had previously seemed of moment was belittled by the indisputable gravity of the present situation, the social importance of a Cabinet Minister could hardly escape a similar diminishment.

Mr Small, then, was living in a solitude to which he had never been accustomed, and which he found unbelievably distasteful. If Ivy had wakened a little earlier he would have welcomed her like a self-abhorrent vacuum opening its doors to a summer breeze. But she slept too long, and ten minutes before she telephoned, he had gone out. He had decided that Tom Hogpool, even though he had not wholly forgiven him, would be better company than none.

The had met, of course, many times since Ivy in the stream of self-interest changed horses; and their relations, rapidly improving from an open quarrel, had now become but little worse than normal. Hogpool had grown richer and richer as the war went on, and he was interested in so many lucrative undertakings, from a new poisonous gas to a new factory making bamboo crosses for soldiers' graves, that his present wealth was almost incalculable. He lived, however, in a smallish flat in Moray Place, for as he accumulated more and more money, and so became more and more interested in it, he grew less and less willing to spend it. He never grudged his own comfort, or immediate luxury. But he had begun to dislike unnecessary display, and even to think it rather wicked.

Mr Hogpool was out, said a man-servant. But Mr Small said that he was in no hurry, and would wait. He was shown into a large richly furnished room, and as he came in a tall girl, of dark and resplendent beauty, turned inquiringly from the window where she had been standing.

Mr Small's first sensation was a jealous and disloyal astonishment. She left Ivy at the post, he thought. And that double-dealing, grab-all, dunghill-blossom Hogpool had body-snatched her! But in a moment he put away these ungentle thoughts; Tom was his friend, and he loved Ivy with a most passionate fidelity. This girl was nothing to him. Absolutely nothing. He could not deny, however, that she was a winner to look at. Swart as a raven, with the flashing beauty of some country that lived closer to the sun than England. Her nose was slightly aquiline, her complexion olive. She had eyes that were darkly luminous under inky brows, and she carried her head proudly ... Mr Small introduced himself with some diffidence, and was much surprised when she replied in a strong American accent.

'Come on in,' she said. 'I've been alone all day, and you just can't think how tired I get of my own company.'

'That must be a unique experience,' said Mr Small gracefully.

'How's that?'

Mr Small explained his compliment, and she appeared to be grateful for it.

'It's sweet of you to say so,' she exclaimed, 'and you must think I'm pretty dumb not to have seen it for myself. But honestly, for that last few months I've been more used to beefs than bokays, and I suppose I've got out of the way of expecting them.'

She had just spent a year in Hollywood, she said, and confessed that all her hopes had been disappointed. It appeared that the moving-picture industry was a lousy racket. Either you didn't get any work in months, or you had to work your pants off. 'When you're on a job, you begin early and end the next morning,' she said. So Hollywood having gone completely sour in her opinion, she had packed up and come home to get a lay-off.

'Home?' inquired Mr Small.

'Sure. Why, you didn't think I was American, did you?'

'Well, you have such a charming American accent ...'

'Why, that's what everybody says, Mr Small, and I just can't understand it! My home town's Bootle – I was born there, and everything – and it seems to me I speak just like I always did.'

'Then Bootle must have changed since I knew it.'

'Oh no, a town doesn't change like that. – But say, you were being funny, weren't you? Aw gee, I'm getting all my signals balled-up. You'll think I'm really dumb in a minute. How about I shake a cocktail? That'll maybe brighten me up a bit.'

Mr Small was beginning to enjoy himself. He had felt a little bashful to begin with, but her rather haughty appearance, the aristocratic poise of her head and the droop of her eyelids, apparently meant nothing at all. Or, to be more accurate, he thought, they indicated a natural dignity, but no tiresome affectation of it. She was positively friendly; not a bit cold and aloof, as he had feared. And he was glad that she was English despite her accent. American girls, so he had always understood, had very expensive habits. Not that it really mattered to him, of course – she was Tom Hogpool's friend, and Ivy was the only woman for whom he cared – but in some way or other it put him more at his ease to know that she was a Bootle girl. It was a friendly town.

'You don't know my name, do you?' she inquired. 'Well, it's Mavis Ramona.'

'That's a good old Lancashire name,' said Mr Small light-heartedly.

'Well, it may be, but I never heard it till I went to Hollywood,' said Mavis earnestly. 'They just invented it for me, because they said I was sort of Spanish looking. – But say, you were kidding again! Well, if you aren't just the regular old kidder!'

With a complacent smile Mr Small accepted a cocktail – a cabinet containing a large assortment of bottles and glasses was part of the furniture of the room – and inquired, 'What's Tom doing with himself these days? I haven't seen him for the last week or two.'

'Oh, he's busy about some new company he's starting,' said Mavis. 'He thinks maybe the war's going to stop, so he's got hold of a patent for making artificial stone. He reckons it'll come in useful for war memorials.'

'There may be something in that,' said Mr Small thoughtfully.

'He's a lousy old mossback,' said Mavis.

'You don't mean Tom?'

'Yeah. I used to know him before I went to America, and he was different then. He'd give a girl a swell time. But now he doesn't think of anything but making money, and I haven't hardly seen him for the last three days. Oh, I know he's busy. They say he's just about as well heeled with sugar as any guy there is nowadays, and that would keep anyone busy. But what's the use of having plenty of jack if you don't kick it in? He's just getting an old tightwad, Mr Small.'

Mr Small, without being dogmatic about it, took it upon himself to defend his old friend's behaviour; but in some curious fashion his rehabilitation of Mr Hogpool's character became an exposition of his own. In temperament, he explained, they were as different as the poles. He admired old Tom for his energy, his commercial genius, his resolute determination to be a rich man; he had shown that a poor boy, if his nature was a bit brutal to start with, and later on became absolutely ruthless, could overcome all the handicaps of poverty, and lack of education, and absence of moral scruple. Yes, Tom was an admirable fellow. But he did not envy him. He himself had been a shy and rather poetical youth, who had grown up with the romantic notion that one ought to be of service to one's fellow-men, and do something, however little, to smooth away the roughness of life for those less fortunate than oneself. Well, to a man like Tom, of course, that sort of ambition was merely silly. But he had stuck to it. He had devoted his life to the service of others – in politics, Miss Ramona – and he thought he could say that his efforts had been attended with some success. And when he spoke of success, he did not, of course, refer to the fact that he was now a Cabinet Minister. . . .

Mavis had not been aware of his rank. 'Well, dog my hide!' she exclaimed with admiration. 'And here I've been talking to you just like you were a guy I'd met-up with in a whistle-stop for visiting firemen!'

The cocktail cabinet was almost as productive as Pandora's

box, and having finished the sidecar that Mavis had first shaken, Mr Small helped her to mix another, equally agreeable, from Bacardi rum, Grand Marnier, and a little lime-juice.

'Mud in your eye!' she observed with growing friendliness.

'Here's to our better acquaintance,' said Mr Small.

By half past seven Mavis had described, with interesting detail, some of the hardships of life in Hollywood; Tom Hogpool had not yet returned; and Mr Small had suggested dinner in the Albyn Hotel. Mavis, having again described Tom Hogpool as an old mossback, said that he deserved whatever was coming to him, and accepted the invitation with pleasing alacrity. In the cab that took them to the hotel she allowed him to put his arm round her, and declared she would rather sit and dunk pretzels in beer with a man she liked, than dine on breasts of guinea-fowl with a guy that didn't appeal to her.

As they walked through the lounge, that was full of lonely men, Mr Small felt again the buoyancy of spirit that he had always experienced when he took Ivy out to dinner; for Mavis attracted the attention of everyone there, and he used all the envious glances, and the rustle of whispered comment, to inflate his self-confidence to its former taut abundance. He entered the restaurant, where again they drew every jealous gaze, with the air of one whom life had acknowledged to be its master.

VIII

In the lounge a stout, pink-faced, bald-headed man, who wore a worried look and a brightly-patterned tweed suit, emitted a softly expressive whistle when Mr Small went by with Mavis. To the two Naval officers who sat at the next table he observed, 'Well, that was a fine bit of stuff, wasn't it? I wouldn't mind putting 'er on the pay-roll, if there was anything in the bank to pay 'er with.'

His chance-got neighbours were Commander Lawless and Lieutenant McCombie; and Lawless in a friendly way replied, 'A nice bit of stuff, as you say. A whitely wanton with a velvet brow, in fact, and two pitch-balls stuck in her face for eyes. You prefer brunettes?'

'Well, I wouldn't go so far as to say I'd specialized,' said the stout worried man.

He sighed, and presently ordered another whisky and soda; and Lawless and McCombie resumed their discussion of the latter's domestic difficulties. His wife had been one of Lysistrata's earliest recruits, and had been sent to Glasgow to assist in the organization of the love-strike there. She was a strong-minded woman – she had been a school-teacher and still believed that humanity needed education – and she had had no hesitation in discarding her domestic responsibilities, which included the care of three children, for the sake of teaching the general public a lesson. She had decided, moreover, that it would do the children good to learn how to look after themselves; there was a girl of eleven, and two boys of six and nine. They were old enough to fend for themselves, she said. And so they had, to their own perfect satisfaction; but the house, said McCombie, looked as though a grizzly bear had littered in it. For a couple of days he had sent Bulmer along, to tidy things up and keep an eye on the youngsters; but now Bulmer, for some mysterious reason, had been borrowed by General Scrymgeour, and there was no one else whom he cared to entrust with a housekeeping job, or who would take it on. He didn't know what the hell to do.

Suddenly their pink-faced neighbour exclaimed, 'And there's another! Oh, mother, buy me one of those!'

A tall fair girl, orchidaceous in her beauty and incongruously partnered by a thick-set red-eared man of brutal appearance, was going through the lounge. A cynosure in any circumstances, she was now, in this melancholy environment of widowed men, the object of such intense and troubled regard as stirs a desert tribe when some new planet scars with silver a long dead segment of the sky; and like a wind, that in a desert speaks only of desolation, a general sigh rose and accompanied her into the restaurant beyond. 'There's more good-looking women in there than I've seen in a week,' said McCombie.

'Strike-breakers, I suppose,' said the pink-faced man.

'Blacklegs,' exclaimed Lawless with a shout of laughter. 'Patriotic piebalds whose honour rooted in dishonour stands.'

'You're drinking too fast,' said McCombie.

'I need it all. I'm so heavily soup-logged I can't answer

my helm. I'm ten inches over the Plimsoll mark in pottages, and drink lightens the load.'

'It's a comfort,' said the pink-faced man with a sigh. 'It helps you to forget.'

'You're drowning a woman's smile, I suppose?'

'No, as matter of fact I'm not worrying about them so much. It's my father-in-law I'm thinking of.'

'I'm delighted to hear it,' said Lawless. 'That's a nice unorthodox note to strike.'

The pink-faced man produced a large visiting card on which was engraved the name *Billy Burstin*. 'That's who I am,' he said. 'I've been playing at the Royal this week, one of the best dates there is, but as soon as I 'eard from my father-in-law about the predicament that he's in – his wife went and left him, to join the strikers, of course, and 'e can't bear living alone – I went to the manager and told 'im I'd 'ave to go. Well, that's when the trouble started. I 'appened to be broke, and he was so annoyed that 'e wouldn't lend me anything. So then I thought I could raise a bit of money on my props, but there isn't a pawnbroker in Edinburgh who'll look at them. They're good costumes too, female of course, through me being a female impersonator, but it seems that every pawnshop is full to the roof with women's clothes. Because that's the first thing that a lot of men did: pawned all the dresses their wives had left behind them.'

Billy Burstin had fame enough to elicit the interest of casual acquaintances. He was a robust comedian whose honest repertory ranged from the Widow Twankey, in the pantomime season, to an hilarious misrepresentation of landladies, termagant widows, and unlovable mothers-in-law. But though he portrayed the most insufferable characters, he had a heart of melting kindness which often left him penniless and still prompted him to succour distress wherever he heard of it. Such was his unhappy condition now. It was, he said, a most pitiable letter that his father-in-law had written.

'Where does he live?' asked Lawless.

'Weston-super-Mare. That's where he went when he retired. 'E was in the profession too.'

'What's the fare?'

'To Weston? About two pound ten. But that wouldn't be enough, because there's my uncle. 'E'd have to come too. He's my dresser, though actually he isn't much use. But I take 'im round with me because it keeps him cheerful. He was a very good operatic tenor in his time, but he tried to commit suicide one night by cutting his throat, and that spoiled his voice for good and all. Gambling was 'is trouble, and still is, for that matter.'

'So you want a fiver? Have you got any money, McCombie? Well, lend me two pounds.'

Taking three pounds from his own pocket-book, and adding two from McCombie's, Lawless said loudly, 'Put money in thy purse. I will do all my abilities in thy behalf, Mr Burstin. A man so tender of his spearside deserved well of the world. You, McCombie, will be a father-in-law yourself some day; would you wish to have a better goodson than Herr Burstin?'

Billy Burstin's gratitude was warm and verbose, but before accepting the money he carefully made a note of Lawless's name and address, and then insisted that he and McCombie should accompany him at once to the railway station, which adjoined the hotel and was accessible by a side door. As they had little better to do, and had drunk enough to be easily indulgent, they followed him after no longer delay than was necessary for the ordering and quick-swallowing of three small whiskies and soda; and he led them decisively to the left-luggage repository.

'I've got them here,' he said, 'and you'll find they're good security.'

'What have you got?' asked Lawless.

'The props, of course.' And with a heave the porter on duty lifted to the counter a strong wicker basket as big as a cabin-trunk.

'But I don't want them! A collection of female costumes isn't any good to me.'

'Then I can't accept your loan. I don't borrow money from strangers, it doesn't matter how friendly they are, except on the best security.'

The anomaly in Billy Burstin's reasoning provoked a rather muddled argument. But it was an amiable quarrel, wholly

unlike the acrimony that had gathered about the table where
Mavis and Mr Small were dining.

The fair-haired orchidaceous girl and her companion of
brutal appearance, who had attracted so much attention as
they went through the lounge were Ivy FitzAubrey and Tom
Hogpool. They had met by chance in the entrance hall of the
hotel. Ivy, by persistent telephoning, had at last discovered
the whereabouts of Mr Small; Tom Hogpool, arriving home
to find Mavis gone, had learnt the name of her captor, put
through a couple of quick calls, and traced them to the same
location. He had driven straight to the hotel, and driven
swiftly; he was one of the few people whose wealth and
national importance permitted them to use a motor-car.

He nodded churlishly to Ivy. 'We've come on the same
errand, have we?' he said.

'It depends on what your errand is,' said Ivy coldly.

'Well, you'll soon see.'

'I've come to look for Mr Small, as a matter of fact.'

'So have I,' said Hogpool.

They said nothing more, but threaded together the populous
lounge – Ivy haughty and Hogpool grim – and entered the
restaurant. Mr Small and Mavis, seated comfortably at a
corner table, were unpleasantly astonished to see them.

Tom Hogpool opened the conversation. 'You dirty foot-
pad!' he exclaimed.

'Now don't lose your buttons, Mr Hogpool,' replied Mavis.

'And you're a slippery piece, aren't you?'

'Well, well, Ivy!' said Mr Small. 'This is a pleasant surprise.
I certainly didn't expect to see you tonight. What's happening
up at the Castle? They haven't called off the strike, have they?
– Now, Tom, there's no need to talk like that, or to look like
that either. I went round to see you a little while ago, and as
you weren't in I asked Miss Ramona to come out and have
dinner with me. So that's all there is to it. And now you and
Miss FitzAubrey had better sit down, and we'll have a little
party.'

'I should choke,' said Ivy decisively.

'You get up and put on your hat,' said Hogpool to Mavis.
'You're coming home with me.'

'Say that again,' she answered imperturbably, 'and we'll give it the horse laugh.'

'You're coming home with me,' he repeated more loudly.

'If you want to give imitations of an Ioway hogcaller, you'd better go outside.'

A waiter, bringing chairs for the newcomers, momentarily interrupted the conversation. Hogpool at first refused to take a seat, but Mr Small, with a sudden access of authority, leaned across the table, and in a low voice, fierce despite the tremor in it, whispered, 'Sit down, Tom! And for God's sake try to behave as if you hadn't been brought up under the kitchen sink!'

Hogpool obeyed. With sullen defiance he looked round the room, and was somewhat abashed – as Mr Small had been – when he saw that nearly everyone present was watching them attentively. Mavis and Ivy were objects of general interest, and the diners at the nearer tables had also remarked their brief but spirited altercation. At the next table a young officer – it was the impetuous Master of Ballantyne – had turned right round in his chair to get a better view of them; and it was obvious that Mavis in particular was the mark of his admiration. Hogpool glared at him, fiercely but ineffectually, and with relief, almost indeed with a feeling of affection, heard Mr Small order another bottle of champagne. He was a low, dirty, sneak-thieving fraud, was old Perce – so he thought – but you couldn't help liking him. When they were boys together it was Percy who'd had the brains, and put him in the way of thinking big. If it hadn't been for Perce he might never have got ambitious, and made a millionaire of himself. But for all that he was damned if he was going to let Perce get away with Mavis. Too bloody true he wasn't.

Mr Small was now using all his charm to make the party a success. He and Mavis were half-way through their dinner, but he halted the procession of courses till Tom and Ivy should have caught up with them, and by a display of unceasing geniality endeavoured to infect the others with the *bonhomie* that he so earnestly simulated. But Ivy and Mavis had not taken to each other. Mavis was doing her best to help on the benevolent efforts of Mr Small, and vigorously laughed at all his jokes. But the more she laughed, the more Ivy disliked her, and tried more earnestly to monopolize Mr Small and divide the party into two.

'Miss Ramona,' said Mr Small with a social smile, 'tells me that she comes of an old Spanish family, and that one of her ancestors was the Grand Inquisitor.'

'I never said any such thing!' declared Mavis. 'I told you I came from Bootle, and so I do. – Aw gee, if he isn't still kidding! Say, this guy's just the greatest old kidder you ever saw.'

Ivy, ignoring this exchange, said earnestly to Mr Small: 'You've no idea what it was like in the Castle! We all had to do parades from morning till night, just like soldiers, and I got that dead-beat I just couldn't go on any longer. And I was feeling very unhappy, of course, being away from you for such a long time. So I went to Lady Lysistrata and just told her that my health wouldn't stand it any longer.'

'Poor little girl,' said Mr Small, combining sympathy with an anxious watch over the other two.

Tom Hogpool had been talking to Mavis in a low voice, and she suddenly exclaimed, 'Oh, for God's sake what's eating you? Lay off that stuff, will you?'

'Tell us that story about the negro and the Southern judge, Miss Ramona,' interposed Mr Small. 'You know, the one you told me a little while ago.'

'Well, there was a nigger called Mose,' said Mavis obediently, 'and the charge against him was operating a mule under the influence of intoxicants . . .'

Ivy put her elbow on the table, and leaning forward turned her shoulder against Mavis. She addressed Mr Small, exclusively, and with an emotion that he could not disregard. 'But all the hardships at the Castle,' she said, 'were nothing to the misery I felt when I got home, and rang you up, and couldn't find you. I just sat and cried for ever so long. And then to come here and see you with another girl! It was enough to break my heart, especially after all I'd gone through.'

To offset disappointment she had, in the intervals of telephoning, drunk a good deal of brandy; and now emotion and brandy and the proximity of a rival had produced in her a state of mind which possibly might find relief in tears, but perhaps in being actively offensive. Mr Small felt fear returning, and looked to Mavis for help.

But Mavis herself was angry now. She had told her story – and it was a good story – to two people who ignored it, and Tom Hogpool who had not laughed. She was going to have her revenge.

She addressed the table in loud and deliberate tones: 'It's a funny thing about blondes. They photograph better than brunettes, but when you see them in the flesh, they're disappointing. I guess there's something phony about them really.'

Knocking over her chair as she rose, Ivy sprang to her feet. For a moment she hovered dangerously between a fit of violent weeping and some horrible display of violence; and then, choosing magnificently the proper riposte, she decided to be dignified. 'I refuse to stay here to be insulted,' she declared; and with a hauteur that even Mavis could not have surpassed, she left them and walked steadily out of the room.

Mr Small, unwilling to create a scene, could not make up his mind what to do; and Hogpool was sullen and indifferent. But in a moment Mavis explained, 'She's stinko, that's what the trouble is. But say, it was my fault for riding her. You stay here, and I'll go fetch her back.'

She also left the room, and as she was about to disappear the Master of Ballantyne rose from the next table, and with a casual air, followed her.

Half-a-minute later Tom Hogpool's face grew suddenly dark and congested with blood. 'That bloody young pup!' he cried. 'He was after Mavis!'

'What are you gassing about, Tom?'

'That young officer at the next table. As soon as Mavis goes, he gets up and goes after her. I'll break his bloody neck for him!'

Clumsily rising, Hogpool with a hot indignant mien hurried out; and Mr Small, with a dreadful feeling that in spite of all his efforts the evening would conclude in some loud scandal, went anxiously in pursuit.

As Hogpool went through the side door that led into the

dark and almost deserted station, Mr Small was but a yard or two behind him. He followed, and in the outer gloom saw Hogpool ponderously running. Two dim-seen figures were on the far side of him. 'Stop him!' shouted Mr Small.

An obstacle of some kind was thrust into Hogpool's path, and tripping over it he fell heavily, and lay still.

'You're a damned fool,' said Lawless. 'You've probably broken his neck.'

Mr McCombie knelt and examined him. 'He's all right,' he said.

After long argument and another drink, Billy Burstin had persuaded them to accept his property basket, and said good-bye. They were still discussing what to do with it when a young woman hurried past them; another young woman; a tall young officer; and then they saw the running figure of Tom Hogpool, and heard the imploring shout of Mr Small. With a strong thrust of his foot, McCombie pushed the property basket in front of the unknown pursuer, and stopped him very effectively.

Mr Small was painfully upset by the sight of his unconscious friend. 'We must get him away from here,' he declared. 'Oh, this is awful! Poor Tom, poor Tom! And the scandal if he's seen in this condition, and I'm with him! You're sure he's not dangerously hurt?'

There was no sign of Mavis and the Master of Ballantyne, but Ivy re-appeared while they were lifting Hogpool from the ground, and watched them prop him in a sitting position on the basket. She had regained her self-control. The night air had calmed her.

'We must take him home, somehow or other,' said Mr Small feverishly.

'His car's up there,' said Ivy, pointing to the station-yard. 'I've just seen it.'

'Thank God!' said Mr Small.

'But I don't know where his chauffeur is.'

'I'll drive it,' said Lawless. 'I'm Phaethon's only heir at this time of night.'

A minute later they were half-lifting, half-pushing Hogpool

into his own magnificent limousine, and Mr Small and Ivy hurriedly followed.

'You'll have to make room for our basket,' said McCombie, and heaved Billy Burstin's properties in beside them. Then he joined Lawless in the front seat.

'I've got a notion,' said the latter, 'that the moon is still in its first quarter.'

'It's nothing of the sort,' said McCombie, and taking out a pocket diary he held it under the dash-board light. 'It was the last quarter four days ago. I thought as much. It was as dark as the inside of a hat last night.'

'I was speaking in metaphor,' Lawless explained. 'And we who use tropes and fancy speaking have a devil in our hearts.'

IX

The fine warm weather, that had lasted nearly a week, was becoming sultry, and at night the sky thickened and from some loury cloud would gush a fall of heavy rain. But the morning brought back tall nacreous skies, and the sun, first gilding cliff and seaside farm, would rise through flawless blue to a hot refulgence; and in this holiday climate the love-strikers in the Castle were fairly well satisfied with a life so largely idle. They lay on the ramparts, like seals on a hot beach, and basked in the sun. But Lysistrata was getting worried. She had hoped that the strike would provoke quick reaction, and achieve a speedy victory. By Fabian strategy, whether deliberate or the result of incompetence and divided council, the men might exhaust the enthusiasm of her troops, and steal success. She wanted them to come into the open, to make some definite move, and expedite the issue. Her own patience, she knew, was wearing thin, and if she could not trust herself to long endurance, what faith could she have in others?

She was waiting, on the night of Mr Small's dinner-party, for the arrival of the unsuspecting Bulmer. A dozen of her most muscular young women, and the reluctant Horrocks, were with her. They stood under the high wall that girdled the Castle Rock. Above them, soot-black against the low sky, loomed the building that once had been the Armoury. The night was warm and dark, and the sky hung close in sombre canopies. The rest of the party felt an agreeable vibration; their nerves had been strung to enjoyment by anticipation of an exciting occurrence; but to Lysistrata the heavy darkness was oppressive, and the seeming stillness of the sky was like the inactivity, that she could not dispel, which filled her mind with doubtful thoughts and the foreboding of defeat. Her impatient spirit demanded some larger happening than the capture of a love-sick sailor – and the event was nearer than she expected.

A few fat drops of rain fell softly. There was no wind, and they fell limp and straight, like flabby little plummets. Then they multiplied, but slowly, and the silence was gently broken by the patter of infinite minute explosions on the stone. In a minute or two there was a downpour, thick and drenching. The water-drops had no longer any separate descent, but came altogether in a deluge, and the nearer sky was full of hissing. The shower appeared to have put out the lights in the city below them.

Far down on the Rock, Julian and Bulmer were huddled on a ledge. They shrank into their clothes, bunching their shoulders, and Julian cursed the untimely rain, that would make the rock slippery and was already adding discomfort to danger. Bulmer, however, regarded the inclemency of the weather with more philosophy. 'If it isn't one bloody thing, it's another,' he remarked, and spat into the darkness. Despite his ardent nature he was a confirmed pessimist.

He had, at first, emphatically refused to take Julian with him. He had, indeed, denied all knowledge of a way into the Castle, and said that Lawless must have misunderstood him. Alternatively he claimed that what he did in his spare time was his own business, and that no one had any right to interfere with him. The offer of a bribe made no impression on his stubborn independence. But then Scrymgeour had taken him in hand, and Bulmer was no match for the General. Scrymgeour, after a friendly word or two, had simply said, 'Now tell me how you manage to get into the Castle'; and Bulmer, in a rumbling voice and a rambling manner, had first protested that what he had done was right, reasonable, and natural, and that being granted, had given a fair description of his route. He had then been told that Colonel Brown would go with him on his next visit, and though plainly averse to company, he had acquiesced in this also. Having been dismissed by Scrymgeour, he reminded Julian of the proffered bribe. It would cost him something to pacify Horrocks, he explained, Julian gave him two pounds, and Bulmer said mournfully, 'It's cheap at the price, buying your way into a castle full of women for a couple of quid.'

The Rock was less difficult to climb than Julian had expected. Not far from the bottom was a short steep pitch, awkward in the darkness, that led to an overhung recess, and thence, edging carefully round an out-thrust corner, they came to what was almost a path. It turned and twisted upward. A thin soil had lodged in crevices and on shelves, and grass had stiffened it. The path, after twenty yards, took them to a smooth slope of rock cut diagonally by a deep crack, and then to a miniature defile, a steep scramble between sharp sides, and so to the ledge where the rain surprised them.

The shower lasted a quarter of an hour, and they were soaked to the skin. When they returned to the ascent they felt little runnels of water trickling down back and sides with every movement, and every movement released from somewhere a draught of coldness. But there was no more real climbing. From the ledge to the shoulder on which the outer wall was built, the ascent was only a rough scramble. It was awkward in places. It needed a little caution, a little stretching and balancing here and there, but it was not difficult; and Julian felt sure that he could lead a picked company to the assault, and from this possibly unguarded, or lightly guarded quarter, take the Castle by surprise.

For a minute they rested beneath the wall. They had agreed that Julian should be the first to enter, for Bulmer was sure that if he went first, and told Horrocks there was an officer with him, she would insist on his immediate return or threaten to raise the alarm. He could never persuade her to let a stranger into the Castle. He was quite certain about this. But if Julian went first, then his entrance would be accomplished before she realized it, and she would need no urging to help Bulmer over the wall. Not affection only, but the embarrassment of being alone with a stranger – for she was a modest creature – would demand the additional presence of her lover. And then, for an hour, Julian would leave them to their own affairs, while he made such a reconnaissance as circumstances might permit ...

'All right,' he muttered, and Bulmer whistled three or four low clear notes. From the other side of the wall came in reply the same notes, but rather tremulous and a trifle off the key, and a long rope leapt snakily over the coping.

It was, thought Julian, absurd to be excited by so trifling an adventure, but despite his disapproval of it, he was conscious of a slight nervous affection as he took hold of the rope and pulled himself up. The quickness of his breathing was not due to muscular effort, and his mouth was unreasonably parched. He would not admit that he was in any degree frightened of the embattled horde of women, whose sanctuary he was invading, but he was very careful and moved quickly to avoid being seen as he crossed the coping. He hugged himself to the stone, wriggled over, caught the rope on the other side, and lowered himself to the ground.

His feet were just touching the pavement when he felt a smooth but muscular arm tighten round his throat and with a vicious jerk pull him backwards. He struggled violently, but could not release himself. He fell, and a person who, from the pressure of her large round knees, must have weighed about twelve stone, knelt upon him, while others pinned him by the arms, and someone clapped a hand over his mouth. In the darkness he could not count his assailants, but they seemed to be numerous, and such was their close pressure and the softness of their damp clothes – together with excited whispering as they hissed instruction to each other – that he felt as though he had been attacked by a flight of infuriated black swans.

He was dazzled by the sudden flash of a small electric torch, and a voice said, 'My God, it isn't him!'

Then another voice exclaimed, 'Look, look!'

Suspecting no harm, Bulmer was coming over the wall with the confidence of one who had done it often before. The silhouette of his head and shoulders appeared above the coping, a leg crossed it, and turning, he gripped the rope and swung himself over. But then a noise of some kind startled him, and looking down he saw by a movement of the darkness that too many people were waiting for him. With a quick movement he had his hands on the coping, and was about to heave himself up, when half-a-dozen women, wildly excited, caught him by the legs and dragged him down. He clung desperately to his hold on the wall, but their weight was too much for him, and letting go he tumbled into a cluster of stout-sided girls who wrapped him round with innumerable hungry arms, as though they had been a giant octopus. But his greatest danger was Horrocks, who, endeavouring to save him from the rough handling of the others, very nearly throttled him.

As soon as Bulmer was dragged down, Lysistrata sent a runner to sound the alarm, and hastily ordering her patrol to tie the prisoners back-to-back, commanded them to line the wall. They waited, fiercely expectant, but minute followed minute and no other darkling enemy threw his invasive leg across the coping. Slowly and half-unwillingly they abandoned their fear of a general attack.

But the alarm had called from their beds the whole garrison, and as Julian and Bulmer, released from their bonds but closely guarded, were marched to the Governor's House, they passed through such a swarm of wild and scantly clad women – club-carrying, fierce of hair and shrilling their defiance.– as no one had ever seen since Boadicea called from Icenian marshes her army of desperate mothers and wolfish girls. Then Julian could no longer deny his fear, but felt in all his veins its gelid current.

X

About eleven o'clock of the following morning, Lysistrata was discussing the situation with her principal lieutenants, Lady Oriole, Mrs Curle, and Mrs Graham. With a pleasing appearance of informality they were seated round a table in the small garden beside the Governor's House, where a large red-and-white umbrella shaded them from the sun; but in spite of its contrary aspect, their discussion was as serious as any that ever took place in boardroom or council hall or government office. They were considering what steps to take next;

and as there seemed no steps to be taken, they were very grave about it.

Their prisoners of the night before had been closely interrogated, and both had refused to give any information whatsoever. It was fairly obvious that Bulmer was guilty of nothing more serious than an improper affection for Horrocks; but what was Colonel Brown's mission? Rose Armour had seen him, and told Lysistrata who he was. She had frankly admitted that he was her lover and agreed to question him in private. But Julian, all the sterner because he had recently been frightened, had rudely told her that she was a traitor, and he wanted nothing to do with her. This was not positively helpful, though it appeared to indicate that he was not, like Bulmer, a lover in search of his desire . . . Then he must be a spy or a scout; and if he were a scout or a spy, he was probably the forerunner of some large assault. Were the men at last going to make a definite move? Lysistrata felt sure of it. Today, for the first time since the occupation of the Castle, the garrison would have neither green vegetables for their luncheon, nor fresh milk for their tea. No tradesmen had called that morning, and the inference was plain: the men were desperate. But what were they going to do? Were they going to sit round the Castle and watch the garrison starve? Or would they launch an attack when they judged the women hungry enough to have lost their fighting spirit? The assault was more probable . . . Then what could be done for the safety of the Castle and the triumph of their cause? Lysistrata and her lieutenants pondered the question long and seriously. But they had done everything, they felt, that could be done; yet they searched their brains for something else; and unhappily could think of nothing more.

This grave perplexity was interrupted by a messenger who announced that Mr Comyn Curle, the Secretary of State for War, was now at the Main Gate, and most earnestly desired an audience of Lady Lysistrata.

'He may have something to say, but I don't think we should count on it,' said Lysistrata thoughtfully.

'Poor man!' exclaimed Mrs Curle. 'Do let him come in. I'm dying to know what he looks like.'

'There's no point in refusing to see him,' said Lady Oriole judicially.

'He may have news of some kind,' suggested Mrs Graham.

Lysistrata smiled. 'I'm just as curious as you are, and I wouldn't dream of sending him away.' She turned to the messenger: 'Tell the sergeant of the guard that I shall be very pleased to see Mr Curle. She had better detail a corporal and two women to bring him here.'

Mr Curle was one of several Ministers who had been much perturbed by the latest decision of the Cabinet. General Scrymgeour had put before them a plan for carrying the Castle by assault; and after long discussion the plan had been approved. But Mr Curle had not approved of it, and he had lain awake all night wondering how to reconcile his duty as a husband – he must save Delia from the attack – with his duty to the Cabinet, whose decision he was bound to keep secret. Could he persuade the women to abandon their strike, now, at the last minute? Could he find argument enough, without the forbidden argument of his secret knowledge, to overcome their dreadful obstinacy? He thought he could. It was not so much the matter, as the manner of the argument, that counted. Eloquence was the thing. It had always been his favourite weapon. And oratory could move mountains.

In preparation for his audience Mr Curle had spent half-an-hour on breathing exercises and a discipline he used for the controlling of his feelings, and he had arrived at the Castle in a very calm and collected frame of mind. But the delay, while a messenger was sent to look for Lysistrata, impaired his equanimity, and he was further upset by the escort with which the sergeant provided him. The corporal was an ash-blonde with a sweet smile and legs of maddening beauty, and the two privates were lovely as houris. He set off, up the long stone causeway, at such a pace that his escort had to skip and double to keep up with him; and some idle members of the garrison, girls strolling to and fro, pretended to believe he was running away, and shouted encouraging remarks as he hurried by. When he reached the garden where Lysistrata and her officers were sitting, he was out of breath and visibly disconcerted.

'Comyn, *darling*!' exclaimed his wife. 'How wretched you're looking! Are you feeling terribly unhappy about it?'

Mr Curle bowed to Lysistrata, and hesitated before taking the deck-chair that he was offered. Such a seat would give him no advantage when speaking. It was difficult to be dominating from a deck-chair. It was inconsistent with rhetoric, and inimical to really compulsive dialectic. But deck-chairs were the only sort available, and despite a feeling that he was thereby admitting defeat, he at last sat down.

'He's just a wreck,' said Mrs Curle to Mrs Graham in a loud whisper. 'They simply can't do without us. Aren't they silly not to stop the war and get us back again?'

'And now, Mr Curle,' said Lysistrata in a firm yet benevolent voice, 'will you tell us the object of your visit? We are glad to see you, and I trust you are not averse to seeing us. But I suppose your mission is important, so we had better waste no time on compliments.'

'My purpose,' said Mr Curle, and cleared his throat. 'My purpose, as you infer, is not a frivolous – well, purpose.'

'Speak up, darling,' said his wife.

'I have come to appeal to you. I have come to ask you to call off the strike. In the interests of the country. The interests of the country are paramount.'

'Is that all you have to say?'

'No,' said Mr Curle. 'No, that isn't all,' he added with an effort.

'Poor darling,' explained his wife, 'he gets so nervous that he can't remember what he wants to say.'

It was lamentably true. His promised eloquence had faded like a rainbow. The spate of irresistible rhetoric, with which he had meant to dislodge the women from resolution and their rocky fastness, had dwindled to the flow of a leaky tap. His arguments, that might have turned the Brahmaputra from its course, were quite forgotten, and language that would have made a planet pause had shrunk to a pair of husky monosyllables. Though eloquence was his favourite weapon, aphasia was his constant foe.

'Let's have some coffee,' said Lady Oriole helpfully, and

presently an orderly brought cups and the apparatus for making it.

Mr Curle recovered some of his composure, but none of the compulsive phrases he had devised. He tried, but did not succeed in moving his audience.

And then he was tempted. Though eloquence had failed him, he had another weapon. He had secret information. If he revealed the imminence of Scrymgeour's attack, and the magnitude of it, the women would surely realize how hopeless was their position, and decide to save their skins. He would give almost anything to save Delia's skin.   But there was a lion in his path, and its name was Honour. He could not be disloyal to his colleagues, nor betray the confidence of the Cabinet. He knew this, and yet was still flirting with temptation, when his wife inquired, 'When are you going to attack us, darling?'

'How did you learn,' he stammered, 'that is to say, who told you about an attack?'

'We have various sources of information,' said Lysistrata quickly.

'Then you know what's going to happen? And what are you going to do? You can't hope to resist.'

'We're certainly not going to surrender,' said Lady Oriole.

'But against double your numbers . . .' Mr Curle bit his lip and blushed like a peony.

'You can't frighten us, darling,' said his wife.

'But please don't think we're ungrateful,' said Lysistrata. 'We shall consider very carefully what you have told us, and I assure you that we shall always be glad to have the benefit of your advice. I had thought, indeed, of inviting you to a conference early next week . . .'

'But that will be too late!' cried Mr Curle. And Lysistrata's lieutenants, who had turned to her in great surprise, now stared at the Secretary for War with the subtle understanding – superior, compassionate, and a little horrified – of those who have taken someone by surprise in a secret place. He had just told them that the assault was to be made almost at once. They felt their nerves tingle, their pulses beat more strongly. And they had the grace to feel rather sorry for Mr Curle, whose embarrassed complexion was intensified by the realization that again he had said too much.

As inconspicuously as possible he began to do his breathing exercises. Deep-breathing, and relax; forced expiration, huff, huff, and again; slowly inspire, count six, and slowly let it go – this regimen was supposed to give self-control, and often indeed produced a certain indifference to the affairs of the extrinsic world. But before his lungs had time to do much good, he saw with astonishment and dismay a tall approaching figure, whose appearance immediately banished the little fragment of equanimity that he had established. Lysistrata and her lieutenants were also surprised. The ponderous tall figure of their new visitor – in spite of the hot weather he wore a morning-coat and top-hat – resembled the high black bow of an ocean liner, and the corporal and the charming escort were like bright-sailed feluccas beside him.

Lysistrata, rising to greet him, said truthfully, 'This is a most unexpected pleasure, Sir Joseph.'

Courteously and with a rich formality, Sir Joseph Rumble acknowledged her welcome and saluted her three lieutenants. Inspired by the same dislike of violence, his mission was similar to that of Mr Curle; but the sight of his colleague gave him no pleasure. His surprise and resentment were not so obvious as the open embarrassment of the Secretary for War, but the florid dignity of his ordinary manner was rather suspiciously exaggerated. It acquired an overlay of irritable pomposity.

He spoke to Mr. Curle with cumbrous irony: 'I must apologize, my dear Curle, if I have intruded upon a domestic visit. For I take it that your presence here is occasioned simply by connubial solicitude?'

'If it is,' said Mr Curle with some spirit, 'then I have more excuse for coming than you have.'

Carefully Sir Joseph lowered himself into a deck-chair, and ignoring his colleague, addressed Lysistrata: 'Though I am the last person in the world to underrate the importance of social observance, it would be idle to pretend that my mission has no more significance than the expression of my deep regard for you and your associates. That it does express my regard, I trust you already believe. That it may fructify in reconciliation of our unhappy differences, I hope to persuade you.'

'I don't think we want to reconcile differences,' said Lysistrata. 'We want to stop the war, and that's not quite the same thing, is it?'

'A rigid definition,' said Sir Joseph, 'is as dangerous and undesirable as a hasty decision. Let us avoid, until they become essential, any pedantic analysis or categorical desideratum. I would go so far as to say, let us avoid any unnecessary clarification, whether of terminology or objective. I have come here to suggest negotiation, to propose a conference, and the only essential elements in negotiation are good will and a *table*. Good will I think we have in abundance, and a table should not be hard to find.'

'I think we'd better have some more coffee,' said Mrs Graham. 'It looks as though we'll be here for the rest of the morning.'

'Again and again,' Sir Joseph continued, 'I have seen an apparently irreconcilable conflict dwindle and fade, and perish ultimately of inanition, when the several protagonists and the appointed mediators have found themselves in joint possession of a *table*. And particularly efficacious is a *round table*. Given good will and a round table, no problem is insoluble, no conflict incurable. I do not claim for myself exceptional wisdom or unusual perspicacity, but long experience has often enabled me to see daylight where to others there was nothing but the dark shadow of insurmountable obstruction; and I feel sure that all our present difficulties would speedily dissolve in the general good will of a *round-table conference*. Will you not authorize me to bring into being such a conference? I beg you to cooperate. We, who have your welfare at heart, desire peace by negotiation, not the unwilling peace of compulsion. It is in the spirit of peace and good will that I make this last-minute appeal.'

'So it *is* a last-minute appeal?' said Lysistrata. 'Then if we refuse to hear it, we may expect the attack immediately?'

Sir Joseph flushed. 'Surely, my dear lady, you are putting upon my words a construction they will not bear. . . . What are you laughing at, Curle?'

'A cat coming out of a bag,' said Mr Curle happily.

'Darling!' said Mrs Curle, 'if you would only look round, you would see a Prime Minister coming out of a clinch. And that's a lot funnier.'

'Good God!' said Lady Oriole, 'the whole Cabinet's coming!'

The sergeant at the Main Gate, having received an order to admit Mr Curle, had seen no reason why Sir Joseph should be kept out; and now, again on her own responsibility, had let in Lord Pippin. She had given him the usual escort, and he, being an old man, had taken the corporal's arm. Mrs Curle's description of this familiarity was a humorous exaggeration; but he had dexterously released himself as soon as he perceived his colleagues.

Both were visibly disconcerted by his arrival, but now Sir Joseph was the more manifestly ill-at-ease. The Premier, however, showed neither surprise nor annoyance at the unexpected presence of his Ministers; though not unnaturally he resented it. His intention was the same as theirs, and he was vexed at its discovery. It was exasperating, too, to find that he and his colleagues were united by a common weakness. It was provoking to be so obviously related to the rest of humanity. But he showed his displeasure only by the malice with which he denied it.

Addressing to each a few friendly words, he shook hands with Lysistrata, Lady Oriole, Mrs Curle, and Mrs Graham. To Mrs Curle, whom he disliked, he was especially amiable. And then turning to Sir Joseph and the Secretary for War, he exclaimed, 'And what a relief, gentlemen, to find you here! Nothing could be calculated to give me greater comfort. On my way hither, I admit, I was doubtful of the wisdom, even of the propriety, of my coming. – The Cabinet, my dear Lady Lysistrata, puts an unbreakable seal upon the mouths of its members, and no one, for any purpose whatsoever, may take private advantage of what he learns in the sanctitude of our joint deliberation. This rule is inviolable; and like all other rules, it is violated quite frequently. My present purpose, if carried into effect, would be at the least an infringement, but if, as I suspect, Sir Joseph and Mr Curle have already warned you of tomorrow's activity, then I may escape recrimination for – ah! telling tales out of school.'

'I resent the allegation!' exclaimed Sir Joseph. 'It is a monstrous and unwarrantable suggestion. I have said no single word about the projected attack.'

'Neither have I,' said Mr Curle.

'Oh, darling!' cried his wife reproachfully.

'Sir Joseph and Mr Curle have been remarkably circumspect,' said Lysistrata hastily. 'You yourself, Lord Pippin, could have been no more discreet. I needn't pretend, however, that we are ignorant of what is going to happen. Tomorrow, with a force that greatly outnumbers ours, you will try to take the Castle by assault. But you need have no fear that we shall ever reproach you for having given away a Cabinet secret. As I told Mr Curle a little while ago, we have many sources of information. For several days I have been expecting an attack, and the news that it is now imminent does not surprise me. Nor, let me add, am I daunted by it.'

This threat of intransigence provoked a new series of arguments. Mr Curle, who prudently avoided his wife, still endeavoured to persuade Lady Oriole that unconditional surrender was the rebels' proper course; for Mrs Curle's benefit Sir Joseph extolled the round table with such orotundity that it almost became visible; and to Lysistrata and Mrs Graham the Prime Minister elaborated a gently Machiavellian proposal of his own. It was that they should abandon the Castle but, if they cared to, continue the strike in the privacy of their homes.

'In a democratic state, such as ours,' he explained, 'it is the undoubted privilege of every citizen to disapprove, if he cares, of the policy of the Government. I will go so far as to say that by the nature of our régime we encourage disapproval – but we retain the right to regulate its expression. The twin foundations of democracy are general suffrage and the secret ballot. That is to say, it is the right of everyone to have an opinion, but the price he pays for that right is a timely reticence. The British Government makes no attempt to discipline the mind of the individual, but clearly it must rule his actions, and prohibit those which are undesirable, lest they interfere

with the liberty of others. We are the jealous custodians of the
liberty of the people, and it is your challenge to liberty, not
your personal opinion, that impels us to take action against
you. If, then, you will peacefully evacuate the Castle, and persuade your associates in other parts of the country in a like
manner to dismiss their garrisons, I promise you that in the
privacy of your own homes you will enjoy the fullest liberty to
think, as you please about the war, about the Government,
about any subject on earth or beyond it. For the mind is
infinite. It is free in nature. It is its own domain, and to that
domain it need set no boundaries. Of all the many fruits of this
land – this England, this jewel set in a silver sea – I think the
acknowledged liberty of the mind is the most precious.'

There was a short silence. The Prime Minister's rosy benignity was disarming, and like the Roman gladiator called
retiarius his weapons included a net. It was difficult to avoid
entanglement.

'You mean,' said Lysistrata carefully, 'that you would
approve our continuing the strike as individuals?'

'No, I should not approve it, but I could not pretend that
the functions of my office would compel me to – ah!'

'Come between husband and wife?' suggested Mrs Graham.

'Precisely. That would be a political innovation of great and
unnecessary danger. The Archbishop, I know, is much perturbed by his responsibilities in this matter, but I must decline
to share them.'

Lady Oriole rose, vigorously stretched herself, and pulled
her habit straight. She had been bored by the discussion,
which she considered quite unnecessary. 'You'll have to excuse me,' she said to Lysistrata. 'I must go and see about the
noon parade. It's late already.'

Mr Curle, deserted, looked longingly at his wife, but resisted
the temptation to take the empty chair beside her – Sir Joseph
was talking of Lady Rumble now, and Delia was being sympathetic – and with a sigh he joined the Prime Minister's
group.

Lysistrata, catching a little of Lady Oriole's impatience, said
brusquely, 'You forget, Lord Pippin, that our avowed intention is to stop the war. Perhaps I have less respect than you for

T–H

the kingdom of the mind, perhaps more. But that doesn't matter for the present. What does matter is the necessity of bringing the war to an end without a moment's unnecessary delay.'

'I agree with you entirely,' said Lord Pippin, and smiled with rosy benevolence. 'A speedy victory is what we all desire. But you cannot stop a war and summon victory as you would summon, let us say, a passing cab.'

'When I'm going anywhere,' said Mrs Graham, rather combatively, 'I don't summon a cab. I take a bus.'

'Indeed.'

'And I've often thought that nearly all the trouble in the world is made by people who do use cabs. Because a man who takes a cab wants it all to himself, but people in buses are content to share them.'

'It is an interesting suggestion . . .'

Lysistrata looked round. The red-haired orderly-room sergeant had silently approached, and now with a little cough demanded her attention. 'There's a girl that's wanting to speak to you,' she whispered. 'She's got bad news. It was Lady Oriole that told me to come and tell you.'

Lysistrata apologized to her visitor, and Mrs Graham resumed her conversation with the Prime Minister. 'I've often wanted to have a good talk about politics with those at the head of affairs,' she explained, 'because it seems to me that you just make a lot of unnecessary difficulty for yourselves. You go about things in the wrong way. When I want a couple of pounds of steak, for instance, I don't go into the country and stick a Union Jack on a bullock, and say, That's mine! I take advantage of the fact that I'm living in the 1940s, and there's a butcher's shop at the corner of the street. Your trouble is that you don't realize we're living in a civilized world with lots of modern conveniences. You're still in the Dark Ages.'

The Prime Minister made a feeble effort to defend himself and his government, but Mrs Graham was too interested in her own thesis to listen to him. She had proved that national politics was no more than a larger sort of housekeeping, and was dealing caustically with the Chancellor of the Exchequer when, much to Lord Pippin's relief, the orderly-room sergeant re-appeared to claim her attention. She had a message from Lysistrata, and Mrs Graham, who was enjoying herself, rose impatiently to hear it.

'That is a very remarkable woman,' said the Prime Minister. 'It would do you good to talk to her, Rumble.'

'Why?' asked Sir Joseph.

'Because she is no more impressed by the wisdom of politicians than I am.'

Mrs Graham returned, and stood for a moment, showing some embarrassment, before she announced: 'I am requested by Lady Lysistrata to thank you for your visit, and to offer her apologies for leaving you.'

'But is she not coming back?'

Again Mrs Graham hesitated. Then she spoke decisively: 'No, she isn't. There's no use your talking any longer, because we've made up our minds. Our policy is *No Surrender*, and we're ready for the fight.'

Not for a minute or two did the Ministers make any attempt to rise and go. Their sense of propriety was shocked and their vanity wounded by this abrupt dismissal; but they could not quite believe that it was seriously intended. They still believed in the rightness of their purpose and their powers of persuasion. They still retained a slight but genuine hope of saving the women, even at the last moment, from the consequence of their folly; and to Mrs Curle and Mrs Graham, who accompanied them to the Main Gate, they repeated all their arguments, and halted on the drawbridge while Sir Joseph with eloquent gestures inscribed a last testimonial to the healing qualities of a round table.

It was unavailing. Sir Joseph and the Prime Minister said a regretful good-bye, but Mr Curle could not trust himself to speak. Slowly they crossed the Esplanade and looked like travellers lost in the gorgeous aisles, loud with parakeets and birds of paradise, of a trumpet-flowered Brazilian forest. For the Noon Parade, of rebel beauty and insurgent laughter, was in full progress.

'It'll be a different sight tomorrow,' said Mrs Graham.

'Very different,' said Mrs Curle, more sober than usual, as she thought of the coming battle.

XI

Staying for a little while to watch the parade, Mrs Graham and Mrs Curle were presently surprised to see company after company called to attention, and come marching back to the Castle. What was the matter? they asked. And the girls, tramping past them, replied, 'The soldiers are coming.'

Swiftly the parade-ground was emptied of all its bright colour. At the far end the multitude of spectators had been dispersed, and the narrowness of Castle Hill was half-blocked by a column of soldiers who stood waiting the order to advance. Lysistrata's Company of Guards – the tall girls in breeches and white shirts, who carried pikes and Lochaber axes – still remained like a strong fence across the Esplanade; and Lady Oriole, blackly defiant in her habit, walked slowly up and down swinging her hunting-crop. Then she gave an order to the Guards, and turning into file, with a swagger in their movement and no look of hurrying, they marched slowly in.

Lady Oriole was the last to retire. 'They've started sooner than we expected,' she said grimly.

'They're not going to attack at once, are they?' asked Mrs Curle.

'No, I don't think so. Tomorrow's the day. But in the meantime they're going to see that we don't escape. There are more troops down in the Gardens, and on the other side as well.'

The soldiers on Castle Hill were called to attention. They advanced on to the Esplanade, and the column divided. The two halves halted, one on either side, about sixty yards from the Main Gate, and after standing at ease for a few minutes, the men were told to fall out. They sat down on the pavement or the parapets, smoking and talking. But sentries were posted over each group, and two patrolled the breadth of the Esplanade, meeting and turning in the middle.

'We're beleaguered!' said Mrs Curle impressively.

'They ought to have done this long ago,' said Mrs Graham.

They turned to go in, but when they were under the archway they heard excited shouting from the young women still loitering on the drawbridge, and hurrying back they saw half a dozen run swiftly to the rescue of a girl who was struggling violently with a pair of sentries. First in the sortie were that redoubtable couple, Miss McNulty and Miss McNab. Before the nearer sentry had realized what was happening, he was down, with blood on his face, from a crack on the skull, and Miss McNab was threatening with her warlike niblick the knot of angry men who came to his help. The other sentry, guarding his head, had got a blow on his elbow that left his arm useless.

Lady Oriole kept a hunting-horn tucked in her bosom. She whipped it out and blew a fierce little blast. 'For'ard!' she yelled. 'For'ard!'

Waving her hunting-crop she led a dozen women to the attack. Mrs Graham followed, and Delia snatched a pike from a hesitant girl. They were just in time. A shock-headed black-avised bombardier had wrested her niblick from McNab, and with a quick jerk heaved her on to his shoulders. He staggered under his burden, and Delia Curle, thrusting fiercely, pricked him in the thigh. He howled with fright and pain, and dropped his prisoner. She rose at once, and swinging a heavy punch at a pot-bellied sergeant of Engineers, kicked a private of the Buffs hard on the shin. 'No more war!' bellowed Lady Oriole, and with her heavy crop opened a great wound on the pimply forehead of a Royal Fusilier.

Now the battle ranged from side to side of the Esplanade, and everywhere the men were getting the worse of it. They had been taken by surprise; they had had no orders to fight, and their only officers were a pair of subalterns who had seen no sterner service than a battalion parade. The men had neither heart for the battle, nor leaders. But within three minutes of the alarm, there were a hundred high-fettled girls cutting and thrusting like Amazons, and with every minute that passed a score of others, fierce as though suckled at a tigress' udder, came racing to help wherever the scuffle was thickest.

Now it was Lady Oriole's hardest task to keep them from wild pursuit, for the men were giving ground. But loudly she blew her horn, loudly commanded, and obeying her like

veterans, the women drew off. Slowly they retired, now linger-
ing defiantly, now cheering and shouting as they went. They
fell back on the Castle. Nonplussed and sullen, the soldiers
made no trial to stay them, nor offered new attack.

The great iron-bolted doors were closed, and Lady Oriole,
her hat askew and breathing heavily, demanded: 'Now
where's that girl who started the trouble? Who is she, and
where has she gone?'

Out of the press of triumphant women came a wild creature
with raven hair and darkly glowing eyes. She was white-
skinned – but her cheek was torn and bloody – and she wore
a faded kilt and a tattered plaid pinned with a great silver
brooch across her shoulder. 'It was I,' she said proudly, in a
high clear voice. 'I am Catriona MacLeod of Rhidorroch.'

'You're very lucky to have got here, Miss MacLeod.'

'I have come from Stirling. There is a Highland army there,
of five thousand women. They are ready to help you in any
way you like.'

'How long would it take them to come here?'

'The time to march forty miles.'

'But how can we send word to them?' asked Delia, who,
since pricking a bombardier with her pike, felt herself a soldier
in earnest, and ready to cope with a soldierly problem. 'We're
closely beleaguered now.'

'Come up to the battlements and let's have a look.'

Following Lady Oriole, they presently looked down from
the upper ramparts, and saw soldiers bivouacked in the
gardens between Princes Street and the Castle; soldiers in all
the roads that girded the Rock; and a column marching to
reinforce the defeated troops on the Esplanade.

'We're tied up like a parcel,' said Mrs Graham.

'Somebody will have to get through their lines,' said Lady
Oriole.

.'I suppose we had better tell Lysistrata, and see what she
thinks,' suggested Mrs Curle.

'Yes,' said Lady Oriole thoughtfully. 'Yes, we ought to tell
her at once. It's a pity, the way things have happened. She got
bad news an hour ago, and it rather knocked her up. An old
friend of hers – she used to think she was in love with him

at one time – died in hospital yesterday. He'd been badly wounded, and death was probably the kindest thing that could happen to him. But she was too damned cut-up about it to see that when I left her. Still, the news of a Highland army at Stirling ought to make her feel more cheerful.'

XII

It was news of the death of Eliot Greene that had taken away Lysistrata from the conference. He had died the night before, and a nurse who had been with him had come to tell of the good end he made. She was waiting in the orderly-room in the Governor's House. She was a pretty fair-haired girl, and she cried at intervals during her story. She had never seen anyone look so happy as Eliot at the moment of his death, she said, and sobbed through a flood of tears: 'He was laughing! He was laughing just before, and then the only difference was that the look on his face got more like someone *remembering* a joke.'

Lysistrata sent word to dismiss the Ministers.

There had been three of them round his bed, said the little fair-haired nurse. There had been herself, and Sister Bliss, and Nurse Fell, and they had all been telling stories of the strike, and laughing like anything. Nurse Fell could make anyone laugh. She was a Cockney. She herself belonged to Glasgow, and Sister Bliss came from Yorkshire. So they heard stories from all over the country, and the whole country was full of jokes about the state the men were in, and the way the women were leading them a dance. You could say anything to Mr Greene. He loved a good joke, and sometimes when Sister used to complain that that wasn't the sort of thing to say before a gentleman – though she was just as bad herself – he would tell them, *Every time you laugh you kill a knave or fox a fool.* But perhaps they made him laugh too much. According to the doctors he died of heart-failure. But Sister said afterwards that from the look on his face you wouldn't think it was failure, but success. . . .

If only he could have lived to see the finish of it, and the war at an end, thought Lysistrata; and realized, as the wish came to her, that she had always shrunk from any serious consideration of Eliot's future. She had never seen him without wondering how he was going to adapt himself, so greatly mutilated, to a life where all his friends were active and afoot; but always, with dismay, she had put the problem from her. She had never been able to visualize him in any picture of the future, nor integrate him in the design for peace that her mind was drawing and re-arranging every day. Even while he was still alive, his place had been receding into the past. He was a country detail in that English landscape which the war had ravished, and he had died to an English sound, of women tattling through the ages on the village green. He had died to a music that would outlast all principalities and powers, to the tumbling echoes of Chaucerian laughter. The little nurse – her eyes were red and her cheeks wet with tears – was right when she would not believe that he had died of the failure of his heart. He had died of his heart's abundance.

XIII

In the narrow lobby of a small house in Leith, two garish and misshapen beings stood irresolute in a discoloured light. There was a hat-stand in the lobby, a toppling piece of furniture hung thickly with coats and ancient waterproofs, and among them a panel of mirror. Looking in the dark glass they saw two faces, grotesque and not their own. They uttered little whimpering noises of fear and protest. One of the figures half-opened the door into the street, but they were still afraid to go out.

They wore fantastic clothes. The one was dressed in a fashion of 1900: a pleated blouse ham-full at the shoulders and high-collared, a long dark dress of ample cut, bell-shaped below a constricted waist, and a pale straw boater skewered to a brown wig. The other was a pantomine figure, the Widow Twankey in a plaid bodice and a cameo brooch, draggle-skirted, long-shawled, wigged in black horse-hair with a white parting half an inch broad. But their faces were alike. – They had been newly shaved, so their cheeks were smooth. – From brow to throat they were the pretty warm white of a girl, with a little red rubbed in below the cheek-bones, and carefully drawn full red lips. Their eyebrows had been shaved, and thin dark crescents drawn above their yellow-flecked but well-mascara'd eyes. But this daintiness, this allure of women's colouring, was shocked and shouted down by their outrageous noses. In the dim light they shone like brothel lamps. They were red as blood, and they seemed to snuffle of sins like scarlet. They were the noses of Gin Lane and the battered clown.

It was McCombie who had painted their noses. His humour was broader than Lawless's, and not so terrible. Lawless had shaved their cheeks and eyebrows, and sprinkled them with perfume.

They had wakened, crapulous both of them, in McCombie's house, already dressed and decorated. Gradually they had re-called the events of the night before. . . . Hogpool had recovered by the time they reached his flat, and they had had a good lot to drink there. Then there had been a quarrel. Hog-pool had accused his old friend Small of taking bribes. His old friend Small retorted that Hogpool sold munitions to the enemy. – Hogpool specified a bribe or two that Small had taken. Small described in detail the latest piece of Hogpool's treachery. – Buffet about, like clowns in a circus, they had smacked each other with base disclosure and fragments of dis-graceful truth. Then Lawless, for no apparent reason save a sudden madness – a hank of yellow hair hung down his fore-head like a fever pennant, and his empty mouth was snarling – Lawless, jumping to his feet, lifted a punch to Hogpool's aching jaw that knocked him out; and McCombie, pulling Small nearer to reach him the better, dealt a blow that was the very marrow of the other.

When they returned to consciousness they were being driven, in Hogpool's car, to McCombie's house in Leith; and Lawless, shouting like a devil at the wheel, was patching with rags of poetry a ruinous device of torture. But then he had taken to laughing – to a fit of laughing wilder than his rage – and no sooner were they bundled into the house than he emptied from a wicker basket a great assortment of female raiment and ordered them to strip. They refused, and were beaten. They were dressed in abominable clothes, painted, and mocked. The savage humour of Lawless frightened them, and when he was tired of their antics they went willingly to bed in a room under the roof. The door was locked, and they slept drunkenly.

But they woke to a day like a nightmare. They were made to scrub floors and cook uneatable messes. There were three children in the house, who jeered at them wherever they went, and tripped them with broom-handles. And Lawless stood over them, with wild hair and a crack-jawed toothless grin, whisky in one hand and a play-book in the other, declaiming of the breeding sun, of bawds and gold, hoar leprosy and sluts with aprons mountant. They grew certain that he was mad, and burnt their own clothes when he told them to. In the early evening, while McCombie held them down, Lawless shaved them and painted them thickly with grease-paint. He shaved their scalps, and stuck wigs on them with hot glue. A little before dark he and McCombie went out and left them. But they had no clothes except the female garments they were wearing, and they were afraid of the streets. Three times they went irresolute to the door, but stood in the lobby and dared not make their escape. Then at last, their jaws slack with terror, they went stumbling out.

A thin rain was falling out of low skies, and the dark street was empty. But they ran, breathlessly, pursued by fear of themselves, for they had been driven out of their familiar shell and were houseless in the rain-swept street. They heard the padding of their printless feet and felt on their necks the hoarse breathing of what they were. A little gangling thieving boy, who had grown into the shabby likeness of a circus lion, and a whimpering gluttonous whelp who had put on the cunning of a hyena and found its stinking appetite, were vagrant now; and clutching their ungirt bellies they clawed at the skirts of their flying hosts. They felt their sides contracting over a void of fear.

They turned into a lane, and a great slouch-hatted figure, leaning against the wall, straightened himself and came roaring after them. The night air scorched their lungs like steam, but they doubled their pace and came into another street where light shone through pale curtains out of plump little taut bow-windows, and looking round they saw that the giant Australian soldier, mad as a rutting camel, was still close behind. Crazy for refuge of any kind, they pushed open a small iron gate and hammered at a pale brown varnished door. It opened, and a bespectacled man with sandy hair and a stringy throat asked what they wanted. 'Safety,' they hoarsely told him. 'Let us in, and we'll tell you.'

There were five other men sitting round a table covered with a thick green cloth with an ornamental fringe. They were knitting. 'You see, we are trying to make the best of things,' said the man with sandy hair.

Hogpool and Small sat on a green sofa that was tightly resilient over hard springs. They were so distressed that they had forgotten their appearance. But the other men stared at them, aghast with a dreadful curiosity. Three were bespectacled and thin, two were bald and soft with pre-senile fat. They looked like home-keeping men. They had been knitting bright wool of different colours, but now they sat staring at Small and Hogpool.

'We are trying to make the best of things,' repeated the man with sandy hair. 'You see, our wives have all left us, so we are studying the domestic arts.' He sniggered uneasily.

Small muttered, 'We were chased by a man. An Australian.'

There was another silence in which Hogpool's laboured breathing sounded like a smithy bellows. Then one of the bespectacled men – he had scanty wet-looking hair over a tall thin forehead – reached tentatively from his chair, and laid a nervous hand on Small's knee. With a dreadful shout Small jumped to his feet, and Hogpool scrambled after him. Nobody tried to stop them, but in their hurry they knocked a vase off the fumed-oak side-board, and wrenched the handle from the outer door. In the street they again took to their heels.

Now they felt that the peopled houses were full of peril, and thought they saw great hairy hands pull back the blind, and cunning eyes stare out. There was danger in the minds of men, and beneath the sober trappings of a town lay darkly a moving jungle where shaggy brutes went prowling through the streets, and panthers crouched upon a window-ledge. When nature littered monsters she concealed their birth in the midst of the flock and clad them in a general fleece, but if their clothes were burnt they ran free, and lycanthropy was no joke.

The rain had stopped and the sky was clearing. In a vaporous bay a few stars were rutilant. Bright red and yellow

beneath a pavement lamp they saw a hawker's barrow –
Brachiano in scarlet letters on the side – and a leash of children,
hungry still, buying pennyworths of ice-cream to cool the hot
night. They tried avoidance, but the children saw them and
came whooping after, and chased them into a juncture of
narrow alleys black between the high walls of a factory. There
the children grew frightened also. Their last cat-call modulated
to a trembling shriek, and leaving their shapeless quarry they
went running back to the lighted barrow. But Hogpool and
Small stayed in the shadows, and slunk soft-footed through
the viewless dark.

Doubtfully they stopped at the corner of a broader road,
and peering round saw in the crack-veined glass of a rubber-
shop their faces glazed and brightly haggard. They chattered
like apes at a reflection in moving water, and hurried clumsily,
scarcely seeing where they went, till the shouting of a dozen
loiterers, idle against the walls of a shuttered pub, startled
them into running again, and they ran for cover. They were
leg-weary, weak in the knees, and their bodies were a marsh of
sweat, but they dared not stop. Limping and shuffling, they
fled from street to lane, past the pale blind faces of empty
shops, and narrow little sombre gardens, and dead grimy
walls. Then they came to a road so broad that it seemed in the
darkness like the sallow water of a great river, the unhurried
Amazon huge and lustreless between forest walls. Hesitant,
they began to cross it, but in the middle halted, their spirit
draining into empty space.

Their selves, that had been dispossessed, became a circling
air that hemmed them in. A host of invisible small mouths
whispered of greed beyond the scope of swine, and lechery,
and shabby lust for power. The darkness was alive and conscious, and the pale unhurried river slid mumbling underfoot.
They stumbled to the other side, and in the blind shop fronts
their lurching shadows kept uneasy pace with them.

They were nearing home now, and the shortest way was
through a sombre crooked lane to the right. But they were
frightened away from that by a noise like the trampling of
male brutes in a stable. They would have to go into the light.
They must risk the breadth and naked side of Princes Street.

Here, where the road narrowed and curved uphill to enter its eastern mouth, there were people on both pavements, and they hurried head-down in the middle of the street. There was some shouting, and a few men turned to follow, but did not molest them.

They had no longer the strength to run. They gathered a little crowd who half encircled them, peering into their faces, and shouting coarsely. They crossed to the open side of Princes Street, and the crowd grew, and followed. But they had made a mistake, for now the mischievous crowd was pressing forward and would not let them cross again to reach any of the streets that led to Hogpool's flat. At the Mound there was a group of men gathered about an all night coffee-stall. They turned to see what the shouting meant, and headed the quarry. An old man offered Hogpool a mutton-pie. He knocked it out of his hand, and the crowd grew angry. They looted the coffee-stall and threw pies and slabs of cake at the fugitives. They were running again now, but slowly and up-hill. It was Small who thought first of the Castle. It was their only refuge. The street behind them was full of jeering pelting men. They had nowhere else to go, and their skirts might get them in.

On the steepness of Ramsay Lane, Hogpool fell, and some-one kicked him. Small dragged him to his feet, and they stumbled on, pushed and jostled by the mob. They had reached the last of their strength, they were sobbing for breath, and their knees were trembling. But they had only a little way to go now.

Where Castle Hill opens into the Esplanade, they were stopped by a picket of soldiers. They were cut off from their refuge. More soldiers hurried up, and drove back the mob. A sergeant peered closely into their faces. In the heat of their sweat the paint had run, and they were smeared with garish colour. He tugged at their wigs, but they were stuck tight with glue. He prodded them in the ribs. 'By God,' he exclaimed, 'they're men!'

'Spies,' said a corporal.

'Spies!' roared the illogical and excited soldiers.

'You're under arrest,' said the sergeant.

The news travelled to the crowd, and someone shouted, 'They're to be shot at dawn.'

'Shot at dawn!' bellowed the crowd with unmannerly glee, while Hogpool and Small, speechless and utterly exhausted, hung limply in the grasp of two unsympathizing privates.

XIV

In the State Prison, over the old Portcullis Gate, Julian sat alone and disconsolate on a wooden bench. A couple of blankets on the floor, a light hanging from the roof, a cup and a dirty plate were all the other furniture of his cell. There was a spider's web in the corner of the roof, but apparently no spider.

Though sorely wounded, Julian's spirit had not been humbled by capture. He felt that he had suffered a gross injustice in being taken prisoner, and he was very angry with the women. He was also angry with himself when he remembered how, for a little while, his heart had been turned to water by the savage spectacle of the garrison in their nightrails running swiftly to guard the walls. It was an ancient fear that he had suffered then – the night-fear of a Roman sentry surprised by women in the Icenian marsh – and irritably he banished the thought of it. He discounted it, for it meant nothing. But he nursed his anger against the women, for it was intolerable that a temporary lieutenant-colonel decorated with the D.S.O. and the M.C., should be prisoner in a hold of petticoats. – He recalled, against his will, that his old ambition was to be a great lover. How unpleasantly ironical to be in the midst of three thousand women, nearly all young, and spending the night alone! – They needed a pretty lesson. Humble pie and the dregs of the cup of humiliation and the smallest of singing should be their lot; and Scrymgeour would deal it to them.

He got up and paced furiously, to and fro, the three yards of his cell. There was only one thing that gave him satisfaction, and that was the way he had rebuffed Rose Armour. He had told her plainly what he thought of her when she came so smooth and friendly to learn the purpose of his venture. He had called her a traitor, and refused to answer a single question.

Or one only, to be truthful, and that had nothing to do with the military situation, nor had his answer been what she expected. But he would give her the same reply if she came back, and tell her without mincing words that he wanted nothing to do with a mutineer.

He threw himself down on his blankets, and stared resentfully at the spider's deserted web.

He heard footsteps, then the lock turning in his door. But he did not look round. The door was closed with a bang, and someone began impudently to whistle a hornpipe. He sat up and saw a slender figure in sailor's uniform. Arms stiffly crossed, and a blue-trousered leg held up like a prancing horse, and whistling still, she began to dance.

'Rose!' he exclaimed. And then coldly: 'What do you want? And why are you dressed like that?'

She struck an attitude. 'I look rather nice, don't you think?'

'No. Where did you get that uniform?'

'It belongs to your friend Bulmer.'

'Nonsense. He's twice your size.'

'You forget that this is a garrison of all the talents. We've got four first-rate dressmakers here, and I got one of them to alter it for me. Don't they fit beautifully behind?'

'I'm sorry, I'm not a judge of dressmaking.'

'Darling, you're not still sulking, are you?'

'I am not aware that I have ever sulked. But if you mean that I'm not disposed for friendly conversation with you, then you're right.'

Rose sat down on the bench and looked unhappy. 'When I came here yesterday,' she said, 'I asked you if you still loved me. And you said no.'

'You can't expect me to love a woman who's a rebel and a traitor.'

'Why not?'

'The reason should be obvious, even to you.'

'Well, it isn't. I never thought that love had anything to do with politics.'

'In a case of this kind. . . .'

'O-o-oh, it's tickling!'

Leaping to her feet, Rose thrust a hand down the front of

her sailor's blouse, and made some rapid adjustment. 'It's this sort of flannel bib they wear,' she explained.

'You haven't told me yet why you are wearing those clothes.'

'You wouldn't answer any of my questions yesterday.'

'Rose, my dear, how could I? I'm an officer in the Army . . .'

'And you're perfectly sweet.'

'Rose . . . Why did you join this wretched strike?'

'Oh, darling, it's too late to ask that now.'

'But it's so nonsensical, and so damnably unfair.'

'Have you missed me terribly?'

'Of course I have.'

'Poor Julian . . . No, because you said you didn't love me any more.'

'I wish to God it was true.'

'Is that the truth now?'

'No.'

'Sweet Julian. You are funny.'

'Rose, my darling!'

'Julian . . . No, you can't. You mustn't do that.'

'We're all alone.'

'I know. But if anyone came. . . .'

'If anyone came! And whose fault is it that we're liable to interruption? If anyone came she might find a prisoner of war making love to one of his gaolers – and she would be so upset.'

'And so would we, darling.'

'My God, Rose, I don't understand you! You're making a joke of it. But I'm in earnest, I'm serious. You can't say that I haven't a sense of humour, but there are certain things that no one can be funny about. A man's feelings, for instance. His real need and belief. Oh, I don't know how to explain it. But listen. Rose, you must try to understand! Before the war I was a schoolmaster. Then I became a soldier, I met you, we fell in love, and I began to live a new life. It was the life I had always wanted – and now you're destroying it. You, who are part of it, perhaps the greatest part, are pulling it to pieces! I can't take that lightly. No man could. And then you say I'm sulking, when my whole heart is full of bitterness and loss.'

'I'm sorry, Julian.'

'You're part of my life, a vital part, and I can't do without you.'

'And I love you too. Honestly and truly.'

'And you see my point of view? I hate talking about it, but I had to make you understand . . . Rose, come here. Oh, don't be silly.'

'Well. . . .'

'We're absolutely alone.'

'Well, just for a minute.'

'You've got the loveliest chin, like the bow of a little ship in clear water.'

'That shows my strength of mind . . . No. Julian, you must be sensible. If we were anywhere else, it would be different.'

'Then let's go somewhere else – you've got the key – let's get out of this damned place.'

'Out of the Castle?'

'Could we do it? You want to be with me, don't you?'

'Of course I do, but . . .'

'Do you know the sentries at the Main Gate? Do you think you could get them out of the way while I slipped through, and then follow me?'

'No, we couldn't do it that way. The Gate's very heavily guarded tonight, because there are soldiers on the Esplanade. There are soldiers all round the Castle now. We're beleaguered, and you're doubly surrounded.'

'The troops wouldn't stop me going through, if I could get out of here. They probably wouldn't stop you either, in that rig-out . . . Rose! Is that why you put it on?'

'What an idea, Julian!'

'Well, it would give you a chance. I suppose you've never done any climbing? If I were by myself I could go down the Rock, but I don't think you could manage it. Though it isn't really difficult.'

'Would a rope be any help?'

'Of course it would. I could take you down perfectly well if you were tied. There aren't more than two or three places that you would find difficult in any case. A rope would solve the whole problem.'

'Well, as a matter of fact, I brought the one that Horrocks used to help you over the wall. It's lying outside the door.'

'Then you were meaning all the time . . .'

'Well, you're not the only one who likes a little affection now and then.'

'Oh, Rose, what a grand girl you are!'

'And you don't wish to God that you weren't in love with me?'

'Where's that rope? I'm not going to waste any more time talking.'

'We'll have to be careful. Wait here for a minute and I'll go and see if there's anyone about.'

The blackness of the sky was broken now by straits and winding gulfs in which a sprinkling of stars glittered brightly. The causeway and the nearer ramparts were seemingly deserted, but Julian, despite his impatience, was cautious now. It was Rose who wanted to hurry. He made her keep to the darkest places, and reconnoitred from every corner. They reached the lower ground behind the old Armoury without seeing anyone, and the wall there was apparently unguarded. Julian whispered that a garrison so careless deserved to be surprised, but Rose answered vaguely that she thought there were plenty of sentries in other places.

From his shoulders she reached the top of the wall, and he heaved her up. She pushed the rope into a crack on the coping, and letting herself down on the other side held it with all her strength while Julian pulled himself up. Sitting on the coping, he released the rope, tied a knot in one end, and jamming the knot into the crevice came down on the outer side. Reaching as high as he could he cut the rope, and they began the descent of the Rock.

Rose had a good head, and showed no sign of fear. She was agile and strong, and they could have gone down with greater speed than they did. But now Julian was very anxious about her safety, and would not let her move until he had explained exactly what she must do, and often put himself into very dangerous positions so that he could help her. He tied and untied her a dozen times, and Rose grew somewhat impatient, though she was touched by his solicitude. They reached the foot of the Rock and the Gardens without mishap or any greater hardship than Julian's nervousness, and to Rose's great relief threw the rope away.

'Now when we come to the picket-line,' he whispered, 'you say nothing. I'll look after that part of the business.'

They walked boldly now, without any attempt at concealment, and were presently challenged: 'Halt! who goes there?'

'Friend,' said Julian sharply. 'And look here, sentry, you'd better keep a brighter look-out than you're doing. I could see you for at least ten seconds before you challenged.'

This little display of authority materially increased his happiness, and slightly exaggerated his military bearing. Rose found it rather difficult to keep up with his long resolute strides. They passed a company of soldiers, lying on the grass, but no one paid any attention to them. They turned west on the road that led through the Gardens. There was another sentry at the gate into Princes Street, but Julian with a soldier's brusque affability wished him good night, and he made no attempt to stop them.

They approached the Albyn Hotel, where Rose had been living before the strike began. She still had her room there.

'But I can't go in dressed like this,' she objected. 'You go first, get the key of my room – it's number 324 – and bring me a coat. There's a big fawn-coloured one in the wardrobe. Hurry, and I'll wait here.'

He hesitated for a moment, for he did not like to leave her alone, but could think of no better plan. 'Then stay here where it's darkest,' he said, 'and don't move.'

Rose waited till Julian had disappeared into the hotel, and then swiftly crossed the road and ran down Queensferry Street. It was one o'clock in the morning, and the town was deserted. Poor Julian, she thought, and looked over her shoulder. There was no one in sight. She took the first turning to the left, and slowed her pace to a fast walk.

She felt very sorry for Julian, but his unhappiness was a small matter compared with the saving of the garrison and the love-strike from defeat. He would be wildly disappointed, but she could atone for that later on. He wasn't difficult to handle, she thought. She was a little ashamed of having deceived him, but delighted with herself because she had done it so well.

For a moment she stood doubtfully at the next corner, but guessed her direction and hurried on. She had a mile or two to go. Her destination was a house in Murrayfield Drive, in the outlying western part of Edinburgh, where she was to ask for Mrs MacLeod of Rhidorroch. Mrs MacLeod would have the latest news of the Highland army. It had been at Stirling when her daughter left it, but that was thirty-six hours ago. And then, wherever the Highland women were, she must reach them without delay, and persuade them to march with all speed to the relief of the Castle.

She found Murrayfield Drive without much trouble, and rang the bell of a tall dark house with a high-pitched roof. Mrs MacLeod herself came to the door. Rose recognized her at once, from her likeness to her daughter, but Mrs MacLeod did not recognize a woman in Rose's clothes, and slammed the door in her face. Frantically Rose beat upon it, and cried, 'I've come from the Castle! The Castle, the Castle!'

Grudgingly the door re-opened, and Rose was dazzled by the beam of an electric torch. Then a rather gruff voice remarked, 'I seem to have made an elementary mistake. Come in, whoever you are. I flattered you, taking you for a man.'

'I don't see there's any flattery in that,' retorted Rose.

'Perhaps there isn't. Still, I don't think much of your women, in the Castle or anywhere else. They ought to have finished this business days ago.'

She led the way into a sitting-room, and said sharply, 'Don't look at the pictures like that. This isn't my house, and I didn't choose the furniture.'

'I'm sorry,' said Rose meekly.

'Now what's been happening at the Castle?'

Rose explained the situation, and Mrs MacLeod remarked, 'So Kate arrived just in time, did she? She ought to have been there sooner. She came here in the early morning, and fainted as soon as she got inside the door. Well, you won't have to go to Stirling tonight; that's one thing you may be glad of.'

The Highland army, she said, had started to move almost as soon as Catriona left it. But it was not taking the direct road to Edinburgh. General Scrymgeour had sent two composite battalions to meet it, who had got as far as Linlithgow, and were halted there, apparently owing to disaffection. In order to avoid them the Highlanders were marching through Fife to North Queensferry, having sent forward a strong force to capture the ferry service. Their only danger by that route was the Navy men at Rosyth, but the Navy was in a state of barely repressed mutiny, so they had discounted the risk. When their main army was expected to cross the Forth, Mrs MacLeod did not know. Her latest news had come with a cyclist early in the afternoon. Since then she had sent as many women as she could mobilize, with food and other comforts, to meet the Highlanders, and in Queensferry, at the Hawes Inn, Rose would find a sensible person called Mrs Moncrieff, who would advise her what to do next.

'And how am I to get there?'

'I've a bicycle waiting for you. And now would you like a drink before you start? Then wait a minute, and I'll get it for you. I'm alone in the house, because I sent every creature I could find to Queensferry.'

She returned with a decanter of sherry and a couple of glasses. 'Had I been in Lady Lysistrata's position,' she said, 'this love-strike would have lasted exactly three days. What's the use of sitting in the Castle doing nothing? Why doesn't she attack? That's what I would have done. On the morning of the third day I would have attacked, and by night the strike would have been over, and the women victorious.'

'But what would you have attacked?' asked Rose.

'Every damned man in the country,' said Mrs. MacLeod of Rhiddorch. 'There isn't a penn'orth of sense in the lot of them. War, my God! I wish they knew as much about it as I do. My husband and both my brothers were killed in the last one, and I took over two crippled estates, paid death duties on both, worked like a slave for twenty years, and now the same sort of nonsense starts all over again. – Have another glass of sherry. – I've got two boys at the front, one has been wounded twice already, and the other has been recommended for the V.C. Six months more, and both will be dead. And you sit in the Castle and do nothing! Even the Highlands would never

have moved if I hadn't told them to. It was I who told them
to attack. That's the only way to win a war; attack, and then
before the other side knows what to think, attack again. Well,
come along and I'll give you your bicycle. Now remember:
Queensferry, the Hawes Inn, and Mrs Moncrieff.'

In a humble but resolute frame of mind – for she had rarely
encountered a person of more forceful temper than Mrs
MacLeod of Rhidorroch – Rose wheeled her bicycle on the
road, mounted, and set off through the darkness in the
direction of Queensferry and the Hawes Inn.

CHAPTER SIX

The Last Battle

I

DRAWING curtains and canopies of mist from the cool earth, the day broke fair and windless. The morning light was opalescent, a whiteness with gleams of topaz in it, and the spires of churches, the roofs of tall buildings, rose like brown rock-islands out of milky vapour. But the upper sky was blue, and above the mounting sun it grew clear as sapphire, while the mist vanished or was gathered into a belt of low-lying cumulus to the east. By nine o'clock the whole sky was brilliant and the day already hot.

From early morning an army had been gathering for the assault on the Castle. Company after company of soldiers had come marching into the Gardens under the northern face of the Rock, and whenever a company or two came in, a company or two – lying peaceably on the grass beneath a tent of idle talk and cigarette smoke – were called to attention and marched out again. Some of them went up the Mound and on to Castle Hill, and some went round the other way into Johnstone Terrace, and up the long flight of steps to the Esplanade. For every military operation of any magnitude is always attended by some confusion, and the law of physics applies also to tactics; to every item of marching there is an equal and opposite item of counter-marching. But eventually, though some of them may still have been in the wrong place, the Castle was entirely surrounded by troops, and on the eastern side of the Esplanade a strong force lay ready to begin the attack.

The soldiers had been drafted from many different regiments. They had been carefully selected and they were all men of good character. But they had no enthusiasm for the task in front of them, though their officers had been at pains to impress them with the serious nature of it. It might, indeed, be one of the crucial battles of the world, but they found it difficult to believe in its importance because the circumstances were so very different from those of other battles. Their weapons, for instance, could hardly be described as soldierly.

General Scrymgeour had found it difficult to persuade the Cabinet to authorize weapons of any sort. The Ministers were still fearful of being arraigned, before the whole world or even their own constituencies, as barbarians and murderers of women. They had categorically forbidden Scrymgeour to employ lethal arms, and to meet their wishes he had devised a kind of club or truncheon made of heavy felt and loaded with sand. These clubs were obviously formidable, but probably not deadly, and the Cabinet, though with some misgiving, had finally approved of them. Every second man carried in addition a large sack. It had been suggested, by Julian Brown, that these would provide useful means of securing prisoners.

The soldiers were almost as uneasy as the Cabinet. They did not like the idea of an organized war against women, though the great majority of them were very angry with the rebels, and hated the love-strike because it had deprived them of so much pleasure. It had robbed them of the only pleasure that put them on the same level of enjoyment as princes and pluto-crats. It was therefore an anti-democratic strike. But the purpose of the strike, said others, was to stop the war, and it was the opinion of many that the war itself was anti-democratic. Britain was in alliance with Germany, and Germany stood for tyranny. After twelve months of fighting the soldiers had started to wonder what they were fighting for; and no one could give any better reason than the need to punish France for the bombing of London. But the punishment, they thought, was hurting themselves as much as the French, and there was no comfort in thinking that it was probably of help to Germany. For Germany's cause, whatever it might be, was certainly not the cause of peace and justice, of freedom and democracy.

The men were uneasy, but their doubtful minds were still in subjection to their loyalty. Their blood was thicker than logic, and England's cause was still theirs though the politicians had taken England down a crooked road. They would grumble but they would not rebel, because they felt that England, in so far as they were England, stood for peace and toleration and a kind of unassuming decency. That was the root of their deeper loyalty. But they were also loyal to their regiments and their own officers, because such loyalty is a natural thing and many of their officers were very fine men. It was, in part, this secondary loyalty that made them dislike the thought of a pitched battle against women; for they feared it would impair the dignity of their regiments. Their colours were glorious with honours won in every quarter of the globe. They had been dyed in the heroism of centuries and brocaded with victories that overstrode the world and filled the pages of Britain's history with such chords of glory as made a music like the supernal harmony of the spheres. Here were regiments that carried on their colours France and India, and there a man whose crest was Egypt. A pair of others pulled red roses from a bush, and stuck the memory of Minden in their coats. They had fought with Clive at Plassey and Wellington at Talavera. They had left their dead in Kabul and Kandahar, they had carried their memory into Africa, they had crossed the desert and taken Jerusalem. Their last, their bitter and most splendid honours, they had won against Germany, who was now their ally . . . And now all this heritage of glory was to be carried into action against a pack of women! They did not like the idea at all, and no one could have persuaded them that the battle for Edinburgh Castle would be of far greater importance than Plassey or Talavera or bloody contests on the Aisne and the Lys and the Somme.

Whistles blew. The soldiers knocked out their pipes and got up. They fell in on their markers, trampling the warm grass, and dressed their ranks. They stood to attention and with disciplined unwatching eyes stared straight in front of them while General Scrymgeour, impassive as they but seeing everything, rode past their unmoving lines. Despite their uneasy hearts and troubled dignity, they could be trusted to obey and do their best. They were loyal, and therefore they would fight a battle of which they were already ashamed, and suffer in a cause they gravely doubted.

II

In the Castle there was neither doubting heart nor any mind that feared the betraying of its dignity. The rebel women were afire with zeal and exultant resolution. The skirmish of the previous morning had given them confidence, and they were determined not only to fight to the utmost of their strength, but to be victorious. They were passionately convinced of the importance of the coming battle. It would be a battle new in history, and Lysistrata had told them it might be more decisive than any storied or stricken field since Marathon.

She had spoken to them on the steepness of the causeway where it turns uphill from the lower part of the Castle to the Citadel. The whole garrison, except the sentries on the wall, had gathered in a great crowd below her. She had told them of the Highland army that was on its way to join them, and charged them to hold the Castle, no matter at what cost, till the Highlanders should come. Then she spoke of the greatness of their cause, and declared her faith in their power to bring happiness and reason to the world.

'From the earliest days of recorded history,' she said, 'of all the many battles that have been fought for one thing or another, those that are remembered with the greatest honour were fought for liberty. And that is what we are fighting for now. You may say that we are free already, and certainly we are not subject to a foreign people, nor do we pay tribute to a conquering enemy. But we are subject to a thing more powerful than any nation, more humiliating than any conquest; and that is error. Though all our faculties were designed for life, we have allowed them to be perverted in the cause of death. Though the right to happiness is surely implicit in the creation of humankind, yet we have allowed that right to be neglected, and suffered our energy to be used in the pursuit of power and wealth, by which the happiness of the many is sacrificed to the doubtful satisfaction of a few. Though beauty and kindness, though justice and the arts flourish only in time of peace, yet our country went willingly into war against France and is devoting all its mind and vigour to the destruction of both these peoples. We are subject to error, and this war is an expression of that error. And so I say that now we women are fighting for freedom, because we are resolved to strike off the shackles of war, and throw down the prison-house of error.

'Most of you, I know, regard our struggle merely as a war

against the men. And in its immediate aspect, so it is. I would
be justified in calling upon you to fight as women against the
stupidity and the crimes of this generation of men. I would be
justified in saying to you: Six and twenty years ago our
mothers brought forth in this country a new womanhood, conceived in liberty, and dedicated to the proposition that men
and women are created equal. Now we are engaged in a great
civil war, testing whether that womanhood, so conceived and
so dedicated, can long endure. And we here highly resolve
that our mothers shall not have lived in vain, that the people
shall, under God, have a new birth of freedom, and that the
government of women, by women, and for women, shall be
established upon earth.

'I would be justified in calling upon you to fight for such a
cause, but I am the more justified in naming to you a greater
cause. It is not dominion for ourselves, nor the rule of women,
that we seek. It is the dominion of love and the rule of sense.
Go to these ramparts and look out upon the land of Britain.
You realize her power, but feed your eyes upon her from day
to day, till love of her shall fill your hearts. And then when all
her greatness shall break upon you, you must first reflect that
it was by courage, a sense of duty, and a feeling of honour in
action that men were enabled to win all this. But you must also
reflect that now greatness has its obligations. It may not stand
still, but must always work to some new benevolence, and the
world is waiting for the leadership that we can give. The world
is in slavery to that same error to which we are subject, and by
winning freedom for ourselves we shall teach freedom to
others. This land of Britain has been given greatness by many
generations of brave and gallant men, and now, by first fighting and defeating error, let women put that greatness to its
proper use. We must have courage as they had courage, and
the sense of duty and the feeling of honour that ennobled
them. But our purpose shall be different. It shall not be wealth
nor power, but the establishment of love, and the securing of
peace upon earth, and the enthronement of good sense.

'Now all this happiness shall be the fruit of freedom, of that
freedom from error which is the only true liberty. But freedom
is first the fruit of valour, and so you may decline none of the

dangers of this war, but seek them out and fight with courage, and all your strength, and unfailing resolution. So long as there shall but a hundred of you remain alive, you must never give consent to subject yourselves again to the dominion of error. For it is not glory, it is not riches nor honours, but liberty that we fight and contend for, which no honest woman will lose but with her life!'

Neither Lysistrata nor her officers had any illusions about the difficulty of holding the Castle and the magnitude of their necessary effort. From dawn they had watched the slow concentration of the army below them, and though they had been warned that the odds against them would be two to one, it was now clear that they would be a lot heavier than that.

In the Gardens where the bulk of the army was gathered the grass was hidden by the mass of khaki, and because the soldiers had trodden down the flower-beds, its drab hue was almost unrelieved. From above it looked as if the ground had been newly ploughed, but among the upturned earth ten thousand points of brass glittered where the sun struck reflection from buttons and buckles and cap-badges.

At about nine o'clock a mission approached the Castle and formally demanded its surrender. It consisted of Mr Pelham-Blair, a Staff Officer, and a sergeant who carried a white flag. They were not admitted. The drawbridge had been lowered, and the Main Gate was blocked and buttressed with baulks of timber. Mr Pelham-Blair had to shout his demand to the ramparts. Lysistrata's reply was drowned in a general cry of 'No surrender!' Hundreds of women, yelling defiance, rose suddenly from behind the battlements with a flourish of white arms like a breaking wave. They stood for more than a minute, wildly hallooing. Three times Lysistrata answered without a chance of being heard. Then the cheering and shouting died away, and Lysistrata called loudly down: 'Until you have stopped the war, we shall never surrender.' Under a new storm of cheering, the mission retired.

Ten minutes later there was a general movement of the troops, and the attack began.

The outermost defence of the Castle was a dry ditch, deep and broad, but in the middle partly spanned by an abutment or mole, from which the drawbridge had given access to a long archway under the Guardhouse. The interval left by the lowering of the drawbridge was not great, and if it could be crossed the arch beyond would shelter a considerable body of men while they attacked the Main Gate. The assault was therefore initiated by a party of Engineers.

Carrying bridging material on to the mole, they first endeavoured to throw a duckboard across the gap, but were assailed from above with such a variety of missiles that they retreated almost immediately. An officer rallied them and again led them forward. From the parapets above and the roof of the Guardhouse they were pelted with hot ashes and kitchen-refuse, and cobble-stones which the women had dug from causeways in the Castle. Much of this bombardment was very wildly directed and did little damage, but the furious shouting and constant shrill crying with which it was accompanied were unnerving, and the Engineers were further disconcerted when two of their number were almost simultaneously stunned by flying cobbles. This success evoked from the women such a demoniacal chorus of delight that the Engineers again retreated.

At their third attempt, however, they managed temporarily to bridge the gap, and three volunteers, running swiftly across the duckboard, reached the safety of the archway beyond. A fourth, attempting to follow them, was not so lucky. He was blinded by a shower of potato peelings, and before he could recover a beef-bone struck him on the head, so that he lost his balance, and falling, clutched at the duckboard, which he dislodged. They fell together into the dry moat.

But the three on the other side were now under shelter, and by means of ropes which were thrown to them began to haul across heavy joists of timber. Meanwhile a flank attack was being made with ladders against the curtain of wall that connected the Guardhouse and the old Portcullis Gate; and in a number of places to the north and west men were attempting, either singly or in small parties, to climb the Rock. But they made little progress. Trundling cobble-stones from the ramparts above them, the women drove them down again, and within half an hour from the start of the engagement the attack had apparently failed. The moat was still unbridged, and the trio of volunteers was isolated under the archway. Three strong joists lay across the gap, but every attempt to plank them had been defeated. Lysistrata had had a score of braziers made out of buckets, and from these, burning on the ramparts above, the unhappy bridge-builders were thickly pelted with red coals. The defenders had also thrown a few bottles of aerated water, which on impact burst like bombs.

The stalemate that threatened was overcome by Scrymgeour himself. Arriving on the Esplanade, he personally directed operations, and by his instruction shields were fashioned out of doors and lengths of corrugated iron, under which the Engineers once more set to work. The bridge was finished, and despite a furious bombardment from above, a dozen men crossed it, armed with axes and sledge-hammers, and set to work on the heavy iron-bolted doors. The attack on the curtain wall was also renewed, and in the Gardens an officer was instigating and encouraging numerous fresh attempts to scale the Rock. None of the climbers progressed far, however, and Lady Oriole, watching from above, began to suspect they were not trying to. She decided that this half-hearted assault was meant only to engage part of the garrison while the main attack took place at the Gate; and she gave orders that ammunition was not to be wasted on it.

The Gate, reinforced by a couple of up-turned lorries and baulks of thick timber, resisted for some time both axe and sledge-hammer. Scrymgeour grew impatient. He ordered a battering-ram to be brought up, the twenty-foot butt-end of a ship's mast, two feet or more in diameter, carried on rope-slings. He himself crossed the bridge scatheless, but the ram was nearly lost in the moat when a flaming brazier was dropped on its crew. One man was badly burnt, and several others, though apparently uninjured, were disconcerted when a few minutes later they found themselves on fire.

In the long archway the thud of the ram echoed softly like the rolling of distant thunder. Presently it was seen that the lower part of the Gate was weakening, for most of the buttressing timbers lay high against the upper half. The great iron hinges were loosened, and the two halves of the Gate met awry. Again and again the ram swung ponderously against the failing door, and then with a tearing protesting sound the one half of it fell gradually outward.

Within the door the stone causeway wound uphill to the Portcullis Gate. To the left the rock, a sheer precipice, rose to the upper part of the Castle; on the other side was the high curtain wall. In this confined space stood a dense horde of women, waiting for the invaders and prepared to resist them by force of numbers. A dozen or so were busy with the defences of the Gate. With blistered hands they held the quivering buttresses in position, and when the up-turned lorries that strengthened the doors were shaken by repeated blows, they thrust new timbers against them, and keenly watched for any weakness. Then they saw, on the one side, the leaning baulks of timber come slowly down, when that half of the Gate fell forward. One of the lorries, up-ended against it, collapsed with the Gate. There was a renewed assault with axe and heavy hammer, and through the confusion of splintered wood and buttresses asprawl, a couple of men came creeping.

From the dense array of the defenders rose a moan of anger, like the thirsty cry of a wolf-pack waiting. Of the women who had been watching the Gate, there was one within a yard of the invaders. She was a Yorkshire woman, red-armed, tow-haired, the mother of a thankless family. She grappled with the soldiers as they got up, both together, and falling with them knocked the wind from the one and thumped the head of the other soundly on the stony road. But following them came a little dark nimble man, who, before she knew what was happening, had stunned her with a blow of his felt club, and dodging among the timber-baulks he quickly accounted for three others, of whom the last was the gallant Miss McNulty. But her fate did not long go unavenged. McNab, her faithful friend, was standing near. She was unarmed, her hands were torn and bleeding. But like a wildcat she leapt at the little dark man, who, retreating from a storm of blows, stumbled and fell. McNab stooped and gripped him by his belt and loosened collar. She exerted her strength and lifted him from the ground. She began to turn, slowly and with short steps, in a close circle. The sweat ran down her face, her eyes were staring and shot with blood. But her pace quickened; her arms, it seemed, grew longer; and the dark man swung round in widening circles. Then with a gasp and a final lift she hurled him against a group of his advancing comrades and scattered them like ninepins. Still sobbing for breath, she took Mc-Nulty's limp hand – two other women were carrying her – and a passage was made for them through the mass of waiting defenders.

By now some thirty men had come through the shattered gate, and every minute others were pouring in. The first arrivals cleared away the sprawling timbers and the broken lorries, and the others assembled in close order on the cause-way. There was a space of about twenty yards between them and the horde of women, and the women stood irresolute. They had been told that their obligation was to defend the Castle, but they did not realize that defence may often be ensured only by swift attack. They had the advantage in numbers, and a vigorous advance might have enabled them to hold and repair the broken Gate; but they failed to see their opportunity and waited till the men had gathered their strength. Then, too late, a tall ungainly girl summoned and led a strong sortie.

Her name was Hepburn, a daughter of the old reiving Border house. A morose and solitary girl, she had been till a week before remarkable only for her gaunt and sturdy frame, and a surly manner that concealed virtues of which no one knew. She was not beautiful and no man had ever loved her. For this failure she had always blamed herself and her appear-ance; but the love-strike had given her a different view of it. From Lysistrata she had learnt that men were not the inefrable judges she had always been taught to think, but fallible and short-sighted beings who rarely knew what was good for them; and for this revelation of their stupidity she now very earnestly hated them all. . . . She had a capacity for affection, she desired children and was clever enough to bring them up sensibly; she was practical and could manage a house; she had taste and education and could, if anyone desired, talk of Auden and Roualt; she had a sweet temper and a sense of duty – but all these riches had gone unnoticed by men because her figure was gaunt and her face plain. Till a week ago she had thought them justified in this neglect, and bitterly resented her ungainly looks; but now she knew it was men's stupidity, their bony lack of understanding and bemused ineptitude, that left her loveless and unfriended. . . . The blood of her reiving fathers grew hot in her veins, and her spirit rose in the flame that had lighted many a Border peel. She turned to the women about her, and they caught her fire. She whipped them to the assault, and laughed as she led them to the fight. The Hepburns were riding again, with Bauld Buccleugh and Kinmont Willie, and four-score ranting troopers from Teviothead and Bemersyde.

But Bauld Buccleugh was short in the arm and hampered by a great depth of bosom, so before she could come to grips with the enemy she was knocked on the head with a sandbag, and that was the end of her fighting for that day. Nor was Kinmont Willie more fortunate, though her long legs took her swiftly over the ground, and her short gymnasium tunic did nothing to hamper her movement. She ran right into the arms of a great ox-eyed, burly-chested, stolid private of the Essex Regiment, who held her fast while another man pulled a sack over her head and down to her knees, where he tied it with a running cord. The raid was defeated, the Borderers tottered and fell beneath the curving blows of soft but heavy loaded truncheons, and one by one the soldiers stuffed them into their ready sacks and tied them round the knees.

But a few of the women, a mere half-dozen, fought their way through the soldiers, and in the blind corner beyond the Gate turned at bay. The Hepburn girl was one of them. A subaltern, with twenty men behind him, called on them to surrender. He was a tall and handsome youth with grave eyes and delicate fine features. He was bareheaded, and his dark hair was wavy as a little pool in the wind. With a sudden shout – of hatred that was strangely charged with another emotion – the Hepburn girl sprang fiercely forward, and with her broken hockey stick struck him heavily on the temple. For a moment she stood looking down at him, and her triumph was half an exquisite remorse. Then she felt a crushing blow on her head, and falling upon her fallen foe, her last thought was to come down upon him as gently as she could. The flood of battle went past them, and they were forgotten.

Now on the causeway there ensued a most desperate mellay. Between the precipitous rock and the outer wall the opposing forces were jammed together like cattle in a pen. There was no room for weapons, no space to swing sandbag or mashie, but soldiers and women fought hand to hand and face to face. The sun poured hotly down, and the narrow canyon was like a baker's oven. But the women were undaunted, and heat-stroke could not conquer men whose regiments had won their glory on the scorching plains of Baluchistan or in the stifling forests of equatorial Africa. They fought grimly, and with method in their grimness. Those in front sought always to get firm hold of a woman, by neck or wrist, and drag her from the ranks. Then she was thrust and hustled to the rear, and there a sack pulled over her and firmly tied. The prisoners, thus securely bagged, were carried out and laid in rows in the archway or on the pavement beyond the bridge. Some forty or fifty of the strongest and most determined of the women were captured and dealt with in this fashion, and the defence grew gradually weaker.

But the men also suffered heavy casualties, and many were stunned by blows or half-smothered in the press. And sometimes when a man had grappled with an opposing girl his eye betrayed him, and the sight of beauty – a flushing cheek, the glimpse of a white and straining bosom, the pretty volute of some delicate distended nostril – went like an arrow to his heart and spoiled him of strength and of his purpose. But another circumstance of the fighting was even more dangerous.

The women had dressed themselves for battle, but most of them had made a party toilet of it, and in the hot close air of the canyon their mingled perfumes were like a heavy enchantment. They put a spell upon the air. It breathed of musk and roses and languorous jessamine. While desperate women struggled with bombardiers and Grenadiers, the oils of santal and cedarwood strove with the attar of bergamot; and above a thousand straining bodies rose the scent of lavender and of rosemary. Now some errant zephyr brought the smell of white lilac, now of orange-blossom; or, to a more discerning nose, of hydrocinnamic aldehyde and the methyl ether of anthranilic acid. But whether of natural origin or the distillation of a laboratory, the enchantment of the air was too powerful for many a simple soldier, and a hundred staggered from the fight, drunk with an odorous thought of Calypso's isle, or the drowsy beauty and the fountains of Zobeida's garden.

The soldiers, however, could with smaller loss suffer casualties twice as heavy as the defenders. Reserves and reinforcements poured steadily through the broken Gate, now undeterred by any bombardment from above, for the refuse buckets were empty, the braziers cold; and steadily they drove the women before them. The attack on the curtain wall, desultory at first, became now more vigorous, and the defenders were thrown into some confusion when a dozen soldiers, reckless of the consequences, came leaping down into the very midst of their tight array. Still they fought stubbornly, and contested every foot they yielded. But then from the rear came a whisper, a growing murmur, a shout of panic. The enemy was inside, the Castle lost! The soldiers had climbed the Rock! Here on the causeway the women would be caught in a trap, with men behind and men in front, and others leaping from the wall above.

They broke and ran. Helter-skelter they fled uphill and through the Portcullis Gate. To their left there were steps in the rock, as steep as the side of a house, that led to the Citadel; but there Lysistrata stood with her Guards about her. Beyond the road, on the level ground before the Hospital and the Governor's House, a battle was loosely raging. The men were out-numbered, but they were chosen troops, and slowly but surely they were driving the women before them.

The fugitives from the lower causeway were halted by Lysistrata's ringing voice. 'What have you lost?' she cried. 'Your wits or your courage? You won't find them that way. There is the enemy, and that's where you'll get your courage back, and your wits too. Every one of those soldiers must be driven out. They came in by the Rock, send them back by the Rock. Remember your manners this time, and so long as there's a man left in the Castle, never turn your backs on him.

Now forward, women! Forward, and remember you're fighting for love and happiness!'

Sullenly at first, the women listened. They wiped their sweaty brows, and pulled resentfully at tattered pieces of their clothing. They were weary and dishevelled. But they took heart again. They grew angry, then combative, ashamed of their retreat and eager to efface its memory in new victory. They reformed their ranks and gathered again into a solid warlike phalanx. Mrs Graham and Miss McNab were now in command, and the battle-torn regiment raised their arms – bare arms leaping out of ragged sleeves – and cheered their order to advance.

Meanwhile Lysistrata had thrown her Guards in a double rank across the road, and before the bristle-hedge of their pikes and halberds, the soldiers were halted, dubious.

The battle in front of the Hospital turned in the women's favour when the veterans from the lower causeway launched their attack. The men gave ground. But they were wisely led, and instead of trying to maintain a hopeless resistance, they broke and scattered. As individuals they were more than a match for the women, and by solitary action they doubled their effectiveness. Their leader was Julian Brown, and their guerrilla tactics were his device. It was he who had previously set hundreds of soldiers to climbing the Rock from all quarters, and so dissipated the attention of the women. But only one in four of his climbers was an actual assailant and these were all mountain-men that he had recruited from Scrymgeour's whole army.

He was fiercely proud of his alpine company. In all history, he thought, no officer had ever commanded such a body of men as these – men from the Cumberland fells and the mountains of Wester Ross, from the slopes of Skiddaw and Beinn Eighe; there were Canadians, short of speech but long of leg, from Tête Jaune and Mount Assiniboine; and New Zealanders from the Crags of Hokonui and the stark uplands of Papahuana, men nimble as goats but of inflexible morality. There were three hundred in all, and every man a mountaineer. Subalterns of the Indian Army, who had spent all their leave on the naked ridges of Kanchenjunga and Nanga Parbat, rubbed shoulders with men who knew every ledge and pinnacle from the Bavarian Wettersteingebirge to the Pic du Midi, from Cimon della Pala to the Sgurr na Bannachdich. A common passion united them, an ardent but ascetic passion, and long days on many a dizzy precipice and vertiginous *aiguille* had given them nerves of steel and made them tough as whale-bone. They had gone up the Castle Rock like firemen up a ladder.

Now their guerilla tactics tired and bewildered the women, and the striking-power of Mrs Graham's phalanx was nullified by the absence of any stable objective. It was harried by constant attack, and spent its strength on charging an enemy that would not stay to receive it. Like a tide running into eddies and overfalls, the battle appeared to have lost all direction, but in twenty different places broke into furious upheaval to show its fierce persistence.

The main force of the invaders was now at close quarters with Lysistrata's Guards. Their pikes and halberds, that might well have defeated an impetuous charge of horse, were less effective against the strong but cautious tactics of infantry. Unbroken, the long line of glinting steel had looked perilous enough, but as soon as the line gave way the Guards were thrown into confusion. A sergeant of the Royal Welch, lithe as a cat, a welterweight champion, had been the first to make a gap in the hedge. He provoked a long-point, side-stepped and got inside, parried a thrust from the rear rank, and leaping sideways flung his weight across half a dozen shafts and brought their heads to the ground. Into the breach came a swarm of men.

Elsewhere a private of the Green Howards, taking a thrust through the fleshy part of his left arm, had caught the pike in his hands and pulled the great tawny freckled girl who wielded it, and would not let it go, out of the line and into a sack that his neighbour held ready. Here was another breach, and three or four men, rushing in, forced it wide open. At close quarters a long-hafted pike gave no defence against the soldiers' clubs, and woman after woman staggered and fell beneath their heavy curving blows. Many of the Guards, dropping their useless weapons, fought with bare hands, and

here and there in a towsy scuffle a sturdy private got the worst
of it from some raging Amazon. Other women, snatching
from the ground a broken shaft or wrenching his truncheon
from a staggered soldier, battled their way to the long steep
flight of steps in the rock, where Lysistrata stood with a sword
in her hand.

Here the remnant of the Guard were fighting fiercely, for
the defence of the steps was a vital matter. They led to the
Citadel, the topmost part of the Castle. They rose steeply, and
were so narrow that two men could hardly stand on them
abreast. Nor was it possible to come at them from either side,
for the rock was precipitous. It was a place that a swordsman
might hold against an army so long as his wrist was strong and
his eye keen. But the women were growing tired, their
weapons were clumsy and heavy in their hands. One by one
they were pulled down, and the soldiers came nearer to
Lysistrata, standing with her sword alone.

About two hundred men had been detailed for the assault
on the steps. The invaders' main army, again reinforced,
pushed forward up the causeway. A detachment was sent to
the assistance of Julian's mountaineers, and the rest wheeled
uphill and came face to face with that part of the garrison
which had not yet been in action. There were more than a
thousand women here, under the command of Lady Oriole.
The greater number were massed in front of Foog's Gate. It
was a strong position, for the road to it rose steeply, and the
women had provided themselves with a store of cobble-stones
for ammunition. Again and again the soldiers charged, and
were beaten back by a heavy fusillade.

By now the sun was almost directly overhead, and the Castle
was bathed in heat. Many of the combatants on both sides had
grown weary, and when they withdrew from the fight the still
hot splendour of the sky abashed them, and they felt a languor
in their bones. The high-pitched Castle was a pinnacle in the
windless sky, far from earth, and the sun pressed close upon it
with plumes of quivering heat. Tired and sweating, their
bones melting in the glare of noon, the laggard soldiers lay,
and the sun that had dissolved their strength now generated in
their blood a strange excitement. They were impatient with

the noise of continuing battle, and they resented the struggling sight of men still swift in action. The burning solitude of the sky possessed them with a kinder passion, and forgetting all other thoughts they looked with longing at the women who lay, weary and dishevelled, in the golden light beside them. Here a bruised and heavy hand touched softly a softer palm, and there a soldier lifted gently to his knees a panting girl. A woman tore from her hanging sleeve a strip of linen to bind a trooper's bleeding head, and others, soldiers and rebel side by side, as though in a trance sat unmoving and stared the one at the other.

But this submission to the heat of the sun had so far been made only by a minority, and elsewhere the battle fiercely continued. On the steps there were still two women who fought in front of Lysistrata, but the one over-reached herself and fell, the other was brought down by a tall limber fellow, strong and truculent, a shoeing-smith in the Gunners, who had thrown off his tunic and shirt and now fought naked to the waist. He had armed himself with the haft of a broken pike, and leaping up the steps he struck hard at Lysistrata. She parried and thrust, but he in turn parried so strongly that she she felt her arm grow numb, and gave ground before him.

But now from above and behind her came a hoarse high shout, and glancing round she saw a huge woman, copper-haired, her great bosom tumultuous in a torn blouse, coming down fast and recklessly to her aid. She carried a great two-handed sword on her shoulder, and pushing past Lysistrata she cried in a rough Glasgow voice, 'Leave yon billie tae me and ma wee Kisser! *Hey-yach!* Up the Celtic! Awa hame, ye naked beast, and put a sark on yer shouthers. *Hey-yeh-yach!*'

Furiously she swung the sword, and the smith gave back in dismay. 'Is this no a bonny wee Kisser?' cried the copper-haired woman over her shoulder. 'I nabbed it the first day we cam here, oot o' yon hall that was full o' spears and trash, and hid it in auld Mons Meg. Up the spoot o' auld Mons Meg. I just minded on where it was, and I thocht tae masel, we'll gie a guff tae the sodgers. Sodgers! I've seen 'em grow! Ay, Christ, ay! *Hey-yey-yach!*'

The smith, a strong and valiant man, had returned to the

attack, but the copper-haired woman swung her sword with such prodigious strength that she beat in his guard and swept him from his feet. She struck with the flat of the blade, and her backward swing took a tall corporal – coming up behind the smith – on the side of the head and toppled him senseless down the stair.

Then, bombastic, she taunted the soldiers and boasted of her strength. 'Come awa', ma lucky lads!' she cried. 'Come awa', fish-guts, pudden-heids, you peelie-wally bastards, you! Come and hae a toss wi' Red Biddy McLafferty o' the Gallowgate in Glasgow! I've knocked the stuffin' oot o' better men than you, and clawed the heid off bluidy Hieland polismen while you were clappin' yer hands at Charlie Chaplin! *Hey-yach!* Here's Red Biddy and her bonny wee Kisser! Come awa', skiters, lang-luggit rottans, ye lousy libbet scrogs! Up the Celtic! Ay, Christ, ay! There's a runt wi' a face like a puddock and a mou' like a spleuchan. Hey, runt, gie ma wee Kisser a wee sook at yer neb! *Hey-yey-yach!*'

Chanting her war-song, Red Biddy held the stair against all comers, and Lysistrata, three steps above her, waited with bitter expectancy. She had trusted to hold out the soldiers longer than this. She had hoped to keep them at bay till the Highlanders came. But the Highland women had forty miles to march. They could not reach the Castle till nightfall at the earliest. And now the soldiers were in possession of all the lower part of the Castle, and the Citadel was threatened from both sides. From her high place on the steps she could watch here and there the eddies and fringes of the battle, and she could see that many of the women, worn out by fighting, had already given up the struggle. In the clear hot air she could see far beyond the ramparts, into the town below, and the road that would bring the relieving Highlanders. But there was no use in looking for them yet, nor for many hours to come.

Now from the soldiers crowded on the steps rose a yell of triumph, for Red Biddy, surprised by one of them clambering up the rock, had turned and swung at him, and missed. The sword struck stone, and so heavy was the blow that the blade broke at the hilt, and Red Biddy was weaponless. But she was still undaunted. She flung the hilt at the jeering faces below her, and with a great gesture wiping the sweat from her streaming brow, rubbed her hands on her thighs and shouted another challenge.

'Come awa', tawpies, toytcrin' yauds!' she cried. 'Come awa', fattrels, clarty hoors! Up the Celtic! It's a stair-heid fecht, and it's stair-heid fechtin' made the name o' Red Biddy McLafferty o' the Gallowgate in Glasgow! *Hey-yeh-yach!* You wi' a mug like a moodly kebbuck, come here an' taste ma loof! *Hey-yach!* Wae gae by the stane that brak the sword, and wae gae by yer hale clamjamfry and a' yer gear and graith. Smell ma nieve! Smell the t'ither, you wi' the grozet een and the grutten mou'. If it's fechtin' you want, it's here by the wamefou' still. Ay, Christ, ay!'

A Canadian sergeant, a grim farmer from the Manitoban prairie, was the first to confront her. He took a savage blow on the face, but gripped her by the arm, and pulled her down into the reaching hands of the soldiers. But Red Biddy was fighting still. She howled her war-cry, and like a boulder that brings an avalanche with it, she swept her enemies before her and tumbled down the rock in the midst of staggered and falling men. But now Lysistrata stood on the stair alone.

The confusion was suddenly stilled, and the angry soldiers made way for an officer. He came swiftly up, and stood two steps below her. It was Scrymgeour, and he was unarmed. Lysistrata raised her sword against him.

'I have come to ask you to surrender,' he said harshly. 'You must know that further resistance is useless, and you will save your people a lot of suffering if you surrender now.'

'There can be no surrender,' said Lysistrata, 'till Britain has proclaimed her peace with France.'

He stood silent for nearly a minute, and Lysistrata lowered her sword. Unmoving, they stood in the golden heat, and in her grave beauty Lysistrata was like the Demeter, calm and lovely in her promise of happiness, that once looked down at the Spartan colonists of Cnidos. The anger died in Scrymgeour's heart, and as though anger had been the upholding skeleton of his strength, his strength grew less. He saw the beauty of Lysistrata, and nothing else. He knew that he loved her, and knew nothing more.

But while they stood, in love and the noonday's cataleptic hold, there rose to the Castle walls a far confusion of noise that held in its midst a shrill high music. The women heard it, and ran to the ramparts. The soldiers heard it, and looked at each other in sudden doubt. It was the noise of an army marching, and the people cheering as it passed, and the music in its midst was the pipers playing.

III

In the very middle of the Castle Esplanade stood a group of elderly gentlemen, darkly clad and of solemn aspect. Despite their obvious importance, they presented a forlorn and desolate appearance, as though they had been forgotten, and having been forgotten, did not know what to do. Which was, indeed the case.

The whole Cabinet was there, except Mr Percy Small who was still in prison, and the Ministers were attended by several secretaries, Private or Parliamentary, and about a dozen junior Ministers who by their serious demeanour did what they could to disguise their present dubiety and comparative youth. They were waiting to hear the result of the battle.

There was a column of soldiers on Castle Hill, and a cordon of policemen at the lower end of the Esplanade. But the Esplanade itself was empty save for the Ministers, and a row of agitated sacks on the pavement near the entrance to the Castle. For some considerable time they had seen no fighting nor any sign of it, nor any movement of troops. They did not know whether the battle was still going on, or whether it had finished, and they were very annoyed because no one had come to tell them.

It was Lord Pippin who finally suggested that they go and see for themselves, and though two or three of the more cautious demurred, the majority of the Ministers were much impressed by the simple good sense of his proposal. They set off in a body, not rapidly indeed, but with a movement that revealed the ponderous resolve by which it was activated.

At the entrance to the Castle they paused to examine the forty or fifty potato-bags which held the earliest batch of prisoners. Many of the occupants were still writhing and heaving, and their heels beat a tattoo on the pavement.

'This is utter barbarism!' exclaimed Mr Curle indignantly, and anxiously surveyed the long row of female legs to see if he could recognize his Delia's.

Several other Ministers also condemned so strict a confinement, and Sir Joseph Rumble, stooping over a well-filled sack, requested a moment's silence. 'This unfortunate woman is trying to tell me something,' he declared.

He and several of his colleagues listened intently. The prisoner had a great deal to say, and her spirit was undiminished by captivity. The expression of the Ministers changed from exaggerated sympathy to the stony aspect of a prosperous congregation when some unfortunate curate preaches from the text, *Thou shalt love thy neighbour as thyself*.

The Chancellor of the Exchequer, a practical man, suggested that it would be a mistake to interfere with the dispositions of the Commander-in-Chief; and the other Ministers, having listened in turn to the voluble prisoner, fully agreed with him. They crossed the bridge and entered the Castle.

In the cul-de-sac to the left of the Gate they were surprised to see a sight very different from anything they had anticipated. A great raw-boned girl, her strong face transfigured by love, was fondling and cosseting a singularly handsome young officer who lay with his head in her lap. She looked up, with lioness defiance, and with protective arms clutched her lover to her breast. The Ministers, abashed, turned the other way, and immediately beheld a Quartermaster-sergeant of the Duke of Wellington's Regiment in the act of kissing a charming girl with lint-white hair and a badly torn frock. In growing embarrassment they hurried up the causeway, but before they had gone twenty yards they saw on either side a dozen couples, soldiers and rebels locked in each other's arms, who either turned and glared at them with manifest displeasure, or, what was worse, ignored them completely.

Even Lord Pippin's equanimity was faintly ruffled. He stopped, and his colleagues stopped with him. The Chancellor of the Exchequer, despite his reputation for Britannic *sangfroid*, nearly jumped out of his morning-coat when a deep

voice immediately behind him murmured, 'Do you love me?'
But turning, he perceived that the speaker was a gunner in the
Royal Artillery, and the person he addressed an exquisite little
creature with bright blue eyes and a fascinating dimple. 'I
propose to go no farther,' he said decisively, and there was a
murmur of approval from the other Ministers.

'I was about to ask Mr Pelham-Blair if he would consent to
investigate for us,' said the Prime Minister. 'If he will be so
kind as to undertake this mission, then I suggest that we
return to the Esplanade and wait for his report.'

Mr Pelham-Blair could not refuse. With a stern expression
he went forward, and with a general sigh of relief the Cabinet
turned in the other direction and hurried out of the Castle.

Silent after their embarrassing experience, they gathered on
the north pavement of the Esplanade, between the statues of
Lord Haig and Queen Victoria's Uncle York. Some of them
removed their hats, and dried perspiring foreheads. Then they
became aware of a multifarious and approaching noise, a
populous clamour that carried with it a combative high-
pealing music; and they saw below them, in Princes Street, a
mass of people of which the centre moved in the discipline of
marching troops and the pomp of an army with banners.

'Another regiment, I suppose,' said the Chancellor of the
Exchequer.

'Reinforcements, I presume,' said Sir Joseph.

'For which side?' inquired the Prime Minister mildly.

'Good God!' exclaimed Mr Curle. 'It's an army of women!'

IV

Half a mile from Queensferry Rose Armour was stopped on
the road by a forward picket of the Highland army, and having
made known her name and mission, was taken without delay
to the Hawes Inn. There, in a large room, she found about
twenty officers in a very cheerful frame of mind, though many
were nearly exhausted by their long day's march, and all were
travel-stained and tired.

So far their plans had been successful. In the late evening a
strong advance-guard had occupied North Queensferry, and
taking prisoner the master and engine-room crew of one of the

ferries, had compelled them to keep steam up. As soon as the first troops of the main army arrived, the crossing was begun, and pickets thrown out to guard the roads. The army had straggled rather badly during the march from Stirling, and the ferry was still crossing with late-comers. Except for pickets and sentries, the women were now sleeping in Dalmeny woods. They were tired out, and it would be impossible to rouse them before morning. But tomorrow they would certainly march to Edinburgh. That was what they had come for, and they were very glad to think they had arrived so opportunely.

Rose Armour was much taken by the appearance and manner of the Highland officers. Most of them wore short kilted skirts and tartan plaids fastened with a big silver brooch. Nearly all the tartans were different, and the room was a blaze of colour, of soft sea-green and the dark green of pine-forests, of broom-yellow and the blue of a faded battle flag, of wine-red and the red of a morning sky. There was a great deal of laughter and excited talk, and Rose found it difficult to remember the ladies' names, for most of them had some territorial appendage: Stewart of Lochroyal, Chisholm of Lyon, Mackenzie of Altnashielachan; there were Mackays and Sinclairs differenced by the title of some lonely hill or wide moor in Caithness or Sutherland; Grants and Gordons called after strath and river-reach of the Spey and the Dee; MacNeils and Macdonalds with the style of an island firth or Atlantic glen – it was as though the wilder half of Scotland itself were in the room, and when Mrs Moncrieff – to whom Rose had been commended by Mrs MacLeod of Rhidorroch – came in followed by the landlady and a maid, the one carrying a tray of glasses, the other a vast silver bowl, then the smell of honey was added to all the heather-names, and they sounded more nobly still. For the bowl held three or four quarts of Athole brose, a specific against fatigue and a liquor in which success might not unworthily be drunk to any mortal cause.

More officers came in, and the colour and the noise increased. Many of the ladies were extremely handsome, and most of them had a very proud and dominating manner, which they combined with a loud good humour. Rose had not yet learnt who was in command of the army, and inquiring of Mrs Moncrieff she was told, 'For God's sake don't ask that question here! We're all in command. There's a dozen more in Dalmeny woods, and half a dozen still in North Queensferry, and there's only one thing we're all frightened of, and that's being second to anyone else. So at present we're a sort of blue-blooded Soviet – but I don't advise you to call anyone Comrade. At the moment we're agreed that the first thing to do is to get to Edinburgh, and we'll fight at the dropping of a handkerchief. But there may be trouble afterwards, unless Lady Lysistrata takes charge.'

It was daylight before the Highland officers went to bed, many in the woods, some in the inn; but all were afoot again in a couple of hours' time. Rose slept soundly on a sofa till she was wakened, and by then the army was on the march. There was no food left in the inn but some dry bread, and she was given a cup of Athole brose to sweeten it. She mounted her bicycle and set off to look for the head of the column.

In the bright sun, beneath a high unclouded sky, the woods of Dalmeny were like a green furnace blazing to cool flame with verdant tongues of beech and sallow, the glow of jade. It was so resplendent a background that any army, marching by, would be diminished that had not breast-plates of silver, and flags of scarlet and gold. The women of the Highlands had no banners. The most of them were dressed in workaday clothes, dusty and drab. So to march equal with the woods they had torn down branches and sprays of greenery, and some carried holly as though it were a banner, belts of ivy, and young saplings like pennants waving. This leafy ornament gave many of them a gay holiday look, but more it trans-figured and turned into maenads flourishing the emblems of a Celtic Dionysos, the divinity of their own mountains. There were women from the outer isles who called to each other in high-pitched Gaelic. It was the speech of an older world, more fierce and jocular than modern tongues. They were the Bacchae, at one with the joyous god, and troop after troop, under the greenery of the torn trees, they marched against those who had neglected his worship for a proud and sterile creed, and forgotten the virtue of country places.

They were the last of the many armies who had come out of the Highlands. Their glens were wasted now, their clachans ruined, but they marched with all the high formidable spirit of their fathers who had sold their valiancy for a day's pay, and made an empire, and taken the wide earth for their tomb. The Highlands had bred soldiers, but little else, and now the remnant women were marching against war because all their history was a tale of war, and war had brought no lasting good to their land. But there was nothing sullen in their determination. They sang as they marched, and hurried to the fight. They were marching under green boughs against a greyness that had darkened men's spirit and chilled the ripe abundance of the world. Like Dionysos they could put on the likeness of a lion when they chose, but their inner heart was in love with jollity. They were raiders, marching for booty, and the booty was their husbands and their lovers and their sons. They wanted to have their men at home. They wanted mirth about them, a house tight against the weather, and some plenishing of meat and meal, of milk and honey. It was little enough that they wanted, but much of that little had been taken from them, or threatened, and so they had risen to fight for it. And their spirit was the spirit that took the clans to red Harlaw, and the spirit that made the Theban women rebel against King Pentheus and his dreary rationalism. There were girls, sloe-eyed, with soft voices and a swift grace of movement; there were shepherds' wives, and wives of gillies and tradesmen in small grey towns; there were burly women, broad of beam, who waddled in their stride, and sweated, and cracked loud jokes in the ancient tongue – and all were ruthless as wolves, devout as saints, in their demand for peace and the home-coming of their men.

It was noon when they came into Edinburgh, and they came like a moving forest in whose leafy rides were pipers playing. They were marching six or eight abreast, and from every company of their mile-long column rose the wild music that had called their fathers to Flodden and Fontenoy and Loos, and among the green branches had still an older sound. A flock of small birds, of finches, tomtits, and yellow-hammers, had followed the marching trees, and the voices of the women, shriller as they neared their goal, were like the baying of the White Hounds on high Cithaeron. Staves, ivy-girt, were raised aloft, and Gaelic vocables had the very sound of 'Iacchos! Iacchos!' From the glens of Ross and Sutherland and the sealochs of the isles, the Bacchanals had come to town.

Crowds gathered, and the hale excitement of the women spread to the watching throng. People ran alongside, cheering. The pipers played more loudly, and the frightened finches and the tomtits fled like coloured motes into the upper air. The Highlanders quickened their pace, shouted, and waved their leafy banners. They were like a forest in a high wind, a forest in a furious summer gale.

At the first noise of their coming the troops in Princes Street Gardens had been hurried out to meet them, and a reserve battalion from Castle Hill came at the double down the Mound. The soldiers formed a line across the road, a solid rampart from pavement to pavement. They stood six deep. They were shoulder to shoulder, redoubtable in their patient discipline. To all appearance their steady ranks were impenetrable.

But the Highlanders did not wait to gather their numbers before they moved to the assault. As soon as their leading company wheeled out of Princes Street, and saw the waiting soldiers, they threw away their green branches and charged with a wild halloo. The unbreakable line bent and quivered before the onslaught. The solid ranks opened and received their files, and before they recovered from the shock the second company was upon them with the fury of an angry sea. Like the high curving waves, dark green and emerald-hearted, hooded with spray, that sweep endlessly out of an Atlantic storm, the Highlanders came wildly surging, company after company, and fell upon the khaki ranks as if they had been a sandy beach. Like seagulls screaming, the pipers played on the outskirts of the fight, and like the undertones of a storm – the churning of boulders and the deep bass of the wind – were the trampling of feet and the muttering sound of strength hoarsely spent. Then suddenly, as suddenly as a squall passes in island seas, the battle was over. The six-fold line of soldiers

broke and scattered. Many fled, and some lay still, but none
resisted. The road lay open, the enemy was dispersed.

Impatiently the women suffered the hurried drilling of their
officers. They gathered again into companies, into a column,
and triumphantly resumed their march. They were, for a little
while, almost silent. The battle, though short enough, had
been arduous, and the hill was steep. They took the nearest
way to the Castle, up the narrow pass of Ramsay Lane, and
turning a blind corner their foremost ranks nearly collided
with a company of elderly gentlemen, dark-suited and emin-
ently respectable, who came hurrying towards them. The
elderly gentlemen stopped in dismay. The women, after a
moment of mute astonishment, uttered a shout of triumph and
derision. They surrounded the Ministers, and seized them with
hard-working hands, gathered them in their great red arms,
and loudly hurried on. Lord Pippin and his colleagues, always
averse from making any rapid decision, had dallied on the
Esplanade a little too long.

A cordon of policemen, a few bewildered soldiers, were
brushed aside, and like a deep river flowing strongly between
straight banks, the Highlanders marched to the Castle. Many
of Lysistrata's garrison had come out to meet them, and standing on either side of the Esplanade, cheered them time and
again. Now the pipers, having got back their breath, tucked
their bags under their arms, and over the tumult of the crowd
and the stormy ground-bass of their drones, soared the Mc-
Crimmon pibroch, *The War of Peace*.

The front of the army halted before the moat and the broken
Gate of the Castle, and successive companies came up on either
side. In the midst of their array were the captured Ministers.
Lysistrata came out and stood on the bridge. She carried,
point down, her husband's surrendered sword. Slowly the
noise of cheering grew less, and a Highland officer, stepping
forward, raised her sword in salute. 'We came in time,' she
said.

'You came in time,' Lysistrata replied. 'And you have
assured us of victory.'

CHAPTER SEVEN

Victory

I

MAJOR GRAHAM, in temporary command of his battalion of
the Royal Scots, deliberately ignored the song that rose from
the column behind him. It was a popular song, but the troops
had been forbidden to sing it because it derided the military
spirit so necessary to an army in the field, and extolled the
simple delights of peace. But Graham had made up his mind
that in certain circumstances his men might sing anything they
liked, and after a morning in the bull-ring he thought it
natural that their choice of a song should be subversive. They
had been out of the line for the last week, and most of their
time had been spent on intensive training for the next battle.
They were seasoned troops, and they resented their ceaseless
instruction in bayonet-fighting, bombing, and Aldershot drill;
so to relieve their feelings they sang, as they went marching
back to their billets:

> I want a quiet life, a lazy-day life,
> I don't want any fighting, and I don't want any pain,
> I want a quiet life!
> But if you doubt my manhood, well, go home and ask
>   your wife –
> I want a real life!
> And I want to see old England once again.

Graham, like everybody else, was worried by the lack of
English news. For nearly a week there had been no delivery of
letters or papers. All leave had been stopped. Soldiers due to
return from leave had not come back, and no drafts had
crossed. The censorship had been complete, and no word of
the love-strike had yet reached the armies abroad. But many
wild rumours had circulated despite the official communiqués
that daily asserted the normality of life in Britain, and described the censorship as a temporary measure necessitated by

the discovery of widespread espionage. Fortunately for discipline, the rumours were so many and various that belief in
any one of them had never time to grow large enough to be
dangerous, before it was dispelled by the eager acceptance of
another, and that was soon ousted by a third. But the soldiers
were worried. They grumbled without much cause, their
temper was brittle and uncertain. There was uneasy defiance in
their voices when they sang:

> I want a nice life, a pipe-and-beer life,
> You can keep your Iron Crosses where the monkey made
>   its name,
> I want a safe life!
> I've had my fill of bombing-raids and seen enough of strife,
> I want my own life,
> And I want to see old Scotland once again!

The song died at once, however, when Graham gave the
order to march at attention, and the Royal Scots wheeled into
camp with all the arrogance of perfect discipline. On the
parade-ground they formed close column, and halted. But the
parade-ground was a scene of great disorder. It was surrounded by soldiers of many different regiments, all noisily
excited, and while his companies were still dressing their ranks,
Graham was approached by the Camp Commandant, an
elderly and agitated Colonel; the Camp Adjutant, a thrice-
wounded and weary Captain; and several other officers, all
showing perturbation according to their nature. The censorship had broken down, and they had just heard of the love-
strike. All the troops had heard of it. An American newspaper
had been smuggled in, and hundreds of copies distributed.
The men had refused to obey orders. They were on the verge
of active mutiny. Could Graham answer for his battalion? The
Commandant would authorize an issue of ten rounds a
man . . .

'No,' said Graham.

The Royal Scots stood unmoving in the midst of tumult.
Their ranks were perfectly dressed, their rifles at the slope
steady in their hands. They wore the rigid impersonal expression of men under absolute discipline – but their eyes

betrayed them. Their eyes had lost the blank look of the drill-ground, they were alive and eager. The other soldiers, pressing closer to the battalion, were shouting news of civil war. The women of Britain were in revolt. They were going to stop the war. There was fighting throughout England and Scotland. The women were fighting. They were besieged in Edinburgh Castle. There was a battle raging in Edinburgh between men and women. Their wives were being attacked . . .

The left-hand man of the front rank of 'A' Company was a tall soldierly fellow called Adam. He wore the ribbon of the Distinguished Conduct Medal, and a red seam on his cheek was the relic of a shrapnel-wound. His eyes grew bright with anger, his face darkened as he listened to broken tidings of the love-strike and the shouted fragments of news. Suddenly he threw down his rifle and marched out of the ranks.

'Where the hell are you going, Adam?' demanded the Company Sergeant-major.

Adam paused for a moment, looked over his shoulder, and bellowed the one word: 'Hame!'

During the weeks of preparation for the love-strike, Lysistrata had managed to establish communication with women in Paris, Berlin, Rome, Moscow, and other capital cities; and the strike had become international. The women of Britain had been the first to rebel, but elsewhere results came quicker. In Paris the strike did not begin till the fifth day after Lysistrata had seized the Castle, but its effect was immediate chaos. For a day or two the news of it was kept from the armies in the field, but further censorship proved impossible.

About the same time as Private Adam of the Royal Scots initiated the homeward march, one of the most distinguished of French generals was presenting decorations for valour in the Place St Denis in Amiens. Three sides of the square were lined with troops, and the General was attended by a numerous Staff. Solemnly he pinned medal after medal on the breasts of the most gallant of France's heroic defenders. Solemnly he kissed the brave cheeks of the bemedalled warriors. Solemnly, in the name of the Republic, he thanked them all for their most valiant service.

At his side an officer read the name of Sergeant Baradat of

the Chasseurs Alpins – it was M. César Baradat, sometime
Minister for Labour, whose fiery eloquence had done so much
to precipitate the war – and proceeded: *Engagé volontaire pour
la durée de la guerre, il a fait preuve en toutes circonstances d'entrain
et de courage. Le 14 juin, est allé sous un feu de mitrailleuses des plus
violents au secours de son Chef de bataillon . . .*'

The General was already pinning the Médaille Militaire on
the broad chest of Sergeant Baradat, when a Colonel of
cavalry – spurs jingling, leather creaking, lungs panting – came
running up and without apology thrust before his eyes a copy
of an America newspaper across the front page of which ran
the streaming headline: LOVE STRIKE SPREADS TO PARIS.

The General took the paper, and read. He uttered an extraordinary noise, a groan of horror shrilling roughly into
anguish, and with shaking hands turned the page towards
Baradat. *'Lisez!'* he exclaimed in quavering tones.

Baradat read; and in his tremendous throat there sounded
the rising growl of an infuriated lion. With instant decision
and a violent gesture, he shouted: *'À Paris!'*

'À l'instant!' said the General hoarsely; and arm-in-arm
they marched in the direction of the capital.

Less immediate, but much more astonishing, was the effect
of the strike – or rather of the news of it – in Italy and Germany. For many years the inhabitants of these countries had
heard no real news of any kind. Their Ministries of Propaganda had supplied them with well-edited statements about
selected occurrences at home and abroad, and these official
bulletins were, on the whole, piously believed. But anything
except official news was held to be at the least a dastardly
perversion, and often a direct reversal of the truth. It was
widely known, for example, that the French always called
white black, and so had the English till the war made them
allies of Germany. When, therefore, the strike broke out in a
small way in Rome and Berlin, and news of it went with all the
swiftness of illicit rumour through the two countries, the
people were at first bewildered. But then the natural perspicacity of the Latin, and the remorseless logic of the Prussian, triumphed over obscurity and they perceived the truth.
The truth must be the direct opposite of that which rumour

stated! It was not their women but their soldiers who had declared a love strike!

Throughout Germany and Italy there was consternation, then terror, then a dreadful anger. The women of these countries had long since been taught that a woman's function was purely domestic, and though at first many had protested against so ancient a restriction, they had become reconciled to it, and now could hardly envisage any other sort of life than that which ran for ever between ample board and double bed. And here was a rebellion that would lay waste the half of their kingdom! Women, they cried, cannot live by bread alone, and from all their towns and villages a monstrous army set forth, more esurient than daughters of the leech, more shameless than Zuleika, and strong with many years of scrubbing, ironing, blanket-washing, and drubbing their ceaseless offspring. Over the parados of every trench on every battlefront of the Fatherland and Roma Rediviva they descended upon their astonished soldiers, and by the slack of their collars and the seat of their small-clothes took them, shouting, home in a pandemonium of topsy-turvy rape; and like Sabine women playing one-good-turn-deserves-another, never relaxed nerve or muscle till they had them safe between bolted door and the reproachful vacancy of the nuptial couch. And that was Italy and Germany out of it.

In Russia the end of the war came with a singular poignancy. The women of the Soviet Union had been trained and accustomed to do anything from managing a boot-factory to hewing forests in Siberia or staffing a university in Transcaucasia. They had acquired a real taste for experiment, and taking to the idea of the love-strike with much enthusiasm, organized it with great efficiency. – It was, of course, unanimous, because unanimity had become second-nature in Russia. – The men were unspeakably dismayed. They realized and admitted that their wives, free-born and equal citizens, had every right to refuse them that gracious office which only a bourgeois mentality could describe as obligatory. Were they to insist on being loved, they would undoubtedly be arraigned as bourgeois, and enemies to the Communist State; but should they acquiesce in not being loved, then their lives would be barren indeed. For love was all they had left that they could call their own. All else in their world had been communized and collectivized, and all their activities had been disciplined according to the habits of the workman Stakhanov: a carpenter who had been used to drive in his nails with five blows of the hammer, must drive them in with two; a team of boilermakers who had always taken three leisurely weeks to create their boilers, were compelled to construct them in one; a poet who had proposed to spend a lifetime in the perfecting of his art, was ordered to produce his punctual canto month by month. That was the Stakhanov system, and the sole activity immune from it was love. A man could still make love at whatever speed he chose, as lazy and light-hearted as he cared to be. And so love had increased in value. It was the one treasure of life, the flower in a slum window, the child of old age, the found shilling of destitution. It was not Venus, proud in white marble or from loud Olympus tormenting a boisterous people; but the hidden bird in its nest, the dream of a workaday world too long and wearily awake. So when the soldiers heard that love was to be taken from them, they did not quarrel and curse and shout. They wept. All over Russia sounded the low wailing of intolerable grief, and if the men had lost every other attribute of manhood, they could still have been known by their tears. The war ended in a passion of fear and remorse, and the soldiers hurried home to beg forgiveness.

In a very short time, indeed, the strike in one way or another achieved the desired result in every warring country but one. The exception was Bulgaria. The Bulgarians proved strangely impervious to female threat, and treated the strike with contemptuous indifference. Austere and disciplined, they continued the war long after everybody else had abandoned it, and for some time it looked as if they might establish their hegemony over all Europe. Fortunately, however, they behaved in a very reasonable manner, and having compelled the World Court to admit their claim to be the victors in the Last Great War, they retired with an enormous indemnity, and decorated Sofia with innumerable statues of their successful generals.

Hostilities were therefore concluded with satisfaction to everyone – except the Ministers, Cabinets, Field Marshals,

Dictators, and Chancelleries of the late-warring states, who for long grumbled at the taking away of authority from their accustomed hands – and the Great Powers discovered that since all had been equally defeated, they could now live together in reasonable amity. No one resented, because few saw it, the enormous Arch of Triumph that overspanned the railway at Dragoman Pass, and bore upon its frieze the gigantic legend: BULGARIA VICTRIX.

II

The marriage of Rose Armour and Julian Brown was celebrated early in August in the Church of St John in Edinburgh. There was as large a congregation as the church would contain, and outside a multitude that entirely filled the confluence of roads at the west end of Princes Street. In a front pew sat Lady Lysistrata and General Scrymgeour. Immediately after his surrender in the Castle he had offered to resign his commission, but as the whole Cabinet had acquiesced in the capitulation he was persuaded to withdraw his offer. 'Consensus facit legem,' the Prime Minister had gravely observed. 'Vir sapit qui pauca loquitur,' he added more cheerfully.

Lord Pippin attended the wedding with several of his colleagues, and in the pew behind him were Major and Mrs Graham, now happily re-united. Mrs Graham was impatiently waiting till the service should be concluded, when she hoped to find a chance of talking to the Prime Minister and resuming her lecture on politics. Not far away was Delia Curle with the Secretary for War on one side of her, and Commander Lawless on the other; and beside Lysistrata were Lady Oriole and her husband, a tall man with a very red face, completely bald, who sang hymns, psalms, and responses with deafening enjoyment. Mrs MacLeod of Rhidorroch, her daughter, and half a hundred other Highland ladies were present, and Lieutenant McCombie was in attendance on his wife, a person of handsome but rather frosty appearance. In all the large and fashionable congregation, however, there was no one more magnificently attired than Mrs McLafferty of the Gallowgate in Glasgow. She had been given a grant of £100 for her valiant defence of the steps, and she had spent it all on entertainment and fine clothing, much of which she wore to the wedding. At intervals during the service she could be heard to mutter, with most reverent amazement, 'Ay, Christ, ay!'

It was generally agreed that Rose Armour had never looked more lovely, and her ten tall bridesmaids attracted much attention. They had all played a prominent part in the defence of the Castle, and the heroic figures of Miss McNab and Miss McNulty were particularly admired; as was the fine emerald in Miss Hepburn's engagement ring. In such an environment it was inevitable that Julian should be more perfunctorily noticed, but it was observed that he carried himself well and spoke clearly when called upon to do so.

When they left the church he was ignored completely, however, and this humiliation was exacerbated by the behaviour of his wife, of which he strongly disapproved; as any new-made husband would have done. The enormous crowd vociferously welcomed her, and would not let her go. They implored, they demanded a song. And Rose, enchanted by their obvious affection, tucked up her wedding-dress, and assisted by a policeman and the ever-helpful Mr Pelham-Blair, climbed to the roof of her waiting limousine, where she clutched her hands in a familiar gesture, and inquired in her sweet husky voice, 'What shall I sing?'

The answer was immediate and unanimous. In the church the organist, intoxicated by the occasion and his own virtuosity, was playing over and over again the Wedding March; and Rose, outside, began to sing her famous codicil to it, in which the delighted multitude presently joined:

> Up in the morning and fry the bacon,
>   Make him a nice cup of tea!
> Who would think yesterday I was forsaken,
>   Now I'm as happy as happy can be?
> If you feel rotten because you're a woman,
>   Seek for a suitable spouse –
> Say what you like, but we're all of us human,
>   And better for having a man in the house!

At the subsequent reception, however, she was commendably serious. She made a speech – it was a good deal longer

than Julian's – in the course of which she said that she ex
pected soon to have very little time for singing, as she ha
agreed to stand for Parliament in the forthcoming Genera
Election. Her constituency was to be Linlithgow, a count
with which she was closely associated inasmuch as she ha
traversed part of it in her ride to the Hawes Inn. Her husband
she added, would also be devoting himself to public work, fo
he had been appointed Assistant Director of Personnel unde
the new Board of National Reconstruction.

The abrupt and unexpected conclusion of the war had released a flood of energy which, in reaction against the purposes
of destruction for which it had been lately dammed, now
turned with immense enthusiasm to the task of rebuilding
Britain closer to the heart's desire of those whose hearts were
benevolently in league with some intelligence. The damage
done by air raids, in the initial phase of the war, had obviously
to be repaired; but the large migration of industry which had
followed the destruction of central London and the removal of
Government, showed clearly that reconstruction must mean
more than rebuilding on old sites and the sedulous refashion-
ing of what had hitherto existed. In its pre-war condition
Britain had been like an ill-loaded tramp-steamer. The Ship of
State had had to navigate the Seven Seas with most of her
cargo lumped into the south-east corner. She had been, in
nautical language, badly *by the head*. But now her cargo was to
be properly stowed, and industry more equally situated
throughout the length and breadth of the country.

With this prospect in view, there was a great resurgence of
local pride, and city after city produced plans for re-building
which combined a stately aspect with every convenience for
those who were to live in them. The old disfigurement of
municipal architecture and industrial sprawling was steadily
to be effaced, and instead would rise proud and spacious cities
whose inhabitants would find comfort to their hands, and
whenever they raised their eyes, delight.

The Board of National Reconstruction gave advice where
it was needed, and coordinated local plans and organization;
but it did not impose any outward uniformity, though it
insisted on the maintenance of certain standards of comfort

nd convenience in domestic building. In this freedom the
cities chose according to local imagination, and built in the
high-rearing pride of splendid competition. Liverpool, as the
gateway by which travellers from the New World should enter
the Old, recaptured the soaring spirit of the Middle Ages and
built itself in a Gothic style that made all the music of its
traffic sound like a fugue of Bach's; and Bradford put on the
magnificence of baroque. In Birmingham a group of architects
gave birth to a new Classicism; and Glasgow rose white and
massive in a sky-scraping forest of concrete and steel. No
more could the traveller go by night from Yorkshire to Ren-
frewshire, from Lancashire to South Wales, and never know
he had moved, such was the grimy squalor that he left, of
railway-station, slum, and paltry offices; and such the dirty
mediocrity to which he came, of factory and Council house
and jerry-built sore of bungalows. But every city was itself,
and took delight in being so; and every town had a face and
spirit of its own.

The triumph of all was London, and much of the reason for
its triumph was the Thames. The Thames was given its proper
due and reverence. London obeyed its course, and presently
every curve and flexure of the river offered noble views of
parks and terraces and stately buildings that adorned its banks.
London shrank to a quarter of its previous size, but became a
capital worthy of the empire over which it ruled, and a
befitting consort for the river that had given it life.

Nor, in the midst of all this rebuilding of the towns, were
the country places neglected. The Highland army that relieved
the Castle had by its victory realized its strength, and its
leaders, preserving remarkable unanimity, had made a series
of demands that were summed-up in the sentence: If people
are to continue to live in the country, then life in the country
must be made as comfortable as life in the town. They had
presented their demands for new roads, electric light, and
modern sanitation with all the fervour of the Reformers set-
ting forth their Confession of Faith; and they had drawn the
rebuke of Sir Joseph Rumble for this undesirable obsession
with material needs. 'I would prefer to see,' he said solemnly,
'a little concern for the life of the spirit.'

To which Mrs MacLeod of Rhidorroch, making her first speech in the new Parliament, replied: 'If you want to see the life of the spirit flourishing as it ought, you'll give it a house with proper drains, good light, food in the larder, and a road to the front door. If you make people live in a pigsty, they'll behave like pigs. Give them decent houses, and most of them will live decent lives. And if they aren't perpetually worrying about where tomorrow's dinner is to come from, then they'll have time to look for spiritual vitamins and a bit of metaphysical protein for their neglected souls.'

There was, of course, much stubborn opposition to all the projected reconstruction and reform; and Lysistrata on one occasion declared: 'Our problem is very much the same as that which confronted Florence Nightingale. We are in the midst of a mental and moral Scutari, and as at the other Scutari, we need plenty of fresh air and release from the dead hand of officialdom.' This release, though not without difficulty, followed the General Election in September. Lord Pippin, for the third time in his career, had announced his political abdication and declared his intention of retiring to his estate in Norfolk, there to live the remainder of his life – as his critics said he had lived the whole of it – in *otium cum dignitate*. Leadership of the Party devolved on Sir Joseph Rumble, whose personality and views were not inspiring. Nearly every seat was contested by women, and four hundred and eighty-three of them were returned to Parliament. Lysistrata accepted the invitation to form a Cabinet, but not without misgiving; for she thought she was pregnant, and if she was she would certainly be brought to bed before the summer recess.

For the first few weeks, however, the new Parliament did very well indeed, and by rapid legislation set moving the innumerable machinery that was to refashion Britain. The women found no difficulty in financing reconstruction. One of the slogans of their election campaign – *If there's plenty for war, there's plenty for peace* – became an axiom of their economic policy; and the Chancellor of the Exchequer, Mrs Graham, compelled the Bank of England and the Treasury to accept her own theory of money.

It was a simple theory, and everybody could understand it.

In her childhood her father had not carried pound notes carefully folded in a leather case, but sovereigns loose in his trouser-pocket. Money – real money – was round. She had always been told that it was made round in order to go round. This she continued to believe, and by virtue of her position insisted that the Bank and the Treasury should subscribe to her faith.

Having thus disposed of a difficulty that had haunted many a Chancellor, and chained with unnecessary padlocks nearly every Exchequer in history, the Government pressed forward with all its schemes in unabated vigour, and the whole country was full of the cheerful sound of building. The exultancy of the returned soldiers, to whom the sudden peace had given years of unexpected life, and the confidence of the women, released by their world-wide victory, filled the land with a new spirit that overleaped all obstacles and sought openly that happiness of which hitherto the most of humankind had hardly dared to dream. Work was a joy, leisure a perpetual holiday, and the merriment of Merry England made room for itself beside the grandeur of Great Britain.

III

This Utopian progress, however, most unhappily received a check. A Miss Willoughby, President of the Board of Education in Lysistrata's Government, tendered her resignation and announced the formation of a New Party. The split was caused by Miss Willoughby's declared intention of introducing a Bill to make Hatton College coeducational. This raised a storm of the most appalling fury, and a gigantic meeting of Old Hattonians, convened in the College itself, published a manifesto that began with the alarming words: '*Over our dead bodies. . . .*'

Lysistrata and most of her Ministers strongly disapproved of the absurd proposal, but Miss Willoughby was obdurate. She was, moreover, a lady with great ability, much charm, and many friends. She had taken the lead, on behalf of spinster Members and their unwedded constituents, in several questions relating to the status of married women, and her so-called New Party eventually consisted of two hundred and eleven of the two hundred and thirty-four spinsters who sat in Parliament. She then enlisted the support of male Members by acknowledging a change of heart with regard to Hatton College, and defeated Lysistrata on an issue that was otherwise of little importance. Miss Willoughby formed a government which lasted three weeks.

Lysistrata was asked to lead another administration, but it was now early March and neither she nor anybody else was in doubt about the interesting nature of her condition. She refused to take office again, and Lady Oriole's government was immediately defeated. Another General Election was inevitable, and without Lysistrata's leadership the Married Women lost a number of seats to the Spinsters, and a hundred and sixty Men were returned. But Miss Willoughby's second administration was unlucky. By midsummer some fifty of her Spinsters had got themselves either married or engaged to be married, which transferred their sympathy to the other side, and much scandal was caused by the flagrant intimacy of one of the Government Whips and the Chief Whip of the male Opposition.

It became evident that as parliamentarians the women had their frailties and limitations. They had shown greatness of vision, charity in alliance with common sense, and a noble conception of the deserts and potentialities of humankind. They had ignored a hundred difficulties that would have daunted men, and triumphed over scores of others. But they had no experience of the long boredom of Parliamentary government, and the House of Commons revealed their weakness. Government followed government and Premier succeeded Premier with depressing frequency, and the country grew more and more impatient with its elected leaders, whose foolish quarrels did nothing but interfere with the great work of rebuilding. The people wanted a stable government, a government that would let them get on with their huge and heroic task; but government after government wasted its time on petty difference and unnecessary dispute. More than once her old troops, the once-embattled women of Britain, implored Lysistrata to come back and lead the country; but Lysistrata, now the mother of a fine boy and determined to

give him both brothers and sisters, could not be persuaded.
She had done her work, she said. She had fought her battle and
helped to create the machinery of reform. It was for others to
keep it working.

There was yet another Election, and the Men increased
their representation to two hundred and eighty-six. They were
now the largest single party, if they could be kept together;
but they could be defeated whenever the women chose to
combine. The country groaned again. It was stability the
people wanted, and stability was still denied them. Only the
most confident of politicians, the most easy and skilful of
statesmen, a man whose brilliance was truly the reflection of
his placid spirit, could find and maintain his balance in a House
so perilously constituted. Sir Joseph had regained his seat, but
Sir Joseph was not good enough. Neither was Mr Curle, nor
young Mr Pelham-Blair. The country groaned, and looked
with anxious eyes at all its unfinished work . . . And then
came news that drew, from Dover to Cape Wrath, a sigh of
relief, and seemed to raise at once each growing house and
half-built bridge to coping-stone and parapet.

The King had sent for Lord Pippin.